blue sky

THE SECOND NOVEL IN THE MORROW GIRLS SERIES

D. BRYANT SIMMONS

Bravebird Publishing | Chicago | 2016

Contact wholesalers about trade sales.
Ingram Content Group (US), Gardner's Books (UK)

Contact publisher about direct sales.
sales@bravebirdpublishing.com
1 (877) 747-6882

Bravebird Publishing
PO Box 235
Chicago Ridge, IL 60415
www.bravebirdpublishing.com

Publisher's Cataloging-in-Publication Data
Bryant Simmons, D., 1983-
Blue Sky / D. Bryant Simmons.
p. cm.
LCCN: 2015907220
ISBN: 978-0-985751-63-0 (softcover)
ISBN: 978-0-985751-64-7 (e-book)
ISBN: 978-1-943989-02-7 (hardcover)
ISNI: 0000000444680132
1. Family Life—Fiction. 2. Coming of Age—Fiction. 3. African American—Fiction
I. Bryant Simmons, D. 1983- II. Title.

First printing 2015.

The Morrow Girls Series is a family saga that captures the lives and exploits of three generations of women.

How to Knock a Bravebird from Her Perch

Blue Sky

How to Kill a Caged Bird

"There was only one thing I wanted after my freedom. My girls."
— *Pecan*

blue sky

MARCH 1983

MYA

MY SISTERS AND I WERE NEVER ALONE with the woman we knew as Aunt Paula until the day my mama disappeared. Aunt Paula sat at the kitchen table with her arm around Jackie.

"She'll be back. Everything'll be okay." She wound the ends of my sister's braids around her finger. Paula only had boys, so spending time with us was how she got her fill of pretty dresses, dolls, and braids. "Your mama will be back before you know it."

It didn't explain anything, but my sisters didn't bothered to question her any further. They heard what they needed. Mama was coming back, and everything would be fine. So, I kept quiet.

The next morning, we went downstairs, expecting to see Mama there in her robe flipping pancakes. We found Paula instead, lining up four paper-bag lunches and smiling. Mama only ever packed us two lunches. One for Nikki, who like most sixth graders, brought her lunch, plus another bag for me and Jackie because we always ate together, and Jackie tended to forget if Mama trusted her with her own lunch. I started to point out Nat didn't need a cold lunch since kindergarteners ate hot lunches, but I decided against it.

"Here you girls go. Now, go learn something."

"Mama be here when we get back?" Jackie asked.

Aunt Paula smiled and nodded.

We raced home, convinced we were due a celebration because Mama had never been gone from us for longer than a few hours. Folks said she was overprotective, never wanting us to go to sleepovers and things. She liked having us close. Up the porch steps we ran, and Nikki took out her key to unlock the door. Silence met us in the foyer. No Mama. No Paula. Jackie took off running, calling out for her like Mama hid in the back somewhere.

"Mama not here?" Nat looked up at me.

Stunned, Nikki couldn't move to even close the door. She peeked over her shoulder at the outside world like maybe we shouldn't be alone in the house, like we might get in trouble.

"Times like this is why you got the key," I reminded her and locked the door behind us. "When Mama's at work. She's at work is all."

When Daddy moved out, Mama started working a lot. At first she worked the afternoon shift, but she got moved to the morning shift, so she could be home around the time we got out of school.

"She'll be here soon." I said.

So, we waited.

We got hungry, so Nikki made us a snack, and we waited some more.

Once suppertime came, Nikki thought we should surprise Mama by making it ourselves. She did most of the work, arguing with Jackie about where Mama kept things and how much of each ingredient was supposed to go in it. I kept watch from the window seat. At the first sight of her, I was gonna yell out, so my sisters would stop fighting and relax. Only, Mama didn't come home.

The next day we got up and did it all again. Only this time when school let out, the principal called us down to her office. Stacks of files and papers covered every inch of the desk with a few on the floor reaching knee-high. The principal was a burly woman with a high-pitched voice. She directed us to the empty chairs and in one long breath, laid out the problem at hand. Nobody answered when the school called our home phone, and the folks at Mama's job claimed she disappeared during her shift three days ago. Then she asked if we knew where Mama was. Asked if we had supervision at home.

"Yes. We're fine," I said.

But she didn't believe me. She said Nat had mentioned it to her teacher who told the secretary who told her.

"Mama must've gone to see somebody about a bike for us."

"Heziah," Jackie piped. Heziah was her answer to every unknown. Just the thought of him made her smile. She loved Mama's boyfriend the way I loved our daddy. "She gone to see Heziah, but she be back soon."

The principal shooed us out of the overcrowded office as she began to make a telephone call.

An hour later, a fiftyish woman in a navy blue suit showed up to take us home. She had two other women with her, both younger and trained to follow orders. They marched us up the stairs and into our bedrooms, lording over us while we each packed one bag a piece. One of the subordinates packed Nat's bag, which didn't sit well with Nikki since she thought she was the one in charge.

I had other concerns. "Where we going? You taking us to our Mama?"

"No. You're going to stay somewhere else for now."

"Where?"

"You'll find out soon enough."

"I'm not going nowhere until my mama get home!" Jackie said, glaring at the woman in defiance. Only one person in our family was as stubborn as Jackie. When my sister put her foot down, she meant it.

"Me neither," Nat said, squeezing tight to her stuffed teddy bear.

"Young lady, I didn't give you a choice. Now...let's go."

"You can't make me! You not my mama."

The front door opened and the standoff ended. Daddy strolled into the foyer, twirling his key around his finger. I was so happy I was about ready to burst. Flew down the stairs and into his bulging arms. Folks said his strength was legendary, and I knew he'd throw down before letting them take us anywhere.

"I missed you, Daddy!"

"Missed you too, baby girl. Where's your Mama?"

The old woman and her sidekicks joined us downstairs. They were still holding on to our bags. I smiled thinking about what was in store for the DCFS woman and her friends. Nobody messed with my daddy.

"Mr. Morrow, hello. I'm Judith Gibson. I work for the Department of Children and Family Services."

"What you want?"

"Do you live in the home?"

"Not at the moment, I don't." His gaze traveled over to Jackie, who dragged the toe of her shoe along a crack in the floor boards. "But I will be soon. Why?"

"We're taking temporary custody of the girls. Now, we don't want to make this harder on them, so please..."

"N'all. They my kids. I'll take 'em until they Mama get home from work."

"She not at work! She gone to get Heziah!" Jackie said. "He's our daddy now! You ain't nothing!"

Daddy's jaw twitched, his chest swelled, and his mouth spat, "You wanna take one of 'em? Take that one. The rest of 'em comin' with me."

"Daddy, where you live?" Nikki whispered.

But his address didn't matter. The social worker had made up her mind before he stepped over the threshold. She took out some fancy document from her purse and held out the sheet of paper, proving we didn't belong to him no more.

He read it over and said, "She lying! I ain't never did nothing like this here...this here letter say! She the one be neglecting them! Where she is? How she gonna say I ain't a fit parent?"

The woman gave a little nod, and one of the younger women disappeared into the kitchen. Daddy didn't mind. He kept right on yelling. Yelled until the police showed up. They tried to calm him down, but they were doing it all wrong. Daddy ain't calm down for anybody but me. They were ushering us toward the front door, but I was trying to stay in his field of vision. My calming powers ain't work otherwise.

"Mya," Jackie's hand clutched mine, and I read the plea in her eyes. Last thing she wanted was to be anywhere near Daddy. My sister's fingers tightened around mine.

Folks always thought we were twins on account of how close we were in age. I nodded and walked with her out to the porch. We were down the steps and almost to the gate before we realized what was happening. Two cars—one tan, the other black. One of the social workers was holding Nat's hand and standing in front of the tan car. Nikki was cowering in the shadows of the black car's rear seat.

Jackie said, "We go together."

"No. You're going to this car, and Mya here is going to the black car."

"We go together," I said.

"You girls need to say your goodbyes."

Jackie's grasp only tightened, and I thought my chest might cave in and crush what was left of my heart. First Daddy left, then Mama, now my sisters. I never hated anyone before, but I hated the smug DCFS woman with every fiber of my body.

"No!" My sister let out a blood curling scream, and I pulled her body to mine, clutching at her clothes.

"Please, if you relax..." The woman was saying as she tried to pry us apart.

"GET OFF ME! YOU GET OFF ME! NO! MYAAAA!"

"Jackie...," I said, mumbling, as she slipped out of my grasp. A stranger's hands were guiding me toward the black sedan. I stumbled over the grass, over the curb, failing to see through the curtain of tears. A car door closed, and a second later, we were moving. Nikki was crying next to me, but she didn't make a move to stop them. She didn't even try.

"Please turn around and sit down. We want you to be safe."

Jackie's cries rang in my ears, but I couldn't make her out. I pressed my fingertips to the rear window, barely able to distinguish her from the other bodies on our front lawn. Even that didn't last very long before we took a right at the corner and sped away from the only home I ever knew.

SPRING 1987

2
PECAN

CAN'T MOVE FORWARD HOLDING ON TO THE past, said the woman in my mirror. I reached high above my head, wrapping a strand of hair from the crown of my head around the spongy blue roller, and snapped the plastic prong in place before reaching for another one. My beauty, which I used to question, now seemed more like fact than fiction. Sure, up close my face showed signs of wear—wrinkles in the corners of my eyes and crescent-shaped indentations framed my full lips, but my skin glided over the hills and valleys of my body with defiant radiance. Smooth as butter under the melancholy hues of midnight. Complementing the crimson gown with its empire waist and black lace trim. Nowadays they considered it vintage but it was brand new when I bought it. Although the youth had long since drained from my eyes, I wouldn't trade none of my scars to get it back. 'Cause for all the old fractures, sprains, and cuts that had healed over I got something couldn't nobody take. I got wiser. And I got Nikki. Mya. Jackie and Nat. Jenna and Callie. With all the pain the past brought me it also gave me my girls, and taught me about miracles. Was a damn miracle what the body could endure.

But still, every night I said those words to myself. Nighttime was when I needed the reminder that nothing good came from holding on to the past. When the day was all said and done, I thought about the things I should've said but didn't. Things I wish I'd done differently or not at all. Ricky Morrow sat at the top of the list. I was down to only ten wishes a day. Ten times I wished I'd never married that man. Ten times I reminded myself I wouldn't have my girls if I hadn't married him. Wasn't fair that they were tied to him. Just looking at 'em sometimes sent me reeling into the past. It helped some that I never had to set eyes on Ricky. Any photograph he was in was safely locked in a box in the attic.

"I could watch you forever." Heziah smiled. "I could die right here and now watching you put curlers in your hair and I'd be a happy man."

"Guess that makes you a simple man then, don't it?"

"As simple as they come."

Heziah Jenkins, was the second man to love me but the first to have my whole heart. He was an honorable man. Came to me when I didn't believe they existed. He saved my soul just by being him. Couldn't write off all men knowing men like Heziah was walking the earth. Couldn't settle for Ricky's sort of love after I'd tasted what Heziah had to offer. Of course he ain't save me from my regular ole man. That was my doin'. I saved myself. After twelve years at the mercy of Ricky Morrow. After bruises I hid and lies I told. After being raped. After having a nervous breakdown and spending months in a psychiatric care facility. After the state took custody of my kids. I saved myself.

"How I get so lucky?" Heziah said as I put the last roller in my hair.

"Well move over, lucky man."

I flicked a hand at him and he laughed while scooting over to his side of the bed. If I splurged at all with the household expenses it was on bedding. On pretty pillows and expensive sheets, because nighttime was the only time I was at the mercy of my thoughts.

"Nice and toasty."

"You're welcome Belinda. See. It's the simple things that make you love me."

"Is it now? Tell me about these simple things."

"Flowers on every occasion. Our anniversary," he ticked off each item one at a time on his fingers. "Mother's Day–,"

"We ain't been married but three years."

"That's three anniversaries, three Mother's days, three birthdays—wait, no. Four birthdays," he paused then quickly added, "Three Valentine's Days too! All of that adds up! Plus every night I warm your side of the bed."

"And I haven't had to change a light bulb in I don't know how long."

"See. Lots of reasons to love me."

"I guess you're right. Okay simple man. I guess I best get around to loving you then."

I laughed more with Heziah than I ever had before. We laughed more than any couple should who's got teenagers that think they grown.

Once the laughter had died down he held me close and we drifted to sleep in each other's arms.

I awoke as the sunlight peeked through the bedroom curtains with only gratitude on my mind. Snuggling deeper into the soft sheets, I counted my blessings. I was free. I had five of my girls back under my roof. And I'd slept peacefully. No dreams about the past.

3
JACKIE

FAST GIRLS ALWAYS GET THEMSELVES INTO TROUBLE," Nikki's bitter drawl bounced off the murky yellow walls of my mama's kitchen. "It's true, Mama," she insisted.

"Don't talk about your sister like that."

Never understood what I did to get on Nikki's bad side, but she was determined to turn everybody against me. Really, she should've been thanking me. She got to be the responsible saint because I played the bad girl so well. Truthfully? She loved every second.

"I-I'm just saying one of these days Jackie's gonna get herself in trouble. Sneaking around doing God knows what."

Nikki didn't swear. Didn't even name call, unless talking about me. She sat at the kitchen table, shelling peas while Mama stood over the stove, seasoning the pork chops. At barely eighteen, my eldest sister dressed like a middle-aged woman of the Christian persuasion. Every blouse buttoned up to her chin, and every skirt hit below her knees. Even her shoes were the ugly missionary variety, as if she needed to advertise her commitment to Jesus Christ. A virtuous Christian woman. Mama never used the word before, but that's all Nikki talked about—her virtue. Far back as I can remember, Nikki was the impressionable one. Didn't even take two years to turn her into a Bible-thumper. She nearly broke her neck accommodating her foster family's outlook. So without warning, we—mainly me—wasn't good enough for her. I didn't say grace before every meal. Didn't go to church. I had too many boyfriends, a flair for the dramatic, and unlike her, I actually dressed my age.

"Hey, Mama," I sashayed into the kitchen, smiling as Nikki's face contorted in disgust at the length of my skirt. "You need some help?" I asked.

"No, baby, I'm fine." Mama studied me from top to bottom and smiled. "Going somewhere?"

"Yep."

I'd paired an electric blue miniskirt with neon yellow tights, a matching bodysuit, and big black belt, which added definition to my youthful waist. Straightened my hair and pulled half into a ponytail on the top of my head and added a pair of thick gold hoop earrings.

"Gina's having a party. Everybody's going."

"You didn't even ask if you could go," Nikki snapped. "Mama, tell her she's gotta ask first. She can't just come running downstairs announcing she's going to some party. It's disrespectful."

"What do you care what I do? You don't even live here."

"See. No respect for anyone."

"Not anyone. Just you."

"All right, you two. Quit it." Mama shook her head. "You two do this every time. And Jackie?"

"Yes, Mama?"

"Boys gonna be at this party?" She'd gone back to the pork chops, turning each piece over to double-check the seasoning covered the meat evenly.

"Boys are everywhere. I mean unless you want me to become a nun and lock myself in a tower somewhere."

"Don't get smart."

"I'm not. I'm simply saying it's basically impossible to avoid boys. Not my fault they exist. Not like I'm searching them out. They find me." I shrugged as the sound of Nikki's scoffing from the kitchen table resonated behind me. "Okay, if it'll make you feel better, I promise not to talk to any of them." I grinned and raised my right hand in a solemn gesture. "I cross my heart."

No surprise when she nodded. My mama was pretty easy to convince. But then she said, "Take your sister with you."

Nikki and I gasped at each other in horror. She couldn't be serious! The oven rattled as Mama extended the door to the open position, allowing her to slide the pan of meat into the heat. She stood, washed her hands, and rubbed them dry on the front of her apron. "Mya. Take Mya with you, and you can go."

Nikki exhaled, and I shared in her relief, if only for a moment....Mya and I didn't share the same friends. We didn't do the same things. She'd be miserable with me.

"Umm...everybody's expecting me, so I don't have time–"

"Well, if that's your choice...we happy to have you stay for supper."

"But, Mama! Mya hates parties! She's not gonna wanna go!"

I unknowingly stumbled on a better argument. Mama didn't want to make Mya do something she didn't wanna do. Nobody did. Mya didn't even have to say anything. If she cut her eyes at you, you knew better than to propose whatever you thought of proposing. Worked on everybody except me.

"How about I ask her, but if she says no, can I go on my own?"

Mama smiled, tilting her head to one side as she said, "I reckon that won't be a problem because you can be downright convincing when you wanna be."

As I climbed the stairs to my sister's bedroom, my brain ran through all possible ideas and strategies. Nothing seemed likely to work. I was a naturally persuasive person, so I'd just have to rely on my instincts. I knocked sweetly and waited for Mya's raspy alto on the other side. I was about to knock again when I heard the sounds of mischief behind me. Instinctively, I understood. The frustration had been a new sensation but was working its way around to being common place. Little sisters. Natalie was a doll. She did a poor job of preparing us for what was to come. I crossed the hall, pushed in the door to my bedroom, and smothered the impulse to scream my head off at the sight of all my makeup and hair products strewn across my bed.

My closet door muffled the giggles. They shushed each other, still having as much fun as when they started. Five girls living under the same roof would be trying for the most patient person, which I was not. Especially when plagued by two devilish three year olds.

I yanked open the closet door. "Get out of my clothes! My stuff! My Room!"

The twins darted around me, running full speed into the hallway. Wasn't the first time I'd caught them playing with my caboodle and wouldn't be the last. Heziah said that they only did it because they looked up to me, that imitation was the sincerest form of flattery, but I found it annoying, and it ruined my mood. Being convincing didn't happen magically. I had to be in the right mindset. I needed to focus. My intention was to approach Mya in a blasé fashion, but even I wasn't that good of an actress, so I decided to use my frustration to my advantage.

"Ugh, do you believe them?" I invited myself into her tiny bedroom and flopped down on her bed.

Mya was the only one of us that was fair-skinned. The rest of us were some shade of brown with a little cocoa or honey sprinkled in, but Mya's fair skin appeared even fairer contrasting with her midnight waves. They were woven into a regal braid and adorned by a purple scrunchie at the base of her neck. Her knees pulled up to meet her chest, as she sat at the head of her bed with her nose buried in a book.

"How come they never get into your stuff? I never see them dressing up in your clothes. It's not fair."

Mya shrugged and turned a page. "My clothes aren't that interesting."

"Whatcha reading?"

"A book."

"Yeah, I see that. What's it about? Is it good?"

"I wouldn't be reading it if it wasn't good."

I nodded. That made sense, and Mya was nothing if not logical. Her attention turned to the page on the right, and I glanced at my watch.

"So...whatcha doing? Got plans for tonight?"

"Why?" She asked without altering her gaze.

"I gotta get outta this house. I'm so sick of...you know...stuff. Don't you ever wanna get out and have some fun?"

She answered my question with the turn of yet another page.

Mya was the star of the girls' track team. She was obsessed with the Black Panthers and spent every minute she wasn't running reading biographies of the more prominent members. Our ideas of fun couldn't have been more different.

"Mya. You should come with me. It'll be fun."

"No, thanks."

"Don't you wanna know where I'm going? It's a little get-together.... Food. Some music. And probably a little dancing."

She finally lowered the book enough to look me in the eye. "You mean a party. Not interested."

"Nope, not a party. It's a get-together."

"Still not interested."

"Aww, come on. I wanna hang out with my sister. We don't spend enough time together."

Her brow furrowed and she laid the book face down on her bed and shifted her legs until she was sitting Indian style. When we were younger, Mya and I had been inseparable, but that was BFC, before foster care. I'd missed her. I truly did. I'd just never said it aloud until then.

"So, what do you say? You gonna come with me?"

"We could hang out here..."

"With Miss Holier-than-Thou downstairs and the twin devils running around? No, thank you. Come on, let's go. Just you and me."

She was still resisting, so I dug deeper.

"Folks are gonna think you're antisocial."

"Maybe I am."

"No, you're not. You're funny and nice and gorgeous. Come with me. I'll...I'll do your chores for a week."

Mya's eyes sparkled. "A month."

"Three weeks. That's it. So, what's it gonna be?"

4
NIKKI

AMAZING HOW NOTHING HAD CHANGED. JACKIE STILL thought rules applied to everybody except her. The world wouldn't function properly without structure and rules. Too bad Mama didn't realize that. Jackie would get away with murder if Mama had her way. So, it was up to me to do the dirty work.

"I wonder what she said to Mya to convince her to go. Most likely sold her a pack of lies. She's a pathological liar."

"What's pathological?" Natalie asked with a mouth full of biscuits and gravy.

Mama sighed, gazing wistfully at the two empty seats on the other side of the dining table.

"Means she lies practically on reflex. Probably isn't even aware she's doing it. That's what happens when a person doesn't have a conscience."

"Nikki...," Mama warned.

"Don't you think you're being a little hard on her?" Heziah's features became stiff. He saw things clearer than Mama, but they both lived in la-la land when it came to Jackie.

"I hope she doesn't start to rub off on Mya. Although Mya isn't the easiest person to influence," I said as I claimed a second helping of green peas. "Isn't that why you wanted her to take Mya? At least Mya doesn't run from one compromising situation to another."

"Let's change the subject. Something more fitting for supper talk."

Mama gave Nat a gentle nudge. "Baby, how was school?"

When Natalie was little, I used to pretend like she was my baby. Even though she was the baby of the family for a while, folks never treated her like that. Not the way they treat the twins. Daddy never paid her any attention whatsoever. He doted on Mya the way Mama doted on Jackie. So, it was up to me to dote on Natalie.

Even at nine years old, her scant frame reminded me of the girlish figures on the covers of magazines. Her dark-brown skin glistened in the dim light of the dining room as she recounted her day. She'd spent the last few years at Jackie's side since they'd been placed in the same foster home, but Natalie didn't share Jackie's moral challenges, making her the perfect sounding board for my suspicions. After supper I helped her clear the table and wash the dishes.

"How come you don't live with us?"

I can't deny the question startled me. I spent as much time as I could with them, but I also juggled church, school, and Darlene and the reverend. Couldn't help being pulled in all sorts of directions.

"Nikki?"

"My school is closer to my other house. You know that." Mama and Heziah had agreed I might as well graduate with my class instead of transferring to a new high school halfway through my last year.

Nat smiled sadly. She was the only one of my sisters who even felt my absence.

"So, what do you think Jackie and Mya are doing right now?"

Nat shrugged then added, "Probably dancing. That's what you do at parties, right?"

I could only imagine.

"What's it like? Your other house? Are they nice?" With a twist of her wrist, she turned the faucet off and began the task of putting the dishes I'd already dried in the cabinets. "Jackie says they brainwashed you with all that religious stuff." She grinned, ready to burst into giggles.

I didn't have a ready-made reply, so I focused on the task in front of me instead.

"Jackie says they got you so uptight, you wouldn't know fun if it bit you on the behind."

My smile gave her permission to let loose a giggle or two. She didn't mean any harm. So, I smiled for her benefit rather than out of any amusement.

"Jackie go to a lot of parties before you guys moved back home?"

"Oh yeah." Nat said. "All the time. Like every weekend."

Right about then the twins came sliding down the stairs. First Callie, then Jenna. I glanced up just in time to see Jenna holding a miniature spiral notebook with pink hearts on its cover. She froze as our eyes connected. Guilt plastered across her face.

Natalie turned, following my gaze, and said, "Hey, that's Jackie's diary."

It wasn't accompanied by a lock or a key. If it weren't for Natalie, I wouldn't have known what I was looking at, but the twins were totally clear on what they had.

Jenna squeezed the squarish notebook to her chest and looked to Callie for help.

"Give it." Nerves made my voice seem snappish, but I meant it as a polite request. I crossed the kitchen and was more or less in the hallway. Snapped my fingers impatiently and reiterated the order. "Hand it over."

5
JACKIE

CURIOSITY BRISTLED THROUGH THE HOUSE PARTY, SPARKING whispered conversations and wayward glances in my direction. I might as well have been the eighth wonder of the world, and I decided Nash Johnson was going to be the one to solve my mystery. He'd been huddled in a dark corner with his friends since I descended the stairs into Gina's basement. Never took his eyes off me. His sly grin eased across his face as I danced with one guy after another.

My current dance partner, Michael Duncan, was an average sort of guy. When he asked, I said yes, planning to dance with him for no more than two songs.

"What's up with your sister? She holding up the wall or what?"

Mya hadn't moved an inch since we arrived. She spent the first ten minutes looking incredibly bored, and then she whipped out a book. Didn't matter to her the basement didn't have proficient lighting.

"She's saving her energy for later."

Michael's crush on me was hardly a secret. Still, I pretended not to notice since it gave me no pleasure to break people's hearts. Nice guys like Mike were better off with somebody like Nikki. Somebody easy and predictable, who only wanted to be of use, that's who he should've been crushing on. Not me.

"You not tired?" he asked after the song ended. We'd been dancing for a good ten minutes.

"Nope," I replied, keeping both eyes glued to Nash and his circle of friends. He removed a silver flask from his pocket. The contents of which flowed quickly into their cups of Kool-Aid, and I was as parched as a rose wilting under the desert sun.

"Thirsty?"

"You read my mind."

"I'll get you a drink." Mike headed toward the refreshment table, probably thanking his lucky stars for the brief reprieve from dancing.

I took the opportunity to move closer to my objective. He saw me coming, and the grin he used to reel me in disappeared. Instead, he offered me a sip from his cup.

"What is it?"

"The good stuff."

Chatter among his friends stopped as all eyes fixed on me. They were about to get their first lesson in the ways of Jacqueline Morrow. I never backed down from a challenge. The plastic cup became flimsy in my grasp as I took my first sip, then another, and before long there was only a drop left.

Nash tossed the cup into the nearest trash and took me by the hand. I used my other one to wipe the last drops from my lips, and that small gesture sent my world into a sort of free fall. Didn't matter to him. In a matter of seconds, he wrapped me up in his arms, and we danced to the scent of his cologne.

"Want some more?" His voice hovered outside my left ear.

"Sure."

"I got some in my coat." He nodded to the small room twenty feet away where everyone piled their coats. "Come on."

I made my steps small and deliberate. No stranger to drunks, I'd seen all possible variations—stumbling left and right, slurring their words. I wasn't about to be one of them. Nobody and nothing would take control of my body.

A door closed behind me as I sunk into the pile of coats. My brain fought fiercely to keep my torso upright, but after a few seconds, it slacked off. I began wondering what kind of liquor he'd given me.

"Here it is," Nash said, sticking a clear bottle, whose label I couldn't read, under my nose. "You wanna drink it slow this time."

"I know that."

We took turns nursing the bottle until the party on the other side of the door melted away and only the room filled with coats existed. He asked me if I ever drank before. I nodded and delighted in the movement that made me feel as if my head had come unscrewed. Next came the giggles. From me. I was sure they belonged to me like it was a fact I'd memorized for a test, but I couldn't recall the moment the giggles actually began or what brought them on. They got louder as his fingers explored my body.

Next thing I knew, my sister stood over me saying, "Get up. Come on. Get up."

"We're having fun. Ain't that right?" Nash protested.

"Get off my sister." Mya's no-nonsense tone grew irritated, and the next moment, Nash moaned in pain.

"You're not reading," I smiled, pointing at her.

We stumbled left and right with me hanging on her like a wet rag, but Mya didn't stumble or succumb to labored breathing. Through the crowd and up the stairs, she carried me until I felt the cool night air on my face.

"D-Don't tell...okay?"

She didn't utter a sound. The only evidence she bothered to listen to me at all was how her grip on me tightened.

"I didn't do anything."

Mya stopped in the middle of the block and withdrew her support, watching me sway side to side in the sobering breeze. "I saw you."

"We talked. We were talking. I couldn't hear him, so he had to—"

"Get on top of you?"

"Lean over. To whisper in my ear."

"You don't even know him." The irritation in her voice bubbled up to the surface until it was all over her perfect face. Like everyone else, I was in awe of my sister, who was neither stupid nor naive. She made a terrible teenager. Always doing the right thing.

"He has a girlfriend."

"Oh no!" The giggles were back.

She rolled her eyes and resumed the task of directing my wayward feet.

"Sing with me, Mya." My body was ripe with the melody of a song I couldn't remember the lyrics to, so I gazed up at the stars asking them for some guidance. "Answer me! They won't tell me. Make them tell me."

"I'm never going to a party with you ever again. Stop laughing."

6
PECAN

"THEY'RE LATE." HEZIAH PACED BACK AND FORTH in front of our bedroom door. He'd refused to put on his pajamas and was still fully dressed down to his shoes.

"I'm sure they okay. Having a good time. Come on and relax."

"I'll relax when I know they're home safe and sound. What time did they leave?"

"Few minutes before supper," I said, easing off the bed to put my hands on his shoulders. Heziah spent more time worrying about things than I did. He worried about money and whether or not the girls should be doing better in school. Always wondering if they needed more. I was still celebrating their return.

"Belinda, I got a bad feeling. You told them to be back by eleven, right?"

"No...not exactly."

"What time did you tell them?"

"I didn't tell them anything other than to have fun and be safe."

Heziah sighed and continued his pacing. "Did you get the address where this party is gonna be or the phone number? You didn't, did you?"

"I trust my girls."

"They're teenagers. You can only trust them so far—" Heziah stood still, his ears perking up at the slightest sound.

A chill ran through me, and I wrapped the light blue robe tighter across my front. The polyester blew easily at the slightest wind. Normally,

I only wore it in the summer months, but that week had been really warm for March. I wasn't expecting the sudden chill that came on that night.

"Heziah, where you going?" I followed him out into the hall and down the stairs. He must've heard the front door opening and closing 'cause they stood in the foyer. Jackie shivered, rubbing her hands up and down her arms, but Mya seemed unfazed. She stood two or three inches taller than Jackie. When did that happen?

"Sorry we're late."

"That's okay, baby. Did you have fun?"

Mya nodded but without any trace of fun on her face. Jackie opened her mouth to say something, but a look from Mya stopped her in her tracks.

"Well, you girls know you're supposed to be home by eleven. Your mama and I were worried."

"I said sorry," Mya snapped, then turned to me and said, "Can we go to bed now?"

"Yeah, baby, go ahead."

It wasn't what Heziah wanted me to say, but I ain't see no need in harping on the time. They got the point. And we all needed to be in bed.

It'd been more than three years since we got married, and I was almost past expecting Heziah to react like Ricky did. I followed behind him a few steps and closed our bedroom door gently so as not to provoke the wild man I was expecting.

"You mad at me?"

Heziah yanked back the covers and flopped down on his side of the bed, kicking off his tired old loafers. He needed new ones, but last week he'd spent sixty dollars buying Nat and the twins winter coats.

"I'm not mad."

"Yeah, you are."

He stood to step out of his pants and took his time hanging them up in the closet. Everything in his half of the closet was organized by color and season. Heziah spent so much time taking care of his stuff that you'd think it was expensive.

"I can take it if you mad. You can say."

"That why you leaning on the door? Afraid to come in the room? To come near me?"

"I ain't. I was...I was pausing."

He sighed and finally turned toward me. The heaviness in his eyes scared me in a whole new kinda way. We'd finally gotten what we wanted. Had each other and our girls. But Heziah was looking at me like it was getting to be more than he bargained for.

"I'm okay. I am. And I know you right...about the girls. I'm too easy on 'em."

"They need limits. They can't do whatever they want, Belinda. It sends the wrong message. To them and to the twins. What do you think's gonna happen when Callie and Jenna get to be that age?"

"You're right. It's just been a long time since I...umm..."

Heziah stopped with only half his shirt unbuttoned and crossed the room to wrap me up in his arms. "You never stopped being their mama. Just 'cause you didn't see them doesn't mean they wasn't still yours."

7
MYA

THE WHISPERS STARTED LONG BEFORE I ENTERED the classroom and didn't stop once their eyes darted in my direction. Jackie and I were a year apart in school. She was a freshman, and I was a sophomore, but that didn't curb my infamous sister's reputation. Even folks in my year were talking about Jackie. She hadn't wasted any time making friends with the guys and enemies of the girls.

"Hey, Mya."

"Hey." I slid into my desk and began rummaging through my backpack for my homework assignment.

"So...you hear about what happened at Gina T's house Saturday?"

"Nope."

Girls in my year only talked to me about two things—sports and Jackie—and they hardly ever wanted to discuss sports.

"You know Virginia, right?"

I didn't. Not by name anyway. If she wasn't on one of the school's athletic teams, then she wasn't really on my radar.

"Well, she's going with Nash. And I heard they got into a huge fight at Gina's party. Something about him cheating on her with some freshman. You ain't hear about it?" She waited for my response, pretending to be an innocent reporter of gossip. "You was at the party, right? I think somebody said they saw you there. You and your sister...what's her name?"

The morning went by a little slower than usual since the catty little girls finally had something meaty to sink their teeth into. I never understood folks' obsession with other folks' lives. Speculating about who did or said what to whom, it all seemed pointless to me. I couldn't care less about who was going with whom, but on that day, I was the only one.

The bell rang, signaling the end of the last morning period, and a flood of students rushed into the hallway. Some of us stood at our lockers, trading our books for lunch money, but most of the bodies were headed to their next class.

"Hey, girl, you coming?" China breezed past me. She was on the track team with me and the closest thing to a friend that I had.

"Yeah," I nodded and intended to follow her toward the cafeteria, but a flash of movement in my peripheral vision resulted in a slight detour.

The crowd was growing fast. Folks shouting ooos and ahhs, bumping against each other as they circled around the spontaneous spectacle that was blocking the hallway. I didn't need to ask. The tightening in my chest was like a sixth sense.

It was her hair that cinched it for me, flying a foot above her head with a vengeance all its own. Jackie spent more time in the mirror than any of us. Her makeup and hair routine took almost an hour. So, when Virginia's fist grabbed a fistful of hair, my first thought was of all the work that went into it. I'd have been extra pissed if somebody tried to undo what took me an hour to create.

Jackie responded in kind, growling as she shoved her opponent into the wall of lockers. That was the first sign that it wasn't an evenly matched fight. My sister had been dodging and throwing punches since she was four years old. Took about thirty seconds before the crowd of onlookers saw the impending slaughter that had Virginia's name on it.

At first I thought the three girls had been thrust forward by the excitement of the crowd, but I was wrong. They knew each other. The three of them and Virginia, they were friends. Friends who stood up for each other when one of them was in trouble. In an instant, the odds had changed. Four against one. Jackie saw it too, but she wasn't any closer to backing down. I took a breath and dove in.

8
PECAN

WHAT THE HELL WAS YOU THINKIN'! HUH? Fightin'? Huh?" I intended to have a nice calm conversation but failed miserably. "You betta look at me when I'm talking to you two!"

"Mama, they started it!"

"Jackie—"

"They did! We just walked by minding our own business!"

Lord knows I loved my child, but she sure set her mind to testing my patience. The social worker said we shouldn't expect the girls to act normal, like nothing had happened, like we hadn't been separated from them for years. So, I was doing my best to be patient and understanding, ignoring the lies that slid so easy off Jackie's tongue and the sadness that had crept up behind Mya's eyes. I hoped it would all work itself out.

"Mya, ain't you got nothing to say?"

The two of 'em sat side by side on the couch, two sides of the same coin: one calm with not a hair outta place and the other with the beginnings of a black eye.

"Mama, you want us to not defend ourselves? That ain't right. Everybody got a right to defend theyself."

"Jackie—"

"We wasn't doing nothing but defending ourselves. Right, Mya?"

Mya sucked her bottom lip into her mouth, chewing on it thoughtfully.

She wasn't as friendly with lies as Jackie was. She hadn't even offered a word in her own defense, staring out the window like she was hoping a familiar face would walk past our house.

"Since you both been suspended, don't think you gonna be sitting around here doing nothing. Got a lot of stuff 'round here that need doing. Come on, let's go. One of you gone sweep up them leaves in the yard, and the other can wash the windows."

"But, Mama—"

"Girl, you say one more thing, and I'm gonna lose my mind!"

Neither one of my girls wore repentance too well. No droopy shoulders and teary eyes from them. So, I ain't expect it and a part of me was ready to give a little anyway.

"I gotta go pick up Nat from school in a little bit. Y'all have your chores done by then, I won't tell your daddy about this." Mya's stare turned ice cold, and I immediately wished I coulda taken it back. "I mean Heziah. I won't tell him."

"Okay." Jackie smiled, taking her sister by the hand. "You'll see, Mama. We're gonna be the best backyard sweepers and window washers you ever seen."

I don't know about 'em being the best, but they was still at it by the time the four of us was headed up the walk to the front porch. Mya worked the leaves into a pyramid while Jackie took a rest from singing and wiping down the windows to meet us at the top stair.

"Hey, Mama, see how hard I been working? Got 'em shining like brand-new now."

Even in her punishment, Jackie couldn't turn off the charm. A good part of the reason I hardly ever bothered with it in the first place. It just rolled off her shoulders like rain off a steep roof.

"Mama, how come they gotta wash windows?"

"They lost their minds is what they did. This is what happens when you lose yo' mind. Now go on inside. Take the twins with you."

Nat got as far as the screen door before turning back to ask Jackie if she wanted some help, and I stopped to watch. Couldn't find the words to explain why that wasn't posed to happen. It was a punishment not a group activity. Jackie saved me from having to explain by simply shaking her head.

"You sure?" Nat's brow wrinkled with concern. Like the manual labor might be too much for her big sister to handle. "Want me to get some clean water?" she asked, already reaching for the handle of the bucket.

Maybe my girls could've used more discipline, but there was one thing they ain't have no shortage of—loyalty.

9 NIKKI

NO ONE WOULD ARGUE THE GOOD REVEREND was an unintelligent man, but he didn't recognize the word no. He allowed one or two not-to-my-knowledges or a few I-don't-think-sos, but never a flat out no. Mya never took to his way of doing things. On occasion it did become a bit irritating, but nothing I couldn't handle.

"Nikki, honey, how's your sister?" Darlene's favorite question. She never stopped missing Mya, but at least, she could say her name without tears in her eyes. "Is she...adjusting all right? Must be weird for her to be back in that house. All those memories."

I wanted to ask why it would be hard for Mya and not for me. The memories belonged to both of us—me more so as the older sister.

"Not too much lemon," she reminded me. Darlene liked her iced tea a specific way.

"Sorry, Mother."

From the day we first arrived on their doorstep, I found myself comparing their lives to what we left behind. Darlene's kitchen didn't differ too much from my mama's. Cozier. Newer appliances. Plus where Mama's kitchen made use of yellow tiles, Darlene's had black and white.

"I'm thinking about whipping up some potato salad to go with dinner tomorrow." Darlene's favorite hint. She smiled in my direction, hoping the added incentive would propel me to mention the possibility to Mya. Mya had nothing but the purest love for potato salad. She would eat anybody's potato salad. Not me. I only liked Mama's.

"Should I peel the potatoes now or..."

"No, I'll do it." Her smile evaporated, leaving only disappointment in its place. "Thank you, dear."

I nodded and slid the pitcher of freshly made iced tea onto the top shelf of the fridge. She still had me. I think it helped.

"So, how are things over there? I mean as far as you can see. They getting back to normal?"

I nodded. A lie because it didn't feel normal. Normal would've been Daddy's cologne wafting through the house. Would've put him at the head of the table, taking seconds and thirds, telling Mama she really put her foot in it this time. Normal would've been waking up in the middle of the night to the sounds of Daddy's temper. Mya and me slipping into bed with Jackie and Nat, the four of us hiding under the covers until the house grew still again. Normal meant watching Mama pack on makeup the next morning. Smiling back at her while she sold us on everything being just fine. Things would never be normal again. Darlene didn't understand that.

"You could mention to your sister the reverend and I would love to get a call from her...whenever she gets a chance."

I nodded. Darlene may've been extraordinary at dropping hints, but she was terrible at picking up on them. Mya didn't need any goading when it came to something she wanted. If she wanted to send word, she would have of her own accord. On top of that, she practically flew out the door when Mama regained custody. The reverend chalked up Mya's eagerness to the freedom waiting for her at home. Darlene, on the other hand, convinced herself that my sister rushing out the door without so much as a nod meant nothing at all. I waited with bated breath for the day when she would have to look that truth in the eye.

"Did I tell you I'm gonna be on the Honor Roll this quarter?"

"Oh, how wonderful."

Darlene served dinner promptly at six–rain or shine. The clock over the stove read 5:53, and dinner rested in the warmer, waiting for the reverend to come home. Darlene took the seat next to me and covered my hand with hers.

"I'm so proud of you. Now all we've gotta do is see you married. I was about your age when the reverend came calling."

"Mmhmm. Actually, there's something I want to talk to you and the reverend about. I..."

Heat rose into my cheeks and intensified. Why did I blush so easily?

I wished she would look away while I got my thoughts together, but she'd picked up the vague scent of romance in the air. "I kinda met someone. He's wonderful—perfect. He's finishing his last year of medical school. He's French and he...well, I think he likes me."

"An older man? Of course, he likes you!" By no measure was Darlene a tall woman, more on the short side, but she jumped up from the table with such vigor the motion added two inches to her height. "This is wonderful! I'm so happy. Thrilled! Oh, wait until the reverend gets wind of this!"

"You think he'll be okay with it?"

If I waited any longer than eighteen to begin dating, then I would've been in danger of becoming an old maid. So, I let out a sigh of relief once Darlene dismissed my moral concerns.

JEAN-LOUIS GRENIER WOULDN'T PASS FOR AN AVERAGE boy. He'd probably never even been a boy. He abided by the ways of a proper, well-bred gentleman. The perfect man and my first suitor. How many girls could lay claim to that? Most of them flung themselves at unworthy boys but not me. I swore never to be cavalier with my body or my heart. After five dates, he picked up on my expectations and began making overtures about the future. Promises of diamonds and expensive vacations lined our conversations, and I smiled politely, careful not to appear too eager. I acted mature for my age. Mature young ladies didn't lose their composure when young men paid them some attention, but when he suggested it was time my family met him, I couldn't contain myself any longer.

"He's going to propose, I think!"

"Mmhmm...," Mya mumbled as she turned the page in her book. She was the first person I trusted with the information.

"You'll be my maid of honor. What color would you like to wear? Oh, and what kind of dress—I know you don't love dresses, but you must wear one. It's just for one night—or day—I'm not sure yet." I gazed up at the ceiling of her bedroom, enjoying the lightness filling my head. "You think it should be an afternoon or evening wedding? What do you think of black-tie?"

"Great," was my sister's quick response.

"Evening is best, right? The twins are gonna be the cutest flower girls, and Natalie can be a junior bridesmaid, and I guess Jackie can be there. Mama would probably make a fuss if I didn't invite her..." All at once panic ripped through my daydream. "Mya?"

"Yeah." She flipped another page and paused long enough to meet my eyeline.

"Umm...you think Mama and Darlene will get along?"

Mya shrugged defiantly as if to say she couldn't care less.

"What about Heziah and the reverend? I mean which one should I have walk me down the aisle? Of course Heziah's been around longer but the reverend...he–"

"Do whatever you want."

"You're right. It's not that big of a deal. The reverend will be happy to do the ceremony, but Heziah...I don't know...since Daddy's not here, I kinda wanna do what he would...I mean you think he'd be pissed if Heziah walked me down the aisle? Considering...you know..."

Mya's book fell a few inches, enough to reveal her pained expression. I could bear no more than a second of my sister's pain and turned away from it. Staring straight ahead at the wall, I silently chided myself for saying too much. It was easy to do with Mya. She only half listened to what you said to her anyway.

"I think you'll like him. Jean-Louis I mean. He's super smart. Like you. All that's left is to keep him away from Jackie until the wedding." I'd meant it as a joke or at least a half joke, but Mya didn't find it funny at all. "You know she can't help but throw herself at everything that moves."

My focus fell to my short, brittle nails, and as if powered by remote, I brought my right hand to my mouth, gnawing at them like a restless dog. A terrible habit. Drove everybody crazy, but I figured the world owed me one vice.

"Mya?"

She moved about the rectangular bedroom, tossed the book, which captivated her only moments before onto a pile of laundry, and dropped to her knees, searching under her bed. Common sense would've been to change the topic, but I forged on ahead anyway.

"Mya."

"What?"

"Jackie say anything about her foster father?"

"Which one?"

"Umm...the last one."

"Nope. Why?"

Common sense beckoned, directing me down a different path, giving me a second chance to leave well enough alone. I simply had to keep quiet, but secrets were never my forte.

"She seduced him." I waited for Mya to deny it. For her to yell at me, accuse me of defamation or slander. I waited for what seemed like forever. "Mya?"

"How you figure?"

"I read it in her diary."

"Let me see it."

Of course she wouldn't take my word for it. She'd want to see it for herself, in black and white. Too bad I didn't have it anymore.

"I gave it to Mama."

10
MYA

SOON AS PRACTICE ENDED, COACH CALLED ME into his tiny closet of an office. He closed the door behind me and told me to sit. Someone told him about the fight. I'd already had one teacher pull me aside to counsel me about my actions. So much to-do over a bunch of silly girls. Folks getting all worried that I might be improperly influenced. Doubted anyone thought to have the same talk with Jackie or the other girls involved in the fight.

"Mya—"

"Yes, coach."

"You're smarter than this. Don't let folks get you in trouble." The file cabinet screeched loudly as he pulled out the drawer second from the top and began thumbing through the files. "Have you given any thought to college?"

I nodded. I had five schools on my short list, all of them out of state.

"Good. There's going to be some college scouts at our next match." The drawer closed, the motion drawing an equal amount of noise. "Here. Study these." He held out a stack of glossy pamphlets with smiling athletes on the covers. "These are some good schools. A worthwhile opportunity for a girl with a good head on her shoulders."

Track was fun, but running had my heart. Didn't need track to run. Didn't need the crowds or my teammates. Had no dreams of the Olympics. I wanted a decent pair of sneakers on my feet and a way out. No more. No less. The competition and training that came with athletic programs had a downside too. Odds were I'd pull something sooner or later. Only a fool would plan to run forever. I nodded as coach continued his speech about college track and kept my logic to myself.

Finally I said, "Thanks, coach."

He nodded and opened one of the brochures to point to the bottom of the financial aid page. "Illinois State holds one scholarship for a girl athlete each year. Just one. Now you keep doing whatcha doing on the track and off and this could be you. Go on home and show this stuff to your folks. I'll be around to answer their questions after this Friday's match if they want."

I didn't expect they'd show. The twins kept Mama busy. Jackie would come. She came to my last match. She spent most of the time flirting with the boy in front of her, but she cheered like it was her full-time job when I crossed the finished line.

"I bet your folks are real proud of you."

"Yeah." I stuffed the brochures into my backpack and slung it over my shoulder. "See ya, coach."

The sun's crest hovered above the horizon of the school's parking lot as I lengthened my stride. Never thought twice about the distance or the time it took to get from point A to point B. Only the blood mattered, rushing from my heart to my feet and back again. The blood broke free inside me, the tiny cells swimming through my body like a broom swishes around dark corners, uncluttering useless thoughts congregating there. I'd been a fan of thoughts my whole life, never would've considered any of them useless. For thoughts and words were so clearly related and I adored words, but I was wrong because words that couldn't be said–shouldn't be said–held no meaning. Not for the person who thought them up and not for anyone who might've heard them. So I ran to keep those thoughts from using up space. Ran hard and fast. Especially when no one was watching. Didn't have to couch my steps out of fear I'd be found out. That someone would say, "Hey, that girl there...the one with the dark hair! She knows!" Surely if they saw me run–the real me, not the me that showed up for track meets–if they saw the real honest-to-God Mya Morrow, the words would escape the cage I'd locked them in. The cage in the dark dusty corner of the farthest reaches of my mind. So, I double-checked, no one was around and adjusted my speed from power walking to a light jog but stopped short when a boy stepped out of the shadows with both hands in his pockets. Ramon. No book bag in sight, but that wasn't unusual since he hardly ever showed up for class.

"Hey."

"Hey. You waiting on me?"

"No," he lied.

Ramon probably could've been my brother in another life. The resemblance gave most folks pause. Same high-yellow complexion and we were both taller than average for our age.

"So...you went to a party last week?"

"Yeah," I slowed my pace so he could keep up. Ramon dared not walk any faster than necessary otherwise his jeans would've sank to the ground.

"Thought you didn't like going to parties." His hands moved deeper into his pockets as if the extra coverage would shield his hurt feelings. "At least that's what you told me."

"I don't."

"You don't what?"

"Like going to parties."

"So why'd you go?"

"Jackie."

"Have fun?" he asked when I didn't explain any further.

"Jealous?"

He shrugged. "What I'm a be jealous for? Ain't like you my girlfriend."

I wished I could've said I hadn't given it that much thought, but I did. I thought about him more than I wanted to admit. I'd even made a chart, listing his pros on one side and cons on the other. The con list was longer.

"You don't need to walk me home. I'm fine on my own."

"I'm not. I'm going to...umm...catch up with my boy. He live up on... umm..." Ramon's hand popped out of his pocket, snapping and pointing as he tried to remember the name of the street. "Over there by...umm..."

Ramon had an ever growing group of friends. Every few months one or two of them were arrested and quickly replaced by new ones. They spent more time hanging out on street corners than they did in school.

"Mya?"

"Yeah."

"I...uhh...I been thinking and—"

"Can I ask you a question?" We were about two blocks from my house. I stopped under the street light and turned to face him. "You wanna be my boyfriend?"

"Why? You want me to be?"

"I asked you first."

To that, he laughed.

"DID YOU HEAR?" JACKIE SLIPPED INTO MY bedroom with a deliciously evil grin on her face. "Miss Holier-than-Thou finally snagged herself a boyfriend. A soon-to-be doctor no less. She's downstairs right now telling Mama how wonderful he is."

I spared a nod and went right back to my homework. About a third of the sophomore class was taking advanced algebra, and I was among the privileged few. My textbook, notes, and workbook made a half circle on the floor around me. They required a bit more concentration than gossiping about Nikki's boyfriend did, but Jackie didn't pay that any mind.

"Guess Miss Goody-Two-Shoes finally gave up the goods."

Even her giggles took on a taunting tone when inspired by Nikki. Why the two of them couldn't get along was beyond me.

Jackie stretched out lengthwise across my bed and rolled on her side so her head rested on top of her fist and bucked her eyes at me. "What? Not my fault she's a prude. I mean what seventeen year old has never had a boyfriend? What's she afraid of? Huh? I mean, you never had a boyfriend, but that's because you're busy with other stuff. What's she busy with? Church? I'm just saying it's weird. If she's gonna be a nun, she should come out and say so. B-B-But she's all freakin' f-f-frigid. I bet she can't even say the word."

"What word?"

"Sex." Jackie's grin disappeared into thin air, but a sly smirk immediately fell in its place. "I bet she thinks it's a sin—or it's for making babies or something like that. Not for fun. Oh no! That would be horrible. I bet she does it in the dark. Fully clothed! Then runs off to shower and pray after! She probably wouldn't even recognize her own pussy if it was staring her in the face."

It wasn't funny. I didn't know any more than Nikki did, so I had no business laughing. I was not gonna laugh. I tightened my facial muscles, forcing them into a stoic expression.

"Know what?" Jackie grinned, holding back her own giggles. "We should have a pussy-vention. Nikki, meet your pussy. Pussy, this is Nikki. Now, you two play nice."

"Jackie!"

"What? It's true!" she said as we both broke into giggles.

"What's so funny?"

I finally regained enough control to wipe the tears from my eyes and focus on the figure darkening my doorway. Heziah grinned from ear to ear, waiting to be let in on the joke.

"Nothing," I muttered.

"Oh, we were just talking about the birds and the bees," Jackie cooed sweetly.

Heziah shifted his weight from one foot to the other. "All right...well, that's...that's...umm...that's good, I guess."

"Damn straight, it's good."

"JACKIE!" I hadn't meant to shout but it slipped out.

"What? Is it supposed to be bad?"

As embarrassed as I was, Heziah was even more so, but he gathered his composure and motioned for Jackie to make room for him to sit next to her on my bed.

"What? What I say?"

She, of course, was aware of exactly what she'd said, but my sister was determined to prolong our embarrassment for as long as she could.

"Well, I've been wanting to talk to you girls about something, and I guess now's as good a time as any. I realize that you're growing up...into young ladies."

"Is this a sex talk?"

"Oh my God, Jackie, shut up!"

Heziah grimaced slightly and glanced over his shoulder at the open door as if he might be expecting reinforcements. A second later, he returned to the matter at hand. "You're both smart, caring, beautiful girls. I want you to be proud of that and make sure that any boy you're...interested in appreciates that too."

"Okay, daddy-o!" Jackie popped up to wrap her arms around his neck. The tension melted from his body, and he hugged her before turning to me.

"Mya, you listening?"

Of course, I was. He was only two feet away. Even if I didn't want to, I couldn't help but listen.

"Mya?"

"Mama's calling us. Come on, Jackie."

I was fully aware that the mess my life had become wasn't Heziah's fault. I'd liked him fine when I was a kid, but that was before my world came apart at the seams. Mama could only shoulder the blame for some of it, so that left plenty for Heziah. The more effort he put into caring about me, the more that blame simmered underneath my skin. I hadn't asked him to care, hadn't asked him for a thing. Nothing he could give me would make up for what I'd lost anyway.

"Why you so mean to him?" Jackie whispered as we went single file down the stairs.

I wasn't exactly mean. I just didn't feel the need to respond to everything he said to me.

"Mya." Her fingers brushed against my shoulder but quickly withdrew before latching on, and Jackie went silent until we were both safely on the first floor. "What'd he ever do to you?" She prodded.

Without so much as a first thought, I spun on my heels to face her and out popped, "What'd he ever do that was so magnificent?"

Silence wasn't easy to come by with Jackie, but that's all she could conjure up because I was right. Wasn't one thing she could point to as a solid piece of evidence that Heziah was some wonderful gift bestowed upon us. Not one thing.

11 NIKKI

"DON'T BE NERVOUS, MA CHÉRIE."

"I'm not."

The hard part was over. Jean-Louis had gotten along wonderfully with the reverend despite the fact that he was eight years my senior and not much of a Christian. Now he just wanted to meet my other family. I wasn't nervous at all. It was going to be easy. I was sure of it. Still, I couldn't stop tugging at the hemline of my brown plaid skirt.

"Did I tell you that Heziah's son is in town?"

In our absence, Louis had become quite comfortable in our house with our mama. He even called her Mama just like we did. It wasn't Christian of me, but I felt the tiniest bit of spite churning in my heart.

"He's a lawyer."

"Oh?"

I nodded, choosing to leave off a few details about Louis's occupation. "He's so educated."

A grimace graced Jean-Louis's African features just as he steered the car onto our street. "Well educated."

"Hmm?"

"I believe you meant to say he is well educated."

"Oh, right. I'm sorry."

"Tell me more about him." We parked a few cars away from the house, and he turned off the ignition but allowed the radio to continue to play. "What is he like?"

I shrugged. I didn't spend much time thinking about Louis. I hadn't even expected him to be there. I was more worried about the other members of my family. Mya would be fine, a little quiet but fine. The twins would be their adorable selves. Natalie was always easy. Where she got her manners from I had no clue. It was hard to believe that she and Jackie came from the same place.

"I told Mama all about you. She was thrilled." I smiled at my slight overstatement.

Mama didn't do thrilled, especially when it came to men. She waited patiently for their true colors to shine through and the waiting made her appear reserved. I just hoped that Jean-Louis wouldn't take it personally.

"And Heziah is extremely smart. Not school smart...I mean, well, sort of...he reads a lot."

"Do not worry, my love," he cooed, lifting my restless hand to his lips. "I will love them as I love you. I promise."

Words of introduction flooded out of my mouth as soon as the front door opened. It was like watching some crazy babbling fool go on and on about a dream he had once. I was sure the moment had gone unnoticed until Heziah gave me his patented pat on the back. Firm and gentle.

"And this is my mama. Mama, this is Jean-Louis Grenier."

"Mrs. Jenkins, what a pleasure it is to meet you. I see where Nicole gets her beauty."

Mama nodded and invited us into the dining room, saying supper was already on the table. They'd added two extra seats, adding up to a total of four mismatching chairs since the dining set only came with six to begin with. We all scooted in bumping elbows and offering up polite smiles.

"Such a cozy home you have here." His gaze roamed the three walls of the dining room.

The twins had taken to snickering every time he said anything. It wasn't long before one of them said, "You talk funny."

"That's 'cause he's from Africa," Natalie explained to them.

"Actually, I'm French. Do you know where France is? It's on the other side of the Atlantic Ocean. In Europe. It is a common misconception. Some people don't realize that Africans have migrated all over the world."

"But you're still African," Mya replied, her cold black eyes staring daggers into his from across the table. "Migrating don't change that."

"Actually, I'm French and I have the passport to prove it."

"Mama, did you do something different to the black-eyed peas? I mean they're usually really good, but this is extraordinary. Don't you think?" I asked, nudging my date.

"Actually, I've nothing to compare them to." He smiled and leaned in to kiss the tip of my nose. "I will have to take your word for it, ma chérie."

"She Nikki, not Sherry," Callie insisted.

"No, no, my dear. It is a saying in my language—"

"African?"

"French," he replied fast as a whip. "It means my dear."

Dinner continued in that manner for half an hour. One assertion followed closely by a correction or challenge. Without the slightest warning, my family was taken over—replaced by a tag team of litigators. The twins were just following the direction of the tide, so I was willing to issue them passes, but Mya refused to let up. Then Louis and Heziah jumped in. It was a miracle that Jean-Louis didn't wither under the weight of their coordinated attack. Neither Mama nor Jackie had a word to spare in his defense, not one word.

"Nicole tells me that you're an attorney."

"I am."

"How is that for you?"

"How is it for me?" Louis's eyebrows reached for the ceiling as he tried to smother the chuckle that was brewing in his throat. "It's fine."

"It is underappreciated here. In Europe it is considered a dignified profession, and they are graciously paid. I have heard Americans say...what is the phrase? Dime a dozen? Am I saying it correctly?"

I nodded, taking a deep breath at the same time. To fill my chest to capacity as if that would protect me from my family's glare. They acted as if I'd brought a traitor into the house instead of a medical student.

"Louis doesn't have that problem. He's undoubtedly appreciated. Overly appreciated even! I mean his clients love him. They're poor, so he's practically doing a public service."

"Oh. Well, that is different."

The plates had been picked clean by then. Only chicken bones remained as proof of our supper. An uncomfortable silence blanketed the table while Mama went around collecting plates. Each plate clanged on top of the others with increasing loudness, offering up their own disapproval. I couldn't believe it. Everything had gone so well at the reverend's house.

12
JACKIE

"WHERE DO YOU THINK SHE FOUND HIM?"

Louis was a better person than me, so he wouldn't have joined in the fun if he was of a sober mind. He chuckled and took another puff from the reefer cigarette before passing it back to me. The crisp night air insured we would be alone out on the front porch. Louis sat in the middle of the top stair and I sat on his right, my knees facing him and my back against the porch post.

"Maybe he was nervous."

"How he gonna just re-name somebody? Did you see Mama's face when he called Nikki Nicole? Whew. I didn't think he was gonna make it outta here alive. I bet you she marries him. That's what happens to girls who don't know any better."

"Jackie."

"What?"

"Be nice."

"Eh. I'd rather be honest." I beckoned for him to pass the contraband in my direction again. Wasn't it enough I'd kept my mouth shut for the entirety of supper?

"How're you doing?"

Louis didn't have Heziah's eyes. His were round, bold, and a bit crass. Whereas, Heziah's were shaped like almonds and always seemed to be laughing.

"Pops said that you moved around a lot."

"Yeah."

"How many times?"

"Eight."

"Damn."

"I'm fine. Girls like me always land on top."

Louis nodded, but my meaning was lost on him. Smart didn't always mean perceptive. I exhaled smoky rings in his direction, and he still wasn't any wiser. I imagined that if I'd had a lollipop or a sucker he wouldn't have been so oblivious to what I was telling him.

"Were they good people?"

"Who? Oh, yeah. Sure. Just swell according to the social worker. But I was a troubled child," I said grinning shamelessly. "Takes a special kinda man to handle me."

"Well, I'm glad they were good to you."

"Mmhmm."

"Do you miss any of them?"

A siren cut through the night as an ambulance charged past our block. I glanced in its direction, wondering where they were headed and what the emergency was. Louis might've said something else, but by then, a comfy fog had settled around my head, blocking out some sounds and some sense. Random thoughts rattled around in my mind. Nikki's boyfriend had parked a few cars down the block. He drove an older model BMW. He was short for a man and lacked any kind of a physique. Not my type at all. I leaned toward taller options.

"How tall are you?"

With the flick of his fingers, Louis tossed the last of the blunt into the front yard and pulled a Ziploc bag from his pocket along with cigarette papers. He could've easily towered over six feet.

"Louis?"

"Hmm?" He was busy rolling another blunt.

"You got a girlfriend?"

"Right now? No." He licked the edge of the paper and sealed it closed. "Why?"

"Like you..."

"Huh?"

I didn't blame him for being confused. I'd meant to relay a coherent thought, but somewhere around the beginning and the end of what I was thinking, my tongue suffered a case of laziness.

"Guys like you..." I tried again, still failing.

"They know you smoke?"

The abrupt change of subject knocked me off balance so much that I actually felt myself teeter from left to right. My feet were still planted firmly on the porch right along with my bottom, but somehow I still managed to be unstable.

"Just be careful who you do it with. Some guys'll take advantage."

The dazed girl in control of my body swooned. He was worried about us, protective even. She gazed into his eyes, searching for proof of his interest.

"Maybe you oughta take a break," he said. "I probably shouldn't have given you any. Go on inside and lie down."

"Come with me?"

"Nah, I'm gonna sit out here for a while. The cool air helps me think."

"Nobody gets high so they can think."

I'd finally managed a well-thought-out statement, and in the midst of my celebration, I was inspired in an unladylike fashion. Louis didn't even see it coming. In his state, it took him a full ten seconds to realize that it wasn't the wind caressing his thigh.

13
PECAN

SNEAKING AND SPYING WASN'T NATURALLY IN ME, so I ended up jumping at every tiny sound my house made. Shoving the heart-covered notebook up under the covers just in case I was about to be caught with it. Some parents wouldn't have thought twice about reading they girls' diaries. I knew that. Nikki knew that too. That's why she looked at me the way she did when she handed it over, like she was challenging me to be a different kinda mama than I had been.

I set my mind to proving her wrong. I could do it. Will alone got me through the first ten pages. They were all about how much Jackie had missed me and missed Mya. The pretty hopeful words of a little girl. I found myself thumbing through the pages wondering how much I could take.

"Belinda, we need to talk." Heziah rushed into our bedroom out of breath and pushed the door closed before moving toward me on the bed. "What you hiding under there?"

"Nothing."

With a quick shake of his head, Heziah dismissed his suspicions and went on with what he figured was more important. "We got a problem. It's Jackie."

"I'm getting real tired of folks telling me she's a problem."

"No, I didn't mean—not like that. She's not the problem. She has a problem. That's what I mean. Haven't you noticed..."

What? I hadn't noticed anything other than she was mostly grown. It was in the way she carried herself, the way she walked from room to room or threw her head back when she laughed. My baby had the confidence of a woman.

"Belinda." His hand reached out for mine, telling me to brace myself for the words coming my way. "I think we oughta have a talk with her. Find out where she is...as far as sex goes."

First Nikki, then Heziah, both of them sure my baby was doing unmentionable things. "Don't look at me like that. I love Jackie, you know I do. But–"

"Ain't no but when you really love somebody. Ain't no thinking bad of 'em for any reason."

"Belinda–"

"I don't wanna hear nobody else bad mouthing her! She's only thirteen. And she been through enough. She not gonna be how you think she should be 'cause she ain't have the life she shoulda had, but that don't mean anything wrong with her!"

Heziah hung his head in what I thought was defeat. Wasn't 'til his eyes zeroed in on me that I realized he was just collecting his thoughts.

"I was locking up downstairs," he began. "And I caught her. With Louis."

"What's that posed to mean? What you saying?"

I could see clear as day that he ain't wanna say any more. He wanted to unsee what he'd seen, but instead he was having to share it with me.

"She wouldn't do that. He's her brother. And he's a good ten years older than her! He should know better!"

Heziah's eyes closed gently, and he exhaled, nodding along with what I was saying to ease the sting of his next few words. "He pushed her away."

SWEETS ARE GOOD FOR THE SOUL WAS something I used to hear Clara say. Usually while she was mixing up some batter for her pineapple upside-down cake. She'd make it when words and water weren't enough to heal whatever was broken. I could almost taste it, but I knew I'd never be able to recreate it. Her recipe was gone with her. So the next day, I did what I could. German chocolate cake.

"Smells good, Mama."

"Thank you, baby."

Nat dropped her backpack in the doorway and cozied up to me, waiting for the first opportunity to lick the spoon. She was the only one of my four to ease back in like she'd never left. She'd always been all smiles. She still was.

"How you doing, baby?"

"Good."

"How's school?"

"Good. My teacher's okay and the kids are pretty cool. My class got the early lunch period today 'cause of our field trip so I got to see the twins. Lashawnda didn't believe that they're my sisters but I told her not all family gotta be the same color. When I have kids they might be like me or like Mya. Right, Mama? You just never know. Can I have some?" She pointed to the mixing bowl I'd basically scraped clean.

I added the chocolate-covered mixers and the spoon, and she carried them over to the kitchen table. Once the cake was in the oven, I sat down too. Nat was alternating between licking her fingers and licking the bowl.

"How you like being a big sister?"

"It's good. I tell them things. And I try to keep 'em from getting in trouble with Jackie. And Nikki too. They don't mean any harm. They just be thinking that everything's a game 'cause they kids. That's how kids are."

"And you don't think that, huh?"

"When I was a little kid, I did."

I wondered how much she remembered about Ricky and what life was like before they were taken from me. It was soothing to think maybe she ain't remember none of it. Well, except for the good parts. Me and her sisters. And Heziah. But it ain't exactly work like that. She had to forget all of it or none of it.

"What's wrong, Mama?"

"Nothing. I'm just thinking about your foster people. The folks that took care of you and Jackie when I was away."

"Which ones?" Her lips made an extra loud pop as she sucked the last of the batter from her fingertips.

"The last ones. Darrel and his wife. What's her name?"

"Catrina, but we called her Cat."

I nodded so as not to scare her. We was just gonna have a quick little chat about these people. And what they did to my girls. "You like 'em?"

"Sure. They was fine. They let me stay in my same school and spend the weekend with my friends. Every weekend if I wanted to."

"Where was Jackie? She go with you?"

"She came with us once, but after that she said she was too old to be hanging out with a bunch of lil' kids."

"But they was good to you? Didn't say or do nothing that made you feel funny?"

Nat shifted an inch or two in her chair then gave me a silly grin. "No. They not what you call funny people. They more serious than funny."

"What about your sister? She get along with 'em?"

She nodded, her gaze gradually wandering from the conversation. I couldn't tell if she was hiding something or if she was just bored. "Mama, how long until the cake's ready?"

"About another hour."

"Okay," she replied, making her way toward the hallway. Nat got a few feet from the doorway of the kitchen and turned back. "Want me to keep an eye on the twins? I already did my homework, so..."

"Yeah, baby, that would be good."

Soon as Nat was out of my sight, I heard a click at the front door and then a whoosh as it closed shut. Mya's quick purposeful stride left the floorboards creaking with each step she took. "Hey Mama," she called halfheartedly as she headed up the stairs.

Was only a few days out the week that Mya didn't have some sort of practice to go to. On those days, she normally came home with Jackie.

"Where's your sister?" I called from the base of the stairs. But when she ain't answer me, I headed up after her. I found her standing over the tiny table in the corner unpacking her backpack. "I said, where's your sister?"

"She's not here?"

"No. She's not here. You didn't see her at school?"

Mya glanced at me for all of two seconds, then went back to what she was doing.

"Mya."

"Yeah."

"Yeah, what? Yeah, you saw her at school?"

"No. Just...yeah. You called my name, so I'm saying yeah."

My fingers found their way to my waist, wiggling and squeezing against the cotton fabric of my dress. I had a sickening feeling in the pit of my stomach. Wherever Jackie was she was in trouble.

"So, you ain't see her at school. Y'all left here together. I saw you."

"Yeah."

"What happened? She leave school early?"

"Ask her."

"She ain't here! That's why I'm asking you! You supposed to keep an eye on her!"

Mya settled on her history textbook and began flipping through the pages. She ain't need no practice at pretending like I wasn't there.

"Mya."

"Yeah." She scooped up the text and her notebook and sat cross-legged on the floor of her bedroom.

"Where she go?"

"How I'm supposed to know? Jackie ain't a baby, Mama. She go where she want."

Getting information from Mya was like trying to get water from a rock. Maybe if I was somebody else she woulda given it up willingly, but I was just me.

"Don't you care about your sister? Care where she is? Care what happen to her?"

"She fine."

"How you know that if you don't know where she is or how she got there?"

I could see the wheels turning in her head. She'd accidentally said too much and was searching for a way out of the corner she was backed into.

"Mya Ann Morrow, don't you even think of lying to me."

14
JACKIE

At thirteen years old, I felt certain Darrel King was a rarity in the world of men. He wore blue jeans rolled up to expose his ankles and bare feet. His black silk shirt rested calmly against his ebony colored skin. Darrel was the only professional I'd ever seen wear his hair in long braids. They fell hard and straight like wooden reeds down his back, daring all that stood before him to turn a blind eye to his will. Darrel made his own rules and expected the world to follow them.

"Miss me?" I asked, snuggled into my corner of the sofa. I wore a denim miniskirt and paired it with one of Nat's tee shirts. My caramel legs and luscious lumps would've been difficult for a priest to ignore. But he sat cool as a cucumber lounging in the fridge, his arm stretched along the back of the sofa, his fingertips resting an inch from my shoulder.

"I see you're finally out of uniform," he said. "Public school, huh? Must make you happy."

It did. Contrary to his opinion, I wasn't cut out for the all-girls academy he was determined to send me to. I was a social being. He, of all people, should understand that.

"How's Cat?"

"She's fine. How's Nat?"

"Good."

Darrel's den occupied a corner in the rear of his house. I thought of it more as a hideaway than a study or office. Vintage posters and abstract paintings covered all four walls with beanbag chairs, overstuffed pillows, and the convertible loveseat arranged in an arc in the center of the room. He and Cat traveled nonstop for years, and the room read like a catalog of their adventures. Summer in Paris. Hong Kong in the spring. A week long excursion down the Nile River. A setting perfect for playing trivia, sipping cappuccino, or cozying up next to the fire to enjoy a foreign film or two. Darrel and Cat were true social beings. Rarely did a week go by without them hosting a gathering for their cultured and posh group of friends–usually with an endless river of cocktails. Didn't take long before I became a permanent fixture at their parties.

"I thought you said you missed me."

"I did." He replied slowly, his stare locked on some point directly in front of him. "I did Jackie."

"So act like it." I said as I changed position. I eased onto his lap and wrapped my arms around his neck. "What happened to all that stuff you said you wanted to do to me?"

His hands coddled my behind as first his nose, then his lips brushed against my neck. "I meant it."

"Good. Prove it."

Darrel's smiles never exposed any teeth, a perfectly formed secret he meant to hide from the world, and it vanished as my thighs straddled his waist. An expression worthy of sex replaced it. We rocked together, pushing our bodies closer until I smothered his, and he was threatening to immerse himself in mine.

"Uhh," I shuddered against his shoulder at the first signs of penetration.

"Mmm, I missed my girl."

Of course, he did. I was young, not exactly naive but still young, and my body was a marvelous thing. Nobody would've argued the contrary–man or woman.

"Good girl, good girl," he growled softly in my ear. "It's mine? Still mine?"

"Yes, Daddy."

A mist of sweat covered his forehead, and his touch went from practiced to desperate. Always a good sign.

Normally, we didn't need to be naked to enjoy each other. Living in such close proximity to his wife and my sister trained us to take what we could even in the briefest moments of privacy. But after being apart for months, Darrel wasn't satisfied with that. He wanted me naked.

"Mmm," he grunted at the sight of my bare breasts and tossed my shirt and bra to the floor. "I hate it when you wear that."

I nodded, remembering his distaste for underwear. They merely got in his way.

"I'm home!" A feminine voice called out as the front door closed shut. She must've seen his car in the driveway because Cat continued having a conversation with her invisible husband even though he never responded to her.

I expected him to withdraw, but the wild man who lived behind his eyes was no longer threatening to come out—he was taking over. He pushed me to the carpet and, in seconds, had dropped his jeans. Now naked from the waist down, he began fucking me like a mad dog in heat.

"Oh, God...yes!" I couldn't help myself.

The door to the den eased open, and the carpet padded her footsteps as they grew closer with each passing second. Darrel's grip seized on to the dark fibers, and my nails cut into the silk on his back. When her footsteps came to a stop, I could feel the explosion building inside me and from his expression, Darrel felt it too.

"Hey, babe, l-look who came to visit me." His chin, square and proud, jerked forward as every muscle above his waist tightened. I gasped feeling the full weight of his being, and he let loose a barrage of swear words as his body went limp.

The room began its topsy-turvy dance, and I delighted in the fact that I couldn't control it. The shadow across the carpet stretched then receded into the darkness, returning a moment later.

"Here, Jackie, let me help you." Cat knelt at my side holding something cold and wet on my thigh. A pink towel which must've seen better days. With calm short strokes, she tended to the evidence between my legs before giving his body the same attention.

Darrel panted silently as he leaned back against the edge of the sofa. Now clean, he pulled his jeans back up to the appropriate height, and the wild man receded to living just behind his eyes.

I took my time raising myself to a standing position, but once I was upright, Cat motioned for me to raise my arms. Her knuckles caressed my skin as she pulled Nat's tee shirt into place. Slowly. Carefully. With a deep appreciation for my supple curves. The cotton stretched over my body, squeezing my breasts in an unladylike manner.

"Now that's what I like," Darrel rose to his full height of six three and pulled me close for a kiss. It was like I never left.

15
PECAN

I STILL HELD OUT HOPE I'D AWAKE TO find this to be a sick twisted dream. The sun would shine brightly through my window, and my girls would be exactly as I'd left 'em. Wasn't they fault time ain't stop when I was locked up in that hospital. Couldn't blame 'em for growing up, but I did. Was natural for kids to grow up, but my girls—Jackie, in particular—didn't grow so much up as she grew in some twisty-turvy direction more or less toward the sky. So, I stood on the corner of Sixteenth and Broadway in my brown trench coat, arms folded tightly, cursing the dark cave I'd been hibernating in. If what Nikki'd been saying was the truth, then I was a new kinda fool since I overlooked what was right in front of my face. So, I stood on the corner willing a rational explanation to come to mind. Had to be another way to explain what everybody was saying. She was just a chile. What did she know about the world? About men? About...

After five minutes passed I crossed the street and knocked on the door. Took a while before anybody came to open it. Long enough for me to entertain the possibility that Jackie currently occupied another corner of the city, surrounded by kids her own age, doing childish things.

"Can I help you?" asked a Chinese woman about my age. She ain't wear a drop of makeup and stood on the other side of the screen door clutching her bathrobe in all the right places.

"Are you Cat?"

"Yes." She stood a little straighter, more curious now than cautious.

"I'm looking for my daughter. Jackie Morrow. She here?"

"Umm..." The woman with the feline name glanced over her shoulder, and I took that to mean a lie would be coming my way. She didn't try to stop me as I brushed past her into the house.

"Jackie!" I took the stairs two at a time, throwing open doors left and right. "Jackie!" Don't know why I thought to search the upstairs first. Call it mother's intuition. "Jacqueline Belinda Morrow!"

"Mama!" The last door in the hall opened and out stepped my chile. Fully dressed to her credit. 'Course that wasn't saying much since she hardly ever fully dressed. "What you doing here?" she asked me more out of embarrassment than fear.

"What you doing in there? He hurt you?"

"What?"

"I come to take you home. Get your stuff."

"I'm just visiting. I can't visit people?"

"Jackie..."

"Visiting ain't a crime."

That's when I put a face to the name. The first time I set eyes on the man, but I knew him. Knew him better than I wanted. The type of man that had no worries. Spent all his days making other folks worry.

"Get over here. Get away from him."

"Mrs. Jenkins, pleasure to meet you. Darrel King." He ain't bother smiling or sticking out his hand or even coming from behind my baby. Just stood there, his eyes locked on mine. "I've heard so much about you," he said.

His little mouse of a woman peeked around the corner behind me. I couldn't eyeball, her but her feet shuffled against the carpet on the second-floor landing. In my head, her eyes grew big, and she clutched her bathrobe even tighter to her tiny chest.

Heziah crossed my mind. He'd probably have been real clear and firm, and he wouldn't have lost control at all.

"I said get ova here!" Before I realized it, I latched on to Jackie's arm and dragged her toward the stairs.

Ricky woulda beat the man to death with his bare hands. Then he'd have done the same to Jackie. She had to have caught that. Made out how lucky she was I came to get her and not somebody else. I only wanted to put some distance between them, but my chile didn't see fit to cut me any slack.

"Mama! Quit! Quit it!" She tried to wrestle free. "I didn't do anything!

I swear!"

Waited until the last stair before turning to face her. As a child she'd never lied to me, but as a teenager most everything out her mouth was a lie, and in that moment, she was determined to prove it to me. Each word came faster than the last and none of 'em held more than a morsel of truth. I couldn't move. Not my feet, nor my lips. And when she finally paused to take a breath, it hit me like a load of bricks.

"What's that? Is that...liquor? You been drinking?"

"No, I–"

"Did that man give you liquor?" She ain't need to answer for me to reckon it was true.

"Oww, Mama..."

But my grip only tightened as we moved closer to the door. Some part of Jackie understood I was saving her because she stopped fighting me. Snatched up her jacket and clutched it to her chest without breaking stride. I took it as a sign I'd broken through. Glanced over my shoulder to make sure I wasn't imagining it, but she avoided my eyes. Still, a mama knows. I caught a glimpse of the scared little girl hiding inside her.

Before we could reach the door, the stairs began to creak. The sound low and heavy like a bear getting up from his slumber, but the bear ain't waste no time getting his bearings, and before long, there he stood.

"Jackie!"

She turned, her eyes dancing gleefully in his direction.

"Was good seeing you." He gave a small nod.

My heart sank. "You stay away from her! You hear me? You come near her again and I-I'll...I'll..."

"Mrs. Jenkins, I'm not sure what you think is going on but–"

"I'll kill you! You stay away from my child! You hear me?"

16
NIKKI

As the eldest child of Pecan and Ricky Morrow, I'd picked up a few things such as the ability to foresee trouble. The twins were smart vivacious girls, but they would never have that ability. They twirled, pranced around the living room, and jumped up and down like they had caught the holy ghost while Natalie narrated their chosen outfits.

"Kee! Kee!"

My eyes were glued to the front door. Mama was missing. Jackie was missing and Mya was silent. She'd curled up in the window seat with a blanket and a book, alternating between ignoring us and keeping watch.

"Kee!" They called again.

"I'm watching. I am."

They twirled in side-by-side circles, then dashed off to change into their next outfit. It was an unsaid rule: bad news was never spoken in their presence. Natalie and I exchanged nervous glances when they weren't looking and pretended like it was normal for Mama to leave in the middle of the afternoon. I quietly reassured myself that it would've been only a matter of time before she found out. Even without my help.

"Think they'll be back soon?" Natalie rocked side to side, pushing her feet together so the bottoms touched. "I'm getting hungry."

I nodded but felt my attention drift to the window seat. With one definitive flick of her wrist, Mya turned a page in her book. Anger wasn't normally one of my sister's emotions, but she did irritated masterfully.

"Mama said she'll be back soon, but I don't know....You think everything's okay?"

I nodded, smiling at Natalie as if she were one of the twins.

"I think Jackie's gonna be in trouble," she confessed, her brow wrinkled in concern. "I hope not, but Mama seemed pretty mad. What'd she do anyway? Just 'cause she ain't come home with Mya?"

This time we both glanced at the occupant of the window seat, but she didn't move, sigh, or utter a sound. She simply read.

"Don't worry about it. I'm sure everything'll work itself out. If they're not back soon, I'll make dinner for everyone."

Mama and Jackie walked through the door exactly forty-two minutes later. Jackie made an unsteady beeline for the stairs, and Mama lingered in the foyer, hanging her coat on the coat rack. It draped over its hook with such resignation that it reminded me of Mama herself—plain old worn-out.

"Everything okay?" I asked, wiping my hands on the apron tied around my waist.

"Fine," was her answer although it couldn't have been further from the truth.

"Heziah called to say he'll be late. I told him you were visiting some neighbors."

Ironically, that was the lie I told Daddy if he called when Mama was with Heziah. She nodded as if she didn't remember and went about putting on her apron. Lying was wrong, and I wasn't a child anymore. And yet, I was still lying to cover up other people's indiscretions.

"Where was she?"

"I don't wanna talk about it, Nikki."

"She was with him wasn't she?"

Mama surveyed the kitchen and the dishes in various stages of preparedness. Smothered chicken, mashed potatoes, and okra. The chicken sat in the skillet on top of the stove. I was about to turn on the burner when they came in.

"What'd she say? I mean how did she explain everything? Were they alone?"

Mama grabbed both oven mitts and lifted the top off the pot to check on the okra. I waited patiently. Daddy liked his extra soft, but the reverend liked his okra with a little bite. I wasn't sure how Heziah liked his.

"How long has she been sneaking off to see him?"

"Nikki! Leave it be!"

My fingers started to tremble as I untied the apron strings. Jackie had run off to do God knows what, and all I'd done was be helpful, yet she was yelling at me. No gratitude for fixing supper. Not even a brief acknowledgment I had been right about her favorite child.

"I...I gotta go before it gets late."

Mama nodded, her attention already drifting.

17 MYA

THE SECOND WEEK OF APRIL MARKED THE beginning of folks looking at me like I was some kinda new manifestation of myself. A group of guys I knew from English class horsed around in the hallway, and one of them accidentally bumped into me. He apologized profusely, then he and his friends practically ran in the other direction.

"Damn girl, what'd you do got them scared of you?"

I shrugged.

"They musta heard." Jackie spun around to face me and arched one mischievous eyebrow as we approached our lockers. "Morrow girls don't take no junk."

Jackie and I adhered to two distinct views on what it meant to be a Morrow girl. Where she saw power and strength, I felt betrayal and grief. A difference we might never be able to reconcile.

"You got practice? After school?" Jackie's locker slammed shut, and she squeezed her mathematics textbook to her chest.

Mama ordered us to walk to and from school together. Every day. No detours. No exceptions. Didn't matter what I had going on in my life or what I felt about it.

"I got somewhere to be."

"Where?" Jackie grinned.

"Somewhere."

"Where?" She persisted, following me down the hall to my homeroom. Ramon stood at the door waiting patiently. "Mya," she gasped with a knowing smile. "Oooo, I'm telling Mama."

It would've been fair since I told on her, so I didn't expect her to keep my secret.

"I'm kidding." Jackie giggled. "Go on, have your little fun. Meet me after, and we'll walk home together."

I'd missed two practices in the last week because it was the only time I could get away. Last time Ramon and I rode a bus downtown and walked to Buckingham Fountain. We held hands. Not the fun Jackie was thinking about.

"Hey, girl."

"Hey."

Since becoming my boyfriend, Ramon hadn't missed one day of school. I suspected he still skipped a few periods here and there, but at least he showed up. I was already a good influence on him.

"Let me see your math homework," he said as we claimed our seats near the window.

"That would be cheating."

"Aww, come on."

Ramon typically got his way with folks. He gave orders on the street, and his friends followed them without question. Even our classmates and teachers tried to stay out of his way.

"I'm not a cheater."

"You want me to fail? Come on, help me out."

The bell rang at precisely eight o'clock to signal the morning announcements. I didn't need the help, but it provided the perfect excuse to end our conversation. Ramon knew, like I did, what the assignment was, and he wasn't stupid. Having a boyfriend was a new sensation. Sometimes it reminded me of having a pet. I'd never had a pet, but I could imagine what it would've been like—lots of worrying. Ramon didn't have the best track record when it came to making decisions. He was involved in a lot of things that were bad for him, but as long as they made him money, he made peace with the risks.

"You mad at me?" he asked me after school.

I shook my head.

We'd taken to walking around the neighborhood. Ramon never crossed State Street, so we walked only so far east before turning in another direction.

"Then what's wrong?" His cold fingers slipped into mine, squeezing our palms together.

"Nothing."

"Bullshit, Mya. What is it?"

"Nothing."

Funny thing about nothing, sometimes it grew from something. See, something became nothing once you got used to it. And nothing and I knew each other well. It haunted my steps regardless of whether I was awake or asleep. It didn't have a name or make a sound, but it was always there.

"SO...WHERE'D YOU GO? WHATCHA DO? SPILL." Jackie assumed I had something juicy to tell. She matched me stride for stride and playfully leaned into me. "I'd tell you."

"I didn't ask."

"But if you did, I'd tell you."

"All we did was walk around and talk."

"Talked?" Jackie peered at me as if observing a fascinating creature she never knew existed.

"Where'd you go?"

I only asked to change the subject. The answer carried little importance to me, but I listened anyway. Jackie spent her last hours with Nash and his friends. She gave vivid descriptions of each boy, popping her bubblegum at the same time. The pink stretchy substance sloshed around her mouth, distracting me from her words.

"You smell funny."

"I do?" Her eyes grew wide, and she spit the wad of gum into the grass before popping in a fresh piece. "How about now?"

"You're okay now."

"Good."

Jackie continued her story all the way home. How she got along so well with Nash and his friends and how they all flirted with her. Between the four of them, they finished off two quarts of Captain Morgan.

"What's it taste like?"

"Umm...it's good when you mix it with stuff like orange juice or fruit punch. You wanna try it? Nash gave me some for later." She pulled a half-empty bottle of Twister Fruit Punch from her backpack and swished the red liquid around the inside of the glass bottle.

"No, thanks."

"You sure?"

I nodded. I could imagine Mama's face when she found out. She paid more attention than usual, studying every inch of Jackie and me. I started to warn Jackie but figured she'd noticed all the extra attention like I had.

"We're home," Jackie called out as we hung up our coats.

Mama was in the kitchen with the twins scooping spoonfuls of dough onto the cookie sheet. First came the German chocolate cake, then chocolate chip cookies, and next would be some type of pie or cheesecake. Some people cleaned or talked incessantly when they were nervous. Mama baked.

"How was school?"

"Fine. I'm thinking about trying out for the talent show," Jackie declared as she took a seat next to Jenna. "And when I win, we can go out to celebrate. It'll be like a family event."

Mama nodded absentmindedly and used her finger to push a chunk off her spoon.

"I'll sing. Or maybe I'll act....No, I'll sing. Did you know I could sing, little Callie?"

Callie shook her head, sending her curly pigtails whooshing against the side of her face.

I was about to excuse myself to finish my homework when it happened. The sound of her backpack unzipping and a muffled clang as the Twister bottle landed on top of the kitchen table. My mouth fell open. Stupid my sister was not, and she couldn't have been so thirsty she needed to have it right then and there. Jackie winked at me, and her fingers lightly grazed the cap as if considering when to open it.

"What should I sing, Mama?"

"Sing? Oh...umm...sing that song about dancing. I like that one."

"What song about dancing? Lots of songs about dancing."

"You know the one." Mama sighed. "With the girl everybody keeps talking about. The skinny one."

They laughed and Mama let herself relax enough to break a smile. "Y'all know who I'm talkin' about! The girl! Houston somebody!"

I'd managed to not care what Jackie did, but I wasn't gonna lie for her. Sitting across from her, watching one gulp after another without telling Mama what really filled the bottle would've been a lie.

"I got homework."

"Oh, you'll knock that out in no time. Come on, hang with us." Jackie gave the cap a quick twist and raised the bottle to her lips. "Family is the most important thing. Right, Mama?"

"Hmm? Oh, yes. That's true. Mya, baby, don't you want to spend some time with us? Instead of always locking yourself up in that room." Mama's face took on a wavering smile, trying to lighten the mood.

But the moments directly after that worked against her. Nobody said anything. They all just looked at me expectantly. Guess I was supposed to grin and lie. Say how much I was dying to have their company. How much fun it was to be around them.

"I got homework."

They could have their little moment of pretend without me.

18
NIKKI

THE GIRL STARING BACK AT ME WORE my face, but she couldn't have been me. Her blouse was buttoned wrong and hung on the outside of her skirt. Her hair matted and pressed against the back of her head. A run a mile long ran down the front of her stockings. But all of that came a distant second.

The bathroom tiles turned into ice-cold rocks under my stockinged feet and got worse once I stepped out of them. The knobs screeched as I turned the water on full blast and flinched as the sound pierced the quiet. Bad enough I'd gotten home late, but if the reverend had seen me...the idea shamed me to my core. I was not going to leave the bathroom until I'd washed the sin from my body.

The basin filled with water until my stockings floated calmly on top. Men didn't have the self-control, we did. Men lived impressionable lives, pulled in arbitrary directions by their private parts. So, setting the tone fell in my lap, and clearly I failed. Worse yet, I compromised my future. Jean-Louis was so close to popping the question. The promise flashed in his eyes every time they moved in my direction. Now what would he think of me?

"Nikki? Is that you?" A soft knock came at the bathroom door. Darlene stood in the hall whispering in the darkness. "Everything all right?"

"Mmhmm." I heard myself sniffle.

"You sure?"

I nodded even though the door stood between us and held my breath until she returned to her bedroom. In the morning, she would ask me how my date went over coffee and Danish, and I'd be a much better liar. I'd smile and recount how romantic the restaurant was and how special I felt. I'd leave out the part where he couldn't keep his hands to himself.

When morning came around, Darlene smiled at me across the kitchen table, and I wondered if she even remembered the night before.

"How's your sister doing? How's Mya?"

"Fine."

"She still getting good grades? I tell everyone all the time how smart she is."

When I first met Darlene, I took one look at her and thought of the Berenstain Bears. Something about my second mother reminded me of the mother bear with her round cheeks.

"I sure hope she doesn't let other folks be a bad influence on her. I like to think both you girls learned a lot about right and wrong from your time with us."

I certainly had, but I couldn't speak for Mya. From what I could tell, the only lesson she learned was obedience wasn't for her. Mya did only what she wanted—no more and no less.

"Nikki?"

"Huh?" I was listening, but my thoughts had begun to wander.

"I do miss having both you girls under the same roof."

I nodded. "We miss it too."

I figured that was better than telling her the truth. Not only had Mya not mentioned Darlene since she left, my sister developed a fascination with parties and boys. That would've been too much for the preacher's wife to handle. So, I lied and changed the subject. "What do you think of Jean-Louis?"

"Oh, he seems like a good man," she nodded as she sipped her coffee. "I do wish he was in the church."

That's when it occurred to me. The answer lied with Jesus. If my soon-to-be fiancé accepted Jesus Christ as his savior, he would be better equipped to fight the devil's temptation. Last night would've ended like all our other dates—with a polite kiss on the cheek.

"It's just that his family never took to religion," I began as the plan took shape in my mind. "I bet he'd be open to it though. I could ask. Maybe bring him to service on Sunday..."

As the reverend would say, takes a strong person to forgive those who have done them harm. So, when Jean-Louis put the small gray box in my hand, I felt ready to put that hormonal incident behind us.

"I love you."

"I love you too." I swallowed hard, my fingers shaking around the jewelry box. We sat in his car with the radio playing softly in the background as the windshield wipers squeaked back and forth, whisking the gentle drizzle away.

"Open it."

I nodded, but my fingers wouldn't cooperate. Would I be able to continue to support the weight of the tiny box? Like all little girls, I waited my whole life for that moment.

"Wait. I wanna say something I..."

I'd agreed to let him take me to dinner for one reason. I'd been a fool to think love was all we needed. God is love, so there can be no love without him, and I meant to say just that.

"I've been thinking and–I mean I spoke to Darlene and–"

His eyes stared deeply into mine as his long dainty fingers began to stroke my hand. A beautiful but otherwise distracting moment.

"Last time I saw you..."

He gave a nod to demonstrate his understanding and squeezed his hands around mine. He never meant to hurt me. He only wanted me to accept how much he cared for me. He loved me, really loved me. The tip of his index finger traced my jawline, drawing a single line from my ear to my chin. It had all been a misunderstanding. I simply wasn't accustomed to having a man pursue me, desire me, so I panicked and overreacted.

"I know you love me–"

"That's right. I do. Why else would I be asking you to marry me?" He smiled, withdrawing his fingers enough to open the small gray box. "Nicole Morrow, will you marry me?"

19
PECAN

"Mama." Jenna hardly ever showed up without her counterpart, so I figured Callie would poke her head in from the hall at any second. "Ooooo..." She pointed at the mess I made of Jackie's bedroom.

"I'm cleaning up. Y'all go back downstairs and play."

"Die-a-ree?" Jenna flopped down on the bed and pointed to the closet. "Die-a-ree!" She smiled, congratulating herself on being helpful.

Was tempting, but I needed more than some words to prove what I thought.

Jackie and Mya would be home at three fifteen. The school let out at three and took 'em a few minutes to get their stuff together and ten minutes to walk home if they walked at Jackie's pace. The clock on her nightstand said a quarter after four but still no sign of them.

I needed some proof I could put my hands on. Condoms, a diaphragm, birth control pills, something she couldn't lie her way out of.

"Mama?" Natalie stood in the doorway with Callie, both of their eyes getting big at the mess.

"Everything's fine. Y'all go on downstairs."

Soon as I said it, Jenna's words whispered in my ears. Her diary. I brushed past the girls and hurried into my bedroom to study the pages. Starting from the beginning wasn't an option. I flipped to the middle and skimmed a few lines. Flipped a few pages and skimmed some more.

"I TOLD YOU," JACKIE SAID AS THE front door opened. "Did you see him staring? You damn near put a spell on him. We should go shopping. Get you outta them jerseys and into some more cute tops."

Their book bags hit, the floor and they went about hanging their coats on the by the door.

"Hey, Mama."

"Wh-Where y'all been?"

"Jackie tried out for the talent show."

"I told you." She grinned. "Guess what? I'm in!"

I shook from head to toe by then. Ain't matter if Jesus himself walked through the door with 'em. I wouldn't have believed one word out their mouths.

"You was 'posed to come straight home. Straight home! Y'all don't listen to a word I say!"

"But I told you—"

"I ain't done!" I realized I was yelling and decided to keep it down so as not to scare the younger ones. Instead I waved the notebook in her face and demanded an explanation. "Answer me."

"Where you get that? It's mine! Give it back!" Jackie reached out to grab it, but I moved faster. The motion actually sent her stumbling forward a few steps. "You can't just be going through my stuff!"

I never was the most cosmopolitan woman, but I recognized liquor when I smelled it, and I couldn't ignore drunk when it stood right in my face. Although Jackie had done a pretty decent job of acting normal up until she stumbled.

"You been to see that man again?"

"What man?" Her top lip curled into a self-satisfied snarl. "You mean that man you said you were gonna kill? That man?"

She didn't lie on me, but for some reason hearing the words aloud sent dread deep into my bones. Was it the reality that I hadn't been lying when I said it? Most folks threw the expression around without any serious intentions. Not me. I'd meant it. Mya inhaled sharply, and in that instant

I saw that it was the past sneaking its way into the present. Somehow after all the harm he'd done, Ricky ended up the victim, and I became a murderer. He could beat me black and blue, whip the skin off Jackie's back, and damn near put Louis in an early grave and somehow my crime dwarfed his. Wasn't fair, but standing before his favorite chile as she looked upon me with them eyes so dark they looked like two lumps of coal, I couldn't say none of that. Instead I fixed my sights on dealing with the issue at hand.

"This ain't about me. It's about you, and this right here gonna stop. You hear me? I mean it. You not gonna be like this. If I gotta walk you home every day, then that's what I'm gonna do. You not gonna be writing him no letters, and you damn sure ain't going nowhere near his house! If I gotta lock you up in your room, then that's what I'm gonna do!"

Jackie started to say something, but Mya took her by the arm and beat her to it. "But Mama, we really went to the tryouts. Jackie sang—"

"Heziah is right. Y'all been getting away with too much around here, and it's gonna stop! You ain't gonna be like them fast girls getting themselves into trouble! So you tell them lil' boyfriends of yours, you can't have boyfriends, you hear? Ain't gonna be nothing but school for you two. Y'all gonna go learn and bring your behinds right back here."

"But, Mama—"

"Mya, you 'But, Mama' me one more time—"

"But we ain't do nothing, and I got practice tomorrow!"

"Not no more, you don't. From now on, you got school and home and that's it."

MYA SLOUCHED DOWN IN HER CHAIR, SHOOTING daggers at me from across the dining table. My daddy would've never let me get away with that. I raked lines into my mashed potatoes, took a small bite, and raked some more lines. I'd loved my daddy something fierce. Still did even though he'd been dead and buried going on twenty years. Little girls and their daddies... I didn't blame Mya for her feelings. Probably would've made it easier if I did.

"Mama, you not listening."

"I hear you, Nikki."

"What I say?"

Heziah lifted his napkin to wipe the gravy from his lips then said, "You were telling us about your male friend. Again."

"Oh, he's just so wonderful, so perfect." Jackie swooned pretending to be Nikki. "I wouldn't know what to do without him."

"Well, he is wonderful," Nikki replied. "I'd be jealous too if I were you."

"Yeah, right. Sure. You ever see me running behind a damn leprechaun you can bet hell's about to freeze over."

"Watch your language," Heziah's eyes darted from Jackie to the twins and back again. "There's no need for all of that."

But Jackie and Nikki never paid nobody else any mind when they got going.

"You just jealous! And he's not a leprechaun! He's average height!"

"For a girl."

"Quit it, you two." Heziah broke in. "Jackie, be nice."

"Not my fault she got low standards. Done hooked up with one of Santa's elves. Boy so short he don't even have to bend over to tie his shoes."

"At least he's not a pervert! At least I'm not s-s-some pervert!"

Jackie wanted to leap over the table and wrap her fingers 'round Nikki's neck.

"What's that supposed to mean?" Heziah immediately took offense as any father would have. His face turned stone cold, the word 'pervert' weighing heavy on his mind.

Still there was a possibility it would all go away. Just needed a good change of subject.

"We gone change the subject. This ain't supper talk. Nikki, how you like being a senior? It's going okay?"

In some ways my girls seemed completely different from how I remembered 'em, but Nikki was still the same in this one way in particular. She loved to tell folks something they wasn't already on top of. So, when she didn't say a word, instead nodded, staring down into her plate, I figured the lil' tiff with Jackie left a bad taste in her mouth.

"Jackie, say you sorry."

"Why I gotta always be the one apologizing to her? She never apologize to me...walking around here like she better than everybody else. Lil' Miss Perfect." Jackie's fork clanged up 'gainst her plate as she leveled her gaze at her sister. "You the one living in a fantasy world. Ain't no man up in the clouds looking down making sure everything go right. The world is a fucked up place, and we live in it, and then we die. In between, we might get to have some fun but that's it."

"Fun...yeah, right," Nikki mumbled under her breath. "You know all about that."

"You ain't no betta than me!"

"At least, I'm not..."

"What? You not what? Say it!"

"You keep going like you is, and...and something bad gonna happen to you! You and your nasty ways! You asking for it! Simple as that."

"That's enough, now y'all stop it. Always biting at each other. You sisters. Act like it."

Before I could say any more, Heziah stood up from the table and ordered Nat and the twins to finish their supper in the kitchen. He wanted to get a handle on what was going on. His stare traveled around the table, giving each one of us a chance to speak up, but nobody did. Me and my girls, we ain't plan to keep things a secret from him, but nothing good would come from letting him in on it. Heziah still thought the world was full of good people, living decent lives.

"What's this talk about a pervert? Somebody say something. Now. Belinda?"

"It's nothing. Really. They acting out."

His skeleton-like fingers stretched out across the table toward us, and he shifted his weight onto his palms. "Are you lying to me? Because family doesn't do that, and we're family."

"See, what you done did!" Nikki exploded. "You gonna ruin Mama's marriage. You don't care about nobody but yourself! Trying to turn Mya into a slut like you! I'm sorry, Mama, but it's true. She's like the snake that went after Adam and Eve. Everything she touch gets ruined."

The anger that gave Jackie such a strong spine wilted away without the slightest warning, so her body had a tough time keeping from slumping forward. And her eyes...hadn't seen such pain in them since...well since her daddy was breathing. Jackie hightailed it for the stairs. Left her chair wobbling from side to side.

"Why you do that?" Mya finally saw fit to open her mouth and that left Nikki speechless. She sat frozen in her seat, while Mya's chair scraped 'gainst the floor. She headed toward the stairs, leaving the three of us alone at the table.

Heziah sighed and sank back onto his chair. The question faded away.

I was lucky to have him, but my luck never stayed good for long.

20
JACKIE

For all my faults, I kept a clean room. Not that anybody could tell from the state it was in. Damn twins. Always messing my stuff up.

"Don't listen to her." Mya tucked one foot underneath herself, and scooted back until she was leaning against my headboard. "Jackie?"

Nat had her own room across the hall, but when we were little me and her used to share the room that now belonged to me. The walls remained the same tangerine color, but I taped posters on all four walls and even across the closet door: Janet Jackson, Paula Abdul, New Edition, Anita Baker, and Luther Vandross. And Prince. I loved me some Prince. His sultry stare seduced me from all angles. In that moment, draped diagonally across the bed, I was happy to get lost in it.

Below, on the floor of my room, Nat squeezed her knees to her tiny chest and rocked back and forth, looking up at me with wide attentive eyes.

"Don't listen to her," Mya said from the head of my bed.

"You mad at me?"

Her brow wrinkled in confusion and soon after smoothed out as she remembered. I got her in trouble. Because of me, she couldn't be on the track team anymore.

"Season's almost over anyway."

"I'm sorry."

She nodded. Wasn't quite forgiveness as much as it was acceptance.

Couldn't undo what had already been done.

"You gotta stop seeing him. And drinking. It ain't good for you."

I nodded because Mya would never understand. The things that made her feel normal everybody cheered. They literally cheered. But me? All that met me was disdain and judgment. Even singing was outlawed now.

"You think I'm a slut?"

Mya shrugged. "What's a slut? Betcha it ain't in the dictionary."

More evidence she could never understand. Wasn't like the word was new to her. Every girl over the age of thirteen was familiar with the word. We'd all been taught to fear it, run from it or even from the thought of it. To be a slut was the worst thing a girl could be, but my farsighted sister took this opportunity to begin a discussion over the definition.

"You not a slut," came Nat's shining voice from down below. "You're just really popular."

THE ARGUMENT BETWEEN MAMA AND HEZIAH BEGAN an hour before lights out and lasted beyond my bedtime. I hesitated to call it an argument because it wasn't anything like what I normally associated with the word. Usually when Mama argued with a man, there was pleading and possibly a scream or two, broken glass, broken bones, stuff like that. But Heziah wasn't like that. I could tell he was upset, but I didn't worry about Mama the way I did whenever Ricky had gotten upset. I'd stopped calling my father "Daddy" the day I figured out what the word meant. A daddy was somebody who loved you and protected you from anything that might cause you pain. He was more than the same blood type. Heziah was my daddy, and he loved my mama, so I didn't worry at all as I slid my window up in the dead of night. I was sure they'd work it out.

What I focused on was the long way down. Nash stood on the ground below, pushing the ladder against the side of the house. It scraped against the frozen ground covered in the midnight chill. The lawn had a slight frost coating each blade of grass. It was unlikely the earth would provide a gracious welcome if I fell from my second-floor window. I never thought I'd get my mama back only to be running away from her.

"I'm not saying that!" Mama said exasperatedly.

The wind blew upward into my face, and I realized I was underdressed. I'd dressed in fuchsia tights, a black miniskirt, and a sweater with a brightly colored abstract pattern that bared my shoulders. Nash had given me his jacket, and it hung down far enough to cover the hem of my skirt. The collar held his scent, and for a moment, I forgot about my fear of heights.

"Don't go."

She'd slipped into my bedroom without a sound—her long black waves tucked behind her ears and cascading toward her waist. Mya's pajamas were black-and-white polka dots, not 'cause she liked them, more so because they had been on sale.

"I'll be back."

But that wasn't the point. She folded her arms under her chest and squinted at me in the darkness of my bedroom. Mya was the one who wasn't afraid of heights or anything else for that matter.

"I promise," I said, straddling the window sill.

21
NIKKI

Most Chicagoans didn't expect late April to have too many beautiful days, but the Lord handed us two in a row. On the second day, I broke the news of my engagement to Darlene and the reverend. They weren't surprised. Darlene said she could tell there was something different about me. I started blushing right there on the spot.

The reverend's house was only a few miles from a forest preserve, and once the sun went down, the parking lot was basically private. Jean-Louis cracked the windows, letting the night breeze infiltrate the warmth of his car. Talk radio played on the stereo, but neither of us was listening to it. I still wanted to wait until our wedding night, but that was getting harder the more time we spent together.

"I have decided on a date."

"You did?" I couldn't hide my genuine surprise. I always figured men needed be dragged down the aisle kicking and screaming.

"Two months on the fourteenth. It's a Saturday."

"Oh. Okay. I was thinking we might wait...a little while...until I get my degree?"

He leaned forward to change the radio station and replied, "Why would we do that? Four years is a long time. An extremely long time."

"Sure, but..." It was a lot to ask, but it would be Mama's first question. She'd want to make sure I finished college because she dropped out of high school to marry my daddy. "I'm already registered for classes this fall. It might not feel like that long."

"It will. Trust me." He shook his head, adding a visual to his words. "No man is going to wait that long for you."

I wanted to ask if he meant for me or for women in general, but I sat quietly looking out the window instead. Wishing for the winter wonderland of picturesque Christmas cards until I felt the pressure of his hand squeezing my thigh. It always began in this way. The strength of his touch would increase steadily until my legs began to part. He poked and clawed at the crotch of my stockings.

"L-Let's not tonight, okay? Let's talk about the wedding. We have so much to do."

He didn't agree, but he didn't disagree either. In fact, he didn't say a word. His body leaned toward me until we were both in the passenger seat with him on top.

"I...I don't think anybody could plan a wedding in two months. H-How about a year? Jean-Louis?"

"Mmmm..." His mouth pressed against mine.

My head turned left and right, fighting to avoid his kiss in favor of the discussion at hand, and a girlish giggle slipped out. "Come on, honey! I'm serious!"

My right cheek was less than an inch from the window. The threat of its coolness veered closer and closer until I felt chills up and down my arms. His fingers pulled at the waistband of my control-top pantyhose. His lips lavished mine with one smothering kiss after another, sending my heart into a frazzled state.

"I am tired of waiting."

I nodded. He'd said as much every time we were alone together. So, I knew my virginity was living on borrowed time.

"A little longer. Nine–six months maybe."

He reached into the darkness beside my seat and yanked at the lever, sending the passenger seat into a reclining position, while his other hand explored a different kind of darkness.

"Jean! Stop!" It came out as a whisper, but he paused long enough for me to catch my breath. My chest rose and fell at a steady pace, relief flooding through my body. Until I made out the sound of a zipper unzipping.

"Give me your hand."

The clock on the dash said 9:52. I'd refused him what he truly wanted, so I swallowed hard and did what he asked, wrapping my trembling fingers around his penis. Ten o'clock came, and I thought my arm was going to fall off.

"Do it! Do it!" He thrusted forward into my grasp.

His feet and knees collided clumsily against mine. I tried to move them out of his way, but my pantyhose were bunched up around my knees, trapping my legs in that position. He seemed to realize this the same moment I did and ripped them in two. His body fit perfectly between my legs.

"I...I think we should stop now. Okay?"

"No."

"No?" I asked, pressing both hands gently against his shoulders. "I... we...we're..."

It was going too far. I began to wonder if he'd even noticed I'd withdrawn my hand, but I figured he had since his thrust had become more direct. Like he was angry at my underwear for being in the way.

"It's late. We have to stop now. I...I have to go home."

"No," He grunted.

Panic settled into my fingertips, pushing harder against his shoulders. My mind was telling me to be more forceful. To let him know I was serious.

"Stop."

There was a tug at the crotch of my underwear and then pressure the likes of which I'd never felt before. Mouthfuls of air invaded my lungs and still I was breathless. The image of a snowman with a carrot nose and buttons for eyes came to mind, and I held on to that until he was finished.

I couldn't go home. So, Jean-Louis drove me to Mama's house, walked me to the door, and kissed me goodbye. I didn't ask him to come in, and he didn't seem to mind. Said he had some charts to fill out before he made rounds tomorrow.

Shivering on the porch, I followed his car with my eyes as he drove off. My feet were numb, and my fingers frozen to the lapel of my coat. It didn't quite fit properly–big in the chest and tight around my middle–but that was normal for me.

I rang the bell. When I was a kid I was the only one of my sisters trusted with a key. Now I was the only one without.

"Hi Nikki!" Natalie pulled the front door open and waved from behind the screen door. "Mama, Nikki's here!"

I knew the heat was on because Jenna ran down the hall wearing only a shirt and a pair of shorts. Her sandy-brown hair fluttered behind her as she skipped down the hall. Mama was in the kitchen wearing a red-and-black checkered turtleneck sweater and black leggings. Six kids and her figure was still intact.

"Hey, baby, what brings you by so late?"

I nodded, still shivering from the memory of the cold. "Can I...can I stay here tonight?"

"Sure, baby. This still your house you know. You'll have to bunk with one of your sisters, but they not gonna mind."

Jackie would. Jackie might smother me in my sleep.

"You okay? You coming down with something?"

I shook my head. I hadn't parted with my coat yet. I was still too cold. So I took a seat at the kitchen table and started counting the floor tiles.

"Is it ready yet?" Jackie lacked basic patience, but that never translated to help in the kitchen. She took a few steps inside the kitchen and stopped when she saw me.

"Almost," Mama answered, putting the final touches of icing on the cake.

She didn't pick up on the look Jackie gave me. She never did.

"Get an extra plate for Nikki."

Jackie turned on her heel, rolling her eyes. My sister had never liked me, not from day one. She came home from the hospital with one goal: to make me invisible. Didn't take her long. All she had to do was cry or laugh or sing, and Mama didn't see anybody but Jackie.

"Mya upstairs?"

"Mmhmm."

I took the stairs carefully as if they might give way under my feet. Almost ran into Heziah as he stepped out of the bathroom. I muttered a greeting and ducked into the second room on the left. Mya was sprawled out on the floor, surrounded by textbooks, with the telephone pressed against her ear.

"Mmhmm," she was saying as I closed the door behind me.

She and Jackie couldn't have been more different, but somehow they still managed to get along. It irritated me. Mya was too smart not to see what I saw. She just never said anything. So, I had to speak up for both of us otherwise Jackie would get away with murder.

"Let me call you back," she said to whoever was on the other end of the line. The receiver clicked against the base, and Mya looked up at me. "Hey."

"Hey."

"You okay?"

I nodded. "I'm getting married."

Mya was quiet. She pushed herself up to a sitting position and crossed her legs Indian style. Bit her lip as she mulled over what to say. Congratulations was traditional, but perhaps my sister didn't know that.

"When?"

"Two months."

22 MYA

EACH BUNDLE OF NERVES IN MY BODY cheered as Ramon tilted his head toward mine, our lips drawing closer together until there wasn't any space between them. Kissing. I was surprised folks made such a big deal about it. Once I got passed the obvious questions about how to do it properly, it was nice. Not stupendous or amazing. Nice. Like chicken.

"You wanna..." His head jerked in the direction of the street.

"Yeah." Sitting on the bleachers was starting to hurt my butt anyway.

The weatherman had promised snow, but I didn't believe him. The sun was out and shining bright. Ramon slipped his fingers between mine, and we walked to the end of the row then down the metal steps until we were level with the baseball field. Ramon didn't know anything about the sport. He knew enough about basketball to convince his friends he was cool, but he didn't care enough to keep up with scores or attend any of our games. He had other things to worry about.

"Gotta go check on things. You coming?"

Jackie wasn't expecting me. She'd said she was going straight home, but that was a lie. Word around the school was Nash had dumped his girlfriend for my more interesting sister although that ain't mean she was with Nash at that moment. You never could tell with Jackie.

"Mya? You coming with me or you going home?"

Mama was gonna blow a gasket when neither me nor Jackie showed up. "I'm going with you."

She'd get over it.

"It won't take long." Ramon lifted the oversized waistband of his jeans, but they slumped down again as soon as his grip relaxed. "Just gonna run by my corner and make sure these fools know what's up. Can't be having 'em thinking they can get away with shit 'cause I ain't around every fucking minute."

"Don't say that."

"What?"

"The f-word."

"Ahh, I forgot." Ramon had one smile. It only came out when he was about to make fun of somebody. "You don't like bad words. You ain't never cursed in your life, have you?"

I didn't see the need. The English language was brimming with a plethora of interesting words.

"That 'cause your daddy a preacher?"

"He wasn't my daddy. I only got one daddy. Ricky Morrow."

"Aight." Ramon's frown quickly turned apologetic for having ruffled my feathers. "So, was he strict?"

"No."

"Would he be cool with me? You think?"

"Doubt it. Daddy ain't like other men being around us."

"You mean you and Jackie."

"No, I mean all of us. Mama too."

"Sound strict to me."

A bronze Cadillac rolled past us, blowing its horn at the car in front of it for driving too slow. The little old lady inside didn't pay any mind to the fact she was holding up traffic.

"Mya?"

I wasn't watching the cars. I was looking at 'em, but I was thinking. Thinking about why what he said had started to piss me off. It had been happening to me more and more. Somebody would say something, sometimes not even to me, but I'd catch it just the same, and then the tickling would start in my fingertips. And make its way up to my elbows, my shoulders, and before long my arms would be ready to explode with energy like two grenades somebody pulled the pins out of.

"Mya."

"I said he wasn't strict."

"Okay, if you say so. I'm just saying sound like he kept a pretty tight hold on y'all."

"You don't know what you're talking about!"

"Hey, wait up!"

It was Mama always trying to rein me in with all the rules about what I couldn't do. Couldn't climb trees. Couldn't stay out past five. Couldn't go too far from our block. She got all uptight about everything. Couldn't even run without her fussing over the possibility of me falling. Of course, she never did that to nobody but me.

Ramon gave up after I crossed the intersection. He would've had to run to keep up with me, and that wasn't gonna happen.

I got home about a minute after that, but I didn't notice until the front door closed behind me. Mama was standing in the foyer waiting with both hands on her hips. Her lips were moving a mile a minute, probably going on and on about me being late and Jackie not being with me. I'd learned to tune folks out when I needed to. Could put them on mute, like they were the television or something.

"Can I go to my room?" I wouldn't have said it if she wasn't standing in my way. I moved left and she went right, mirroring me. Blocking my path on purpose. So now I was trapped on top of being pissed off.

"Answer me."

"I got homework."

"It can wait. You gonna tell me where you been and where your sister is. Tell me right now!"

"I been where I always am. In my skin, and Jackie where she always is—in her skin."

"Girl." Mama wagged her finger at me. "Don't you get smart now. Y'all don't know how lucky you is that it's me and not somebody else standing here."

Lucky? I was lucky?

"Now, I'm your mama, and I know you think you know everything, but you gone have to trust me when I say I know what's best. If your daddy was here, he wouldn't even try to talk some sense into you—"

"You shut up talkin' about my daddy!"

One of the twins started to whine, but neither me nor Mama turned to see which one. We stared at each other. Locked onto one another, veering toward the past. Few seconds later, her gaze dropped to the floor, and she sent me to my room. I obliged happily.

THE THUMP STARTLED ME, BUT I WAS already awake. I had been staring at the ceiling. Thinking. The idea felt almost easy as long as it stayed cozy inside my mind. So, I knew if it was going to be real, I needed to hear it aloud.

My sheet and blanket fell silently to my lap as I rose from my bed. The thumping was less distinct now, similar to a rustling or shuffling. With my eyes closed, I matched the sounds to her movements as I tiptoed down the hall. She'd waited until the crack of dawn to climb in through the window of her bedroom.

If it were me, I would've climbed the sturdy old oak that put down roots on the left side of the house, but Jackie was not me. She most likely got the ladder from the shed and pushed it up against the house.

"Good Lord!" she exclaimed as I slipped into the darkness with her. "Damn, Mya. Make a sound why don't you."

"Sorry."

"You about scared me to death."

She was the one sneaking around in the dead of night, but I scared her? Jackie kicked her shoes in the general direction of her closet, took a few stumbling steps toward her bed, collapsing in a pile of faint giggles.

"Oh, Mya, Mya, Mya..." She grinned at the plain white ceiling above us. "You're my favorite, you know that?"

I did. It wasn't hard to figure out. Nat and the twins were too young, and she couldn't stand Nikki. That left me.

"Girls don't like me." She confided with a smile. "I don't know why. I'm cool. Right?"

"Yeah." I nodded and got into bed next to her. "I need to talk to you about something."

"But wherever I go they don't like me. I want a girlfriend. Do you have a girlfriend? That girl...what's her name? The one with the braids. Asia or Africa or something."

"China."

"Right. I want me a China. Boys are only temporary, but girlfriends, they last forever. You could be my girlfriend."

"I'm your sister."

"You are, aren't you?" She smiled dreamily and gently pushed my hair off my face. "You're smarter than me. And prettier."

"Stop that." I shook my head against her pillow, trying to keep her from fondling my face.

Jackie giggled. "Mya's soooo pretty." She swiped her finger against my nose playfully. "I got me the prettiest sister there is."

"Jackie—"

"When we grow up you can be the model, and I'll handle all the money."

"You drunk?"

"A little," she admitted, still smiling. "I'll be your manager. We'll go all over the world." She yawned.

"I gotta ask you something. About...about sex."

"Okay."

"What's it like?"

She shrugged and went back to studying the ceiling. I thought I'd lost her again to one of her silly fantasies, but at that moment, she said, "It's like floating on a sea of nothingness, hoping something will fill you up, but nothing ever does."

I was hoping for a more definitive answer. Before I could ask a more direct question, she began twisting and turning, cozying up to me. Her hair stretched out behind her as she buried the left side of her face in her pillow and stretched one arm over my stomach. I probably should've tried harder to look after her. Jackie liked to think she didn't need it, but she did.

23
PECAN

RUINED. THE SOCIAL WORKER SAID. WIELDED THE word 'gainst me like a weapon. From her point of view, I'd ruined Jackie, or I'd let her be ruined. Either way, it was my fault.

Heziah sighed as another bottle clinked in the trash can. Vodka, gin, tequila—some even mixed with juice or fruit punch. All perfectly sized to fit in her backpack.

"I was afraid of this. Belinda? You see this? This makes..." He paused to count. "Five bottles."

I nodded.

"We can't ignore this. We gotta do something."

I nodded again. I'd been holding my breath, waiting to find a box of condoms, thinking that was as bad as it could get.

"It's them foster people. They got her drinking."

Heziah ain't believe me. He still lived in a world where folks was basically good. He moved on to her closet, sticking his head in the darkness among her clothes. "Why would they do that, Belinda?"

"To make it easier to...umm...it ain't her fault."

"Okay, whose fault is it?"

He emerged from the closet holding a travel mug. Popped the top and took a sniff. "Let's go."

We'd kicked the girls outta their rooms and told 'em to wait downstairs. They set about occupying themselves for the last twenty minutes.

"What are you gonna do?"

"I'm going to confront her and make sure she understands this is unacceptable. I don't know if they have rehab places for girls her age, but I'll look into it."

"Rehab?"

Heziah responded with a look of pure impatience.

"I mean...maybe we could talk to her first. I don't wanna send her away."

"We may not have a choice. She needs help."

"I'll help her. I'm her mama. She had a tough go of it, and she needs some time to adjust. I'll talk to her, and everything'll be okay. I promise."

Was a silly thing to promise. I ain't have no control over what Jackie did. Truth be told, I was all talked out.

The scene downstairs ached of girlhood innocence. So much so that I thought maybe Heziah might rethink what he said. Mya sat in the window seat, like always, her nose between the pages of somebody's life story. Nat and the twins were on the floor, playing a board game. Jackie mighta been playing with 'em, but she was concentrating more so on painting Jenna's toes a bright pink. They were good girls. I silently pleaded with Heziah to remember that.

"Okay, everyone, your mama and I need to talk to Jackie."

"What I do now?"

"Y'all go on back upstairs."

A hearty sigh came from the window seat, and a thud as the book closed. "You told us to come down here. Now we gotta go back upstairs? Make up your mind."

"Mya."

"What?" She spat, not the least bit shamed by my reprimand.

She and Jackie must've gotten together and decided they was both gonna do their parts to drive us mad.

"Do as we say." Heziah's voice took on the tone he usually reserved for the twins. Full of what my daddy called authority. Ricky'd used it all the time. With me and with them, but Heziah wasn't Ricky.

Mya walked right up to us, failing to tame the lion inside her that was dying for a fight.

"Do I need to repeat myself?" Heziah's voice didn't waver an inch.

"I dunno." She shrugged. "Do you?"

"Mya!"

Everyone stopped. The game stopped being put away. The nail polish wand paused in midair. I'd only ever been embarrassed by my kids one other time.

"You apologize to Heziah right now."

"Sorry," she said, passing us on her way to the stairs.

Her sisters were quick to follow after that. They didn't even wanna look like they were being smart.

"I don't know what's gotten into her," I heard myself whisper.

He gritted his teeth and got on with it. The talk. He motioned for Jackie to get up from the floor and sit next to him on the couch. I sat in one of the armchairs off to the side, wondering when Heziah had time to think up what he was saying. I knew more about what Jackie was up to, and I couldn't have put things as clearly as he did. Suppose I never was good at explaining things. Part of me felt like it would make it worse to hear the words aloud. So, I kept quiet to hide from all the pain they would cause.

"You wanna send me away."

"No, that's not what I'm saying. I want you to go somewhere where people can help you deal with this—"

"I-I'll stop. I won't do it no more. Okay?"

I nodded, smiling at her from where I sat, but Heziah kept concentrating on the coffee table. Magazines lay lazily across it, and the bottle of neon pink nail polish sat on one corner.

"Tell me the last time you drank." He uttered the words without lifting his gaze.

Jackie stuttered through her lie then smiled at him sheepishly. She was sure she could stop at any time.

"I believe her. Heziah? You hear me? This a family matter. We don't need no strangers butting in."

"Belinda—"

"She said she gone stop. She get it now."

Jackie nodded enthusiastically, right on cue. "And I won't see Darrel any more. I promise. For real this time. I gotta new boyfriend now anyway."

Shock, followed by confusion, and finally disgust changed Heziah's features. It all came clear to him, and he aged a decade right on the spot. "Did you know about this?" he asked me.

Jackie started to say something, but her mouth fell open as she realized I hadn't told him what I knew. Her eyes grew large with panic. Then filled up with blame. She blamed herself for all of it.

"I...I was going to tell you," I said carefully. "I was."

"I'm calling the police."

"No!" Jackie leapt to her feet, following him to the phone in the kitchen. "Don't! Please!"

Heziah stopped with his hand on the receiver. "Did you have sex with this man?"

"No..."

"Did he force you?"

"No."

"I don't believe you." He lifted the handset to his ear and pressed down on the number nine.

"Mama! Do something! Stop him! Please."

24
JACKIE

DARREL WOULD NEVER FORGIVE ME, I THOUGHT as the words slipped out of the policeman's mouth. The officer was trying to project passivity, keeping his voice at an even tone no matter what my answers were, but it was all an act. Every so often the corner of his mouth would flinch and a spark livened up his eyes. He probably had daughters of his own.

"It was just sex."

"Jackie!" Mama sat in her favorite arm chair, looking horrified. Couldn't tell if it was because she didn't want me to say it aloud or if she didn't want it to be true. She hugged her elbows and shivered, shaking her head slightly.

Heziah stood next to her. He let his hand drop onto her shoulder and gave it a little squeeze.

"We only did it once or twice." I glanced over at them again, thinking the lie would make them feel better. It didn't.

"Do you remember the dates?"

"No."

"It's in her diary," Mama whispered to the floor.

"No, it's not," I lied with a straight face.

The policeman nodded and kept on writing his report. He thought I was a victim, like Mama did. That I'd been hurt in some way by Darrel. That tickled me at first, and then it made me mad. Who did she think I was? I wasn't some poor defenseless puppy. I coulda said no to him. I simply didn't want to.

"What's going to happen now? Are you going to arrest him?" Heziah wanted to know.

"Right now, we're investigating."

"She told you what he did." Heziah glared.

It occurred to me I'd never seen him mad before.

"He needs to be behind bars."

"He didn't do anything!" I threw my hands in the air.

"Jackie, be quiet," was all he said before turning back to the policeman. "Do I need to speak to your supervisor? Because as far as I know, it is against the law for a forty-something man to...to...be with a teenage girl."

The cop nodded and rose from his position on the sofa next to me. He didn't need convincing. He was on their side.

"It's procedure to talk to all the parties involved. I'll be in touch. Oh, and if I could get that diary..."

"I threw it away."

It was Mama's turn to glare now. "Go get it," she demanded. Mama never demanded anything. She always asked nicely.

They didn't even bother waiting until I left the room before discussing me. Mama apologized to the cop. Again. He took it upon himself to explain girls like me—girls who had been through what I had with Darrel—we sometimes tried to protect our abusers. I rolled my eyes and climbed the stairs. My sisters waited for me at the top.

"Don't worry. They're overreacting. It's no big deal."

I knew abuse. Ricky made sure of that. Because of him I could smelling it in the air. Saw it hidden in the smiles of women on the street. Nobody knew it like I did except for mama. I paused with my most cherished belonging in my hands and considered if there was a resolution I hadn't thought of before. Darrel wasn't Ricky. He didn't deal in fear. Only thing he'd ever inspired in me was lust. Maybe my diary would convince them.

My sisters lurked in my doorway, watching me.

"Are you going to jail?"

"No, Nat. I'm not going anywhere." I smiled. "Everything's gonna be okay."

The officer took my diary and assured my parents once again he'd be in touch. Mama walked him to the door, thanking him for coming by like he was a neighbor who stopped off to loan her some milk.

I was happy to be rid of the man and expected things to go back to normal now that he was gone, but those pitiful expressions didn't want to leave their faces.

"What now? I answered his questions. Gave him my diary. What more you want from me?"

"Jackie—"

"You want me to say I'm sorry. Fine. I'm sorry. I won't ever have sex again."

"Don't say that!" Mama snapped. "You—You too young to know 'bout that! He...what he did was...he..." She took a deep breath and forced her arms down by her sides, so they were straight as arrows. "He raped you."

"No, he didn't. I'm a big girl. I knew what I was doing. You just don't wanna accept it. Wanna keep treating me like a child, but I'm not a child no more, Mama. I'm not."

"You are! And you not having no more boyfriends!" She played with the syllables of the last word, so I'd know she didn't actually believe that was an adequate title. "Ain't none of you gonna have no boyfriends!"

"Belinda—" Heziah made a move to talk some sense into her, but when Mama got going wasn't no stopping her.

"I'm your mama, and it's my job to protect you. So, I'm saying no. You stay away from these men. And boys. And quit drinking!"

"Should I become a nun too?"

Mama looked like she wanted to hit me. She took a few steps forward and bit her lip.

"Jackie, go upstairs. I think we all need some time to think and calm down. Right, Belinda?"

Mama didn't answer. She blinked, exhaling through pursed lips.

Heziah lifted his head in the direction of the stairs and said, "Go on. We'll talk more tomorrow."

Tomorrow came, but there wasn't much talking. They were waiting on me downstairs. Said Mya should go on to school without me. Then Heziah told me about this place in Cicero for troubled girls. Said I'd have people to talk to who knew what to say to help me understand things better. The time away would give me some space from the Darrel situation, he said. Mama didn't say anything. She sat next to him clutching her hands on her lap.

"But I did what you wanted. I'm sorry I was smart. I take it back."

"It's not a punishment. We're trying to help you."

"Sending me away ain't helping me! It's...sending me away. Mama? Mama, please? I'll be good. I promise." I knelt down in front of her desperate for her to look at me, but she closed her eyes instead.

Heziah did all the talking.

"We've already made the arrangements. They'll be here to pick you up soon."

"Don't make me go. Mama? Please? I don't...I didn't mean to..."

She sniffled and took my hands in hers, sharing my tears. She loved me, sure. Still didn't stop her from handing me over to strangers.

25
NIKKI

BELINDA, TALK TO ME. PLEASE. IT'S BEEN two days." Heziah's voice cracked like maybe he was coming down with a cold.

I felt bad for him. Looked like Mama was torturing him good. She'd look at him, sigh, and finally turn her attention elsewhere. It'd been like that all through dinner. Heziah would make a comment—an innocent comment about the weather or something—and look to Mama, hoping some of the ice around her heart would thaw a little. Of course, it didn't happen. We made it through dinner without anybody saying too much of anything, all of us watching the empty chair where Jackie used to sit.

"How long you gonna punish me? You don't think I feel bad enough already?"

He was trailing Mama around their bedroom while she got ready for bed. Their door was open a crack, but I don't think either one of them noticed.

"Hey, look at me."

"Don't you lay a hand on me!"

"Belinda—"

"I mean it!"

Didn't seem fair. All he'd done was tell the truth. She'd never acted like that with Daddy, and he did a whole lot worse. That's the way Mama was when it came to Jackie. She threw all the rules out the window.

"You not supposed to be eavesdropping." Nat leaned against her doorway, wearing a nightgown that used to belong to Mya. The cotton was so worn it was more like a collection of fuzzy little balls of thread than actual fabric. The yellow stars had faded, and the ruffle hem fell above her ankles. "That's rude," she said without the slightest bit of judgment on her face. She was quietly informing me of something I needed to know.

"I'm not."

"You spending the night again?"

I hadn't planned on it. I'd planned to tell everybody my big news, but they were all so down I was having second thoughts.

"You could sleep in Jackie's room."

"You still here?" Mya appeared, wrapped up in her bathrobe, holding a clean washcloth.

"She's gonna stay in Jackie's room."

Mya hesitated before pushing open the door to the bathroom. Threw a short glance my way, which wasn't encouraging in the least, and inhaled through her mouth. She needn't worry. Not like I thought I could replace Jackie.

"I'm going home, but I wanted to talk to Mama about something first."

She nodded and proceeded to close the bathroom door behind her. She didn't care about my reasons, but I didn't take it personally. That's how Mya was. If it didn't involve her directly, she didn't get all worked up over it.

Nat abruptly stood at attention, her ears pricking up, then just as quickly, she ducked back into her bedroom. A second later Mama was marching toward the bathroom.

"Mya's in there."

"Oh."

I waited for her to ask why I was still hanging around. A few seconds passed, and neither of us said anything.

"You waiting to go in?" she finally asked.

"No. Actually, I was waiting for you."

"Mmhmm." Mama's eyes passed over me from head to toe, but I wouldn't have been surprised if she wasn't seeing me at all. She had a lot on her mind.

"Umm...whatcha think of Jean-Louis? You like him?"

"Don't know him."

Men didn't have a good track record with Mama, so I didn't expect her to be ecstatic at the mere mention of my boyfriend. Plus, given the tension between her and Heziah, I probably shoulda waited, but the wedding was going to be in less than two months.

"He really liked you."

She cut her eyes at me like she could smell the lie on my breath.

"He was just saying how much he loved visiting with everyone. And the food he liked that too. And he...umm...he loves...me."

"Mmhmm." She shifted her weight to her right hip and crossed her arms under her chest.

"He's gonna make a lot of money. He's gonna be a surgeon, you know. And he would take good care of me."

"I ain't raise you to have some man take care of you. You take care of you."

She hadn't raised me at all, I wanted to say, but I smiled and banished the thought from my mind. Instead I said, "I think Daddy woulda liked him, and Daddy didn't like hardly anybody," I said it with a smile so bright, my cheeks started hurting.

"What you trying to tell me, Nikki?"

"We...we getting married."

Whatever she was feeling before up and evaporated. Sheer panic took its place. Why she'd panicked when she didn't even know him, I don't know. Wasn't like she had some incriminating information to hold against him.

"Lord, have mercy. Y'all trying to put me in an early grave!" She gasped, shaking her head.

"Well, this way you don't have to worry about me no more."

"You are not getting married. You are too damn young."

"You was my age when you married Daddy."

"That's why I know what I'm talking about! Nikki..." Mama closed her eyes, counting slowly to ten and back again.

"I'm gonna be nineteen this year."

"Don't be stupid."

I nodded as the tears began to trickle down my cheeks. There it was—

exactly what she thought of me. She'd never have said that to Mya or Jackie or anybody but me.

"That boy don't love you. He wanna own you."

Why couldn't she be happy for me? I was on the verge of living happily ever after. Didn't I deserve that?

"Nikki, baby..." She took a step forward but stopped when I took a step back. "You gotta listen to your mama, okay? I know what I'm talking about."

"You don't even know him. You just said so, and maybe...maybe you don't know me either. Maybe you just too bitter."

26
MYA

ALL MY LIFE FOLKS BEEN LOOKING AT me with expectation. Daddy expecting me to be like him. Mama expecting the same. And the world, they expected me to be right. Do right—whatever that means. If you're smart, you're 'posed to have a huge career and make lots of money. Good at sports? Become a famous athlete.

None of my sisters had to carry expectations like I did. Nikki thought she did, but that was all in her head. And Jackie did whatever she wanted, telling folks what they wanted to hear along the way. Nat and the twins, well, they got away with being cute and polite.

So, when coach gave me that look of pure disappointment, a part of me roared up inside, ready to proclaim my right to be free. To be whomever I wanted to be. Even if I didn't end up being all that I could be.

"I can talk to your mama if you want. Explain about your potential, and the opportunities you'll have if you keep running this season."

"That's okay."

I'd made up my mind, and Mama's wishes didn't have much to do with it. I'd grown tired of track and wasn't looking forward to softball or volleyball either.

"Mya." Coach glanced over my shoulder to the far end of the gym, then slowly drew his gaze back to me. "This about that boy?"

Ramon was waiting for me on the bleachers.

"I gotta go. See ya, coach."

The team would have to do without me. Hell, they'd just met me. They didn't own me.

China stopped mid-lap to watch me walk out the gym. I thought maybe I shoulda waved, but since she didn't, I didn't either.

"Ready?"

"Yeah."

RAMON'S PEOPLE WERE DIFFERENT FROM ALL THE folks I'd ever met. His mama insisted he bring home money, and she wasn't talking about the part-time McDonald's kinda money. She was the same way with Ramon's big brother, Tyrone. So when Tyrone got locked up for dealing, Ramon took over his corner.

Folks came by in cars and on foot, all of 'em wanting an ounce or two to tide them over until the end of the week. Some of 'em even begged, tried to negotiate discounts, or promised favors. But Ramon's mama couldn't take no favors to the store, and discounts wasn't gonna buy her name brand clothes and shoes. That's the way she put it, and he repeated her word for word.

I wasn't in a hurry to get home. With Jackie gone, the house felt even more empty than usual. Seemed like every room held a memory of somebody that wasn't there anymore.

A rusted green hooptie pulled up to the curb, and one of Ramon's friends stuck his head in the driver's window to collect the cash before signaling for the boy across the street to get the requested quantity. Ramon joked I was his lookout girl 'cause I picked up on everything around me. There was a rhythm to things. That made it easy to spot outsiders: folks that were new to our neighborhood and the occasional cop. I'd gotten so good at it that I worried something bad would happen to him if I wasn't there.

"Hey, man, whatcha looking at?" Ramon ran in my direction, bouncing lightly on the balls of his feet like he was tiptoeing down the sidewalk. "What? Something wrong with yo' eyes?"

A blue hatchback with the Indiana plates stopped at the stop sign a block away. It lingered at the intersection longer than was necessary, but that was normal for cautious customers. Behind me, a woman came out the three-flat with two or three brats in tow. She was chiding them about taking care of their shoes, saying she'd spent a hundred dollars on each pair, and they'd better be grateful. I paid attention to all that, plus the two girls who were a few years older than me standing at the bus stop. Saw that and I didn't see him—the man Ramon was accusing of staring at me.

"What you looking at, man?"

I'd seen him before, but I couldn't place where. His dusty forest-green jacket looked vaguely familiar. His face was framed by short dreadlocks screaming for some maintenance, and his general demeanor was in need of some soap and water.

"Hey, I'm talking to you, man." Ramon pushed the dark-skinned visitor's shopping cart sideways. It didn't topple over, but that was sheer luck.

Jackie had left behind more than half of her wardrobe, and I figured she wouldn't miss some of the more modest pieces. But modest for her was still revealing on me, well, when compared to what I usually wore.

"I look where I want."

"You looking at her? Huh? What you need to do is look at a bar of soap!"

The corner erupted in laughter, echoing against my back as I walked against the tide. Ramon wasn't all that mad, but that didn't stop him from acting like it. He was paranoid about folks thinking he was soft.

"Leave him alone."

My boyfriend did a double take. I guess he expected I'd be impressed by the display. "Go back to where you was," he ordered for his friends' benefit though.

"You shouldn't be here," the dark stranger was saying. His blood-stained eyes poured into mine. "This ain't no place for a nice girl."

What made him think I was a nice girl? Ramon looked at him then at me, wondering if we knew each other. I was wondering the same thing.

"Aight, man, whatever. Go on. Be about yo' business."

Wasn't until dark that I realized the homeless guy's words were still hanging around even though he'd long since departed. Ramon hadn't said one word to me. Couldn't even look my way for too long. Made it an awkward walk home. Me watching him, and him watching the cars, people, stray dogs, anything other than me.

"Wanna have sex?"

"Here?"

"No. Over there."

"In the bushes? Seriously?"

"Better than your place. At least ain't nobody listening over there. And nobody's out here sightseeing this time of night, so they not gonna spot us."

Wasn't any happiness behind his smile, so I wasn't surprised when he shook his head. Had to be the first time any boy anywhere had turned down sex. "Your people gonna be looking for you."

It was a terrible excuse. He knew I wasn't in any hurry to get home.

"You sure?" I stopped about twenty feet from the house and crossed my arms behind his neck, daring to be seen kissing him. That was all it took for him to change his mind.

27 PECAN

I HATED TO ADMIT IT, BUT MAYBE THAT social worker was right—I'd ruined my girls. At the very least, I'd lost 'em. Nikki wouldn't listen to me. She was gone. Jackie was gone. And Mya never really returned home. Her body was with us, but when she looked at me, I ain't see my girl anymore. Wasn't any recognition in her eyes. Like all the love had drained right outta her. The love she had for me...

"Mommy, is this like money?" Nat sat at the kitchen table going through my purse. She'd settled on my checkbook and was flipping through the pages. "Can I have some?"

"Ask yo' daddy." I stood over the stove, stirring the spaghetti sauce.

"How old are you?"

"Thirty-seven."

"Is that old? How old is Daddy? You're..." She gazed up at the ceiling, counting on her fingers. "You're nine years older than Louis! 'Cause he's twenty-eight. How old's Hazel?"

Heziah's firstborn was a myth to us. In all the time we'd been together, I'd never laid eyes on the girl.

"Ask your daddy."

"Don't you know?"

"She's in her thirties, I think. About thirty."

She giggled. "And you're her mommy! If you were only seven years older than me, you'd be..."

"Well, I ain't. So you don't gotta worry about that. Go tell your sisters it's time to wash up for supper."

The twins weren't ruined. Nat wasn't ruined either. But that wasn't proof of my mothering. I reckon it was the opposite. They had the least amount of time with me.

I was jolted forward, and the sauce made a short puckering noise as the spoon fell from my hand into it. Nat had wrapped herself around my waist, hugging it with the strength of somebody twice her age.

"You'll feel better, Mommy. You'll see. When Jackie gets back from her treatment, everybody will feel better."

Jackie's treatment was supposed to last thirty days. I ain't know if I would make it that long.

"Hey." Heziah strolled down the hall, shuffling through the mail.

I went back to the spaghetti.

"Got the first bill for that place." He sucked in loudly and held his breath as he pried open the envelope. "Better be worth it."

"Was your idea..."

"I know. I'm just saying I hope they know what they're doing." He didn't have to explain anything to me, and I didn't want him to sit but he did it anyway. "I'll see if I can't get some extra hours at the plant."

"Mmhmm."

Heziah had taken a second job at a plastics factory on the far south side. It was so far east, he might as well have been going to Indiana.

"I can work."

"That's not what we decided. The girls need you here."

Wasn't like I was doing much good. Obviously.

"At least until things settle down."

Heziah rose with the weight of the world on his shoulders, and for a second, I forgot to blame him for the hole in my heart.

"Well, we'll see..." His rational self decided to make an appearance. "Maybe you could get something part-time. We gonna have a wedding to pay for too."

I snapped the dial to the right, turning off the stove, and removed the sauce from the heat. I ain't wanna get wind of nothing else about no wedding!

"What you think of this guy?" Heziah was wearing his concerned face. "He seems all right, don't you think? A little full of himself, but..."

I hated him. He was Ricky in a smaller package. If I'd have known who Nikki was bringing to supper, I woulda sprinkled a lil' poison on his plate. Got rid of him from the get-go.

"Belinda?"

"He's fine."

He nodded. "I sure wish she'd wait until she was older."

"It's them crazy church folks. Got her thinking she gotta be married to have sex." That and she was desperate to feel loved. But I ain't say that. Woulda been too much like inviting him to poke at an old wound of mine. My firstborn ain't feel loved...

"Hmm. Maybe..." Heziah tapped his chin thoughtfully.

I got a few plates from the cabinet and stacked them on the kitchen table. Next came silverware.

"Maybe you should have a talk with her. You know...tell her about it from a woman's perspective."

"She doesn't listen to me."

He nodded. The truth hurt enough without him having to agree with me.

We sat down to supper with two empty spaces instead of one. Mya was missing. I was too spent to throw a decent-sized fit. Pushed the food around my plate until I heard the front door open and close. Heziah studied me from the other end of the table. He always sat facing in with his back to the hallway. I liked to look out and see the living room on the opposite side of the house. The girls sat along the sides between us. Nikki hadn't stopped looking at me with them big sad eyes of hers. Like she was gonna guilt me into denying what I saw in that boy of hers. It was right at that moment I felt the urge to give Clara a call. She'd have backed me up. She'd have seen it too.

"Oooo, Mya late for dinner." Nat teased.

"So," my mostly silent daughter said before sitting next to Jackie's empty seat.

I wasn't quite sure if she was giving us the silent treatment or if it was her usual quietness. Everything seemed more quiet since Jackie left.

"Try to be on time," Heziah said to her.

"She supposed to be home right after school, Daddy."

"Is that true?" His question was to me.

I nodded.

"Well?" Heziah waited a proper length of time for an explanation but none came. "Mya?"

"What?"

"Why were you late? Where were you?"

She helped herself to a spoonful of collard greens and began breaking up the cornbread into pieces over her greens, so she could mash them together with her fork.

"She always late, Daddy. Since Jackie started her treatment."

"Shut up," Mya snapped, and Nat looked hurt by the threat in her sister's words.

"Don't tell your sister to shut up. We don't use that word in this house."

"It ain't a word," she muttered.

"Excuse me?"

"It ain't a word. It's a phrase."

"We don't use that phrase in this house."

When Ricky was in a bad mood, I could feel it coming. Like rain in May. It'd be all in the air. Was only a matter of time before enough things got under his skin to make him do what he'd already set his mind to doing. Mya was taking a page out of her daddy's book. She kept looking straight ahead. She was sitting to Heziah's right, directly in his path, so she had to concentrate real hard on avoiding his gaze. Nikki looked like she might fall to pieces under the weight of her sister's glare even though Mya's stare wasn't truly aimed at her. Her fork scooped up a mouthful of greens dotted with bits of yellow cornbread and she sucked it all down. She mighta been hungry, but I suspected her appetite came from the ball of anger growing up inside her. It was time to change the subject.

"Mya, I'm still waiting for an answer. If your mama told you to come straight home, you should have a good reason for not doing that."

"That another rule for this house?"

Everybody's jaws clamped shut. The twins' eyes grew two sizes, and they looked at each other to make sure they'd both heard right.

"Mya has track practice." Nat gave a lil' smile, meant to encourage the peace. "Right, sis?"

"Nope. I quit."

"B-Because Mama told her to." Nat was determined to save her sister.

"Nat, baby, don't you got something you wanna ask your daddy?"

"Hmm?" She'd forgot all about our conversation. "Oh, yeah. Umm... Daddy, how old is Hazel?"

When he didn't answer right away, Callie said, "Daddy?"

I hadn't said anything else, but I was begging Heziah to let it go. Wasn't no good gonna come from pressing Mya at that point.

HEZIAH AND ME AIN'T NEED TO BE all lovey-dovey to make love. We both had enough experience with marriage to know it wasn't always about that. We was slipping away from each other, so we did our best to hold on to what we had. Took longer than usual, but when we finished, he hugged me to him and let me cry on his chest.

"I'm sorry, Belinda. It'll get better."

I managed a nod between sniffles. Before I could get too comfortable, I reminded myself to go to the washroom. If I ain't go before bed, I'd be up in the middle of the night. Heziah stirred only slightly as I wrapped myself up in my robe and stepped out into the hall.

The quiet filled up all the empty space around me, and I breathed a sigh of relief. Thinking of my girls sleeping soundly in their beds, having nice dreams. Couldn't peek in on Nikki or Jackie so I started with Mya. Her door was closed, but the lock ain't work, so I turned the knob slow so as not to wake her with the sound. Felt the breeze before I saw her bed was empty and the window was open.

I'd done my best by her and still failed. What did she want from me? I went to the window and pushed it shut. Maybe I had overreacted a bit with the track thing. She'd always liked running. I sighed and sank into her bed. Well, I wasn't too big to admit my mistakes. Mya was a good girl, especially considering all that had happened.

28
JACKIE

MYA CONFESSED IN ONE LONG BREATH AND promptly retreated into her own world. She stretched her long muscular legs out in front of her until her feet disappeared under my bed. She sat with her back against the wall and stared listlessly at the tops of her sneakers. My roommate could sleep through a tornado, so she never knew about my sister's late night visits. Couldn't imagine Mama approving, so she had to be in the dark too, which made it our secret. Been a long time since we had secrets to keep from the world.

"You want me to talk to her for you?"

Mya shook her head slightly.

"I'd tell her with you, if you wanted, but they say I can't leave for another two weeks. Mya?"

No longer could I pretend her solitude was natural. Quiet she'd always been, at times even something of a loner, but there was a happiness to her before. She was as content on her own as she was with us, but not anymore. It was painfully obvious that she was as far from content as she could be.

"Ramon wants me to keep it."

I hadn't even known they were doing it. Weren't sisters supposed to tell each other things like that?

"Jackie."

"Huh? Oh. Umm...Mama gonna be mad, but she'll help you. She

would...," I insisted, expecting her to argue the contrary. "Me too. I'd babysit. I'm good with kids. Don't know why but the little suckers can't get enough of me."

I desperately wanted to ask her how this happened. Mya of all people? The smart one? I was the wild child. If anybody was gonna get knocked up and ruin her life, it was supposed to be me. I eased off the bed, so we sat side by side. An apology burrowed its way into my chest.

"I had to quit track."

"You can rejoin next year."

"I'll need new clothes."

"You can borrow some of Nikki's. Not like you actually care what you look like."

She smiled at my lame attempt at a joke. "Ain't you mad?" she asked.

Took me a minute to realize she frowned on my behalf and not actually at me.

"She sent you here."

I shrugged, and my hair brushed across my shoulders, reminding me of how much time passed since I cared about my appearance.

"Was more so Heziah's decision, and he only sent me here because he was trying to help."

"Whatever," Mya muttered to the darkness.

The Palmetto Rehabilitation Facility wasn't so bad. Lots of girls. In fact, there were only girls. About fifty of us. In two weeks' time, I'd made lots of new friends. Some from all corners of the city, most originated from the suburbs. We sat around talking most of the time—to each other and to our counselor. Once a week they let us paint or draw, and we could relax in front of the television until nine o'clock.

"You think it'll hurt?"

"Darrel said it doesn't."

"Ever had one?"

"No." Again, I felt the urge to apologize. I should've had more to add. My sister needed me. "I'm sorry."

"Not your fault," she said simply. "I think..." Mya folded her lips inward, uncertain if she wanted to let the words out. "I think I got...you know...on purpose. To get back at Mama."

Didn't get how that worked exactly, but I nodded and listened.

"Can't go around dictating to people. Even if they are your kids. It ain't right. How'd she feel if somebody was trying to control everything she did?"

"I'm sorry."

"Stop saying that." She rolled her eyes. "Ain't your fault." A tremor ran through Mya, and she ground her teeth in frustration. "If she'd never left us, you wouldn't be in here, and I wouldn't be..."

"You don't know that."

"Yeah, I do."

The guilt closed in around me as soon as I saw the pain on my sister's face. We shared almost everything. Had the same memories, same teachers, same parents. Yet, we couldn't share this. She blamed Mama. I blamed Ricky. Couldn't even talk about what happened without being afraid to rupture the other's wound. So, my favorite sister carried her feelings alone, all this time and even though we sat side by side, she was still alone.

My eyes dropped to the floor. "Mama didn't wanna be separated from us..."

"How you know?" she snapped. "She tell you that?"

"Lots of stuff people can't say. Doesn't make any of it less true."

"Exactly. She disappeared! Walked straight out the door and ain't come back!" Mya finally choked out, "Least she could've done was let daddy take us..." And then it happened. My sister–the beautiful smart strong one, who never let anybody see her sweat–cried. Fell over into the fetal position, sobbing quietly. "I miss him."

Made sense. He'd loved her.

"Shh...," I said, stroking her hair softly. "It's okay."

"No, it's not," she choked out. Shaking her head vigorously. "Not okay... it's not..."

29 MYA

I RETURNED TO FIND MAMA ASLEEP ON MY bed. Her mouth hung open with drool sliding down her cheek. Made me want to hit something. So, standing in my bedroom, watching Mama snore peacefully, I knocked over the cup which held my pencils. She snorted and sat straight up.

"Mya." She wiped the slobber away with the back of her hand. "Where you been, baby?"

"Out. Obviously."

"What you doing?"

"Getting my stuff for school." I needed to change into clean clothes, get my books and things together.

"Come sit next to me?" Her hand hovered over my bed like she was afraid to touch it. She could sleep under the covers but couldn't touch them.

Pissed me off even more.

"Mya? Please, baby?"

"I gotta go."

Her eyes began to water, and I thought I might explode. What did she have to cry about? She got exactly what she wanted.

"I'm still your mama. You not gonna get another one. I'm it."

"Great."

"Baby...," she whispered as I turned my back to her. "I'm so glad to have you home. You know that? I missed you girls. I love y'all. Love you so much–"

"I'm pregnant."

Her mouth dropped open again only this time wasn't any sound.

"I had sex a bunch of times and now I'm pregnant."

"No–"

"Yeah. And he's in a gang. And he sells drugs."

"Mya!" She erupted and shot to her feet. She lifted both hands to her hairline, pulling her hair back as she uttered nonsense.

Didn't matter to me what she said anyway. I won. The bitterness drained from my fingertips one drop at a time. Surely that was cause for celebration.

"Stop smiling! This ain't funny!"

Mama hadn't caught on yet but I finally had a victory. Me, Mya Morrow. She paced from the window to the door, breathing heavy and murmuring about the new rules she was gonna impose. She didn't see I was done with all her rules.

"We can fix this. Mama will–You young. You made a mistake. Y'all been through a lot. It's okay. Okay? Mama'll help you."

Red flashed before my eyes, like the fire burning under the surface of my skin got a burst of oxygen. "Didn't ask for your help."

She stopped pacing. "What? Oh. You want to...well...'course, it's an option too."

"No, I'm keeping it."

I'd made up my mind finally. Looking at Mama, I couldn't do what she did. I wouldn't leave my kid for somebody else to raise, leave her in the world all alone, and I wasn't gonna become a murderer.

"Don't need nothing from you."

Mama's hand flew to cover her mouth, and her chest caved in like I'd hit her there. Another victory.

"What's that supposed to mean? Mya..."

I stuffed the contents of my bureau into my book bag. Dragged my suitcase from the floor of my closet and flung it open.

"You gonna need me!"

I shook my head no. I needed her four years ago. Now, I didn't need anybody.

"Yes, you are!" she cried. "You girls think everything so easy....Think you can do whatever...well, you ain't grown! Not yet. You—"

"Don't have to be grown to work out the truth."

"Is that so? And what exactly is the truth, huh?" She struggled to find a natural-looking pose. Folding her arms, shifting her weight, trying to give the impression she was in the right. "I know you loved your daddy, but he...he...I...things just happened the way they had to...I'm sorry, but—"

"You not sorry! You ran off! Ran off with Heziah and started a whole new family!"

"Mya, baby, that ain't what happened."

"Then what happened? Huh? You get amnesia? You forget about us? What kinda mama just disappears on her kids? What kinda mama choose her boyfriend over her kids?"

"That ain't what happened! Your daddy...he..."

But she didn't have an excuse. Just stood there staring at me, her lips moving but not finding any words.

"You ruined my life." I said under my breath.

"When you older we'll talk about this." She finally said. "Not right now. When you older."

"How old I gotta be?"

"Mya—

"How old I gotta be for you to tell me why...why you killed my daddy?"

I waited, milking every second of silence. Watching her features for even the slightest indication of remorse. But Mama ain't deal in apologies. Would've been like paying bills with promises. More than that, she'd never loved him. We all knew it. I used to wonder what came first—him hitting her or her not loving him. More questions that would never be answered. Not that it mattered. It all came down to this one point: she made the choices she did in spite of what those choices did to us.

"How could you? When you knew...you knew what it would do to me!"

More silence. Weighed more than the last one. So heavy, it seemed improbable for it to be hanging on by a thread, but it did. Swinging gently back and forth, taunting me. The moment of no return had finally come. If anything was unforgivable, this had to be it. Some things folks just don't get to come back from.

SUMMER 1987

30 MYA

RAMON'S FAMILY SPREAD FAR AND WIDE, AND none of them had a better grasp on their lives than he did. His sisters, nine and ten, ran in and out the house on a constant basis. Which made his mother and grandmother incredibly tense, yelling for somebody to shut the damn door every ten minutes or so. And his brother was hardly ever home, but he had two cousins who occasionally slept on the floor of whatever room they passed out in. All of which, I could handle. At least they were real. Nobody in his family tried to be anything other than what they were: gangbangers, dope fiends, ex-dope fiend alcoholic mothers, whatever the case may be. His people didn't have all those complicated layers to be pulled back to get a straight answer. Of course, their unambiguous nature came with its own issue. None of them could make heads or tails of me.

"Morning." Ramon's grandmother's voice croaked out into the earliness of the kitchen.

I nodded, closed the basement door quietly behind me, and moved on to whatever was sizzling on the stove. His people were good about always having something cooking.

"Where's Baby?"

"Getting ready," I swallowed my first and second bite of a sausage patty.

Ramon was a middle child, but they all called him Baby for some reason. Could've been because they favored him. Nobody could stand the girls. They were horrible vicious little things and not even their mother denied it, but Ramon was different. His mama said it was because he had a different daddy. His daddy was about something, not like her other kids' daddies. Ramon's daddy worked for the Chicago Transit Authority and had a wife and two other kids on the west side. Ramon never saw fit to comment on it even when his mama would bring it up, so I left it alone too.

"Some eggs on the stove too if you want." His grandma studied me. "Can't eat only meat. Gotta have something else to go with it."

"Eggs meat too."

"No they ain't. Eggs is eggs. All you do is eat the meat. Don't want nothing but some meat."

The last few weeks I couldn't seem to get enough meat. Didn't matter what animal the meat came from. At the mere mention of a chop or strip or patty, my mouth started watering. I finished off the second sausage patty at a slightly more subdued pace.

"At least get some toast." The old woman stood shakily and hobbled over to the bread box on top of the fridge. "You know meat expensive. Tell Baby he gotta bring some more home or you gonna eat us outta house and home. Got six mouths to feed now you here. You think about getting yo'self a job?"

I shook my head and took a seat at the tiny kitchen table in the corner. The fridge hummed so loud next to me I could pretend well enough I didn't hear the woman and all her nonsense. I'd moved outta Mama's house, but I still went to school every day. Did my homework. Hung out with Jackie. She'd even talked me into joining a few after-school clubs. Said not running didn't mean I couldn't have fun. After school I caught up with Ramon, and we headed home together. I wouldn't complain if the rest of my life followed the same pattern, at least until graduation. Didn't matter how much his people kept saying I needed a job to contribute. Ramon said the opposite. Said I was going to school and that was all. He contributed enough for the both of us, and I agreed with him.

"Hey, Mama." Neferteri didn't have much going for her in the looks department. She traipsed into the kitchen, dragging her slippers along the way. Years of drug abuse had taken its toll on her body. She drooped from head to toe more than her age should've allowed. Cursed with missing teeth, incessant scratching, and random dark spots too big to be freckles, Nefeteri wasn't a catch by anybody's standards. The dirty pink slippers swished across the mustard yellow laminate floors. It was better to focus on something specific when Nefeteri came into the room. "What da fuck happened to all the fucking sausages?"

The two women communicated silently then turned on me.

"Look here, lil' girl, I know you think you special, but this here is my house. Don't nobody be eating up all my shit b'fore I can get to it."

"Still some left."

"I told her. I told her she gonna have to get a job. Contribute 'round here."

The creaking of the stairs above our heads put an end to the conversation. Ramon hurried into the kitchen, smelling fresh and clean. "Morning," he announced to all the female energy in the room. "Mmm. I smell sausages?"

"Here, Baby. You can have these two." Neferteri wasn't shy. She batted her eyes when it suited her and draped herself against any man who held the keys to something she wanted. Didn't matter to her if it was some guy she met in a club or her own son. Her game stayed the same. Her grasp on her robe relaxed long enough to give her chest some air, and she handed him a grease-stained paper towel with the two lumps in it.

"Can I get one more?"

"Sure, you can...we gonna need some money to go shopping though."

Ramon nodded, eased a wad of bills into her hand, and kept his eyes trained on something safer than the view of his mother. "Mya, you eat?"

"Don't she look like she ate? Or ain't you noticed?"

I took it to mean I had sausage grease on my face and went to grab a paper towel.

"She sure is healthy. Eating all the time." Grandma's lips wished around against her gums as if to reassure herself she still had her two precious teeth.

"You know, Mya...if you ain't careful, you not gonna get that cute lil' figure back. Then what you gonna do?" Neferteri planted a wet kiss on her baby's cheek and headed upstairs with her plate.

The walk to school was a little longer than usual. I checked my watch at the halfway point to confirm it. Ramon wasn't walking his usual speed. He still had the sausages wrapped up in the greasy paper towel, clutching his fingers tightly around them. Staring at nothing in particular, it seemed. Just the sidewalk.

"What you thinking about?" I asked.

"Nothing."

He seemed to shake out of the trance long enough to offer me one of his sausages. I chewed and swallowed, watching as the other kids hurried past us, running just so they wouldn't be late.

"I'm gonna be late."

"Yeah?"

"Yeah." With a loud suck of my thumb, I drew his attention finally, but he was still concentrating on something else. "You look mad. You mad at me?"

"No. You mad at me?"

I shrugged and helped myself to his last sausage. "Why I'm gonna be mad at you?"

"'Cause," was all he said. His eyes drifted down my body, and he said, "Can't tell all that much. 'Specially when you wear big tee shirts. I can go by the mall...get you some more..."

"Okay. And some bacon. I want some bacon."

A hard whistle blew, the leftover vibrations ringing in our ears. The crossing guard wasn't the patient type. She waved us on persistently, but Ramon didn't budge. Held tightly to my hand and kept me planted firmly at his side. His lips parted, but only silence came out.

"I gotta get to school."

"I know...wait, okay? For a second?"

Given the woman in the neon vest's impatience, I wasn't sure I could wait much longer. "Okay. What is it?"

"Maybe you oughta go back home."

I dropped his hand without a word and reset my steps in the right direction. We'd gone three months without him saying it, but there it was.

"Mya! Wait!"

The regret on his face wasn't enough to temper my emotions. They were wild and unpredictable, my emotions. They grunted inside me and shoved him with undue force before taking off toward the crosswalk.

"Mya!" he called again, running to catch up. "I'm just saying...maybe you'd be better off..."

"I hate you!" Of course, I didn't but I said it anyway.

"I just...I dunno...I'm just saying they can take care of you."

"You wanna break up with me? Just say so and I'll go!"

"Huh? I'm just trying to look out for you. Make sure you okay. It's my fault..."

"What?" My chest rose and fell, finally finding a steady rhythm, my feelings calming to a simmer instead of a raging boil. "What's your fault?"

"That." His finger made a clear arrow to my growing stomach. "I should've...I should've been careful. I got rubbers. I just didn't..."

"Rubbers?"

Ramon let out a groan that drew attention from the last few students running through the crosswalk. I turned casually, curious if I recognized any but I didn't. Whenever anybody said the word rubber, I automatically thought of rain. Rain and my rubber boots. I did not think of sex. So, I waited anxiously for him to draw the connection between the baby and rubbers, but Ramon was too embarrassed. His fair complexion burned bright red, and for the life of me, I couldn't understand why.

"You gotta go. You gonna be late."

"I'm already late. You gonna tell me?"

"I...yeah..."

I waited, both hands on my hips. "Tell me already! What's rubbers have to do with babies and sex?"

"They are...protection. You know, like condoms. Come on, Mya! You really don't know this?"

I shrugged. "Don't know why you'd call them rubbers. They not made of rubber."

"Yeah they are." He frowned.

"Not all of 'em. Not the ones you got. Says it right on the box."

"Forget it."

I shrugged. "You the one brought it up."

"Forget I said anything!"

"Fine," I said, happy to get back to walking.

Folks always making up words that didn't make sense. Didn't they know there were enough words in the English language? Why couldn't they say exactly what they meant? It confused me. Meant I had to think twice about things I, otherwise, understood.

"I gotta go to school. See ya later."

One thing school had taught me was for every question, there was a book with the answer. I was already late, so I wandered into the library and began searching. Didn't find anything about rubbers, and when I asked the librarian for her assistance, she had the same reaction as Ramon. After an hour with the card catalog, I found one book with illustrations, black and white, of course, but I didn't mind. Learned all the technical names for areas were once-vague ideas—like uterus, fetus, placenta. By lunch time, I was immersed in another book detailing everything could possibly go wrong during pregnancy, and it was there, I felt the first pangs of motherhood. I eased my hand under the table to rest against the bump, which was suddenly more than just a bump. A baby. My baby. The book said my baby had ears and nails. The thought made me giggle in my quiet corner of the library.

Tiny little ears and tiny little nails filled my dreams. Followed by endless black waves and eyes the color of the darkest chocolate known to man. So pleasant the dreams were I didn't mind how often they came. I couldn't seem to sit still for more than ten minutes without drifting off into one of those dreams. It frustrated my teachers nonstop, but eventually they understood.

"Mya, have a seat."

The principal's office hadn't changed at all since I'd been sent there with Jackie. Tall windows matched by equally tall stacks of files and papers. Sitting in the middle of it all made me nervous. So much disorganization. Even in the basement, me and Ramon managed to do better with our things.

"Your teachers tell me you're one of our brightest students." The woman sat down, almost disappearing behind a mountain of paperwork.

Worried I'd have to have a conversation with pages instead of a person, I scooted my chair to the left.

"Mya? Are you pregnant?"

It seemed like a trick question. The answer was obvious, but the woman stared at me over the top of her glasses while holding her breath.

A trick question but still a serious one, so I took my time with the response. Considered every possible outcome and said, "No."

"No? You're not pregnant? Because your teachers say your work has begun to suffer. You are an A student getting C+ grades. You fall asleep during class. And..." Her fingers flicked almost musically in my direction. "You certainly appear pregnant."

"Am I in trouble?"

"In trouble?"

"Yeah. I break some kinda rule or something?"

"By being pregnant or falling asleep in class?" the principal asked but quickly dismissed the matter altogether. "Well, Mya. By all other accounts, you seem like a good girl, but we can't ignore this." Her drawer was open and closed before I even knew what was happening, and the woman handed me a pamphlet. "Girls like you find themselves more comfortable in a different setting."

Lots of smiling faces and a few cute little babies graced the laminated pages. I took a quick gander at it and handed it back. "No. I'm gonna stay here."

"I've already called your parents. I'm waiting for them to get back to me, but you're old enough now you can comprehend the value in this. You'll learn things you need to know. Like how to change a diaper."

"I know how to change a diaper," I replied and paused long enough to give her time to come up with something I hadn't already mastered by the age of ten.

"It's going to get harder if you stay here. Our sister facility will give you the support you need."

"I can take care of myself. I don't need support. I'm fine."

"Let's wait and see what your parents think, hmm?"

That's when it hit me—Mama and Heziah were what was standing between me and things going wrong. Not their physical being, but the idea of them. The idea they were still in my life meant the principal, my teachers, and all the other adults who cared enough to wonder didn't have to worry. If they knew the truth, that I was only a few irate words from being homeless, then they'd be considerably worried. Worried enough to make important phone calls to people with authority. They'd put me back in foster care and take my baby from me. I couldn't have that.

"I gotta pee."

The principal quickly agreed. Pointed to the open door, and I walked out. Out of the office. Hurried down the hall to my locker, slipped on my coat, and headed out of the school never to return.

I had to be careful, not just for me, but for my baby too. I thought about it so much that my nice comfy dreams turned into nightmares of screaming babies and blindness. I'd wake up sweating and completely out of breath. When I tried to explain it to Ramon, he just told me to go back to sleep. He didn't get it. How could he? He didn't know what I did, that at any moment somebody could knock on the door and take me away. I lay awake, staring at the pipes running over our heads. We needed a plan. Some place to go where nobody would find us and the baby seemed to agree. I gasped as the little flutter turned into something of a more definitive nature.

"Ramon. Ramon. Wake up."

"Wh-What?"

I took his hand and placed it flat against the side of my belly. "Feel it? That right there? That's the baby. She's kicking."

"Mmhmm. Can I go back to sleep now?"

I lifted my shirt to get a clearer view. Scrutinized every inch for thirty minutes straight, waiting for the next kick. When my patience finally started to drain, I decided to provoke the little miracle. Figured if I could see the kick, then she could see the opposite motion. So I poked my stomach. Poke. Kick. Poke. Kick. The two of us went back and forth for a few minutes before my grin turned into rolling bouts of laughter. A quick glance at Ramon's peaceful body, and I thought better of letting him in on the joke. It was ours. Something special between her and me. For some reason, the miracle didn't belong to Ramon the same way it belonged to me. She was my baby. I found myself wondering if that was how I got my name. Did Mama feel the same way? Did she feel like I belonged mostly to her?

"Mia," I said it aloud for the first time. "That's what I'm gonna call you. 'Cause you're mine. All mine."

31
MYA

SAYING NO WAS NOT ENOUGH. RAMON WAS insistent. He stood dutifully by my side as I got familiar with the cold steel. The handgun weighed more than I thought it would, and its weight took up most of my contemplation. Wondering about how many pieces made up the weapon. Somebody had to be awfully meticulous to design a gun. After five minutes, I hadn't even gotten around to thinking about pulling the trigger yet.

"Good. Now point it at the pillow." Ramon was growing impatient. He pointed to the bed, giving me the order for the third time.

"No. I'm done." I held it out, waited for him to take it and shove it back into the waistband of his jeans, but he didn't.

"Point it at the pillow. Or-or point it at the wall or the column or the freakin' pipe, I don't care. Just point it."

"But–"

"Ain't no point in just holding it. Never gonna be a time where you gonna need to just hold it. If you got it, folks gonna expect you to use it. So point it at the freakin' pillow!"

"Fine." My arms extended out in front of me, and I pointed the heavy thing at our bed. "Happy?" The nose of the gun wavered from left to right as I spent more energy looking at Ramon than the intended target.

"Don't be afraid of it. It ain't gonna bite you."

"I don't even want it. What I'm supposed to do with it?"

"It's only for a lil' while until I can straighten some stuff out...so take it. Okay?" He didn't wait for me to agree before taking it out of my hands and dropping it into my book bag. "I loaded it already. You just gotta point and shoot. This weekend I'm gonna take you out to practice. Don't forget it's up in here. Okay? Can't be leaving your bag open for everybody to be all up in it."

"I know that."

Couldn't help being irritated. Was he trying to protect me in his own way? Sure. But all I paid attention to was somebody telling me the obvious. Only stupid people needed to be told the obvious. I made slow circles against my stomach, calming myself and Mia. The cheap mattress moaned and groaned under my weight. It wasn't made for comfort, and the last few months handed me all the proof I needed of that fact. Stubborn springs found their way into my back regardless of my position, but I wasn't about to yield to the tired old thing. Eventually, I'd find a groove.

"Where you going today?"

"Library." It was where I went every day. The public library made me feel like less of a high school dropout. Packed myself a sandwich and read to my heart's content. Was better than school to tell the truth.

"Good," he replied.

"So, I got your permission?"

"Don't be snapping me up. I'm just asking."

I sighed and arched my back. "Sorry."

"I'll come by 'round four to walk you home."

Started to say I didn't need an escort. I'd been walking all over Chicago most of my life. 'Cause I was a little heavier didn't make me less capable. He shook the wrinkles from his favorite shirt and sank into the bed beside me, his shoulders slumped forward, his eyes glazed over in contemplation.

"What stuff?" I asked, delayed confusion wrinkling my brow. "You said you had to straighten stuff out. What stuff?"

Ramon shrugged and pulled his tee shirt over his head. "Stuff. Dude over on Dorchester got it up in his head he gonna take my corner. It ain't gonna happen, but he going around telling folks different."

"Take your corner?"

"It ain't gonna happen. He see how we making good money and think he gonna get in on it. So...uhh...you shouldn't come around for a while." Guilt kept his gaze planted firmly on the basement floor.

"But I got my trusty gun." I smiled, my version of a joke. "And I know how to point it and everything."

"Real funny, Mya."

But I could tell he was serious. He never brought up the streets to me, so it must've been a big deal for him to do so that morning. His was a dangerous business. I'd have to get him away from it if I wanted to keep him safe. Step one would've been to break the hold his family had on him. So he'd be free to be who he actually was instead of whom they wanted him to be. We'd have to go somewhere far away from them. Montana crossed my mind. I'd seen it on a map. Traced the state's borders with my finger and imagined we were there. Lots of open fields meant lots of space to run. I imagined teaching the baby to climb trees and pretending to be a monkey on the way up. Montana. I liked that it started with an M and ended with an a, like my name. Montana, it would be.

The branch librarian had gotten so used to seeing me pop in and out during the day, she glanced up and smiled. She wasn't like the school librarian. She didn't blush at all my questions.

"This is our geography section. Anything you want to know about Montana will probably be in here," she said, gesturing to the row of books at eye level. "I'll check and see if we have any state history books on it."

I nodded my thanks and grabbed the first few books. The library was usually empty, so I had my pick of tables, but I always chose the same one—by the window with its very own light hanging overhead. It sat a little ways off from the others. It was perfect.

I decided to start from the beginning, and by the time I'd read up to the twentieth century, my neck was begging for a break, my back ached in all the usual places, and my behind was numb. It was a bright sunny day. The kind of day you didn't wanna spend cooped up inside. So, I packed up my book bag and let the sunshine spill over my face.

Montana trickled through my thoughts as I walked. School was but a distant memory. I wasn't going back. There would be no going back, only forward. To Montana. Thoughts came about what I would do once we got there. Where we would live...if Ramon would be happy there. His happiness didn't outweighed what I knew to be true—Montana equaled freedom. Fresh air and wide open spaces and nobody to worry about us. Nobody would even know I was there.

Before I knew it I was only a few blocks from home. Mama's home. I stopped at the corner, wondering if I should dare to walk down the street. What if she saw me? What if I saw her? I missed my sisters. Missed watching Jackie and Nikki get on each other's nerves. Missed Nat's smile, even missed the twins. I'd miss them even more if I moved to Montana. I turned the corner and walked on. The house was quiet, and for the first time in a long time, I thought what it would be like to sleep in my own bed. Still had my key. Had Mama changed the locks? No. That wasn't Mama's style. She wasn't spiteful or vindictive. I sighed and turned the next corner, headed toward the high school. Maybe I'd catch Jackie when she got out.

Didn't occur to me I'd have to pass Ramon's corner before I got to the school. Didn't think about the danger lurking there. The danger he'd tried to warn me about, protect me from. No, I was too busy thinking about other things. It wasn't until I approached the block that I heard it. If lightning had sound, this was it. Sounded like a car backfiring. Not once. Not twice. Over and over the sound cracked open the bright shiny day. I was close enough to see the action but too far away to do anything about it. Too far away to stop them. The people-sized blobs ran in all directions. Some of them hiding behind parked cars, others simply running for their lives. Arms locked around me, steady and sure, and pulled me to the ground as the gunshots came closer. We landed hard in the shadow of a two-flat, and a putrid scent invaded my nostrils. The god-awful smell occupied my mind, not the bullets whizzing over our heads, until it was silent again.

"Let me go." I wrestled free from his grip, crawling to get a better view of the devastation at the corner.

"Nothing you can do, now."

The arid stench was coming from the homeless man I'd seen lingering around. The one who said I had no business being on that corner. It wasn't his place to say such things to me. What did he know? Sirens called out in the background. Neighbors finally peeked out their windows, gasping at the bodies that bloodied the sidewalks. A few screams sliced through the eerie silence as I managed to get to my feet, stumbling over one then the other as sirens engulfed the area. They must've been coming from all directions, surrounding the massacre. Some of the slain faces I recognized, but they weren't important enough to garner a pause. I was looking for one face in particular, hoping and praying he wasn't there. Maybe he'd taken a short walk to the liquor store for snacks...it was possible, I thought. A glimpse of the bold colors up ahead nearly stopped my heart. A red-and-yellow shirt, a shirt I knew. I'd seen him wear it at least once a week since the day I met him. The ground rose up to meet me, and my hands hovered over the bullet holes steeped in blood.

"Ain't nothing you can do," the voice said again. "He's gone."

"Shut up."

"I'm just saying...you can't help him none."

"Shut up! Shut up! Leave...leave me alone!" I still couldn't bring myself to actually touch him. My hands shook so badly, I finally gave up and lowered them against my thighs.

"The police coming. You wanna be here when they get here?"

Dazed, I shook my head. Police meant worries. More folks worrying about me, trying to fix me. Send me where I didn't wanna be. "No."

"Want me to help you up?" The smelly stranger kept his word. Walking steady and slow, we put much needed distance between ourselves and the blood spilled. "You got somewhere to go?"

For the first time, I got a load of the man who saved my life. A black forest covered his chin and half his face, his dark green coat was dying for a bath. He needed help more than I did.

"He dead?" I heard myself ask.

The man nodded. "Yeah, he dead. Where your people at? Want me to call 'em or take you there?"

"No. I can...I can...by myself."

SUMMER 1991

32
NIKKI

MARRIAGE DIDN'T SEEM TO ENDEAR MOTHER NATURE in my favor. Each month she rained on my parade. My spirit had grown weary from the roller coaster of ups and downs. Jean-Louis's urologist gave him a clean bill of health. The problem was me. My husband wanted me to have it confirmed officially, but I didn't need any laboratory or tests to tell me what I knew in my heart. I would never have a family of my own.

"You're young. Give it time, " Darlene advised. "The Lord will provide. He always does," she said.

The two of us were a pair—both infertile. Her butter knife spread the moist cake layers into a thin slice as she put her guilty claim on seconds. Chocolate cake with vanilla frosting was the reverend's favorite. He would expect to come home to at least three-fourths of his cake still standing.

"Can't be genetic."

Darlene forced a smile. She still didn't like any mention of my other family. "No, probably not," she added after swallowing a big bite.

Mama had six girls. Mya had one, and Jackie was gonna get knocked up any day now.

"It's only been two years. Give it time."

"Four. We've been married four years. Last month made four." With one whisk of my finger, I claimed a dollop of creamy white frosting and sucked it clean off. My midsection had grown steadily each year of my marriage, swelling with emptiness.

"By then, you could be bouncing around here with your own baby!" Darlene was insistent on pretending to be hopeful.

"It's not fair."

"What does Jean say?" Darlene couldn't bring herself to say his full name, and she pronounced it jean, like the denim. Each time it made me cringe. I'd imagine Jean-Louis sitting across from me, arching one eyebrow in disapproval. He thought it was obvious the correct pronunciation was John. Nobody named their son jean Louis.

"He made me an appointment to see a specialist."

Actually, he'd made me three appointments. The first two I'd accidentally forgotten about. I was considering forgetting about the third.

"You should go. Have faith." Her gaze shortened as if she were a little girl about to ask for candy. "You could have your sister go with you. How is Mya?"

"Fine." It was a lie but a merciful one. Nothing good would come of me telling her the truth.

Darlene rose from her seat at the kitchen table and lumbered over to the pantry, returning with a fully gift wrapped box. "I picked this up from Marshall Field's. It's for the baby." She'd hid it in the pantry, so the reverend wouldn't find it. "Give it to her for me?"

The reverend never thought much of my sister. He thought she was unruly and ungrateful. She didn't exactly change his mind by getting pregnant at sixteen.

"Sure." I accepted the box and mentally probed my schedule for time to donate the gift to someone who would accept it.

A resounding beep filled the tight little kitchen, and my heart skipped a beat as I reached for the phone. Jean-Louis's code popped up on my beeper. He must've been between patients. He hated to be kept waiting.

"Where are you?"

"At the reverend's."

Darlene was pretending not to listen, perfecting the curly ribbons of the gift wrapping with her big black scissors. She made a respectable effort to stay out of my marriage.

"Did you want something?"

"I will be home late."

"Oh, okay. Should I leave your dinner out?"

"No."

I DIDN'T KNOW ONE WOMAN WHO WAS as lucky as I was. I had a beautiful house, a husband who gave me money whenever I asked—I had a great life. Better than my mama ever had. Better than anybody I knew. I reminded myself of this as the garage door ticked up.

I pulled my Honda into our vacant three-car garage next to where Jean-Louis's Ferrari would've been. He worked long hours to take care of me, so I tried not to complain. Twice a year he took me on vacation. Last year, we'd spent four days in Hawaii before he got called back to Chicago to see a patient. He was a very dedicated surgeon.

I'd thought seeing my house would've made Mama proud. I had only the best finishes: sparkling black granite countertops, mile-high cathedral ceilings, and Italian white marble floors throughout the first floor. It all felt very expensive and clean. At least it did to me. I thought she'd have been impressed. Maybe even admit she'd been wrong about Jean-Louis, but Mama had squinted her eyes and gritted her teeth as she took it all in. She hated it.

My sisters loved it. Nat and the twins oooed and ahhed appropriately. Jackie said it felt like a museum.

"I'm home," I called to no one in particular.

There was a bedroom right off the kitchen I thought might serve some purpose once Mama got on in years. I'd decorated it with her in mind and envisioned complementing the garden-themed wallpaper and white wicker furniture with fresh-cut flowers every day. Mama would love it, and so would I. It was, after all, my duty as the oldest. Wasn't like Mya or Jackie would ever think to do such a thing.

Of course upon seeing the room, Mama wasn't the least bit grateful. She nodded and forced a smile after I explained its purpose, but the stench of her disapproval didn't dare abate. She was determined to hate everything about my life.

33 PECAN

"MAMA!" JACKIE'S VOICE BOUNDED THROUGH THE FRONT door and down the hall. "Mama!" She wore a smile so wide I thought she might swallow me up whole. "Put that down," she demanded, taking the dishtowel from me and tossing it to the floor.

"Girl, you lost your mind? I gotta clean the dishes with that. You wanna eat off the floor?"

"I got good news, Mama!" She took my hand, twirling under my arm and in a circle around me.

"What's going on?"

Nat was first down the steps, soon after came Heziah and the twins. Jackie was so full of giggles by that point she could barely get it out.

"I'm gonna be a star." She beamed.

"Oh, good Lord."

"I am, Mama! The band gotta a gig," she declared.

We'd spent the better part of every waking moment trying to impress on her that what she needed was a solid education. A steady stream of doors would open for her if she took her studies seriously. She said all the right things, but I think it was mostly to satisfy us.

"You need to be thinking about school."

"I am, Mama," she said, dismissing it at the same time. I knew my chile. She wasn't thinking no more about college than a cat thought about cheese.

"What kinda band?" Callie wanted to know.

Didn't matter. I mean Jackie had a real nice singing voice, she did, but she had other things going for her too. Like her brain which wasn't gonna give out. It was gonna make her some good money, so she would never have to depend on nobody to take care of her.

Jackie let go of me and moved on to dancing with her lil' sisters. They ain't know enough to do more than laugh when she did, smile when she did.

Heziah wrapped one arm around me and whispered in my ear, "Let it go." His smile said he was about ready to give up. He wasn't gonna hold out on college, seeing how happy this band thing made her.

She was eighteen years old. Technically an adult, but she was more stubborn than grown. Wasn't in me to just let it go.

"Oh, Mama, come on! You not gonna be happy for me?" She pretended to pout. "When I get rich and famous, you know I'm gonna buy you a big pretty house. Twice as big as this one!" She bat her eyes at me, then moved on to Heziah. "And a whole acre of land, so Daddy can plant flowers and vegetables, and y'all can sit out there in the garden drinking wine and flirting!"

Was hard not to at least smile at that.

I WASN'T GONNA BE AROUND FOREVER, SO I had to get my girls squared away. The years had been kind to 'em in some ways, but it only took one misstep to put 'em on the road to misfortune.

"You worry too much," Heziah was saying as he pulled back the covers. "They are doing good. Nothing bad's gonna happen."

I nodded, for his sake. We was never gonna think along the same paths. Heziah still thought the world was full of roses and rainbows. I knew better.

"Belinda, you gotta learn to take the good. Can't go around expecting things to go bad."

Nikki had married that little troll of a man. Mya was God knows where. Jackie was...well...she was working on herself, as she put it. Nat and the twins was up next, but if I ain't get my oldest three squared away, I ain't have the slightest bit of confidence that I could handle the next three.

"Stop worrying," he demanded, pulling me close to his chest for a quick hug.

"It ain't gone work."

"What?"

"Holding me close. You ain't gone rub off on me." If it hadn't happened in ten years, it wasn't gonna happen.

"This is about Jackie ain't it?"

"She got her heart set on this music thing." I sighed and flung a fresh blanket over our bed, smoothed it over the mattress and tucked it tight. "Won't listen to nobody..." Just like Nikki. Just like Mya. Damn Ricky and his stubborn genes.

"She'll come around."

"Oh, yeah? When? I'll put it on my calendar."

He laughed, taking the pillows, which were for decoration, from the head of the bed. "Soon enough. We give her some space, and she'll make the right decision on her own. You'll see."

Space. I wasn't good at space, not where my girls were concerned. Space had nearly taken them from me one too many times. Space was the reason I'd never set eyes on my only grandchild. I still felt too young to be a grandma but didn't change the fact I was one.

"She needs time," Heziah said.

"She done had four years."

"Jackie?" His forehead wrinkled with confusion, then relaxed a moment later. "Belinda—"

Heziah's chest swelled, and he squeezed me to him until the air whistled between his lips. He couldn't lie to me, but I wish he would've. Wish he could've stopped me from killing Ricky. I still wanted him dead, but I wish it hadn't been me that done it. Then maybe my child wouldn't hate me.

34
MYA

MIA ANGEL MORROW WAS BORN AT COOK County Hospital after twelve hours of sweat, blood, and tears. She came out half screaming, half laughing, with big eyes dark as coal and a head full of curly hair to match. She was mine. There was no doubt about it.

From that moment on, everything I did was about her. I didn't trust anyone. Not daycare people, not my sisters, not my mama. Not even the old lady who volunteered at the soup kitchen. She never left my side. Maybe I wasn't the most cheerful child to begin with, but having my own to look after made me harder. Who was going to protect her, feed her? When she had a problem, who was going to know the solution better than her mama? So, it wasn't long before I developed a sixth sense—about people, places, even times of day. A long list of rules I lived by.

Rule number one. Guard the facts. Our first names were privileged information, and our last name was totally off limits. Folks regularly referred to us as the girl with the baby, and I was perfectly content with that. As far as government agencies were concerned, I lived at home with Mama, her new husband, and my sisters. Jackie got my mail for me. I didn't bother with a lie or the truth when it came to other interested parties, and eventually, they stopped asking.

Rule number two. Be prepared. Count the exits and how many steps it will take to get to each one. Keep the big blade in your bag and the small one in your underwear with anything else of value.

Rule number three. When in doubt, the answer is no. You want me to hold her while you go to the bathroom? No. You want a ride somewhere? No.

No such thing as a free lunch, my daddy used to say. He was wrong a million different ways, but he got a few things right.

"Mommy, where Dee?"

"I don't know," I uttered, taking her hand in mine as we hurried across the street. Mia was always asking me where the mysterious soldier boy was. She worried about him when she shoulda been worrying about putting one foot in front of the other. Holding on to her and pushing the shopping cart with everything we owned was hard enough without having to think about where soldier boy had disappeared to. "He'll show up."

I meant it to soothe her mind, but she immediately took to searching the crowded street for his face.

"Oww, Mommy."

"We gotta hurry." Things went much faster when she used to fit in my cart, but at four years old, Mia was tall for her age and very restless. Everybody said she was like me.

"Dee be there?"

"Yeah." I didn't really know one way or the other, but she'd move faster if she had something specific to move toward. Getting to the shelter before they closed the doors wasn't enough of an incentive for her. Long as she had us, she thought sleeping on park benches and in public restrooms was an adventure.

The line at St. Ann's Rectory stretched down the block and around the corner. Women with teenagers. A few whole families, but most folks were single. A few of them waved when they saw us coming. Mia waved back. She waved to everybody regardless of whether they were actually looking at her.

"Dee here?"

"Inside."

She was gonna throw a fit when she found out I was lying, but by then, we'd have a roof over our heads. Easier to deal with her fits when we were stationary.

"We gonna sleep with Dee?"

Two days ago I'd woken up at four in the morning to find he had skipped out of our studio apartment with all our money. All the money I'd been saving to get us a real place and pay the back rent we owed our current landlord. It was the last straw for the man who sublet us the studio.

"Mommy." She tugged at my hand. "Dee be there when we sleep?"

"If he's here."

"If?" The tears began to crowd in the corners of her eyes. "Who gonna look over us, if he not?"

My daughter may not have understood all the intricacies of living on the street, but she got the danger, and soldier boy had spoiled her—always showing up in the nick of time. When she was a baby, she couldn't sleep if she wasn't right with me. I couldn't be lying in the bed next to her. She had to be right on my chest, and it had to be quiet, but eventually, even those conditions weren't enough.

"Who watch us, Mommy?"

"I will."

She looked doubtful.

MIA COULD ROAR LIKE NO CHILD I'D ever seen. She reminded me of the cartoon babies, sprouting tears from their eyes with their mouths wide open. Her pint-sized fists went to work pounding on anything within reach, even her own legs. Once she'd had enough of that, her claws came out.

"Stop scratching yourself!"

You'd think the pain would make her think twice about what she was doing but not my child. She could be bleeding and wouldn't feel a damn thing.

"Mia. Stop."

The cots around us began to stir. Nobody was gonna sleep 'til she got it outta her system.

"I want Dee!"

"He ain't here. Now lie down and go to sleep."

"I want Dee!"

She was two seconds into her favorite chant.

"Here," I whipped out her stuffed Elmo and thrust it into her chest for her to hug. The chant died a resistant death. "Go on, take it. He wants to sleep with you."

"She really loves her daddy." The old woman behind me chuckled.

Dee wasn't her daddy, but I ain't feel the need to correct the woman. I'd spent enough time trying to impart the distinction on Mia, but it didn't seem to matter to her. Ramon was only a word. I imagined her daddy turning in his grave but nothing I could do about it. The soldier boy was flesh and blood. Gave her Skittles even when she was bad. Mia loved him like he was her one and only friend. She might've loved Ramon like that if he'd lived.

"We see Dee in the morning?"

"Yeah."

"Okay. I go to sleep now."

35
JACKIE

"YOU NOT SCARED TO SING IN FRONT of lots of people?"

"Nope."

Callie shuddered at the thought. Her hands perched on top of her knees. She sat back on her heels, following my direction to tilt her head to the side.

"I would be. How many people are gonna be there?"

My littlest sister was too young to come to the club. Technically, I was too young, but I convinced the owner to overlook that.

"Are you gonna wear the red dress?"

"Mmhmm." I had a mouthful of rubber bands and was desperately trying to cajole the slippery ends of her hair into a neat cornroll. Mama had given up on braiding the twins' hair, but that's what they wanted. All their friends had braids.

Callie shuddered again between my knees. "Don't wear heels. You might fall."

The twins were growing out of their adorable phase and making their way toward beautiful. It was obvious even at seven years old. Didn't see even the tiniest bit of Heziah in them. They seem to have sprung up, deciding for themselves what features they would have, like grapes on a vine taking in the influences of everything around them.

"I wish I could see you. You gonna be the only one singing?"

"Maybe I'll sneak you in. Get you all dressed up. Throw some makeup on ya..."

She giggled.

"You'll just be a shorter version of me. There. I'm done."

She was up and at the full-length mirror on the back of my door in seconds, patting her head and admiring my work. "I look okay?"

"You look gorgeous! Now I gotta get ready. Off to bed you go. Go on."

Mama had given me a curfew of eleven, but I wasn't supposed to be at the club until ten. I figured she'd make an exception since I was doing something responsible like working. How else was I supposed to pay for the fancy college she wanted to send me to?

I held up the red dress by its straps and envisioned what I'd look like. It was like lipstick and fire had a baby and rolled her in glitter. Nobody was gonna ignore me, and to make sure of it, the band was wearing black.

"Knock, knock."

"Hiya, daddy-o."

Heziah watched as I laid the dress across my bed and went about pairing it with the right accessories. "You need a ride?"

"Nope. Kem's gonna come get me."

"Ahh. Right. Kem."

Kem Delgado was our lead guitarist. He had the desperado thing going on, so most people thought he was a bad boy. Truth was Kem was a good Catholic boy, and his bad boy side ain't hold a candle to mine.

"And...umm..." Heziah swallowed deliberately and made room for himself on my bed. "Who is he again?"

"The guitarist."

"No, I mean to you. Who is he to you?"

"My guitarist." I grinned. I knew what he was getting at, and he knew I knew. That's what made it so much fun.

"You know your curfew's—"

"Don't you want me to make some money?"

He nodded slowly, but he clearly wasn't convinced. "This club you're going to...is there going to be alcohol?"

"The grocery store's got alcohol too. You let me go there."

"Jackie—"

"I'll be careful. I promise. No booze. Not even a sip. Not even a drop."

He nodded again, and his gaze drifted over to the outfit I was dying to put on. His fatherly eyes racking up another set of concerns. The neckline wasn't subtle, but none of my necklines ever were, and it was short. Upper thigh short.

"I'm wearing really tall boots with it."

"And a long coat, I hope."

KEM AND I REALLY WERE JUST BANDMATES. Friendly bandmates. Friendly bandmates that everyone assumed were having sex. We weren't. Which isn't to say I didn't enjoy trying.

"Well, don't you look very mysterious?"

A very responsible driver, Kem smirked but kept his gaze on the road in front of us.

"How do you see through all this hair?" His black curls slipped easily between my fingers as I pushed them out of his face. A second later they'd stubbornly returned to their previous positions on his chiseled cheekbones.

"How do I look? You like my dress?"

"Of course, mami."

"It looks good on me, right?"

That garnered a turn of his head, so he could look me in the eyes. "Are you fishing for compliments?"

"No." I put on my best pout. "Although, I wouldn't have to fish if somebody wasn't so stingy with 'em."

Kem chuckled softly and stroked his goatee. "You know you're beautiful. You don't need me to say it."

I decided not to press the issue. If I had, he'd undoubtedly have played the we're just friends card he was so fond of. In Kem's world, friends didn't remark on each other's appearances, they didn't exchange lustful glances, and they did not have sex. I wasn't a very good friend.

Bobby Francesco, the fat little man who owned the rundown Club Francesco, met us at the door to his dirty jazz club which, to be fair, might've been something back in the day.

"You're Late!" the owner screamed, blissfully ignorant of the fact the club's best days were behind it.

"No, we're on time. See. On time. You said ten o'clock. It's ten o'clock." Never mind the confusing rule that ten minutes early was actually being on time.

His club was home to as many dust mites as it had cracks in the ceiling. These cracks stopped and started and ran down the walls until they'd satisfactorily marked off their territory. The black-and-white tiles that made up the floor were once perfectly spaced, but the effort was overshadowed by the chipped corners and tiles so loose they rocked under your feet like a seesaw. And the smell—dank and musty. Most of the chairs looked like a strong wind could destroy them, and when I accidentally bumped into a table, the damn thing wobbled back and forth for a good hour. Nobody said a word, but I was pretty sure it wasn't normal behavior in the House of Blues. Club Francesco was like its meek physically challenged younger brother.

The grumpy old goat grumbled for us to get on stage then waddled his flabby self toward the dark corridor lit by a series of amber-colored lights to spend the evening in his office, crunching numbers. There was probably a time when he was all about the music, but those days had come and gone. The old man had bills to pay. Period.

I started to say as much to Kem, but he'd already began to make his way to the stage. I say began because he got stopped by a table of giggling co-eds. A blonde. A brunette and a girl with pink streaks in her hair. I was thankfully out of earshot. It was a familiar scene. Kem and his inconsequential little bobbleheads. He would never allow himself to fall in love with one of them, and he didn't call any of them his friends either.

Clark and Jess took notice from the stage as they readied their instruments. They had briefly considered adding a second singer, but I put that idea to rest pretty quickly. Why would they need another girl when I was more than enough? Kem had just smiled at the floor when I said that. Clark and Jess howled into the night like two coyotes, but they didn't disagree with me. They were both old enough to be my father and doted on me like I was a rambunctious puppy.

The bartender was a thin and friendly looking guy with a well-groomed afro. He wore traditional bartender attire—clean white shirt, black tuxedo vest, and black pants. The warm hue cast from the squarish lanterns that mounted the surrounding walls made his teeth look dingy, but I assumed in the bright light of day, they looked white.

"Want me to take your coat?"

"Yeah, thanks."

He hadn't taken his eyes off me since we walked through the door. He wrapped my raincoat into a ball and shoved it beneath the bar. Then offered me a drink.

"It's on the house," he said after I refused. "I'm Mo and you are?"

"Jackie."

"Good to meet you, Jackie."

I wore the dress and played the role, but male attention had become a double-edged sword. I couldn't go anywhere, do anything, without wondering what their intentions were. Wondering if entertaining their affections would put me in danger of disgracing myself.

"Here." He shot a short glass filled with a lemonade-colored liquid across the bar toward me. "Maybe this is more your speed. It's my specialty."

Kem's little fan club giggled in delight as he took the stage and pulled his hair back with a rubber band. He could drive with the black tendrils framing his face, but he couldn't play like that. Clark, a big teddy bear of a guy, sat poised behind his drums waiting. His eyes searing into mine. He knew how I felt about Kem.

"Come on, take a sip. Help me think of a name for it."

36 MYA

MIA WAS TOO YOUNG FOR SCHOOL OR daycare. I didn't trust people with her anyway. Folks just saw a cute little toddler until she blindsided 'em with the truth. Nobody handled her like I did.

"Mommy, you got pretty hair. I got hair like you?"

It was shorter but basically the same. A blessing straight from my father, like my complexion. "Read your book."

"I don't wanna. When we gonna find Dee?"

I wasn't about to admit it to a four year old, but I was starting to worry about him myself. Couldn't stay mad at him for no real stretch of time. Besides, I should've known better than to hide the money where he could find it.

The world flew by the windows in front of us and behind us. The Dan Ryan Expressway was busiest during rush hour. Folks trying to get from the south side to downtown and back. The cars' headlights made one long blur of light as the El sped from one stop to the next.

"I like the train," Mia announced for the hundredth time. She turned the pages in her book, interpreting the pictures. Sometimes she managed to thread together a story that actually made sense. Most times not.

I watched her, waiting to hear whether this was one of those times.

"I not gonna sleep 'til we find him."

"Yeah, you will."

"No, I won't."

She didn't talk like a regular four year old. Didn't look at me like one either. I'd been in charge of kids before. Natalie. Some of the kids at the reverend's church. All of 'em was more scared of me than my own daughter was.

"Mia, you gotta sleep. Your body needs it."

"No, Mommy."

"Yes."

"No!"

That could've gone on forever. With Mia holding her sleep hostage or at least determined to do so. She'd eventually fall out, and I'd be there to catch her. By the time she realized what had happened, she'd be in la-la land.

"We go get Dee now?"

"Yeah."

Soldier boy liked to disappear on the south side. Pissed me off I had to go back there to find him. Last thing I needed was to bump into somebody I knew from my previous life. That's what I called the time before I left home.

I had a good idea of where to find him. He'd gotten away with almost a thousand dollars. It was enough for him to stay doped up for a few weeks. If I got to him soon enough, maybe I could reclaim most of my savings.

"Dee miss me. I can tell. He missing me right now. He miss you too, Mommy."

My best bet was a vacant three-flat on King Drive. It didn't have any numbers on the outside, so I never remembered the actual address. Only recognized it when I came upon it. It wasn't the kinda place to take a little kid. Even if she was Mia Morrow.

Both Jackie and Nikki came with baggage. Neither one of 'em was me. Jackie was always teetering on the edge of her sobriety. Nikki was miserable, married to a man I ain't trust as far as I could throw his little ass. If Natalie were older and had her own place, she would've been my first choice for a babysitter.

"There she is! The cutest little niece in the whole wide world!"

"Hi, auntie."

Jackie hoisted Mia onto her hip and gave her a loud smooch on the cheek.

"She hasn't eaten yet."

"Don't worry, I got it." Jackie nodded to the table, telling me to leave Mia's bag there. "Whatcha want? Want a Happy Meal?"

McDonald's was safe. I met everybody at McDonald's. Meant I ain't have to worry about them telling certain folks where I was 'cause they didn't know themselves.

"I'll be back in a few hours."

"Mommy, I go with you."

"No, you stay here with Jackie."

"No, I go with you."

Jackie tried not to smile. She wasn't so good at that. I was better.

"No. You stay here. With Jackie. I'll be back."

"No," Mia began to roar.

"You don't wanna be with me?" Jackie gave her best wounded look. That my sister was good at. She could make a dragon feel guilty for the fire he breathed. "I wanna be with you. I think we could have lots of fun together. Don't you usually have fun with me?"

"Yeah."

"Then why don't we hang out while your mama goes to do whatever she's gonna do." Jackie winked. She still thought everything secretive had to do with sex. "Okay? Deal?"

"I want a Happy Meal."

DARIEN WAS WOUNDED IN THE LEG DURING a mission to some far off land he wasn't supposed to talk about. He was lucky because nothing was left of the soldier standing next to him. He said Private Bird was a really good guy.

That Bird was the type to crack jokes even in the middle of a thunderstorm. He'd taunt the lightning and poke at the thunder. He had a young wife and a baby on the way. Bird was the one who was supposed to come home, but Dee made it instead.

He'd been honorably discharged from the army two years before we met. For all the lip service folks did to the troops, the services for veterans were limited and seriously backlogged. By the time he got around to seeing a doctor regularly it was too late. He'd found another way to manage the pain and the guilt. So for two years, he pushed that squeaky old shopping cart all around the neighborhood, collecting cans and anything else he might sell for food or drugs. I was sixteen, standing on Ramon's corner looking out for the police when he walked by. He was one of Ramon's regulars, but he tried not to come by when I was around. For some reason, seeing me there made it harder for him to get his fix. He never could explain to me why that was. He ain't know me. I ain't know him. We'd never even spoke, but if he saw me, then he had to walk on by.

That was what he was intent on doing, but Ramon noticed him anyway. The permanent shadow that covered his eyes, the ratty old jacket reeking of incense and funk, and the mangled dreadlocks which were meant to be a cultural statement. Ramon hadn't liked the way he was looking at me, but Dee didn't care. He kept on looking from a distance, mostly.

The three-flat on King Drive was built of blonde bricks and gray mortar. It was surrounded by a nonexistent yard. The kind of landscaping which looked like it had never been alive to begin with. A vacant lot stood on its left and a small bungalow, squatting beneath overgrown trees and bushes, on its right. The apartments inside were abandoned long ago. Junkies couldn't get high properly in absolute darkness, so the flicker of candlelight appeared in random sequence throughout the various windows, most of which were boarded up.

A few of 'em were lurking on the porch, like gargoyles standing watch over their castle. Their glazed over stares fixed on me, and there was no way to tell whether their next move would come from paranoia, murderous intent, fear, or some combination of all three. Didn't do any good to stop, so I climbed the steps, prepared for the possibility I'd have to fight my way inside. I didn't.

There'd been a fire in the building some years back, and the walls and floor were still charred from it. The scent of human depravity covered any lingering hints of smoke. Bodies laid slumped over makeshift mattresses and each other, some with only the moonlight to keep 'em company. Darien hadn't gone a day without that faded green jacket. It was because of that jacket I could pick him out of a crowd of a hundred people. I did a quick scan of the first floor and moved on to the stairs. The steps were an altogether inconsistent bunch. Some of 'em did their job well enough while others had given up a long time ago. Had to take my time, careful to avoid places where the wood had fallen apart, leaving empty pockets of darkness anybody could've fallen into.

Don't get me wrong, I ain't no hero. I'd heard of the terrible things that happened in that building. Little girls getting raped. Folks dying and nobody even caring. In spite of common knowledge, I wasn't worried. I hadn't been a lil' girl for some time, and I had no intentions of dying. If it came down to it, I was more worried about the damage I could do than what would be done to me. See, I'd always known I couldn't be hurt, not physically. Bad things happened all around me, and I managed to escape it unscathed. Darien and I had that in common.

I found him huddled in a corner of the smallest bedroom on the second floor. A writhing lump under the army surplus coat. The patch labeled Lt. Allen was all that was left of his time in the service. The coat covered most of his body, leaving a few dreads and his legs to stick out. A slow moan rustled beneath the dense but dirty cotton when I pushed my foot into his thigh.

"It's me," I whispered and leaned over to sling his arm around my shoulders. "Come on. Get up."

He didn't argue. His head drooped forward and a long string of saliva dropped to the floor. He tripped over his own feet, mumbling about Uncle Sam and destiny. I focused on guiding him down the stairs. I'd have to check his pockets later to find out how much of our money he'd blown.

37
PECAN

"Mama, do me a favor?" Jackie went on to ask for something, but I was too busy staring at the little girl holding her hand. "Mama?"

"I not 'posed to be here," the little one said, reprimanding her babysitter.

She wore faded blue jeans that were too long for her, but they had been rolled up, so she didn't step on 'em, a tee shirt that fit a smidge better, but was clearly meant for a boy, and sneakers which were so big they flip flopped on her feet. Still, she was beautiful. She was Mya.

"Mommy said stay at McDonald's."

"I know, but I gotta get to work now," Jackie's eyes pleaded with me. "I waited as long as I could. I don't know what happened to her."

"She go get Dee."

"She keeps saying that. I don't know what it means. Here." She handed over my grandchild then, as a last thought, turned back before taking the first step upstairs. "Mia, this is your grandma. Say hi."

"What's a grandma?"

"Me. I'm a grandma."

"Why?" Before I could answer, she seemed to remember a more important question. "You know Dee? My Mommy go get him. She gonna be mad when she can't find me."

I didn't doubt that at all.

"You not gonna like her when she mad." She was warning me. "She get real big and strong."

"Mama, who's that?" Jenna asked from the top of the stairs, rubbing her eyes sleepily.

Heziah and I hadn't exactly told the twins why Mya left, only that she wanted to live somewhere else. They didn't know Mya had been pregnant. What they knew about the deed wasn't much to begin with so explaining how their sister got in the family way wasn't high on our list of things to do.

"Go back to bed." I went back to being amazed by the lil' girl who looked so much like my own child. Coulda been her sixteen years ago. "You hungry?"

She nodded, so off we went to the kitchen.

Heziah came down eventually, and I explained who she was while she devoured a box of RITZ Crackers. He stuck out his hand and introduced himself as her grandfather. She waved and went right back to her midnight snack.

"You two can have the bed. I'll sleep on the sofa."

"You sure?"

"Yep."

I had my baby back. Maybe for an hour, maybe for a night, but she was all mine.

38
JACKIE

KEM WAS A NATURAL ON STAGE. He seduced the women in the audience with every strum of his guitar. Didn't even have to look directly at them. They swooned in their seats with moist panties and eyes so big you'd think they were lusting after a mouth-watering steak, and their men were too focused on me to notice.

After the first set, we climbed down from the stage to a thunderous applause. I smiled my thanks and headed to the bar while the guys disappeared into the dark corridor that led to the closet posing as a dressing room. Mo greeted me with his special, this time in a martini glass adorned with two olives.

"Heard a rumor 'bout ya."

"About me?"

He gloated at his newfound knowledge. "Heard you just a baby."

"I ain't been a baby for eighteen years." Couldn't have been. Not with Ricky Morrow leering over me. The foggy liquid swirled around coating the inside of the glass. I suspected the liquor of choice was gin, but Mo wasn't giving up any parts of his secret recipe.

Mo spread his fingers against the bar, leaning forward with all one hundred and fifty pounds of his weight. He was a decent-looking guy and acted enough like a gentleman that I couldn't put my finger on what I was shying away from.

"Bet you got a boyfriend, huh?"

"Not technically."

"What about the pretty boy that be on stage with you?"

"Just friends."

"So, he ain't gonna mind if I call you sometime."

I caught a glimpse of Kem out of the corner of my eye. He sauntered to the opening of the dark corridor and looked out over the crowd with a tiny cigarette perched between his lips. He held it between his thumb and index finger and took a slow puff. Even from ten feet away, I could tell it wasn't filled with tobacco. I'd smelled it before in his car and immediately recognized it although it had been a while since I indulged in the herb.

"I'll be back," I said before gulping down my drink. Kem saw me weaving through the wobbly tables toward him and smiled.

"Nice set, huh, mami?"

"I think that's illegal."

His eyebrows arched to the ceiling, and he nodded to the blunt between his fingers. "Are you going to turn me in?"

"I'm thinking about it," I confessed, leaning against the other side of the hallway. "

I'd chosen metallic gold pants and a black sequined tank with black stilettos that put me almost eye to eye with him. Kem's gaze dropped to the floor as he took another drag. I was almost certain he was admiring my legs. Rings of smoke floated calmly across the space between us, and he lifted his prized possession an inch, offering to share it with me.

"Isn't that a gateway drug?"

"Gateway to what?"

I shrugged.

Kem pressed it again between his lips, this time savoring the experience as his smoldering stare climbed up my body. A ruckus rose up in the audience, but we barely noticed. He offered it to me again, and this time, I moved to his side of the hall and took it between my fingers as I'd seen him do then feigned innocence.

"You'll have to teach me." I said.

39
PECAN

"FORTY-ONE AIN'T OLD."

"I didn't say it was."

My doctor was the dumbest smart man I'd ever met. Sure, he had plenty of degrees and such, but he ain't know one thing about how to talk to folks. Couldn't fix his lips to offer an apology. Didn't even look me in the eye. Just kept right on squeezing my right tit.

Mia sat in the chair by the door, flipping the pages in one of the fashion magazines. I wasn't too sure if she knew what she was looking at or if she was acting like the folks she'd seen in the waiting room.

"I'm still a woman."

It was a ridiculous argument to make. Of course, he knew that, but I couldn't help being offended by his pointing out maybe I should be thinking 'bout the change.

"Belinda, I'm not saying it's around the corner, but you might start to notice some changes. Do you know when your mother began menopause?"

I ain't even know if the woman was alive.

"That could give us some indication...umm..." His thought trailed off as his pasty-white forehead was suddenly overcome by wrinkles. "Have you been examining yourself?"

"What?"

"Your breast. Have you been giving yourself those exams we talked about?"

His fingers went back to digging into me with a new kinda focus. Pain shot through my underarm, and I almost slapped him for it. Then I remembered who he was—the doctor.

"Why? What's wrong?"

That's when he smiled. The paper gown rustled all up in my ear as I covered myself up. I ain't need no degree to know when folks was smiling to cover up bad news.

"We're just going to run some tests." His pen clicked and he began writing in the folder with my name written 'cross the label. "I found something. Could be nothing. We'll see," the smile said.

MAYBE THERE WAS FOLKS SOMEPLACE WHO HAD it easy. Folks who wasn't nothing like me. They woke up with smiles on they faces and nothing but good memories in they heads. When bad stuff happened they thought "Oh no!" instead of sucking they tongues and going "I knew it." They was probably out there.

"Hey, where you going, good looking?"

Sitting 'round the Christmas tree, singing songs with their kids—who, of course, loved them to death.

"Can I come?" He was leaning half out the car. Don't know how the fool managed to be driving in a straight line at the same time. "You too fine to be taking the bus. You gotta man, sweet thang?"

I was about three blocks from my house, and last thing I wanted was for this idiot to follow me to my door but glaring at him ain't seem to work.

"You leave my grandma alone!" Mia barked at the fool in the big brown Oldsmobile.

It had rust stains on the doors and around the headlights. Ain't look too sound. Like maybe it might veer onto the sidewalk if you looked at it the wrong way.

"Before you make me mad!" She ran right up to the curb, and I had to grab her by the back of her collar to keep her back.

"Ignore him, now. He outta his mind. Don't know what he saying." I could smell the liquor from ten feet away.

"Grandma?"

He howled with laughter, and the car screeched to a stop as his foot slipped from the accelerator to the brake. Only made 'im rev up the engine to keep up with us.

"Don't you have other folks to bother? Go on now! Get!"

We was coming up on our block, and I was tempted to make a run for it. Then I saw her. All grown up and beautiful. 'Course she ain't dress like it, but some things is hard to cover up even with hand-me-downs. She'd been sitting on the porch but was moving toward the gate to meet us.

"Mommy!" Mia took off running, and Mya scooped her up in her arms. Whispered something in her ear, then placed her gently on her feet.

"You left me!" Mia's protest didn't get much of a reaction from Mya, who was now staring at me. "Mommy! You left me! You said you never leave me! You promised!"

"I know. But I came back, didn't I? So, I ain't really leave you."

"Yes, you did. You left me."

Mya's whole body sighed, and she gave in. "I'm sorry."

"Don't do it again!"

"I won't."

"You promise?"

She nodded, patting Mia's head at the same time. Was like I wasn't even there, but I ain't mind. I was seeing something I'd been waiting years to see. I almost started crying right there on the spot.

"Hey, sweet thing—"

"Shut up! Go on and leave me be!"

His raggedy ole car was halfway down the block before I realized I'd gripped my purse strap so tight I coulda whipped it at his passenger window, and it wouldn't've taken nothing but a second. "Crazy folks..."

Except Mya wasn't looking at me like she knew what I was talking about. She was thinking I was the crazy one.

"He been trailing behind us ever since we got off the bus."

She just stared. Face hard as stone.

"Mommy, this my grandma."

The corners of her mouth turned up in an almost smirk. It was funny.

This lil' girl introducing me to my own chile. Funny in the heartbreaking kinda way.

"Where's Jackie?"

Wasn't quite three o'clock yet. Jackie ain't get outta bed before noon, and she ain't even think about getting dressed and out the door before four.

"She should be at home. You ring the bell?"

Mya nodded and took lil' Mia by the hand. "I gotta get her stuff. Then we can go."

"You ain't gotta go right now....Could stay a while."

I hadn't seen her in so long the memory I had of her was starting to get fuzzy around the edges, but the real her–the one standing in front of me–she was about too heavy for my heart to take, and still I ain't wanna let her go.

"Mommy, how many grandmas I got? And where Dee?"

"Shh," was all Mya spared.

Mia moved on to other questions. "I hungry. We gonna eat?"

"I'll make y'all some lunch."

With a tiny nod of her head, my child agreed to let me feed them, but she coulda changed her mind the second things ain't go the way she wanted.

Mya was never a picky eater. She had her favorites, but she'd eat basically anything somebody put in fronta her. That much hadn't changed. I made 'em each a turkey sandwich, then pulled some frozen steaks out to defrost. Thinking maybe she might stay around for supper if she knew what to expect. She'd grown a few inches. Was taller than me but not quite as tall as her daddy was. Still had his features–even had his smirk with the right portion of violence attached to it. When she was a girl, it was easy to think she ain't mean it. She wasn't a little girl no more.

"How you been?"

"Fine." Her answer rang with resentment.

"I been asking your sisters about you. They tell you?"

She nodded and took a healthy bite out of her sandwich.

"The young ones really miss having you around. You know? They doing good though. The twins going into third grade. They real excited 'bout it too. They off spending the day with some of their friends, and Nat's gonna be a freshman. You girls grow up so fast."

Lil' Mia looked from me to her mama, smudges of mustard covered her cheeks and lips. Obviously, Mya hadn't seen no point in teaching the chile table manners. She smacked her lips just as loud as you please, then had the nerve to burp like a grown ass man. If I hadn't've heard foosteps on the stairs, I mighta reprimanded her. By the time Jackie slumped into the kitchen, I was glad I didn't. Mya wouldn't have taken too kindly to that.

"Morning, Mama."

She wore sweat pants rolled up to her knees and a tee shirt she'd cut up so it hung off her shoulder and showed off her midriff. Jackie rubbed her eyes fiercely, then plopped down in the chair next to Mia. She'd yawned and tugged at the elastic band of her sports bra before she realized we wasn't alone in the kitchen.

"Hey," Jackie greeted her sister.

In the blink of an eye, the somber chile who was mostly familiar to me disappeared, and what sat in her place chilled me to the bone.

"I told you to wait."

"Aww, Mya...come on...it's too early for—"

"It ain't early. What about wait here you ain't understand? Huh? Next time you think you can just take my child—"

"Not my fault you took so long. I had to work. She's okay. Right, baby? You okay?"

Mia took another bite and gave an impressive imitation of her mama's blank expression.

Jackie continued with her defense. "Besides, she ain't never met Mama."

My heart skipped a beat. I spun toward the window over the sink, letting the sunshine warm my face. Hoping it could convince the tears to stay away.

"You don't do what I tell you to do, then I can't trust you." Mya's gruff tone began to tremble under the weight of her anger.

I closed my eyes, trying to be one with the sun. Nobody hated the sun. It was welcome wherever it went. I could be the sun. If I hadn't married Ricky, I coulda been the sun.

"Need somebody I can count on..."

"You want me to apologize 'cause you fucked up? Hell, I ain't the reason you were late."

Mya had an advantage in that Jackie was only a few seconds outta her sleep, but that ain't last long. The two of them was each other's favorite—hardly ever had a moment of discord between them—so when it happened, they tended to overreact.

"I shoulda asked Nikki."

"Fine! Next time ask Nikki! See if I care."

"MMM," HEZIAH'S VOICE VIBRATED AGAINST MY EAR. As far as husbands go, he was the best. And he loved me. Loved me and my girls, despite all the trouble we brought into his life.

"Belinda? Where you at?"

I took a deep breath, forcing myself to concentrate on what it felt like to be kissed by the best husband there ever was. To be underneath him, feel his body hot and sweaty on top of me, pushing deep into me. I was not gonna be thinking about Mya and the hardness she saved just for me or the grandchild I'd finally met or the doctor's words. We'll see. Couldn't be positive, n'all he had to point out the obvious. If I was gonna die, then yeah, we'd see. If I was gonna live, we'd see that too. We'll see. Who told the man to say such a stupid thing? He couldn't think of nothing better to say?

"Belinda." Heziah frowned down at me.

"I'm here. I am. I'm close."

He started in again.

I wasn't about to tell nobody until I had to. My girls had been through enough. Heziah too. Wasn't no sense in getting everybody all worked up when we didn't know anything for sure.

40
NIKKI

DARLENE HAD WANTED TO ACCOMPANY ME TO my doctor's appointment, but she didn't complain when I told her Mama was coming with me instead. She wished me luck which just made me feel worse.

"What time these people supposed to see you?"

Mama never had a big voice, but over the years, it had become dead and brittle, like she was just waiting for an opportunity to snap somebody up. Jean-Louis said it was because she was bitter. He said he didn't see how I could've come from her.

She flipped another page in the magazine she'd chosen. That made thirteen pages she'd turned without really looking at any of them.

"Nikki?"

"Soon, Mama."

"You should go on up there and ask 'em how many folks in front of you."

"I'll just wait."

She sighed and muttered to herself, clearly disappointed in my decision. I wasn't bold enough for my mama. I didn't yell at folks even when they did me wrong, and I forgave too easily.

"Nicole Grenier," the nurse called, and I shot up from my chair. She led us back to examining room B and asked me to get undressed. She tried to reassure me with a smile when she saw I wasn't too comfortable with that idea. Then she pulled the curtain around the bed, so I'd have some privacy.

"Why they calling you Nicole?"

"Huh?" I prayed she wouldn't push the issue and carefully reached behind my back to unhook my brassiere.

"That ain't your name. Last I remember I named you Nikki."

"Must've been a clerical error." I patted myself down to make sure the hospital gown was fastened securely then slipped on my sweater for good measure. "How's Heziah?"

"Fine. He's fine. Working like a dog." She studied me over the top of her magazine once I pulled the curtain back. "How's that husband of yours?"

"He's good."

She nodded, completely satisfied with the short exchange. She didn't really want to know anyway.

"I heard Jackie's working in some club over in the Woodlawn area. Is that a good idea? Shouldn't she be some place where...where people don't... umm..."

"She's doing just fine."

I nodded.

"How come that husband of yours ain't come with you to this here doctor appointment? He too busy to see about his wife?"

"Mama."

"I'm just saying raising kids ain't an easy job even with help, and he ain't exactly around much."

"He works hard, taking care of me. Just like Heziah does for you."

She closed her magazine at that. She didn't want to be reminded of Heziah. Heziah, who she'd left my daddy for and started a whole new life with, complete with two new babies.

The doctor appeared shortly after that. Asked me some questions about my cycle and how often me and my husband...

Mama sat in the corner, hands folded, and ankles crossed.

"You're only twenty-three. So, is there any history of infertility in your family?"

I almost laughed at that. For most of my childhood it seemed like Mama was pregnant. Couldn't go two years without Daddy wanting another kid, preferably a boy.

"Ain't nothing wrong with us. Nikki just fine. She just need to relax. If it's meant to be, it'll be."

I'd been married for four years. I had a beautiful house and a wonderful husband who wanted kids. Destiny had a weird sense of humor.

"We'll run some tests and see what comes up."

I agreed quietly and listened as he rattled off hormones that needed to be checked and conditions that needed to be ruled out. "

"Don't worry, Nicole. We'll figure this out and get you pregnant before you know it."

Mama eyed the man through narrow slits like he was threatening my life.

41
MYA

DEE! I MISS YOU!" MIA BOLTED ACROSS the room, weaving in and around folks, and flew into his arms. "I told Mommy to get you," she declared, telling on me.

I would've done it eventually. Her pestering just got it done faster is all.

When I caught up to them, she was situated on his knee, explaining all about the grandma she'd just met. He was straight enough to pretend to listen, but I doubted he was really hearing anything she said.

"And then we went to the docta and he was touching on her and she got mad, and then we got off the bus and this guy in a car..." She paused long enough to swallow. "And she got mad again. She get mad a lot. Just like Mommy."

"I'll bet." He grinned at me. "Was she pretty like your Mommy too?"

"No. She darker."

"Like me?"

"Not that dark."

The other folks at the table turned to study my child, grinning at her. She was funny even though she ain't know it.

"Being dark ain't the same as being ugly," I claimed the seat next to them and set my sights on the bowl of soup Darien pushed in front of me.

He probably hadn't eaten in days, but that never seemed to faze him none. "Mia, you hear me? Just because somebody brown skinned don't mean they ain't pretty."

"Where you go?" She demanded to know of Darien.

"You hear your Mommy? She's trying to tell you something."

"Next time you not go without me. Okay? Me and Mommy. Okay?"

"Okay."

For the umpteenth time, I prayed there wouldn't be a next time. Wished this would be the last time I had to drag him outta some dope house and get him straight while Mia wasn't looking. In a few years, she was gonna start noticing stuff.

"I don't wanna be by myself."

"You won't be." Darien's arms closed in around her, squeezing her tight. It was a promise he'd already made a million times. To her and to me. I was still waiting for the day I believed him.

Mia's little head suddenly popped up, and she said brightly, "If I get a baby sister, I won't be, right?"

Panic gripped my chest. The last thing Darien and I wanted was a baby. A baby that cried at all hours of the night, and when he wasn't doing that, he was hanging off my tit. Last thing we needed was a baby. But Darien grinned from ear to ear and winked at me.

"Ain't gonna happen," I said, cleaning the bottom of the Styrofoam bowl with a slice of white bread. Mia fixed her face to jump-start her campaign for a baby. She'd only seen them from a distance. She didn't have one clue what they were really like. But ignorance never stopped her from roaring.

"Come on." My chair scraped against the floor of the church basement as I took her by the hand, leading her off of Darien's knee. "Let's go get you some soup before it's all gone."

"I don't want no soup! I want a baby!"

"Too bad. 'Cause what you're getting is some soup."

We got in line behind an old white woman with crumbs in her hair. At first I thought it was dandruff, but nope, it was crumbs. Cookie crumbs from the looks of 'em. Sugar, maybe butter cookies. Mia turned her nose up and yanked on my hand to get my attention. She pointed at the woman's behind.

"Shh."

Sometimes my child reminded me of my sisters. She was having a Jackie moment right then. Wanting to say stuff she had no business saying. So, the woman wasn't the freshest-smelling person. It happened.

She must've felt our attention on her back 'cause she turned around with a glazed look in her eye and grinned at me like she recognized me. I could've ignored that, but then her gaze fell to Mia, and her eyes lit up like it was Christmas morning, and my chile was her one and only present.

"Oooo, aren't you precious? The cutest little thing..." She reached out with both hands.

Mia promptly recoiled and said, "You stink," before I could utter a word.

42
JACKIE

AT FIRST IT WAS LIKE A PESKY mosquito that wouldn't go away. A week later it had become the monkey on my back. Who does she think she is? Talking to me like that! If she weren't my sister, her ass woulda been grass.

"Mami, take a break. Sit down. Relax."

Kem's apartment was clear across town on the north side. Technically one bedroom, but it spanned the entire first floor of his building with a long hallway connecting the living room to the kitchen, dining room, and bedroom. It was furnished in typical bachelor fashion. Futons and tables in functional positions around the room. He had an end table holding up his remotes. A coffee table he perched his feet upon. And a smaller end table by the door whose job was to keep his keys from getting lost. None of it was color coordinated. There were stacks of books and magazines in every corner, and boxes filled with the same he had yet to unpack.

I paced around the coffee table, taking care to step over his legs and maintain my righteous indignation.

"She always thought she was all that!"

"Who?"

"Mya!"

Kem took a quick puff then raised the blunt, so I wouldn't have to bend over to hit it. "Here, mami. This will help."

"I don't need any help."

Kem thought I was having a reaction to the cocaine. It was my first time, but I was sure my sudden irritability and lack of appetite had nothing to do with that. He took another hit for himself, then placed it gently in the ashtray near his feet. A graceful twirl of his hand and his guitar whipped into place across his knee, ready to sing out whatever chords Kem's heart desired.

"If she can't depend on me...who the fuck does she think she is?"

His fingers drummed out a melody that reminded me of a girl skipping through a meadow on a summer afternoon.

"She ain't my mama. I'll tell you that much."

His melody turned on a dime, instead taking on the life of a stormy night in June. Then found its intended direction somewhere in between the two extremes.

"That's pretty."

He began to hum to it, and I realized I'd never heard him sing before. I sunk into the futon next to him and was about to say as much when the first verse flowed from his lips in a language I didn't understand. If I weren't in love with Kem Delgado, I would've been.

"I didn't know you could sing. Did you write that?"

He smiled and began again from the top. Mesmerized by his mouth, I hummed along with him, harmonizing while I did my best to memorize the lyrics.

An hour later, we were working on the bridge. "We sound great together, don't you think?"

He'd wrapped another blunt, and we were halfway through it. His guitar leaned against the back of the futon, and I stretched out with my head on his lap. My bare feet wiggled free, flexing against the cold metal of the futon's arm. I wore a denim miniskirt and an old tee shirt that was a few sizes too small. Kem placed the blunt between my lips then let his hand rest on my stomach. I was reasonably sure he'd heard me.

"We make a good team," he finally admitted.

"What else have you been holding out on me Mr. Delgado?"

"I don't know what you mean."

"Yeah, you do." I reached up to return the blunt to his mouth, exhaling smoke at the same time. "I bet you have all sorts of talents."

His cheeks sunk into his face as he inhaled one puff then another, attempting to dim his senses. That was all the proof I needed. I suddenly felt light-headed, struggling to find my balance in an upright position, but I was gonna persevere. I stood, only to kneel between his legs.

He was on his third puff before he made a move to shield his zipper. “What are you doing?”

It was pretty damn obvious what I was doing. His body went rigid and so did his crotch. The heater hissed in the corner, spewing steam into the room. I pulled the zipper down slowly, and he didn’t try to stop me this time. He sat frozen in place. His hair fell across his eyes, and he moistened his lips. I wondered how long it had been since a woman had pleased him in that way. And I wondered if he would return the favor.

43
NIKKI

MAMA ASKED ME WHY I WANTED A baby so bad. It was completely ironic coming from her—the mother of six girls. I twirled my thumbs, listening to David Letterman give his top ten list about something or another, and considered my mama's words. I'd been undressed and tucked into bed for two hours, but I wanted to be awake when Jean-Louis came home. I tried to be awake to see him off in the morning and to give him relations in the evening if he wanted it. It was the least I could do, considering how hard he worked.

Don't nobody work that hard, Mama had said, giving me the stink eye. She couldn't give my husband any kind of credit.

I wore a knee-length black slip, my version of lingerie. The silky fabric put me in a wifely state of mind. The audience erupted in laughter as Dave got up to number five on his list.

If I had a baby, I'd probably be pooped out by now. Or maybe I'd have someone to sit up with me and watch late night television. Either way, my life would be completely different.

"You are still awake."

"How was your day?"

He gave a tired nod and tugged at his tie until the knot began to fall apart. I crossed the room to help him with the buttons of his shirt and caught a glimpse his disappointment. Over the last three years, he'd gotten thinner, and I'd picked up a few pounds. They all sat in my midsection as if to remind him that I should be with child by now.

"How did your appointment go?"

"Fine. They're running some tests. Hormones and things. If everything checks out, they'll want to retest you before doing anything too invasive with me."

He sighed and disappeared into the connecting bathroom. The water came on in a rush, and I imagined him glaring at the mirror as he brushed his teeth. This whole issue was hard on him. He'd married me thinking I was completely healthy.

"I'm sure everything'll come out fine." I smiled, intertwining my fingers over my stomach. "It's probably just something small."

"Mmhmm." He returned minus his shirt and pants, strolled past me, and climbed into his side of the bed.

"Mama said I'm probably fine. I just need to relax."

"And is that her medical opinion? What else did she tell you?"

His face took on a stern quality. Reminded me of an angry bee. The first few times I'd seen it, I wanted to laugh. I was over that impulse now.

"Did she say anything about me?"

I shook my head and hurried to the doorway to hit the light switch before joining him in bed.

"She did not say it was my fault? That there's something wrong with me?"

Mama clearly thought there was something wrong with him, but the flaw didn't have anything to do with his ability to procreate.

"I don't think it's you. It's probably me." His hand felt warm inside mine. My fingers were notorious for being cold. "Honey, you hear me?"

"I don't know why you insisted on taking her with you. She only has negative things to say about us."

"I wouldn't have if somebody else had offered to come."

From time to time, I made unwise choices with my words. Or at least that's how he put it. Meaning I said something I shouldn't have said. This was one of those times.

"Who are you speaking of?"

"Let's just go to sleep." I released his hand and sunk down further underneath the fluffy duvet.

"You would like to go to sleep?"

"It's late," I replied, snuggling into my pillow.

Jean-Louis didn't waste a moment whipping back the covers. He claimed his pillow and the blanket from the foot of our bed and stormed out the room.

I shouldn't have made him feel guilty for not attending my doctor's appointment. I hadn't even asked him to go because I knew what the answer was going to be. He didn't have a choice. He had to work. Besides, men didn't want to sit around talking about fertility. Then, on top of that, I made that little comment about the time. I rolled onto my back and stared at the ceiling, imagining how I'd make it up to him in the morning.

44 MYA

FOR THE MOST PART, I'D ALWAYS BEEN good at minding my own business. One time I saw kids in my class cheating on a spelling test. They knew I saw and, from that day on, watched me like I was a volcano about to erupt, but I never said anything about their misconduct. And I didn't get all worked up when Daddy and Mama fought. Didn't cry like Nikki or get mad like Jackie, and I wasn't oblivious like Nat. I saw it, whatever it was, clearly. Wasn't saddled with all the emotion my sisters got so wrapped up in. I saw people and situations exactly for what they were—an ability which doubled as a blessing and a curse.

Darien carried everything that meant anything to him in a tattered brown book bag that had been thrown in the gutter and kicked off many curbs by mean-spirited folks. Inside this book bag was a toothbrush, a washcloth, a few odds and ends, and a notebook he'd had since his time in the service. He probably wasn't the only soldier to take up writing poetry, but I suspected he was the only one to keep at after he was discharged.

"What you think?" His voice stretched out into the darkness, quietly nudging me awake.

"It's nice."

"It's about dying, Mya."

Poetry wasn't my thing. I'd read about every book I'd ever heard of but could never get into poetry.

We slept fully clothed on an old mattress piled high with blankets.

Even in St. Mary's basement, you had to be ready to move in a split second if the situation demanded. Mia slept soundly between us—arms spread, legs spread, her body forming a little X with her limbs.

A yawn slipped out even though I was doing my best to be attentive. Darien liked to converse in the wee hours of the morning. It was either that or sex. I preferred the conversation. No chance of getting pregnant that way.

"Mya?"

"I'm listening."

"How come your eyes closed?"

"I'm just resting them. I hear you."

"Before I die, I want a son."

I nodded, easing into the silent lull of snores and dreams.

"MOMMY!"

I sprung up, both hands stretched out in front of me, and fixed my face to do battle with whatever had threatened my sleep.

A warm little bundle crawled into my lap and wrapped her arms around my neck, whimpering. Whenever she was scared, Mia wrapped her legs and arms around me with a vicious vice grip. She'd grown stronger since the last time.

The sounds of a scuffle began to close in from the outer reaches of my consciousness. Fluorescent lights flooded the space, inspiring frustrated moans from various cots around the room, but the lights were necessary to see the fight. Couldn't break up a fight if you couldn't see it.

"He tried to get me," Mia whispered in my ear.

The light had temporarily blinded me, but now I could make out the figures clearly. The big one was a simple-looking white boy who might've been a transplant from Iowa or Wisconsin or at least he looked like it. A farm boy who was more used to farm animals than people. He thrashed and wrestled a smaller, darker figure to the floor. Darien.

"He was gonna get me, Mommy."

The priest and nuns were shouting for them to stop at the other end of the room. By the time they made it to us, it would've been too late. Not that the peaceful, well-meaning folks of St. Mary's could've put a stop to it anyway.

"Sit here."

Mia didn't wanna let go, but I didn't give her much of a choice. A flick of my wrist and the switchblade that slept with me popped out, the overhead fluorescents glinting off the shiny surface.

"Get off him or you gonna lose something real dear to ya."

The pointy end poked at the inseam of his overalls, and the big oaf magically regained his senses. Darien crawled from underneath him, panting and wiping his forehead with his sleeve.

Father so-and-so was appalled. Weapons were strictly forbidden. Thieves and predators not so much. Maybe the religious man thought he had a shot at saving them. Couldn't redeem a knife. It only had one purpose.

The sun had barely begun her morning ascent when the kind do-gooders of St. Mary's put us out on the street. Mia was clinging to both me and Darien, even as he hurled cuss words and threats at the big wooden doors as they closed shut.

The big oaf meandered west while we headed in the opposite direction.

"Mommy, I sleepy."

45 NIKKI

"MAYBE SHE'LL GO BACK TO SCHOOL."

"Maybe you'll go back to school," came Jackie's retort.

I hadn't meant anything by it. It was common sense. Mya was smart enough to accept the logic. She just needed to act on it. How else was she going to take care of herself and my niece? She certainly couldn't depend on that shiftless man she'd attached herself to.

"A high school diploma is kinda important when you want a job," I said.

We sat at the dining table shelling peas with Mama and Natalie. Mama had gotten it into her head we needed to have a big Sunday dinner as a family. That meant black-eyed peas, string beans with potatoes and salt pork, mustard and turnip greens, cornbread, potato salad, fried chicken, fried fish, and possibly ham. It was four o'clock on Saturday afternoon, and I wasn't so sure we were going to get it all done in time.

"What do you know about getting a job? Thought that little Napoleon of yours forbid you from that sort of thing."

Jackie was equally as talented as Mama when it came to twisting positive things into negative ones. She sat across from me in shorts that showed more leg than cloth and a shirt that hung so far off her shoulder we could all see her black underwear. When Heziah walked by, I actually blushed on her behalf.

"Maybe she is working." Natalie was eternally the family optimist. "Or maybe she'll come back home. Or both!"

"Not gonna happen," Jackie mumbled without the slightest hesitation.

Mama hadn't said a word since the topic of conversation had turned to Mya but didn't mean she didn't feel anything. It was obvious to anybody who bothered to pay attention.

"She could have my room. I don't mind." Natalie was persistent, but her energy was wasted on us. We weren't the ones who needed convincing.

"She's too proud," I said.

"Some people ain't proud enough," Jackie spoke with the accuracy of a sharpshooter, and she aimed her words directly at my heart.

"You girls make sure your sister shows up tomorrow. And I don't wanna hear no fighting. We gonna have us a nice supper. Be real loving to each other. Like a family."

"Can I bring a date?"

"Oh, Lord."

I couldn't help it, and a giggle slipped out. Mama looked so tired at the thought of Jackie dating.

"What? Nikki's gonna bring that little gremlin, and I can't bring Kem?"

"Hey! He's not—"

"I thought you and him was just friends."

"We were. We are. Can I bring him? Puh-lease, Mommy? He's so-oh beautiful. Wait until you see, Mama. You're gonna love him."

Mama gave her consent, but she clearly wasn't thrilled about it. I wondered if she intended to keep Jackie single for the rest of her life. By no means did I support my sister's wild and crazy love life, but even I acknowledged she needed to date if she was ever going to get married. That was the only way to ensure Jackie didn't end up one of those women with questionable morals. Maybe this Kem was going to be the one to get her to settle down.

"What kind of name is Kem for a man?"

Sly giggles came from Natalie's direction, but she put a prompt end to it once Jackie turned her way.

"He's named after his mother."

"So, he does realize it's a female name?"

"Mama, tell Nikki to be nice."

She could call my husband every name in the book, but I asked one measly little question, and all of a sudden, I was the bad guy.

"Where you going?" Mama paused after the snap of a string bean.

I'd run outta beans, so I was headed to the kitchen to get start on the corn on the cob. She seemed to realize shortly after I stood up. Once they thought I was out of earshot, I heard a thud then the rattle of silverware like something hard had landed on the table. Natalie's giggles got louder, and then Mama's voice crawled in underneath it all.

"Stop being so hard on her."

"Not my fault she married a toad."

"I mean it. She's your sister. That should be enough for you to have some sympathy for her. It ain't easy being so unhappy."

46
JACKIE

THE SECOND TIME ON THE FERRIS WHEEL of love was completely different than my first. I was more mature, and Kem Delgado was nothing like Darrel King.

I traced the rim of my shot glass with my index finger and smiled at the thought. Kem was perfect, head-to-toe perfect. I'd seen the proof. There was no way he didn't feel it too. His searing dark eyes looked at me as if they could see into my soul. As if they wanted to be inside of my soul. Men didn't look at women like that unless they wanted to be with them.

"Another one?" Mo stood poised with a half-empty bottle of Jose Cuervo.

I nodded and began searching the club for Kem's silhouette while he poured.

"You should let me take you out."

The fourth shot eased on down my throat at a leisurely speed. The shots plus the few beers I'd had before the first set and the joints we'd smoked in the car were weighing me down. Even my thoughts were slurred.

"Take you to a nice restaurant. Or we could go on back to my place. Have some dessert." His clammy hand slid over the mahogany bar and plunked down on top of mine. "I won't tell if you don't."

I'd made up my mind before he'd said a word, but the rejection had gotten lost on the road to my mouth. I managed a nod and tried to focus on pointing my feet in the right direction.

"You okay, mami?"

"Oh! There you are." I couldn't help grinning. Every time I saw him, heard his voice, or his presence graced my thoughts I smiled like a ticklish child.

Mo moved on to tend to actual paying customers, and Kem helped me to the storage room, which had been cleared out to function as a dressing room. Four folding chairs and two tables on either side of a mirror occupied the space. The lighting was so bad, I wouldn't dare attempt to put makeup on in there. I'd probably come out looking like a rosy-cheeked clown.

"What's so funny?" Kem asked as he lowered me into one of the folding chairs and turned the other so he was sitting in front of me. "You've got an admirer."

"I do?"

"Mo."

"Oh. I guess so." My fingertips slowly danced up the length of his thigh. "I've got other things on my mind."

"I'm flattered."

"You should be."

He pushed his hand into his hair, but the dark tendrils predictable returned to their positions a moment later. "You are...drunk," he said.

I laughed so loud the sound made me jump out of my skin. And that only made me laugh harder. A dense fog had begun to settle over me. I wasn't entirely sure where it came from or when it set in, but there it was. There was a brief second of clarity brought on by the screeching of one of the tables as Kem labored to pull it closer to us. He unfolded a small square of wax paper and began tapping out two white lines.

"You cannot go on stage like that. Here."

"Are you jealous, Kem Delgado?"

"Jealous?"

"I won't be mad if you are."

His laugh didn't actually come with sound, so at first, I thought I was imagining it, but nope, he was laughing at me. Or the thought of loving me...

"Don't laugh. I'm serious. I want you to tell me these things."

"Why would I be jealous?" His accent grew thicker than usual, and he kissed me quickly on the cheek. "You are free to do as you please. Just as I am."

"Wait. What?"

My head was pounding. Kem was right. I couldn't be expected to perform in my state. I couldn't even have a simple conversation. He held out a straw for me, and the first line disappeared through it. The second was for good measure. I needed to make it through the entire set, not just the first few songs.

"Are you busy tomorrow? Wanna have dinner at my place? Meet my people?"

"I would love to, mami."

47
PECAN

SUPPER WAS MORE OR LESS DONE. I was putting the last touches on it when Callie said, "Mommy, where Jackie go?" The twins wanted to go everywhere Jackie went. Didn't seem to faze them she was a good ten years older than them.

"She's on the porch with her friend. But y'all stay in here!"

They froze in the midst of dashing for the door, pretending to be statues. It was for their own good. No telling what they would've walked in on.

"Food ready?" Heziah strolled into the kitchen and lifted the lid on the gravy pot. He couldn't get enough of my gravy.

"Just about. Be nice if somebody set the table."

"Girls, you hear your mama?"

"Yes, Daddy." Off they went, each cradling a stack of plates in their arms.

Heziah turned back to me and rested his hand on the middle of my back. He ain't have to say it. I knew. I hadn't stopped thinking about it since the nurse called to reschedule the test.

"You okay?"

I nodded and moved from the stove to the fridge, pretending to search for something.

"Pecan?"

He'd never called me that. Not once since the day I met him. It was my daddy's nickname for me 'cause of how much he loved pecan pie. Ricky'd called me Pecan every day we was married. Every day that he beat me. Heziah had always called me Belinda.

"Everything's going to be all right. You hear me? You gotta think positive."

THEY CAME IN FROM OUTSIDE SMELLING FUNNY. Wasn't a smell I was familiar with, but it seemed to be coming more from Jackie than him. He hugged me warmly, and I got to see what Jackie saw in him up close and personal. A perfect smile and full-bodied voice with a delicate accent, and he looked on my girl with such affection. Couldn't be mad at that. They sat across from Nikki and her husband who looked more like a brother and sister that had had enough of each other.

The seating arrangements went like this—me and Heziah in our regular spots at the ends of the table, then the twins on my right and left facing each other, Natalie and Mya, Nikki and the devil, and Jackie and Kem closest to Heziah.

"Where's my beautiful little niece?" Jackie asked.

Mya chewed a forkful of greens, then added a bite of fried chicken to her mouth, swallowed and said, "She's fine. Safe."

My quiet child had turned into a secretive little thing, but I thought since the ice was broken maybe she'd start bringing my grandbaby around.

"So. How are you?" Heziah nodded to her.

"Fine."

"She's obviously hungry." Jackie grinned. "Damn girl, leave some for the rest of us."

Nikki was bursting with nervous energy, like everything her sisters said brought shame upon the table. She always got like that whenever the little maniac was around. I expected her to jump up and explain Mya didn't usually eat so fast, that she must've been in a hurry, but Nikki didn't.

Heziah was better at making conversation than I was, so he went around the table chatting up everybody until I'd built up the courage to say what I wanted to say. By then, we was on to dessert. Sweet potato pie.

“Mama, you make the best pie.” Nat was naturally thin and never gave a thought to having a second slice.

“Thank you, baby.”

“Yes, everything was delicious, Mrs. Jenkins. Thank you for inviting me.”

“You’re welcome Kem. Glad you could come.”

Jackie beamed, batting her eyes at him. The sight of my girl so full of love brought tears to my eyes. My troubled child had finally found happiness. Once I got the others squared away, I could be at peace with whatever happened to me.

“Mommy, what’s wrong?”

“Nothing. You and Jenna go on upstairs and get ready for bed. Go on now.”

Telling the twins was gonna require a little more strength than I had at the moment. They looked over their shoulders, pouting at us, but did as they were told, and Heziah walked around the table to Jenna’s chair. He took my hand.

“What’s wrong? Mama?”

“My doctor found a lump.”

48 MYA

JACKIE STARTED CRYING ON THE SPOT. NIKKI took a little longer, stuttering about how medicine had come a long way and looked at the idiot she'd married for confirmation. Kem politely excused himself and the miniature fool followed his lead.

"Why? How could this happen? Haven't we been through enough!" Jackie didn't have to try to be dramatic. It was her natural state of being.

"Your mama's gonna be just fine. She's got a really good doctor—"

Natalie flew across the room and threw herself in Mama's lap. They were acting like she was dying. Wasn't even sure if she had it yet. Besides, being sick wasn't the same as being dead. Dead meant there wasn't any hope. No chance of ever seeing somebody again. Hearing their voice or their laugh or seeing their smile. No chance they'd be there for the most important day of your life, the best or the worst days either. Mama wasn't dead or dying. She probably wasn't even sick.

"I'm fine." She was saying, patting Nat on the head. "I feel just fine. And the doctors gonna take some of it out next week to run some tests on it. Find out what it is."

"Wh-Who's your doctor? Maybe Jean-Louis can recommend somebody. You should have the best."

"Yeah, Mama."

It was the first time Nikki and Jackie had ever agreed on anything.

"You need anything? I can take you to your appointments, " Nikki volunteered.

"Me too." Nat and Jackie chimed in.

Nat was too young to drive and Jackie still hadn't passed the test so I don't know exactly how either one thought she was gonna take anybody anywhere, but Mama seemed touched by the gesture. Heziah too, until he looked at me. His eyebrows lifted like he was expecting me to proclaim "me three!"

"I don't want y'all to worry. I ain't going nowhere. I promise."

ALL THE SHELTERS I KNEW OF CLOSED their doors before it got dark, basically giving grown folks a curfew. Nikki was headed in my direction, so she offered to give me a ride. I told her she could drop me off at Ogden and North Avenue. I'd walk from there.

Mama hugged us all goodbye, whispering in my ear she was glad I came. Heziah nodded his goodbye, and Jackie squeezed me so hard I ain't think she was ever gonna let go.

Nikki's little man had driven his ruby-red sports car. It was brand-new even though he had her driving a used Honda. I climbed into the cramped backseat and off we went.

The two of them rattled on, putting on a good show for me and themselves. Nikki trying to prove he cared at all about what was happening to Mama. While he was set on demonstrating how much he knew about cancer treatment. They both got on my nerves after about five minutes.

The air conditioning was on full blast. It had to be about eighty degrees outside. Darien had said he was gonna wait for me before going in the shelter, but I hoped he wouldn't. Mia's allergies had been acting up.

"Mya, you okay?"

"Fine."

"Where can we drop you?"

I'd already told her Ogden and North Ave. I hated repeating myself.

"You sure you're okay?" Nikki turned all the way around to look at me.

Her studious gaze made me feel trapped in the tiny car. I hated when people stared at me.

"It's okay to be upset you know...to be scared..."

Translation. She wanted me to be scared, to be a nervous wreck, to be crying my eyes out. They all did. I was sorry to disappoint them. It wasn't like I wanted Mama to die. I wanted her to live. I didn't want her to go skipping off to have a fairy tale ending, but I wanted her to live.

"Mya? You gotta make your peace with her. Now more than ever."

"I said I'm fine."

GOOD SHEPHERD SHELTER CLOSED ITS DOORS AT nine o'clock, but you had to get in line hours before then. Not before five o'clock though—their way of encouraging folks to work. They gave the first one hundred people blue tickets, and you had until nine to get settled in before they locked the doors. Darien and Mia got in line at 5:05, and he talked one of the volunteers into giving him an extra ticket. Most folks didn't need a lot of convincing that Mia wasn't his daughter. They didn't look anything alike. So, it was really easy for them to believe her mama was on her way.

I got there at 8:53.

"Mommy, what take you so long?" Mia demanded, hands on her hips. She couldn't tell time yet, but she could read Darien pretty good, and he'd been worried.

Good Shepherd was a decent deal. The closest we got to having any sort of privacy. Every family got its own room as long as there were at least three people in the family. The rooms put you in the mindset of a jail cell more so than a bedroom. The concrete walls were separated by five or six feet across and nine feet lengthwise. Was like sleeping in a tomb with a bunk bed. There was a sink perched on the wall with its pipes exposed and no cabinetry to speak of. Darien went down to the men's washroom, and me and Mia took turns washing up at the sink.

Mia stretched her hands up over her head, so I could pull off her shirt. "Mommy, if I have a little sister can we name her Candy?"

"No."

"I like candy."

"I'll get you a dog." I offered without thinking as I sniffed her clothes to see if she might get away with another wear before washing them.

"When?"

Nope. Definitely needed to be washed. "Someday."

"Can I have a sister and a dog?"

"A dog is better." I sighed, lathering up her wash cloth.

"But you got sisters. I want sisters too."

"You can borrow mine."

"I don't want yours. I want mine."

"You can have cousins."

"Are they girls?"

"Yes."

"When?"

"I don't know. Soon."

"How I get cousins?"

"You have to be really good, and one day they'll magically appear."

"Magically appear?"

"Yup."

I'd won. That would probably buy me a few more months before she started in again.

I got Mia tucked in and Darien started reading to her from his collection of poetry while I got to work on our clothes. Didn't bother separating anything. We had two bars of soap for us and one bar of laundry soap. The water wasn't quite warm, so it didn't really matter. By the time I'd washed everything and hung what I could on the loud radiator under the window, Mia had drifted off, snoring soundly on the top bunk, and Darien was writing in his notebook beneath her.

"How'd it go?"

"Fine. Mama thinks she got cancer."

His mouth dropped open.

"She's fine."

"Can't be fine and have cancer at the same time, Mya. It don't work like that."

I wasn't in the mood to argue. Pulled my tank top over my head. Stepped outta my jeans, and tossed my underwear into the sink. A lump developed in my throat, and my palms began to burn a rosy red from rubbing the ends together so hard.

"Mya."

"You gonna tell me I should be upset?"

"No."

"Good."

"Mya?"

"She was looking for Mia. Wanted to see her."

He nodded. "Makes sense."

I scrubbed my legs, arms. Rinsed, lathered, and started again on my middle. "Nikki cried. And Natalie. And Jackie."

He nodded again and closed his notebook.

"Not me."

"Not you," Darien repeated it, but he wasn't surprised. "You don't cry."

"It's not my fault. I try." I scrubbed between my legs and moved on to my backside. There was a humility thing some people had, I didn't have it. I didn't get embarrassed. I didn't sugar coat the truth for anybody. And I hadn't cried in years.

He took the washcloth out of my hands and rinsed it thoroughly before wiping the soap from my body. He'd clear the foamy white suds from one section, dunk the towel in the face bowl, and start on another. When I was clean I sat down on the bottom bunk and he took his time applying lotion. Massaging my flesh with the same tenderness he used the first time we had sex.

"She'll be okay, you know."

"I know."

"But maybe you should try to see her more often."

Darien hadn't seen his family in more than seven years, but he didn't want that for me. Said he wished things had gone differently between them, and he didn't want me to make the same mistakes he'd made. It was like comparing apples and oranges. Our situations were completely different. Wasn't like his mother had murdered his father.

"Mya, what're you thinking?"

The bottle of lotion was almost empty. It fell over onto its side when I placed it on the concrete floor.

We'd waited until I was eighteen because Darien said he couldn't make love to a child. I'd told him I was a Morrow girl. I didn't remember being a child. But he was determined to wait. Two years of sleeping in separate rooms, separate beds, sometimes separate bedtimes. Two years and not so much as a kiss. We belonged to him, Mia and I. He'd tell anyone who dared to do us harm he would kill them where they stood first. He'd protected us. Always protected us. From prying eyes, blistering cold, and bullets. Covered my pregnant body from the same bullets that had ended Ramon's life. I owed him everything, but for two years he made a ritual of refusing my body.

"Stand up."

He obeyed, dropping his pants and everything else except his socks and pressed his naked body on top of mine. We kissed—hard and passionate—and within a minute, I was guiding him inside me.

49
JACKIE

JESSE'S GARAGE WAS STILL GROOVE CENTRAL FOR us. We practiced there when the club wasn't available. And after sweating it out for six songs, the brisk air had turned steamy, and my hair had no tolerance for steamy goddamn air.

"Come on, baby girl. You can't change the lineup at the drop of a hat." Jesse hated surprises. He was as persuasive as I was and used to getting his way when it came to the nuts and bolts of our performances. But I wasn't in a compromising mindset.

"I'm singing, right? Well, I don't wanna keep singing the same old songs every night. When you decide you wanna be the lead singer, then you can sing whatever you want."

"Now, hold on. Let's calm down." Clark held up both hands, shifting his weight from one butt cheek to the other on the tiny stool behind his drum set.

"Hey, little girl. You don't own this band!"

"Fine! Then you don't need me, right? You can do it on your own? Let me see you get up on stage and shake your ass and keep folks comin' back for more!"

Clark rose to his full height and gently tried to guide our smaller bandmate to a different corner, pleading silently with Kem to do the same for me.

"Mami–"

"I'm fine!" I paced from the corner of the garage that held Jesse's tools to where his lawnmower sat doused in spider webs. "He's the one that treats me like I belong to him! Like I'm only around to take orders! I don't get to have an opinion! I'm not a real musician like the rest of y'all!"

"He didn't say that."

"What about our song? Don't you wanna sing it?"

At the other end of the garage, I thought I caught one word. Diva. Jesse was trying to convince Clark he'd been right all along. Adding a girl to the group was trouble.

"Fine. I quit."

I didn't have to scream to be heard that time.

"You don't mean that." Kem looked so pained, I felt a flash of guilt, but another second and I was right back to being pissed.

"Just wait." He grabbed my arm as I leaned over to collect my things. "Let me talk to him."

The tears had already began to fall. It was too late. My heart would never feel the same. It'd been broken too many times to heal itself so easily.

As soon as Kem turned, I slapped the garage door opener and slipped out. I was halfway down the alley before he caught up to me. It wasn't the best neighborhood, so he insisted on driving me home. He believed that given some time to cool off everything could go back to normal. I knew better.

"I'm going to college anyway. I won't have time to sing."

His car rolled to a stop at a yellow light, and he stared at me befuddled. "Music is who you are. I don't believe you can walk away so easily."

"I have college."

"You never mentioned it."

I hadn't given it much thought since I got the acceptance letter in the mail a few months back, but Mama had. She really wanted me to go. Wasn't much I did gave her peace of mind. The least I could do was take my behind to school. Study something safe like accounting.

"Maybe you should not make decisions right now."

"Why not? 'Cause my mama's sick?"

Kem didn't want to say it, but that's what he was thinking.

I went searching my purse for some tissue and came up empty. "You got any tissue?" I asked, pulling the lever for his glove compartment at the same time.

Kem must've been concentrating on driving because he didn't panic or utter one guilt-laden word. It was like he'd forgotten that the evidence was there.

"What's this?"

He steered the car into a turn. Glanced over to see what I was holding and said, "It's an earring, no?"

"Whose earring?"

He looked again. "Not yours?"

"No, it's not mine. You think I'd be asking if it was mine? Think I don't know my own stuff when I see it?"

"Then it belongs to my friend," he said slowly.

"What kind of friend?"

"This is not the time to discuss this. You are upset."

"No shit, I'm upset! Are you...are you cheating on me?"

Kem let out a guttural sigh and began to maneuver the car into a parallel park on my block. His fingers brushed lightly against my shoulder as he positioned himself to see out of the rear window, and my first instinct was one of violence. I hadn't felt such hatred for another person in a long time.

"Answer me."

"No. I am not cheating on you."

"Liar."

I wanted to storm out of the car. March up the walk and slam my front door closed. I wanted him to know the pain I felt. I wanted it all in his face so he couldn't ignore it.

"Jackie..."

"Touch me again, and you'll regret it."

One thing about being a Morrow girl, we knew our way around some threats.

"Let me explain. I never said we were exclusive. It is not a reflection on you. You are wonderful—"

"Damn right, I am."

"But, I am not...I don't believe...I don't believe monogamy is for me. I'm poly."

"You're what?"

"Poly. Polyamorous. It means I am open to falling in love with more than one partner."

"You mean you're a man." The door handle had a propensity for sticking, so I had to pull at it extra hard and thrust my shoulder against the door to get it to open. "You're a selfish, greedy, son-of-a-bitch. Stay away from me."

My feet found the curb, and his passenger door rattled as I threw it closed. The glass resisted, refusing to break even though I'd put all I had into the motion. The trek to the door was a blur of wind and blame. Blaming myself for thinking my heart would be safe with him. I felt his eyes on me the whole way. Even after I'd locked the door behind me, I suspected he was still watching me. Did he think I was gonna change my mind and come running back? I stood frozen in the dark foyer listening for the sound of his car pulling away from the curb. If he knew what was good for him he'd do it. Only way I was going back out there was with my hands wrapped around a bat.

"Baby?"

Mama was waiting up for me. She'd been sitting in the window seat watching from the living room. She stood and wrapped her frayed yellow robe tighter around herself and met me in the foyer.

It was selfish to cry in front of her, but I couldn't stop myself. The tighter she held me, the more the tears burned my eyes. I tried to explain them away, but she shushed me and stroked my hair.

"Belinda?" Heziah stood at the top of the stairs. "Everything okay?"

"We're fine. Go on back to bed."

50
PECAN

Did it hurt?" Callie was worried. She sat at the foot of the hospital bed tracing imaginary circles across the pale blue blanket covering me.

"I'm fine, baby."

I'd wanted the twins to go to school like any other day, but Heziah had brought them to the hospital instead.

The doctor had already come by to say they got a good-sized sample, and the results would be in soon.

"Mommy, I'm hungry. What's for dinner?" The twins were identical, but sometimes their personalities took over and made them resemble different people. Right then, Jenna reminded me of Mya.

"Your mama's gonna stay here for a little while."

"Why?" She sat in the chair next to Heziah, her head tilted to the side as she looked up at him in wonder. "She's all better now."

"She's gonna be very tired for a few days. She needs to rest."

There was a quick rap at the door and the nurse, a simple girl with a head full of tight brown curls, stood in the doorway. "Now, Mrs. Jenkins exactly how many daughters do you have?" She smiled.

And Nat, Nikki, and Jackie slipped past her into the room. Heziah swallowed each of them up in a hug.

"Mama, you okay?"

I nodded, but I was still a little drowsy, so I wasn't real sure if my head was doing as I intended. Nikki's arms were wrapped around a potted plant, and Nat still had her book bag slung over one shoulder. At least one of my girls made it to school.

"They fixed her." Jenna brought the others up to speed. "She's all better now, but she gotta rest."

Heziah grimaced ever so slightly, so they'd know it was just a little girl's version of the truth. This was only the beginning. I'd have to wait to find out if what they took out was really cancer. Still, I was a lucky girl to have my family around me at that moment. All the folks who loved me.

"Where's Mya?"

Everybody held their breath, but the silence wasn't answer enough for my youngest. She had a ways to go before life showed her that asking questions could be just as hurtful as an angry hand.

"Mama, how come Mya's not here?"

NIGHTTIME IN THE HOSPITAL CAME ON SUDDENLY and dragged on. Supper was ground meat and gravy with soupy mashed potatoes, steamed broccoli, and a dinner roll. The old woman in the bed next to mine gobbled hers down while flipping the television channels. She was closest to the window, which gave me a good view of the hallway. I was sure I wasn't looking for her, but when I caught a glimpse of the lean figure at the nurse's station my heart skipped a beat. She wore black combat boots, one of which was missing laces, so it flopped lazily with each step she took, dark pants that was probably the lower half of some civil servant's uniform, and a yellow tank top. Her features softened the closer she got until she looked more like me than her daddy.

"Hi, Mama."

"Hi, baby. You doing all right?"

Her mouth twisted up as she fought the impulse to smile and possibly even laugh. I was probably the only patient more worried about her visitor than herself.

"I'm fine." Her left arm flexed slightly as she dragged the chair from the doorway to my bedside. She sat and unfolded a tan piece of paper before handing it to me. "Mia made this for you."

It was a crayon drawing of a box with a ribbon on it and the words "Get Wall," scrawled across the top.

"You missed your sisters. They were here earlier."

"I figured." Her eyes locked onto my supper tray. "You not gonna eat that?"

"You can have it."

Mya took her time breaking out the fork and knife from their plastic prison, paused long enough to say grace then took a bite. The old lady was snoring soundly and had left the television tuned to the news. We watched the weather and a report on a fire downtown.

The two of us hadn't been alone together since that day she packed her suitcase and left. Hadn't had a conversation that nobody else was in on. It hit me this might be the last time. I might not ever get another chance to say the things I needed to say.

"Visiting hours are over." My new nurse was a full-bodied blonde and ain't bother with a spick of makeup. She claimed my tray without looking at me or Mya and walked out the room.

Mya stared gloomily at my feet, the same spot Callie had been tracing with her finger. "I'm gonna stay," Mya said.

Ten minutes later the no-nonsense nurse reappeared, checked my vitals, and repeated herself. Visiting hours ended at ten o'clock. No exceptions. Mya nodded slightly and leaned back in her chair, lifting one foot so her ankle rested on top of her knee. The boot without laces hung defiantly in the air.

"I'm sorry," the nurse said.

"I'm staying," Mya said.

The plain-faced woman went from an expression of duty to irritation. She'd probably been on her feet for a good ten hours and just wanted to be done with her shift so she could go home. I felt sorry for her. She didn't know who she was dealing with. If Mya ain't wanna do something, she didn't do it. Wasn't much wiggle room in that.

"Fine." The nurse relented.

I AWOKE WITH A START LIKE SOMEBODY had jerked me awake. The sun was shining bright as ever and the noisy old woman in the bed next to me was gone. The doctor stood over me with his stethoscope pressed against the crook in my arm, listening. The chair where Mya had slept was empty. The doctor wanted to examine the site, or so he said as he peeled back the bandage.

"Mmm, good." He nodded, prodding my flesh. "Any pain?"

I nodded.

He motioned to the nurse standing at the foot of my bed and rattled off some instructions. Was right then that I saw Mya standing by the window, holding a paper cup with steam rising off the top. Her eyes met mine.

"Mrs. Jenkins, the incision looks good. Would you like to know the results of the biopsy now or do you want to wait for your family to return?"

Mya returned to sit at my bedside as if to say my family had never left. The doctor covered his surprise with a smile and waited for my answer.

"Tell me now."

The very next second, the doctor's face turned grim. It was cancer. I had cancer. He recited some numbers for me, none of which made any sense. Then he turned hopeful.

"We can begin treatment today, before you go home."

51 NIKKI

THE LAST THING MAMA NEEDED WAS TO go home. She needed rest. Somebody to take care of her. I stood back to admire my work and decided to fluff the pillows one more time. She'd have her own bathroom, and she was only about ten feet from the kitchen. She'd love it.

"Nicole. What are you up to?"

"Mama's gonna come stay with us for a while. Until she's feeling better."

"I don't think that's the best idea."

I smiled anyway. He'd had the same opinion when I suggested that Mya and Mia come stay with us for a while. I'd caved on that one, but I would not cave on this.

"You won't have to do anything. I'll take care of her."

"I don't think that's the best idea." Jean-Louis loved to repeat himself, each repetition weighing more than the last until it was no longer an opinion but a fact.

"If she goes home, she's going to feel like she has to take care of everybody else. This way she can relax and get her strength up."

"She will be farther from her family here."

"I'm her family."

"Oh? I thought you were my family."

"I am..."

"Then you must understand it is not the best idea. If my opinion means anything..."

The room had been my project for about a year. I'd chosen the color palette with Mama in mind, knowing that she needed a cheerful environment to balance out her outlook. Bright yellow and white furniture with fresh-cut flowers was precisely the prescription. All I needed was a few days, maybe a week, and Mama would be a new woman. She'd finally be happy.

"Nicole, are you listening to me?" He crossed the room and took both my arms in his hands. My husband had the grip of a man twice his size.

"I made up my mind," I said, going limp at the same time.

His fingers shifted slightly until his fingernails were digging into my skin, and his stare bored into my head. His hold tightened a bit as my instincts took over. It was useless, trying to wiggle out of his grasp, but I still tried from time to time.

"Nicole."

"She's my mama and I want her here."

His eyes tightened as his hold began to relax enough for me to slip free. It would be a short-lived victory, but I didn't care. For the first time in years, I was gonna get my mama all to myself.

"So THIS IS WHERE IT ALL HAPPENS." Jackie giggled as she sauntered around my bedroom like a model on a runway.

I'd been tricked into giving a tour of the upstairs. And Jackie couldn't help herself. She'd remarked on our his and hers towels, and now, she was eyeing the size of my bed. Mama looked like she was gonna bite Jackie's head off.

My sister bent over and pressed one finger into the foot of my bed and withdrew it with a hiss. "Ooo, hot!" She grinned. Nothing gave her more pleasure than to tease and embarrass me. "How big is this thing?"

"It's a California king."

"That's shorter than a normal king, right?"

"Don't start."

"What? What I say? Where is his royal highness by the way?"

A chill settled on my neck and arms. I was always prone to cold. That was why I lived in sweaters, even in the summer.

"Mama, wait for us." I didn't need to hurry to beat her to the stairs. She said she was fine, but she hadn't quite regained her normal stride yet. "Let me help you."

"Thank you, baby."

"Hey, Mama, at least you not on the same floor as them. Don't have to deal with all that married folks business probably keeps Nikki up all night. Is it true what they say about Africans being wild in the sack?"

We were halfway down the stairs, and I was seriously tempted to let go of Mama's hand, so I could slap some sense into her favorite child.

"Oh what I'd do for a Mandingo of my very own!"

"Don't you have any shame? Mama doesn't wanna hear all that."

"What I say?" Jackie shrugged helplessly.

Why she even insisted on coming with us was beyond me. She didn't have a ride back to the city and I sure wasn't gonna leave Mama to drive her back.

"You hungry, Mama? I can make you something."

"Maybe a little something." She smiled and disappeared into her new bedroom.

Jackie's behind stuck out from behind the refrigerator door, waving side to side as she hummed. She apparently didn't need an invitation to raid my fridge.

"What in the world is this?"

"Tofu," I snapped and returned the package to its proper place.

"See. I told you that man is crazy. Got you eating stuff ain't even food. You know Mama's not gonna eat that."

I was counting on it. Mama was my excuse to eat normal food. Jean-Louis and I had discussed my eating habits and decided a healthier lifestyle might improve my fertility.

Jackie's forehead caved into a frown as she watched me lay out the ingredients for a ham sandwich. "What happened? He tell you you needed to lose weight?"

"No."

"Liar."

"He wants me to be healthy. We're trying to have a baby you know."

She nodded, but in true Jackie fashion, her mind had already jumped to the next topic. "I want some ice cream. With hot fudge and crushed peanuts. Got any of that?"

Obviously, I didn't. I'd just explained that.

"Nikki?"

"Hmm." I sliced Mama's sandwich from corner to corner exactly the way she liked it, then went looking in the pantry for a bag of chips. All I found was some rice cakes.

"You like being married?"

At first I thought she was gearing up to aim another assault at me. Poke fun at how happy I was not. But something in her voice was different. Softer. I hated to admit it, but Jackie and Mya were alike in that way. Neither one of them really did gentle. Not like me. I'd never seen either of them anything less than supremely confident.

"Why you ask?"

She shrugged. "Just wondered." She glanced over her shoulder toward Mama's bedroom. "You think I'm the marrying kind? I mean—"

"Of course, you are."

I hadn't always had the nicest things to say about Jackie, but I didn't see any reason why she couldn't end up as somebody's wife. My sister didn't appear eased at all by my answer.

"This about Kem?"

"We broke up." The crack in her voice was barely audible as she forced a smile. "I'm dating somebody else now. This guy from the club. The bartender. He's crazy about me."

"And you think you might want to marry him?"

She shrugged, put a piece of lunchmeat into her mouth, and chewed thoughtfully. Wasn't like she had trouble meeting people. All she had to do was set her mind to getting married, and she probably would be.

"Well, is he nice? Does he have any ambition beyond bartending?"

Jackie shrugged again.

"What exactly do you know about the man?"

"He makes a mean martini."

"Oh, for heaven's sake..."

52 JACKIE

HARDER. HARDER."

I wasn't a big fan of bossy sex, but I couldn't take another lackluster performance. Given the way he talked, I expected Mo to have much more umph in his...stroke.

"Ugh..." He began to tremble, but I hauled off and slapped him. That put an end to that. I was gonna get what I came for.

His belt buckle clicked against the concrete floor of the storage room as he doubled his efforts between my thighs. Bottles rattled inside the boxes I was sitting on. Saturday afternoon was the day he did inventory for the club. It was also the day the band came in to rehearse. They hadn't showed up yet.

"Faster."

Mo was in decent shape but sweating profusely. Muttering about how good I felt and how much he loved me. It was our fourth date.

"Faster."

He was a nice enough guy. Nothing really wrong with him, except he needed directions, and he fell in love with me before I had a chance to learn his last name or his first name for that matter. I was dying to know what Mo was short for.

"Oh, God, yes. Damn, girl..."

Morris? He didn't look like a Morris, but then I'd never met one.

"I...I love you so fucking much...yeah..."

Morton?

Maybe it was something that didn't have Mo in it. Maybe the Mo came from a characteristic I wasn't yet aware of like a big hairy mole on his back or maybe when he was little he would always ask for more of something.

He panted against my neck with breath so hot I felt like I was sandwiched between a wall and a furnace.

"Okay," I pushed softly against his chest, savoring the fresh air the moment he stepped back. "Thanks."

He nodded, starry-eyed and spellbound by what my pussy had done to him. His sad little thing dangled stiffly between his thighs, peeking out from underneath the front of his tee shirt. Without his usual tuxedo, Mo wasn't really as attractive as I remembered.

His belt buckle jingled for the last time as he pushed it back into the last loop and secured it around his waist. My panties had landed in a dusty corner. Dust particles lifted into the air as I stuffed them into my purse. Mo was a grinning fool and entirely too proud of himself given his repeat performance. I shook the wrinkles from my summer dress and quickly adjusted the slim straps. The blue-and-white print swirled across my chest and around my waist before stopping abruptly mid-thigh.

"You gonna hang around? Wait for me to finish inventory?"

I nodded and slid back onto the wooden crate. I'd spent the previous evening preparing for this moment. Got Mama to straighten my hair and wrap it up in her rollers. Wore my brand-new white sandals and made up my face three different ways before deciding on a look. I damn sure wasn't leaving before the coup de grace.

"You hear that?" I asked. "You thirsty? I'm thirsty."

The storage room was only twenty feet or so from the front door of the club. The sound of the door opening and closing didn't have far to travel.

"I'm gonna get something from the bar," I said over my shoulder.

Had they arrived on time, they would've caught one of my better performances. I had been ready to throw down as if Mo was the best lover I'd ever had.

Clark bumped into a table and the noise filled the empty club a thousand times over. The big guy was the first to see me. A wide grin spread across his face, and for a second, I forgot all about the confrontation that had ousted me from the group and met his smile with one of my own.

"Jackie!"

"Hey."

"Hey, ya'll look who it is."

Jess gave a nod and returned his attention to the sheet music perched over his keyboard.

"You look pretty. Don't she look pretty?" Clark would always be a fan of mine. He was like a big old teddy bear. "What you doing here? All dressed up. Gotta date?" He pulled me into a big bear hug then released me so I had a direct view of Kem. "Or you here to see this guy?"

Kem's expression turned hopeful, and my heart nearly stopped. I'd played the scene over and over in my head. Knew exactly what I was going to say, but at that moment, all my preparation went out the window.

"Oh hey y'all," said a voice from behind me. The voice strained as if dragging a steer behind him and exhaled as a wooden crate met the floor. "How long you gonna be practicing for?" The voice came closer until the hairs on the back of my neck began to stand up. He wrapped his arms around my waist. "Me and Jackie gonna try to get outta here soon."

Clark arched an eyebrow and let his gaze fall to the floor. It was Kem who replied. Assuring my new boyfriend that they wouldn't be there for too long.

"SLOW DOWN, MAMA, I CAN'T HEAR YOU."

She'd insisted on having the telephone number to the club, but I never expected she'd call it. The owner's office was unlocked but held nothing of worth besides the file cabinets and boxes of memories. I sat in the ornery old guy's chair and tried to tune out the music in the background.

"Wait. He said what?"

All I could make out was Mama was upset, and it had something to do with Nikki's husband. She wanted to come home, but Heziah had taken the twins and Nat to Cleveland to visit his other kids.

"I don't understand. Why can't Nikki drive you? She...she's where?"

I gave up and promised to be there as soon as I could. My new boyfriend was taking notes on which bottles of liquor needed to be restocked. Clipboard in hand, he scrolled down the list scribbling in the appropriate boxes how much and when. His pen tapped rhythmically to the beat as I tried to be heard over it.

"I can't leave right now. I've still got two more shipments." The band chose that moment to take a break, so I could hear him perfectly and so could they.

"Can I borrow your car?"

"You can't drive."

"Yes, I can." Technically, I didn't have a license, but I'd been a passenger enough times that I knew what I was getting myself into. "Come on, please."

"Sorry, babe. Let me finish here and I'll take you."

"Is something wrong?" Kem stood at the bar, chugging a bottle of water.

"We're fine," came Mo's short reply.

I was most definitely not fine and said as much. Didn't take longer than thirty seconds before Kem agreed to drive me out to the suburbs. To which, Mo gritted his teeth and took me by the arm to put some distance between us and Kem.

"Just wait, okay? I'll take you."

I wasn't waiting. I wasn't the patient type to begin with, least of all when it concerned people I loved.

"I don't want you going with him."

"Why not?"

"It ain't right, okay? You wait and I'll take you. I'm your man now. Not him."

Kem's steady gaze never shifted. He swung his car keys around his index finger, waiting patiently, and I thought I might have caught the tiniest bit of jealousy in his eyes.

"How is your mother?"

"Good. She's good."

"That's nice."

"Mmhmm."

Kem was driving like a little old lady. Slow and steady. Never tailgating. Never speeding through a yellow light. I wondered if he'd always driven that way or if it was a new development. Maybe he was stretching out the trip.

"How's things with you? How's your...friend?"

We came to a stop under a red light, and he dropped his head against his left shoulder, eyeing me with a subtle smile. "She is fine. So, you are dating Mo now?"

"Yeah. He's nice. Good kisser."

"He seemed upset."

He was gonna have to get over it. Or not. Either way was fine with me.

"He did not want you to come with me?"

"Nope. Something about how I'm his now. He doesn't like to share. Gets jealous. Nothing like you. Right?"

Kem gave a silent nod and drummed his fingers against the steering wheel as one of his favorite songs came on the radio.

"He's in love with me. Tells me all the time. Not sure if I feel the same way. I might be one of those people that takes a long time to...umm...you know."

"Fall in love?" The smile in his voice provoked a tickle in my heart. Was he making fun of me or was he flirting with me?

"That's the house right there."

53
PECAN

"Mama, please. Call her back and tell her it was a mistake."

I was gonna do no such thing. And kept throwing things into my suitcase to prove it. I was going home. No need in staying some place I wasn't wanted.

"He didn't mean it!"

Nikki was a nervous wreck, tugging at the sleeves of her sweater, holding herself so tight like she was afraid she might break into a million pieces otherwise.

"He just—that's how he jokes. You can't take him seriously."

I took him seriously all right. If I stayed, I wasn't real sure he would've seen another morning. He'd been careful enough not to do anything too bad in front of me, but I knew more than most folks. I knew what to look for. And I wasn't about to sit around and pretend like I hadn't seen what I did.

Wasn't no love in his eyes when he looked at my child. He was gone more hours of the day than he was there. When he did come home, he walked through the door and ain't bother to speak to nobody. Nikki had to say something first. Offer him some food. Ask him about his day. Not once did the fool do the same for her. Had her on a short string. If he even smelled her about to do something he didn't like, he shot her a look, and she just stopped dead in her tracks. Once he even smiled when he did it. Then asked her to join him upstairs. I'd listened real hard, but I didn't hear anything. No screaming or things breaking, didn't hear the sound of fist against flesh.

Nothing. Which meant one thing–he was good at hitting her with his words. Probably ain't even have to raise his voice.

"Mama, Jackie gonna make a bigger deal outta this than it is."

Nikki came around to my side of the bed and gently laid her hands on my arms. She was more worried about folks finding out than how she was gonna get out.

"I failed you. Failed as your mama. I'm sorry."

"What? No. What are you talking about? I'm fine. Everything's fine."

I studied her eyes, hoping for some sign she was lying to me and breathed a sigh of relief when I saw a little bit there. At least she wasn't so far gone she actually believed it was fine. Fine to have a husband that ain't consider her feelings. Demanding she do as he pleased without so much as a thought to what she wanted. He was so twisted up in his superior-ness that he ain't even think there was anything wrong with it. I wondered what kinda woman his mama was.

"Mama, I can make us a really nice dinner. Everything'll be okay. Don't go. I like having you here. You need to rest."

"I'm just fine. Jackie gonna come get me."

"She not gonna take care of you like I will! She too busy chasing men–"

"I don't wanna hear no slander!"

"I'm sorry." Nikki swallowed hard and took a second to gather herself. "Just don't tell Jackie."

"Don't tell your sister? Don't tell her what? That he call himself joking about putting me out? I don't need a damn thing from that man!"

Nikki shushed me like I was an irate child and looked over her shoulder to the doorway. I wanted to scream. Scream until I got through to her. How did this happen? How did my girl...

The doorbell rang.

My child looked like she was about to burst into tears. Mad as I was, I pulled her to me and squeezed as hard as I could. Nikki always been the one I worried about most. She ain't have the direction or the groundedness that her sisters did. She was sweet and light, going whichever way the wind told her to go. She'd always been sensitive, but I ain't expect her to get so emotional.

"Please, Mama. D-D-Don't leave me."

She could've come with me. Wouldn't have taken no extra effort, but she didn't want to leave. She just wanted me to stay. Then it hit me.

"You pregnant?"

The sobs stopped and she squeezed her eyes shut. "I think so...maybe." Then she whispered, "Things are tough right now, but when I have this baby, everything'll get better. It'll make us closer."

Folks could say all they wanted about me staying with Ricky, but at least I knew better. Knew better than to think what he was giving was real love. I may not have known how to get outta it right away, but I knew that. I wasn't walking around talking about how much he loved me and how good he was to me. And I expected better for my girls.

"It's a mistake. You hear me? You having his baby is gonna ruin your life."

"Don't say that!"

"Pack yourself a bag and come on home with me."

"Mama..."

But that was my one and only offer. I'd spent too much of my life living under the thumb of some man. Wasn't about to do it again.

54
MYA

MIA KNEW THE DRILL AND SAT QUIETLY on the bench at the front of the store while I settled in on lane seven. Counting the change and then the bills and making a note of both amounts. The manager wanted only cashiers that had high school diplomas, so I didn't get as many hours as most of the girls, even though I was the best at math. He paid me cash, thinking I wouldn't find out that my wage wasn't quite minimum wage. I'd been all set to quit, but then Darien took off with the rent money. Couldn't get a new apartment if we ain't have one job between us. Besides, there were other perks too.

"Mya, your little girl is so cute!"

Simone Robinson was a big-boned girl with long blue fake fingernails. She said the same thing every time she saw us.

"But why you always dressing her up in boy clothes? Huh? My girlfriend just had a baby, and they getting rid of all her oldest's clothes. I'm gonna bring this angel some pretty dresses."

"You don't have to do that."

"But you want some pretty dresses, don't you?" She leaned over to smile in my child's face.

"No," Mia replied promptly without looking up from her coloring book.

Dresses weren't practical for our living situation. Pants could be worn year-round. I wasn't gonna be trekking around the north side in a snow storm with a bag full of clothes she couldn't wear for months. She got pants because if they were too long, they could be rolled up, and she could wear them regardless of the season.

"She look like a mini you. Just a waste of all that prettiness." Simone took up at the cash register in lane eight, and her drawer chimed as she began counting her money.

When time for my break came around, I took Mia and headed to the back of the store and through the swinging double doors. The warehouse was always as cold as the inside of a freezer, so we had to hurry. She trailed me around holding open a plastic bag as I piled in almost rotten and easily discarded food. When the bag didn't have any more room, I told her to stay put while I went looking around the corner.

"Ain't no food over there, Mommy!"

But I wasn't looking for food. Items were delivered from each company and sorted by aisle. I found the toiletry aisle and did a quick sweep for any boxes that had been damaged during the delivery. There were none. So I swiped three perfectly good toothbrushes, a tube of toothpaste, and a pregnancy test.

"I GOT GOOD NEWS! Y'ALL READY? READY to hear it?" Darien grinned from ear to ear. "You are now looking at the new custodial engineer for Paisley Elementary."

Mia leapt off the top bunk and into his arms, shouting "Yay" at the top of her lungs.

I could tell he'd been holding something in all day. I'd just assumed it was something bad. I leaned forward on the lower bunk, placing my elbows on my knees with both feet facing each other, and watched the two of them celebrate.

"Mya, you not gonna say anything?" He lowered Mia to her feet but still held her little hands in his, swinging both her arms back and forth. She giggled like mad. "Mya? Say something."

"Good timing."

55
NIKKI

SHE NEVER CALLED ME. NEVER, UNLESS SHE was looking for Mya, and even then we didn't stay on the phone that long. This time she'd made it clear she had an agenda. Twelve minutes and counting. She wasn't going to understand. I knew that going into it. Knew she was going to tell me I was crazy. She probably didn't give any thought to having a baby or a family. So, I prepared myself for her to echo Mama's sentiments, but all she seemed to want to talk about was the past.

"Mmhmm, I remember—" I said, holding the phone between my cheek and shoulder. It was hard to get a word in when Jackie really got going. "Yeah, Daddy got like that before a fight." And after. All the time really, but I didn't get a chance to add any of that.

When she took a breath, I managed to sneak in, "I...I wouldn't say that. I mean he was just really unhappy."

Jackie was determined to paint Daddy as the worst man on the planet. She'd used the word abusive at least three times already. He had more bad days than good, but I wasn't ready to make him the evil villain Jackie believed he was. He'd done some good things too. I sighed and tossed the chopped vegetables into the pot of stew, then readjusted the phone against my other shoulder.

"Well, he did take care of us....No, I'm not making excuses—I'm not. I'm just saying..."

"And Mama gave him four kids, that didn't turn him into a joy to be around!"

I pictured Jackie standing in the kitchen with one hand on her hip, waving the other about in various expressive gestures, while Mama stood at the stove pretending not to listen. She'd probably put Jackie up to it. This little trip down memory lane was turning into a lecture. Pressing my thumb and fingertips against my temple, I tried to massage away the migraine I felt coming on.

"Nikki. You listening to me?"

I knew she wouldn't understand. She was probably jealous, thinking she'd never have a husband of her own.

"Nikki."

"What?"

She suddenly got quiet. Gathering her points for another argument probably. But this is where Mama and I differed. Mama had never forgiven Daddy. She'd put up with him for years but never forgave him, she'd stopped loving him the moment he made a mistake. Marriage was for life. I was committed to my husband. I was gonna love him no matter what.

"Does he hit you?" Her words filled my ear, echoing and airy, as if she'd cupped her hand around the receiver. "Nikki?"

"No! Never!"

"I don't believe you."

"Well, I'm not lying, and I don't care if you believe me or not! It's my life and I don't owe anybody any explanations!"

56
JACKIE

I COULDN'T TALK MYSELF OUT OF IT. I didn't want to be there, but I needed to see him. I had already rung the bell when it occurred to me that maybe he wasn't alone.

"Hola," a static-filled voice burst from the speaker.

"It's me. Jackie."

The door let out a long buzz, and I hurried into the inner sanctum of Kem's apartment building. He met me at the door to his apartment wearing only jeans. No shirt, no socks. Just jeans and a smile.

"Sorry to show up like this. I was in the neighborhood, so I thought..." I smiled and glanced around the living room for signs of a woman or girlfriend or whatever he called her.

"I am glad you did. Come. Sit."

He shoved the assortment of magazines and bills to the floor and offered up the futon. The same futon we'd made love on. I walked to the window instead and looked down onto the street.

I'd called Mya's job, but they said she wasn't on the schedule until Tuesday. I couldn't wait three days to get what I was feeling off my chest. Couldn't talk about it with Mama. It would make her worry more. My boyfriend came to mind, but I quickly dismissed that possibility.

"You all right?"

"My father was abusive."

Kem lingered in my shadow, watching me as I watched the world on the other side of the glass. He didn't say anything, just listened as I confessed. It wasn't my sin, it was Ricky Morrow's, but I carried it with me like a wound that needed to be sheltered from the rain. A secret that everyone knew but wasn't allowed to speak of. He beat my mother. Terrorized her. And when she wasn't around, he took it out on me. Not Nikki. Not Natalie. Definitely not Mya. Just me. And then my mother killed him.

"I am sorry, mami."

"My sister's husband is abusive." I searched his eyes for an answer. An instinct about what I should do. Should I talk to her again? Should I run him over with a car? What?

"How do you know?"

"I just do. She says he isn't but...I just do. You have anything to drink?"

He nodded and led the way to the kitchen, broke the seal on a bottle of rum, then took two glasses from the cabinet. "Forgiveness isn't just for the person who did wrong. Hard to move on if you don't forgive."

I finished my drink in one gulp. "Anything stronger?"

I AWOKE WITH A START. SAT STRAIGHT up in bed, clutching the sheets to my chest, certain that it was all a dream. A toilet flushed nearby, and I glanced around the room. It was vaguely familiar. Magazines and books were stacked against the far wall, laundry littered the floor, and the bed consisted of a mattress with a box spring.

"You are awake." Kem stepped into the darkness and closed the door gently behind him. He was without apparel.

"What happened? What time is it?"

His eyes darted to the tray posing as a bedside table. On it was a digital clock. It said 2:37.

"Twelve hours? I've been here twelve hours!"

It all came flooding back. Nikki. My father. The booze and the cocaine. Sex. And more booze. At least I hadn't tossed my cookies. That much was certain. Kem slid into bed next to me and held me close, leaving moist kisses from my shoulder to my neck. I'd heard of men who lost their erections when intoxicated. Kem was not one of them. His love was relentless. Hard and soft, passionate and caring. If I wasn't already in love with him, I would've been. It was like he set my body on fire and then saved my soul by putting it out.

"Stop."

"Do you want to talk more?"

Had we talked? What did we say?

"Jackie? What's wrong?"

"I...I have a boyfriend." I broke free, fumbling at the foot of the bed for my underwear.

"That doesn't change how I feel about you or how you feel about me."

"I..." I kicked listlessly at the ball of sheets surrounding my feet and did my best to resist the warmth of his touch. I figured I had about a fifty-fifty chance that I could get out of his bed and out of his apartment without falling into his arms again.

"Mami?"

"I need my clothes. Where...where are they?" I trembled openly and swore under my breath as my body betrayed me.

Kem's kiss had settled on my neck, and his hands molded against my breasts, coddling them as if they were two soft mounds of clay.

"You do not need clothes."

Oh, but I definitely did. I needed them, so that people wouldn't stare at me as I walked down the street.

"You have me. I will keep you warm. I will protect you."

He sniffed and brushed the white powder from his nose before snorting another line and passing the handheld mirror to me. Some couples did pillow talk after lovemaking. We did lines.

57
PECAN

I WISH YOU WOULD'VE TOLD ME. I WOULD'VE liked to go with you."

"But it would've meant taking more time off work."

"I don't care about that, Belinda. This is your health we're talking about."

My health. I was sick and tired of thinking about my health. The girls watched attentively from their places around the dining table. Once I made up my mind to lie, I'd intended to tell Heziah the truth later on in private, but that was before he started to read me the riot act. Now, I was having second thoughts.

"I told you. Doctor said everything's fine. I'm fine. It was all a mistake. Nat, you hear from Jackie? She say anything about being late for supper?"

Nat was now the oldest of my children. With Nikki and Mya off living their own lives and Jackie God knows where, it left Nat and the twins. She shook her head. It wasn't like Jackie not to call.

"She's an adult now, Belinda."

"Being eighteen don't make her an adult."

We still had two slices of Jackie's birthday cake in the fridge. I wasn't ready to start calling her an adult.

"Mommy, the doctor said you not sick anymore?"

Callie took after Heziah. Never quite believing what somebody said unless she could rephrase it into her own words. She'd make a brilliant lawyer or maybe a psychiatrist 'cause she was full of questions and doubted every answer that came her way.

"He said I'm just fine."

I ain't feel no shame in lying to my girls. They had the rest of their lives to be sad.

AFTER SUPPER, HEZIAH CAME UP BEHIND ME as I was washing the dishes. Hugged me so tight, I knew he knew. The years had been kind to us. As married folks we'd learned to read each other. He must've known about my lie from the very beginning.

"Tell me again," he whispered.

I turned to face him, held his face in my hands. "I ain't never gonna leave you. Even if I ain't here..."

"No."

"Heziah—"

"No. You said you were fine. That the doctor said...what did he say?"

"It don't matter what he said."

"Of course, it does!" He wanted to yell, wanted to scream at the top of his lungs, but he smothered the impulse and lowered his voice. "Tell me."

The doctor had spent a good ten minutes telling me how they was learning new things all the time about cancer. That there was experimental treatments I could have. That they could zap my tits with some fancy ray that would kill all the cancer. They could keeping giving me chemotherapy, and it would make me sick as a dog, make all my hair fall out, but I'd have a shot at beating it. Or they could just cut my tittie off.

"What are you gonna do?" Heziah looked at me with eyes so big I thought about the puppies I saw in the window of pet stores. "Pecan."

I nodded. "I had one of their so-called treatments, and I ain't gonna torture myself no more with it."

"You just gonna give up?"

"I'm gonna be normal. Keep my wits about me. Long as I can. I don't want my girls to see me falling apart." I pivoted back to the dishes and turned the faucet on full blast. Some things was worse than death. Dying slow and making my girls and Heziah watch was one of them.

58
PECAN

"MAMA, BUY ME A CAR."

"What?"

Jackie grinned and kept on stirring the greens for me. "Buy me a car, and I'll get rid of him. Probably wouldn't even have to drive that fast to knock his little ass down."

"Jackie, stop!"

"What? Like you weren't thinking it too!"

I wasn't. Running him over seemed like too much work. I was partial to a scoop of rat poison in his lemonade.

"Knock who down?" Nat suddenly appeared in the doorway. She'd begun her ascent to womanhood or so I was told. All I saw was my little chocolate baby begging me to pick her up. She took up position next to me, her back against the countertop. Quick as a cat, she stole a slice of tomato, smiling at me guiltily as it disappeared. "Who's gonna get knocked down?"

"Nikki's little toy husband."

"Jackie."

"Why? What he do?" Nat sucked her fingers dry.

I didn't need to give her another warning. Jackie knew better than to divulge all the dirty details to her baby sister.

"How come nobody tells me anything? I'm not a baby you know."

Of course, she was. She was a baby. Jackie was a baby. They was all babies.

"Mama." Nat stamped her foot and pouted, proving my point. "What'd he do?"

"Nothing, baby. You do your homework?"

My child let out a growl like she was a lion warning some other lion to stay away from her cubs. Then she stormed upstairs. Jackie thought it was funny. Her laughter filled the kitchen until the sound of Nat's bedroom door slamming shut put a stop to it.

"Ooo, she's mad now."

If I'd had a sister growing up, I liked to think I would've been more sensitive to her feelings, but my girls got they sensitivity from Ricky. Made them poke fun when they should've been sympathizing. Made them be careless when they should've been careful.

"You think Daddy'll let me borrow his car?"

"Just finish up them greens. You need to be thinking on college and signing up for them classes this fall."

"Yes, Mama." Jackie grinned.

SUPPER WAS OVER AND DONE WITH WHEN I walked in on them. Sitting on the sofa, whispering in soft tones. Both of them looked up with great big teary eyes soon as I walked into the room. Don't know why I expected Heziah to keep things to himself.

"Is it true?" Jackie was sobbing.

Damn man. Why he couldn't let sleeping dogs lie? He had to go and be all familiar with the truth. Lies had they place too. World wouldn't keep turning if folks didn't tell lies every now and then.

"Mama." Jackie stood and crossed the room, threw her arms around me, clinging to me like the baby she was. "Mama, no..."

"I'm fine. It's fine."

She brushed her wet nose against my shoulder, then stood back enough to press me with her eyes. Eyes she'd gotten from me.

"Y-You gotta do whatever the doctor said. Whatever he says is best. Promise me."

Couldn't say no to that. Couldn't tell my child that it wouldn't make any difference. So, I nodded and said, "I promise, baby."

59 MYA

TWO BEDROOMS AND AN EAT-IN KITCHEN WERE plenty. More than we'd ever had before. The floors sparkled from their recent waxing, and each room smelled of a fresh coat of paint. Darien nodded somberly as the landlord explained the fees associated with the application, but his eyes danced about excitedly. Was probably the same look George Jefferson had when he was just about to move on up. Mia bounded around the room, mimicking a galloping pony—an outward expression of Darien's controlled enthusiasm.

"What do you think?" He turned to face me and whispered, so the old lady wouldn't hear.

"It's big."

He agreed, then fixed his gaze to study what I was thinking but not saying. "You think it's too much."

I thought it was gonna be a long way to fall when reality caught up with us. There was a laundry room in the basement and mailboxes in the entryway. Didn't even have to go outside.

"We have a credit requirement," the woman informed us, but she kept her eye on Mia, as if my child might break something in the furniture-less apartment. "Do you know your score?"

"It's good," Darien lied.

"How long have you been at your current job?"

"A while," he lied again.

Usually, I was the one who made contact with landlords, but he'd expressed a burgeoning interest in all things related to responsibility. So, I hung back. Crossed my arms against my chest and squeezed, hoping to dull the impulse to take over the appointment. Mia disappeared into one of the bedrooms, and I followed. The distance was a good idea. I could barely hear the negotiations that were taking place, which made it easier to be less critical.

"Mommy, I sleep here, and the baby sleep there." She pointed to the corner near the closet then spun two hundred and seventy degrees to point under the window. "And you and Dee sleep over there."

"I think we would sleep across the hall."

"No, you sleep there. Me here. And baby over there."

I sighed. How many kids didn't understand the concept of separate bedrooms? Probably just mine.

"So...what do my girls think?" He was grinning. "Should we take it?"

"How much is the rent?"

He hooked an arm around my waist and whispered that the woman wanted eight hundred, but he'd talked her down to seven fifty. A typewriter appeared in my head, keeping a very specific list of expenses complete with realistic minimum and maximum costs. If his custodial position turned out to be permanent, we'd have to work something out for childcare 'cause I wasn't about to give up my job, part-time as it was.

"Don't worry so much." He was still grinning. "I got this."

"Smile, Mommy. Dee got it."

I was surrounded by delusional fools and children. And somehow I'd ended up as the bad guy. The disciplinarian. The realist. The adult. I was the one charged with keeping the truth from them. What stood before us was a nice vacation from the norm, but as with all vacations, it would eventually come to an end.

"YOU SHOULD LEAVE HIM. YOU DON'T NEED him," Nikki said between bites of lettuce and croûtons. She'd ordered lobster to take home to her little Napoleon and subjected herself to a salad. "It's not like you're married to him."

"Because if she was married to him, then she'd have to stay, right?" Jackie snarked. "She'd owe him the rest of her life?"

Nikki rolled her eyes and reached for the frosty water glass to the right of her plate.

I often wondered if we'd been born in a different order, would they be closer. Maybe if Jackie had been the second child, then Daddy would've loved her as much as he loved me, and she wouldn't be so sensitive. Or if she'd been fourth instead of Nat, then Nikki would've carried her around like she was a doll instead of treating Jackie like she'd stolen her spotlight. Although none of that would've worked in the end. The problem was their personalities—oil and water.

"You can't be with somebody thinking you gonna fix them. Mya, you hear me?"

"You should talk. I don't think you need to be giving anybody relationship advice," Jackie said.

Nikki feigned a gasp and replied, "I was going to say the exact same thing to you!"

"I'm not leaving him." They both turned, expecting me to elaborate which I had no plans to do. Five minutes passed. Five minutes of them watching me take a bite of my cheeseburger, swallow, grab a few fries, swallow, and gulp down unsweetened iced tea.

They spent the next thirty minutes taking turns changing the subject. Jackie spoke to me as if Nikki weren't at the table and Nikki did the same. Topics went from Mia to Jackie's impending collegiate attendance to Nikki's pursuit of motherhood to Jackie's love triangle. Nikki was clearly disgusted by our sister's vivid explanation, which tickled Jackie endlessly.

The Irish pub was on my side of town, between the suburbs where Nikki lived and the south side where Jackie still lived with Mama. It was a cross between a highbrow restaurant and a neighborhood bar. The kind of establishment that offered filet mignon as well as a decent burger. Nikki'd chosen it. She was the more thoughtful of us, considering carefully what would be the most neutral location for our get-together. Men lingered at the bar and roamed around the room, sparing suggestive glances at our table. They outnumbered us six to one. A phenomenon that had plagued me since we sat down. I nodded, pretending to listen to the current conversation, but I was actually trying to figure out the reason that so many men were unattached and present.

"Babies ain't Band-Aids."

"You sound like Mama."

"Well, it's true. You're crazy if you think everything's gonna be all roses just 'cause you have a baby."

"Just shut up, Jackie. I didn't ask your opinion."

"Don't tell me to shut up! You—"

The men began to converge toward three tables pushed together. Robust laughter emanated from the group, and they raised their glasses in a toast. It was a bachelor party. I smiled, congratulating myself for having figured it out.

"Nikki's knocked up," Jackie claimed pointedly, staring at me. "Did you know that?"

I didn't.

"Aren't you gonna congratulate her?" She sounded pissed, like I'd offended her with my silence.

"Shouldn't we all congratulate her? Throw her a congratulations-you're-having-a-little-asshole party?"

Maybe it wouldn't be an asshole. There was a fifty-fifty chance that the kid would take after Nikki. But something told me not to point that out.

"You're just jealous," came Nikki's usual retort.

"Of you? Seriously? If I woke up one morning with your life, I'd shoot myself."

Nikki's eyes began to water, and Jackie paused for a sip of her martini. She'd ordered a rum and Coke to begin with then progressed down the menu to the martini section. She'd barely touched her food, and four drinks later, I expected she was about to move on to the coffee liquors.

"Y-You're so mean."

"I'm just being honest. Right, Mya? I mean am I lying? Better to be dead than with a man who beats you."

"He doesn't hit me!"

"Why are we here?"

"What?"

I repeated myself, and Jackie squirmed in her chair. Nikki had forgotten that Jackie had called this meeting for a reason. A reason she refused to divulge until we met in person. At which time my sister decided to pick a fight. Obviously the reason for this little powwow was one she was dreading.

"What is it?"

She motioned for the waiter to bring her a refill, then began tapping her nails against the empty glass. "It's Mama."

"She's fine," Nikki insisted. "It was all a mistake. She told me when I picked her up from the hospital."

Mama had lied. Surprise, surprise. I took another bite of my burger while Jackie laid out the truth for Nikki. Mama had cancer. She was not "just fine" as she liked to put it. Nikki looked to me to share in her shock, but I was never a very good actress.

"She lied to me?"

"That's right, Nikki. Make it all about you."

"Did you know? Mya?"

I took no pleasure in telling my sisters the truth. I was the first to know. Mama had clearly trusted I would keep quiet about it, not because she favored me, but because I could. Everybody knew I was the only one of my sisters that could keep a secret. Just wish she would've told me it was supposed to be a secret.

"So, everybody knew except me..."

Jackie was growing more irritated with Nikki's focus every second that passed, so I moved the conversation along. "Is that it? That's what you wanted to tell us?"

"No." She paused to accept her fifth drink and waited until the waiter had disappeared. "Mama wants us there when she tells Nat and the twins. Wants us to put on a good face so they don't worry."

I nodded. "Just tell me when."

"WHAT DID YOUR SISTERS SAY ABOUT THE baby?"

"Nothing."

Darien jerked around to face me then sat at the foot of the lower bunk. "How could they say nothing?"

"I didn't tell them."

I wiggled my back to the cement wall and waited for him to ease into bed next to me and ask me why not. He didn't do either. His profile was dominated by his nose that was both wide and pointy. His dreads fell forward over his shoulder as his stare lingered on the floor.

"It wasn't good timing."

60
JACKIE

IN OUR JOURNEY FROM ONE FOSTER HOME to another, Nat was my charge. If she had a problem with her homework or a classmate or squirted ketchup on her sweater, I was the one she looked to for a solution. I taught her to tie her shoes, to whistle "Twinkle, Twinkle, Little Star," and I was the one who introduced her to the cute little girl card and taught her how to use it. If it wasn't for Natalie, I might've become an entirely self-absorbed person. She saved me from myself, and not a day of her life had passed that I wasn't there for, so we were both disappointed that I was going to be living on campus.

She sat in the center of my bed with droopy eyes as I tried on my third outfit of the night. My little sister had learned well. She started with a plea for practicality. Commuting to school would obviously be cheaper than paying room and board. Then she hit me with the sentimentality.

"But, if you go...I'll be here all by myself."

If it had been up to me, I would've told her the truth: Mama had made me promise. She wanted me to enjoy college life because she never got that chance. I couldn't say no. Not now. Just like I wasn't about to break Nat's heart with the truth. I'd leave that for Mama to do.

I stretched the black-and-white striped spandex over my body and turned to look at my ass in the full-length mirror. It was normally hard to ignore, but even more so given the graphic print.

"Jackie!"

I sighed and flopped down next to her, applying wet kisses across her forehead. "Come on, get up."

My mattress squeaked in agreement, and I dragged her before my closet. At fourteen years old, Nat was already my height. Minus my curves. I settled on a purple spandex miniskirt and a sheer sleeveless blouse with a black-and-white print.

"Put that on, and then I'll do your makeup."

"I..." She giggled, clutching the pieces in both hands. "I can't wear this. Mama would kill me."

"Then I guess we're not gonna tell her. Come on, sis, let's go have us a good time."

FRIDAY NIGHTS AT CLUB FRANCESCO MEANT WALL-TO-WALL bodies. Squeezing through the crowd, I bumped elbows with a few regulars who complained that I wasn't on stage.

"It couldn't be helped," I explained.

Nat beamed in my wake and uttered, "This place is awesome."

The tables and chairs had seen better days, and the floor tiles were chipped in so many places it was easy to mistake them for a pattern. My sister's eyes glazed over, taking it all in. I suppose the quaint charm had a certain amount of appeal.

"Can we sit near the stage?" She didn't even wait for my answer before weaving through the collection of unsteady tables to claim the only available one in the first row. "There's Kem." She waved eagerly as I joined her.

He gave her a slow smile and a wink. My sister swooned like the teenage schoolgirl she was.

"Hey Jackie. Mo sent this." One of the waitresses stopped at our table to unburden her tray. A tall fruity cocktail, Mo had created especially for me, a shot of tequila, and a Shirley Temple for Nat.

"Who's Mo?"

"My boyfriend."

"I thought Kem was your boyfriend."

The waitress smirked and went back to her duties, taking orders from the tables around us.

"Not anymore. I'm with Mo now."

"But I like Kem." She pouted, eyeing her drink suspiciously as if it would be a betrayal of Kem if she took a sip. "What kinda name is Mo anyway?"

I shrugged and knocked back the tequila. I didn't disagree with my sister on any particular point.

"Is that alcohol?" She asked.

"Nope."

"You're not supposed to be drinking alcohol."

There were a lot of things I did that I wasn't supposed to do. So, I smiled and explained that I could handle a few drinks now and then. Besides it was a special occasion. How many times was my little sister gonna have her first time in a bar?

"Then I want some too."

No...The word slurred itself from one end of my brain to the other. Mama would kill me. Heziah would kill me. I was definitely supposed to say no to that request. I removed the straw from the tall cocktail glass and gulped down the fruity drink.

"Don't say I'm too young 'cause I'm here. Just like you. And...and I just wanna taste it."

She must've seen the no in my eyes fixing to make itself heard because all the pleading evaporated from her voice, and she played the only other card she had. "Bet Mama would be real mad to find out you drinking again."

61 NIKKI

IT HAD TO BE A MISTAKE. I was pregnant. I was sure of it. My chest was swollen and tender, I'd never felt more tired, and I was two weeks late. I stared at the white stick waiting for the second line to appear. Maybe the test was defective.

"Nicole."

"Coming!" I flushed the toilet and hurried to wash my hands. The woman in the mirror looked closer to forty than twenty-three.

"Nicole." A quick knock came on the bathroom door.

I simply needed to find a hiding place for the test with the defective results. Last thing I needed was Jean-Louis to see it.

"Hi." I smiled and yanked the door open so fast the air lifted a piece of my bangs. "Sorry. I'm ready."

We were going to meet one of his colleagues at an Italian restaurant nearby. He took a moment to take in my outfit then sighed with disappointment. His colleague wasn't married, but he was sure to bring a date. Probably a girl with no aspirations and a size two body.

"Here." He thrust the telephone into my hand and spun on his heel. "We are leaving in two minutes," he called over his shoulder.

"Hello?"

Mama's voice came on the line. She said she wanted to remind me that

Nat had to be at school tomorrow for freshman orientation. Apparently, Nat and Jackie were both spending the evening with me, and Mama didn't want them up too late.

"Don't worry, Mama." Killed me to lie for them, but the last thing Mama needed was an extra reason to worry.

62
JACKIE

MAYBE THIS GIRLFRIEND OF HIS DIDN'T ACTUALLY exist. He never mentioned her. Never brought her around. No one I knew had ever laid eyes on her.

Kem parted the crowd of adoring women, smiling shyly at their overtures, and disappeared down the dark corridor alone.

Nat let out a perky burp and covered her mouth in surprise. "Oops."

Beer had that effect on me too, which was why I preferred harder liquor. But I'd sequestered my baby sister to Budweiser and similar frothy options.

"Can I have...some of yours?"

Madonna's words, "like a virgin," came to mind, and I shook my head. One was enough.

"Puh-lease!"

"I said no. Stop begging."

Mo was surrounded by wanting customers. It was the perfect opportunity to slip out unnoticed.

"Where you going? I'm coming too."

"No. Sit here. I'll be back."

He was alone in the dressing room, his finger whisking against his gums, and a line of cocaine stretched across the mirror on his lap.

"Want some company?"

The last line disappeared up his nose. My ex-boyfriend and current lover wasn't in a sharing mood. He closed the door behind me and attacked the distance between us with slow silent steps. If we'd ever truly been friends, those days were long gone. The hairs along my spine stood at attention as my body anticipated his touch. Strong. Soft. Sweet. Where did a good Catholic boy from Columbia get such lovemaking skills? His fingertips whisked gently across my shoulders, and I resisted the impulse to shiver instead moving out of his reach.

"Not talking, huh? That's fine. Good actually." My mind grasped aimlessly for something to say and out popped, "I wanted to talk about what happened. Last time."

I didn't want to talk. He didn't want to talk. By all indications, he couldn't talk, and I apparently couldn't shut up.

"We shouldn't do that. What we did. The other day."

Even as I said it my heart began its protest. What did I know? My heart was the expert in all things Kem Delgado, and she didn't like being told no. I centered my gaze on his nose, carefully avoiding the eyes that were still working their magic on me.

"I've gotta boyfriend."

"I do not care. Do you?"

Of course, I did.

"Mami?" He was again within reach.

"I'm not a cheater."

Yes, you are! Cheater, cheater, cheater! screamed my heart. I was dating Mo, sure enough, but she had never given her consent. Never wavered for a moment. Still hung up on the beautiful brooding guitarist...

"Don't do that."

"What?"

"Touch me." That's right. I got dressed and dragged my fabulous ass down here just to tell you not to touch me.

"You don't like it when I touch you here? How about here?" He grinned, enjoying the tease as much as the touch. "You're not talking, mami."

The table nudged my behind, reminding me there was nowhere to run. It's top, clean and oh-so inviting, sliding underneath me without a plan or an order; my thighs spread upon contact with the flat surface. Why had

I come back here? What did I think was going to happen?

"I am going to kiss you."

"Okay."

Kissing wasn't cheating.

BETWEEN THE MOANS, THERE WAS A THUD. His palm slammed against the table in defiance, never would he succumb so easily. He would fight it. He would win.

"Mmm, that's it, papi." My legs floundered around his waist, my naked bottom streaking across the table. "D-Don't stop. Don't stop."

Somewhere between the panting and the prayers of ecstasy, I was aware of a third person in the dressing room. A figure dressed in black and white, hurling expletives at us. Kem pulled away from me, turning to see where the words were coming from. It all happened so fast. I ducked for a second to pull my dress down, and by the time, I looked up Kem was leaning right to dodge Mo's fist. The miss threw Mo off balance, and his second attempt at contact was even less successful. They continued in that manner. It looked something like a ritualistic dance. Mo's fists went flying, and Kem responded with sweeping blocks and graceful dodges. I was vaguely aware that I should've been cheering for the home team, but my boyfriend's defeat was too damn hilarious. Ricky Morrow came to mind, and I wondered if he was looking down on the scene, grumbling about Mo's lack of technique. It was official. Not only was I a cheater, but I was caught. Thank goodness for the liquor padding my senses, otherwise I might've been able to see my way through the haze of sex I was reluctant to abandon.

"Hey," Kem called, worry seeping into his voice.

Mo had turned his attention to me. His lying, cheating, alcoholic, girlfriend. Only he chose a more colorful word than girlfriend. It didn't bother me that he was only a foot or two away. As much as I despised it, Ricky Morrow's blood ran through my veins. Even though my blood was probably two parts liquor and one part narcotics, that still left enough Morrow chick to handle his tepid ass. But it didn't get that far. Kem locked Mo's neck in the crook of his arm and dragged him backward.

"You don't touch her." He released Mo and quickly stepped between us.

"You can have her! I don't give a shit anymore!"

My heart sank. Mo didn't want me? So much for all that love he claimed to have. He stormed out of the dressing room, and Kem turned to face me. My heart went a flutter. Kem loved me. Kem wanted me.

"Are you okay, mami?"

I nodded and nearly knocked the wind out of him with one kiss. Desperate I'd never been, but there I was hanging off his body, clutching to his clothes with a fever that would've embarrassed a modest woman. We made it back to his apartment in a frantically aroused state, tossing clothing and underwear along the way to his bedroom. It wasn't until the next morning that I realized I'd forgotten something. Someone.

63 NIKKI

"ARE YOU INSANE? YOU JUST LEFT HER!"

"But I-I'm okay, Nikki..."

"No, you're not. You're scarred and don't even know it. What if I wasn't here when she called? What if I couldn't get to her in time? Are you listening to me?"

Natalie sat on the ottoman between us, shoulders slumped forward, carrying the burden of the disaster that was last night. I would've confiscated the disgusting outfit she was wearing, but there was no way she'd fit into anything I owned. It wasn't her fault. Not by an inch. The rumpled sex kitten hiding behind black sunglasses was to blame. She'd probably dragged my innocent little sister to that club and abandoned her for the very same reason—she was a self-involved little thing. Doped up on God knows what.

Jackie folded both arms against her chest and sighed. "I'm sorry Nat. You're okay, right?"

Real apologies didn't come from behind sunglasses, but Nat didn't seem to mind. She still looked on Jackie as if she were a rock star.

"Do you know how lucky you are that nothing bad happened to her? What were you thinking taking her to that place anyway? You have seriously lost your mind!"

Jackie's left hand went to her temple, and she asked me to keep it down.

"I will not!"

"God, Nikki! I made a mistake! As you love to point out, I'm not perfect. Come on Nat. Let's go."

"How are you getting home?" I followed behind them, hands firmly planted on my hips.

Jackie didn't bother with an answer, she opened my front door and led the way to the sedan parked at the curb. Kem Delgado was waiting behind the wheel. He was up and out of the car in time to open the passenger door and the one behind it. Had everyone fooled with that gentleman routine, but not me. I could see straight through it. He was as bad as Jackie, and she was never going to change as long as he was in her life.

64
PECAN

"MOMMY?"

The outline of one of the twins appeared in the doorway, but I couldn't keep my eyes open long enough to see her face.

"She's gotta rest, Callie," came Jackie's voice along with the weight of the big homemade quilt Clara had made years ago. It was the fifth layer Jackie had piled on me, and I was still freezing. "You want something?"

It was time for their afternoon snack. I'd promised them popcorn and Kool-Aid.

"No, Mama. Stay in bed." Jackie tucked me in tight and promised to be back in a minute.

Aunt Clara had done the same ten years before. Put me to bed, tended to my wounds, and made sure my girls had everything they needed until I got my strength back. *Pecan girl, God must've been feeling real good the day he made you*, she'd said. Clara would be almost seventy now. I wondered how Mississippi was treating her. We'd lost touch after everything happened with Ricky.

"Mommy, you want some?" Jenna held out a freezer bag filled with freshly popped corn.

I shook my head, or at least, I meant to. Every part of me was shaking, so I guess that counted.

"You hiding under the covers?" She giggled and jumped onto the bed, spilling popcorn along the way. "I'm gonna hide with you."

The first treatment didn't go as they planned, so they switched up protocols. The doctor said I might have some new side effects. Gave me a long list of them. So far I was only having chills, but they ain't have any intention of letting up any time soon.

"Jackie's boyfriend is downstairs. He's gonna go get us some pizza. You want some pizza?"

Jackie's boyfriend..."W-Who's that, b-b-baby?"

"Kem."

Kem was her boyfriend now?

"Mommy, you shaking." Jenna rested her head against the pile of blankets.

"I'm f-f-fine baby. D-Don't worry."

Lyrics to a song I didn't recognize wafted into my bedroom followed by a beat that was somewhat familiar. Somebody must've turned up the volume 'cause after ten seconds, I could hear it more clearly. It was one of Stevie Wonder's songs.

"Come on, dance with us." Nat poked her head into my room. "Come on." She didn't wait before taking Jenna by the hand.

From the sound of it, I figured she had both the twins dancing in the hallway. The music was coming from the boom box in Jackie's room.

"How you feeling now, Mama?"

"Fine."

Jackie sat on the floor beside my bed, watching me attentively. "If you feel like eating, let me know, and I'll fix you something."

"Mmhmm...," slipped from my lips as I sunk into the darkness.

DADDY STOOD OVER ME, LOOKING DOWN PATIENTLY as I came to. He knew everything that had happened since we last saw each other and forgave me for my less than honorable moments. I hadn't been blessed with his strength, or so I thought, but he fixed his face to tell me otherwise. I had survived his passing. Survived Ricky. Got my girls back. And he meant to impart on me that I had everything I'd ever wanted at the edge of my fingertips. I just had to reach for it.

"Am I dying?"

He smiled, stroking my face. "Pecan."

How long had it been since I heard his voice?

"You done good," he said sternly. "But you ain't finished. Go on now. Make yourself useful."

Tears flowed down my face, and my heart filled with love.

"It's okay, Belinda. Just let it out."

The floor was hard, like stones rubbing against my bare knees. Rubbing as I fought my body's convulsions, fought to stay upright over the toilet.

"I got you," Heziah said, as I lurched forward into the toilet bowl.

I ain't even remember eating, but at some point I must have.

"Okay, I think that's it. Relax now."

The rocks that were trying to rub my knees raw a second ago, up and decided to be nice and cool my forehead instead. The sound of water filled the sink basin, and a cool towel pressed against my lips. Heziah's face came into view.

"Am I dreaming?"

"Not at the moment, no." He settled into the cramped space between tub and toilet. "We'll just sit here for a minute and relax."

The house was too quiet to be daylight hours. The girls must've been sleeping in their beds. "I saw my daddy."

He smiled, "Oh yeah? Did you tell him about me?"

"Didn't have to."

Heziah chuckled softly. "Well, I sure hope that's a good thing."

DECEMBER 1991

65 MYA

"MOMMY, WHAT'S THAT?"

"It's...it's a penis."

"Eww."

Mia's arm stretched out with a fresh diaper dangling from her fingertips. She'd seen me change quite a few of her baby brother's diapers but was just getting around to paying attention.

"Can we go in the pool?" She took up her usual position outside the only window, which was painted shut.

The two-story motel circled around a parking lot and a pool that should've been drained and tarped over since the snow had begun to fall, but the manager at Lakeview Terrace had better things to do.

Lakeview Terrace didn't have a view or a lake, but what it did have was two U-shaped floors with substandard rooms surrounding its cesspool—the site of disputes, parties, and everything in between. One night I even saw the guy from room 112 jacking off into it.

"Can I? Puh-lease?"

"No."

Alan was a good baby, nothing like his sister was. She'd yipped and yapped and fought with me over everything—medicine, diaper changes, and anything else that seemed to matter. But Alan just cooed, sucking his fingers and toes.

"How come?"

"'Cause I said so."

"But I'm hot."

"No, you're not."

"Yes, I am!"

She wasn't. She couldn't have been. It was forty degrees outside and only fifteen degrees warmer in our room.

"When Dee get back?"

The school needed him before the kids got there and long after they went home. It was good for him, but meant I was stuck in that tiny motel room for longer than I could stand.

"How come the floor stink?"

"Don't lie on it. Stand up."

Mia pushed her nose into the decrepit green carpeting to make sure she'd located the source of the stench. Then jerked back and coughed. It wasn't just the mildewed carpeting. The dresser drawers smelled of smoke and the blankets of dust and disinfectant. It all mingled together and filled the room, prompting coughing fits every few hours.

"Where Dee go?"

"Work."

"When he come back?"

"Soon."

Having full-time work should've been our ticket to a halfway decent life. There was more money coming in, at least theoretically.

"When soon?"

"Soon soon."

"How come he not coming upstairs?"

Alan was drifting off to sleep, rubbing his face against the clean towel stretched across the bed he shared with his sister. So, I stood and joined Mia at the window. Just in time to see Darien slip into one of the rooms on the first floor.

"Why he go there? He forget where we are?"

"Stay here."

"No, I go too."

Mia weighed about thirty pounds, and I felt each one as I lifted her onto the foot of the bed. "Stay here. Do not move. Do not open the door."

I made it to the staircase and was all set to take the steps two at a time when it hit me. I'd left my new baby alone with his four-year-old sister in a motel that housed the lowest of lowlives, all to chase some sense into a man that was twice my age. I turned on my heels and returned to our room to pack.

"We go get Dee now?"

"No." I braced myself for what was coming next. Mia stood at my side, watching in horror as I stuffed our things into a duffel bag.

"We can't go without Dee!"

Her bottom lip began to tremble, her eyes watering. I'd never wanted to separate them, but it was for her own good. Someday she'd understand.

66
JACKIE

"DO YOU HAVE TO GO? STAY. STAY with me."

Any other man would've been flattered to have a naked woman in his bed begging for him to return to it, but Kem was on the verge of becoming irritated.

"I told you. I have to go. I gave my word."

He did tell me. And I'd decided that two hours of lovemaking would be enough to change his plans.

"Is the sky gonna fall if you don't meet her tonight?"

He didn't bother to answer.

"Is she more important than me?"

"Don't do that." He was no longer dangling along the edge of irritability. He had jumped in with both feet. "You knew." He sighed and stepped into his jeans one foot at a time. "Do you want me to break my word?"

I wanted him all to myself, but I'd technically given up on that desire. Officially, he was free to date any woman he wanted. And I was equally as free. I spent more time at his apartment than I did my dorm room. He knew every curve and scar on my body. And I was learning Spanish for him. We ended every night with "I love you" and began every morning with a kiss. But still...

I tucked the sheet under my arms and across my chest. He was sexually spent, so I was reasonably sure he wasn't going to sex up what's-her-face. "What time are you coming back?"

"I am not sure." He sifted through his pile of laundry, sniffing out a tee shirt that was generally presentable. Kem had a long list of talents, but domestic matters weren't included.

"Is she still depressed?"

I wasn't supposed to know that, but I'd overheard him expressing concern about the amount of medication she was taking. And it didn't take a psychic to see that all the joy had seeped out of their relationship. A big part of me rejoiced in that. The rest of me was riddled with impatience. Anyone could see the end was coming. It was just taking its sweet old time.

"She is having a hard time," he admitted and settled on a black tee shirt with an image of a rock band in white on the front. He pushed his hair back from his face, and his eyes did a sweep of the bedroom floor, searching for something. "My shoes. You moved them?"

"In the closet." Shoes belonged in the closet, along with coats, clothes, and nifty little things called hangers. "Maybe I can come with you?"

It was a subtle shift. A pause. A curious expression. And then he took the bait.

"What do you mean?"

"I can go with you. If you like her, I'll probably like her too. At least, we'd be together. You. Me. And her."

"You have a test to study for, no?"

I did.

"You study. Get some sleep. And I'll be back before you know it."

Our lips met briefly, and I forced a smile as he disappeared into the hallway. Studying required a certain amount of brainpower. As the front door closed and locked, my mind began a familiar trek. Imagining what's-her-face. How she wore her hair, whether she was taller than me, thinner than me. Did she greet him with a hug or a kiss? Where would they go? A groan escaped my lips, and my feet hit the floor. I thought I had him for a second there. What man didn't want two girls in his bed? Studying was impossible.

I dressed quickly in black-and-silver striped tights and a black spandex minidress. Then lit a joint and took up watch next to the picture window overlooking the street below. Dusk was on the horizon, and a bursting orange glow hovered in the distance. Happy hour. It was my second favorite time of day. Half-priced drinks and exhausted professionals looking for a distraction before returning to the monotony of their everyday lives. I finished off the joint and snatched my keys from the hook by the door.

THE WORLD SPUN AROUND ME LIKE A merry-go-round with dark bottles, tall and short, and smiling faces that were cheering me on one minute and taunting me the next.

"Get it, girl!"

He was a heavyset dwarf of a man with tiny sweaty hands that had an affinity for my hips. He wasn't my type, but he was generous, and I was living on a student's budget. His belly bumped against my midsection, jiggling as he attempted to keep up with me.

"Another round for my girlfriend here!"

A man I'd just met had called me his girlfriend while the man I loved was off with another girl. I wished I was anywhere except for Martin's Pub. It was only a block or two from Kem's apartment. The heavy wooden door opened with a whoosh, and I glanced in its direction. Maybe he'd come and find me. He'd end his date early and save me from the overly affectionate oompa-lumpa.

"Hey, wanna get outta here? I know another place downtown. Real nice. Got the best cocktails in the city."

I heard my mama's voice in my head screaming a very clear no.

"Whatcha say, pretty girl?"

He didn't sound like a crazy person. His voice was all I had to go on since my vision had been blurry for the last thirty minutes.

"Aww, come on," he whispered against my neck while his fat little hands squeezed my waist. "I wanna get to know you better."

Kem knew me better than anybody outside of my mama. Did he use lines like that to pick up girls? Doubtful.

"I gotta..." My mouth went dry, and I did my best to stand absolutely still with my most serious expression. "Study. Go home. I gotta...go home."

"I'll take you."

A hearty, very pointed laugh jumped out of my chest and danced in his face. Accepting free drinks from the fat midget was one thing, but he wasn't getting anywhere near my honey pot.

I HAD A SPECIAL RELATIONSHIP WITH THE moon. It rose and shimmered for me, and I sang for it. Sang all the way down the street. In low sultry tones and a few high-pitched operatic notes thrown in for good measure. Cars whizzed by, their passengers shaking their heads, laughing at the girl with the big voice, but I didn't take it personally. I tripped over a crack in the sidewalk and the hairs on the back of my neck stood up. The street was suddenly quiet, but whispers wafted through the silence. And footsteps fell behind me. They quickened as I caught sight of Kem's building until they were running after me. One, two, possibly three sets of feet. I turned the corner, wishing I had the coordination of my sober self and was suddenly thrust into the bushes of a neighboring flat. Shadows, tall and lean, stood over me then dove into my pockets, frantically tugging at my clothes.

"No! Help!"

My plea was met by a fist. And then a kick and two more.

67 NIKKI

OF COURSE, YOU CAN STAY HERE. YOU should've called me, and I would've gone to get you all."

Mya just stared at me, determined not to give anything away. She'd grown even more secretive since getting knocked up the second time. My homeless sister with the pride of a Titan didn't even have to try to get pregnant. She had two kids out of wedlock, and I was married with none.

"We've got plenty of room." I smiled.

"You sure?" She peered around the corner cautiously.

"He's not here. I mean he's working a double shift at the hospital. Give me that baby. He's so precious." I couldn't believe she'd named him after that man.

Mya slung a large duffel bag and a smaller one over her shoulder, then took Mia by the hand and followed me upstairs. We truly did have more than enough room, but Mya seemed reluctant to give the kids their own room.

"Fine." She finally relented and lifted Mia onto the foot of the bed, systematically removing her shoes, socks, and jeans.

"How Dee gonna find us?"

"Go to sleep," she said softly and kissed her daughter's forehead.

With Alan safely tucked away in a laundry basket, Mya began her own bedtime ritual. I trailed behind her to the bathroom, watching as she splashed cold water on her face and squeezed toothpaste onto her toothbrush.

"So, what happened?"

"Nothing," she lied to my reflection in the mirror.

"Nothing? You just thought you'd show up on my doorstep in the middle of the night?"

She rinsed her mouth and spit into the face bowl. "How are you, Nikki?"

"Where's Darien?"

"Where's Jean-Louis?"

"Working..." She'd heard me the first time I said it, and her expression said she wasn't buying it. "H-He works really hard. He's the best heart surgeon at the hospital, so..."

"We won't be here long."

I had to remind myself not to be offended. It was just Mya being Mya. She didn't believe anything unless she had firsthand knowledge of it. And she wasn't big on long discussions. I followed a few steps behind her as she returned to the second guest room.

"How's Mama?" my sister asked.

"Good. Gaining weight and growing hair. You should go see her. When you get a chance."

Mya nodded and shed her clothes before yanking back the bedding. Her hand rested against the three hundred-thread count sheets and the fluffy down comforter, examining it. My sister—the smart one, the beautiful one, the one that everybody loved—she'd never seen a bed so nice.

"How's Jackie?" I asked, making conversation.

She sank into the exquisite sheets and thick down comforter. "Fine, I guess."

I understood. Even if you saw Jackie every day, there was no telling exactly how she was. Well, other than being high. That much was a given.

"Mya? You okay?"

"I'm a hypocrite."

"That's an awful word. Don't say that."

"I took them from him. He loves them. They love him. And I took them."

"You're their mother. You're just doing what's best for them."

Mya glared at me as if I'd just accused her of being the worst person on the planet.

68
PECAN

"Jenna that's enough," Heziah was saying. He was always telling her when enough was enough. Didn't always stop her though. She giggled, zigzagging from the living room to the dining room chasing Callie with a spray bottle of Arm and Hammer.

It was long past the bedtime Heziah had set for them, but that wasn't so unusual. I stood watch from the second-floor landing, watching the three of them dart from one side of the hallway to the other and back again. I'd been fighting the urge to say "I told you so." The twins had him wrapped around their little bitty fingers just like the older ones had me.

"California Jenkins!"

She froze, and a second later, Jenna did the same. They stood side by side in matching nightgowns, looking up at me with wide innocent eyes.

"Y'all must've lost your minds. You know what time it is? Don't make me have to come down there."

Right then the telephone rang, and Heziah disappeared into the kitchen to answer it.

The twins took the stairs in single file, each one blaming the other for getting in trouble. They went down easy enough after that. Kissed them both goodnight and checked in on Nat before I ran into a panic-stricken Heziah.

WHEN HEZIAH ASKED THE SECURITY GUARD TO point us in the direction of the emergency room, she was stunned. She looked right past him and at me. I ain't have time to put on my wig, so I was like a walking advertisement for cancer.

"Miss?" He tried again.

She collected herself and pointed us to the double doors to the right and handed us two passes. Folks was practically sitting on top of each other waiting to be seen. Heziah went right to the desk, but I couldn't help studying all the faces, hoping to see my baby.

"Belinda. She's this way."

I never had any love for hospitals, but after all my treatments were successful, I thought maybe we might be able to be friends. But when I saw Jackie curled up under a mountain of blankets, I knew it would never happen. I was gonna always hate hospitals.

"Hi, Mama. Hi, Daddy." My girl tried to smile under the weight of all the swelling and bruising. She'd rolled herself up into a knot either outta fear or chill.

Heziah squeezed her shoulder and asked her what happened. My girl tried again to smile. Said she was robbed on her way home.

"Home? Or school?" Heziah wanted to know as if it would make a difference. Jackie didn't answer. "You were walking by yourself? Where? Did somebody call the police? When did this happen?"

"Heziah..."

He took the hint well, nodded, and pushed the only chair, so it sat next to Jackie's bed then went about finding a second one for himself.

"It's okay, baby. You gonna be just fine."

Tears made tracks down her cheeks, and her warm fingers grasped onto mine. It had happened again, and once again, I wasn't there to stop it. To protect my child.

The doctor said Jackie had a few bruised ribs plus cuts and a black eye. One of Kem's neighbors had called the police, and the boys had run off at the first siren before they could do any real damage.

"Real damage. What's that supposed to mean?" Heziah glared at the man, then glanced down at Jackie.

She was fixated on the machine that sat over her shoulder beeping.

"Oh," he gasped, and tears threatened to break free from his eyes.

We listened in silence as the doctor continued with instructions to care for Jackie's wounds. Instructions I'd never heard before but knew better than he did.

They'd taken Jackie's clothes and given her a sweat-suit that probably came from the lost and found. She huddled against Heziah, and I walked a few steps ahead of them, opening doors and doing my best to shield her from prying eyes.

"MAMA, WHO'S AT THE DOOR?" NAT STUMBLED out of her bedroom, rubbing her eyes.

"Nobody. Go on back to bed." I guided her gently and she didn't resist. I wrapped my robe tighter around me and tied the sash into a knot. Had to lift both my robe and nightgown, so they wouldn't trip me up on the way downstairs. Wasn't appropriate attire to receive company, but I ain't have a choice.

Heziah was already on edge, and he sounded as if he was about to lose it.

"Where were you, huh? You just leave my daughter to roam the streets at night by herself!"

It was a ridiculous accusation. One that he wouldn't have made if he'd had a night to sleep on it.

"Where were you when she was being attacked by three thugs?"

"Heziah."

He stood over an equally distraught Kem and turned ever so slightly in my direction. We ain't need to make eye contact. He knew he'd gone too far. He sighed and headed toward the stairs.

Kem held his head in his hands, and as Heziah's feet climbed to the second floor, Kem slowly withdrew his fingers until I could see his face. He loved my girl, I was sure. It was easy to feel guilt for something that wasn't your doing when you loved the person hurt by it.

"Is she...? Did they...?"

"Just a few cuts and bruises. She's gonna be just fine."

He nodded, more for my sake than his own.

I sat next to him, squeezing my knees together, and took his hand in mine. Jackie had seen and felt enough pain in her young life for any mama to feel the burden of that failure. But I knew my girl. I'd raised her. And wasn't no man or even three strong enough to break her. Not in this life or the next.

MYA

I DON'T REMEMBER GIVING MY PERMISSION FOR THIS. Don't remember you even asking. You just moved them in."

Nikki hushed him, but he continued without altering his tone or volume. My sister's husband was what my daddy would've called too big for his britches. And Nikki wasn't big enough to put the little man in his place.

Mia sat on the floor playing with a clean white bunny that Nikki'd given her two hours before. It still had the tag on it. Nikki'd handed it over, talking about Easter, which sparked a question-and-answer session that covered both the resurrection of Jesus Christ and the Easter egg hunt. Mia didn't understand the importance of either, but she liked the bunny's soft fur.

"If anything comes up missing, you're paying for it."

Nikki agreed hurriedly and begged him to keep his voice down. "Mommy, we live here now? Where Dee gonna sleep?"

"Shh. Time for bed."

Mia hopped up into the center of the bed and pretended to fall asleep. She'd spent one night in a separate room and apparently that was enough. I wasn't about to fight her on it. Truth was I felt better knowing she was within arm's reach anyway.

"I'm sleep now, Mommy."

"Okay." I lingered at the bedroom door and opened it an inch more. Nikki's bedroom was directly across the hall. The argument had stopped.

"I really sleep now, Mommy. See."

"Mmhmm."

The quiet was a suspicious end to the conflict. That is until I heard the bed creak followed by a long moan. I closed the door and turned my attention to the little girl claiming to be asleep while she jumped up and down on the bed.

"WHAT WILL THE NEIGHBORS SAY? GET HIM OFF MY LAWN! ARE YOU GOING TO SIT ON YOUR HANDS WHILE THEY EMBARRASS ME?"

I was caught off guard by the exchange. Awakened from a deep slumber by the irate little voice that was becoming too familiar.

"I'LL CALL THE POLICE! I WILL!"

I was almost vertical when Nikki slipped into the room. She smiled and stuttered, apologizing if the noise woke me up, then waved me over to the window. Darien stood on the front lawn looking up at us.

"I told him you weren't here, but I don't think he believed me."

Of course, he didn't. She was a terrible liar.

"Do you want me to get rid of him?"

"And by you, you mean Jean-Louis?"

She nodded.

Even if he were high as a kite, Darien would've been too much for her little Napoleon. The angry little man would've been put down in a matter of seconds.

"No, I'll handle it."

"You don't have to. We can call the police. They'll make him go away."

And Darien would've gotten a police record as a parting gift. He wasn't the type to leave easy without having his say.

"No. I've got it."

Nikki watched restlessly as I pulled on a pair of tube socks and reached for the doorknob. "That's it? You're going down there like that?"

I wasn't really big on sleepwear. I wore to bed what most folks considered workout attire. My sister didn't approve. She shed her own robe and handed it to me.

"Our neighbors are a little touchy."

"They've never seen arms and legs before?"

"Mya, please."

I'd made her life hard enough, so I took the robe and hurried downstairs. The little dictator was pacing at the front door. He wanted to issue an order to me, but good sense kept his mouth closed. When I opened the door, Darien was standing on the doorstep.

"What are you doing here?"

"I...I wanna see you—talk to you."

The morning sun fell across my eyes, and he stepped in its path to shade me from it.

"I read your note."

"Good."

"I fucked up."

"Yeah." I crossed my arms against my chest and waited to hear something I didn't already know.

"I slipped. Just once. But I'll get straight. For you. If you come back to me."

"I'm done, Darien."

He understood and chewed his bottom lip as he studied the blades of freshly cut grass that had blown across the stone pathway. "Please, Mya. Forgive me. I need you."

A forgiving wind blew my hair across my face, and I tucked the rebellious strands behind my ear. I'd never struggled with forgiveness. Even when logic told me the grievance was bound to happen again. I forgave anyway. I just didn't forget.

70
JACKIE

THEY ARRIVED WITH A SPRING BOUQUET AND their cheer-up smiles, but that didn't last long. Nikki couldn't possibly relinquish her title as the family wet blanket. She distracted me with talk about God never giving people more than they could handle while Mya sniffed the drink at my bedside. Once Mya had confirmed that it was indeed water and not vodka or some other clear poison, she moved on to studying her surroundings. She hadn't been in my bedroom since before Mia was born. It looked exactly the same, minus a few details.

Mya poked around my dresser then turned to me with a frown. "Where's all your stuff?"

"At Kem's. Mostly. Where's my little nephew?"

"Downstairs with Mama."

"If you move back here, then it'll be just like old times. Mama won't mind."

Mya seemed to think it over, but Nikki interrupted with some jazz about Mama being swamped as it was with her recovering from having cancer and taking care of Nat, the twins, and now me. Not to mention, Mama wanted Aunt Clara to move back up here and everybody knew it was only a matter of time before it happened. Mama simply couldn't handle another three mouths to feed.

"Well, I won't be here that long. Probably be back at Kem's in a few days."

"Oh? And how is Kem?" Nikki's fake smile asked. She stood in the corner folding my laundry. "Are you two getting married finally?"

It was a struggle just to see out of both eyes, so I couldn't roll them the way I wanted, but Mya made that unnecessary anyway.

"Leave her be."

"I'm just saying...milk...cow...free. That's it. That's all I'm gonna say." Nikki lifted the neat pile of pants she'd created and placed them into the second drawer in my dresser.

If Kem had proposed, I probably would've said yes, but I wasn't about to hold my breath. Seemed unlikely that a man who didn't believe in monogamy would want to get married.

"Well? How is he?"

"He's fine."

"That's good," she replied, smiling harder still. "You might want to give some thought to cleaning up your act. Just because your friend does something doesn't mean you have to join in."

Nikki suffered from self-imposed memory loss. When it was convenient, she forgot the most obvious details about people and life just so she could impose her own version. That's how she managed to delude herself into thinking that her own life was so fabulous, and I was the type of chick to do anything because of some man.

"I think you're smart enough to know that," she was saying as she began folding my underwear.

I glanced at Mya and said, "I think she just gave me a compliment."

"None of this would've happened if you made better choices. You're not a kid anymore. Somebody's gotta tell you these things, and if it has to be me then so be it."

"Saint Nikki."

"I'm just looking out for you."

In the most uncharacteristic fashion, Mya sucked her tongue and shook her head just slightly. Nikki was too involved in her advice to notice. Mya was the one with a bottomless well of patience. Even as kids, she had a soft spot for Nikki. Mya could listen as Nikki droned on and on without even an inkling of irritation or agreement. Normally.

"I'm hungry," I announced.

Nikki sighed and glanced at Mya before making a big show of

volunteering to go downstairs. Couldn't be a saint while people starved right in front of her. Once we heard the stairs creak, Mya sat at the edge of my bed and exhaled.

Mya, like me, had been blessed with Mama's figure—shapely and lean—but she wasn't at all aware it seemed. She wore army fatigue pants and a black sweater. It wasn't that she was hiding her body exactly, but she damn sure wasn't trying to present it in the most attractive light. If we'd had a few more years under the same roof, I probably would've been a good influence on her.

"Stop critiquing my clothes."

"What? I'm not..."

She sighed and rolled her eyes. "Terrible liar."

"I am not. I'm a fabulous liar."

She laughed, dropping her head into her chest. Giving me that girl-you-so-crazy look. I didn't mind since it was the first moment in twenty-four hours that I didn't feel like a charity case.

"You...umm...remember what they looked like? The guys that attacked you."

And just like that the moment was over.

"Jackie?" Mya's gaze turned hard. "Tall? Short? Black or white?"

I could've lied. Given a very detailed description of men that didn't exist. Mya wouldn't have known the difference. She was just making conversation.

"Do you remember?"

I didn't. I barely remembered leaving Kem's apartment. The scent of cigarette smoke and sounds of a jukebox whispered to me in my dreams while fuzzy faces and lights danced around me. And then there was the cool night air.

"Were you high?" Mya had a bad habit of asking questions that she already knew the answer to.

"I called Kem a bunch of times, but he's not answering the phone. Mama says he came by last night. It might be nice if somebody I trusted went to check on him."

Mya's chest rose two inches then fell gently as she struggled to find her usual blank expression. But too much was going on in her head. She tilted her head left and right, stretching her neck.

"He didn't do anything wrong. He wasn't even there."

"I know." But the neck exercise continued.

"And I'd never do something just 'cause some guy told me to. Or wanted me to. I do what I want. Just like you. I ain't a puppet."

Mya rose and gulped down the glass of tepid water that Mama had brought me that morning. "Nikki is," my favorite sister finally admitted, "she lets him run her like some kinda servant."

In all our years, Mya hadn't said one bad word about Nikki, but something had changed. Her black eyes seared into mine, giving me chills. It wasn't anger exactly. Anger was hot. Mya's stare was cool as ice. Calculating. And lethal. Somebody else might've been scared by the brutality that threatened to lay itself across my bedspread but not me.

"You wanna kill him? I know where we can hide the body."

Mya was tickled and tempted if I wasn't mistaken. Even so she shook her head and hit me with one undeniable truth. "Nikki would miss him too much."

71
NIKKI

PINK, WHITE, GRAY, AND BLUE WITH FURRY coats and happy expressions, they sat in the darkest corner of my basement tucked against Jean-Louis's tool kit. A bag of stuffed animals. It was probably the child in me that laughed at the sight. The wife in me was finally vindicated. My husband was a good man. He'd taken the time to purchase toys for my sister's kids. I hurried to the washing machine, leaving the load of laundry I had pre-soaked on top of the dryer and seized the bag of toys covered in a thin layer of dust. Nothing for a newborn, but then newborns didn't need toys. I wondered if Mia had even seen a toy before. She was totally enamored by the stuffed bunny I'd given her.

And then a life unfolded before me, a life I thought would never be mine. It suddenly all made sense. Mya was meant to come live with us. A year maybe even two, and then I'd help her find an apartment nearby. The school district was amazing, and Mia and little Alan would grow up with every advantage. Jean-Louis would be the absolute best father figure. Maybe the boy would grow up and want to be a doctor too. Happiness rarely brought tears to my eyes, but standing in the dewy basement of my immaculate home, I let them flow freely.

Mya sat at the kitchen counter, pouring a bowl of cereal for Mia. She hadn't yet adjusted to her new surroundings although she hid that fact from me reasonably well. Never complaining. Never asking for anything and only taking what was offered. Now that Jean-Louis was fully on board, my sister was sure to feel welcomed in my home.

"What?" she asked. "Laundry usually make you this happy?"

"No." Clearly Jean-Louis wanted to be the one to present his gifts, and I would let him. "I'm just a happy person. Happy to have my sister in my kitchen."

Mya gave a silent nod.

"I was thinking...," I began, placing a paper towel in the puddles of milk in front of Mia's bowl. "We could get Mia a toddler bed for the bedroom upstairs, the one facing east. She'll need a little area where she can color and play, have tea parties, and stuff."

Mya's lips remained shut as she studied me, but that didn't deter me.

"And, of course, we'd outfit the smaller bedroom as a nursery for Alan. What colors would you prefer? Blue and white or green and brown? I've seen some very pretty ones in catalogs."

"That's...umm..."

"I don't want you to worry about it. I'll take care of everything."

Mya took a breath and smiled a smile that had little to do with her happiness, but it was a first step.

"Just think about it, okay?"

She nodded.

"Mommy, when we go get Dee?"

"Shh," came Mya's quick reply. "Eat your cereal."

"I save some for Dee."

Further proof that he was no-good for them. My beautiful little niece felt like she needed to deprive herself of nutrition for his sake. He was supposed to be taking care of her, not the other way around! I smiled as the righteous glow of God's grace fell upon me. It wasn't the way I'd planned, but surely he knew best. God had provided. They needed me.

DAVID LETTERMAN WAS INTRODUCING A CELEBRITY I'D never heard of, but I could only devote a fraction of my attention to the television. I scanned the index of my book of daily devotions for a passage that would fit the day I'd had and sank into the clean bedding on my bed. Besides the occasional cry of a baby, the house was quiet. The clock flashed 11:47, marking fifteen hours since I'd laid eyes on my husband. Working such long hours made him terribly tired. When did he have time to go shopping for toys? Didn't matter. As soon as he walked through the door, I was going to spend the rest of the night showing my appreciation.

There was a creak on the stairs, and I looked up in time to see Jean-Louis close the door of our bedroom. His tie hung loosely from his neck as he placed his medical bag by the door.

"You're home. How was your day?"

"It was long."

"Did you eat? Want me to warm you something up?"

"No, no. I'm fine."

Restless, my knees began bouncing beneath the sheets, and I sat my devotional book aside, waiting for him to focus entirely on me. "Honey? Is there anything you want to tell me?"

He mumbled something from inside the walk-in closet that didn't sound like what I was expecting, so I eased out of bed and tiptoed across the carpet.

"Honey?"

He was wearing only his underwear and buttoning his sleepshirt. "Something...about the basement?"

"Did it flood?"

"No."

"Then no, I do not know what you're talking about."

"Something in the basement, maybe? Something sweet and furry?"

"Nicole, what are trying to say?"

"I found the toys!" I couldn't contain it any longer. My cheeks hurt from the smile that had taken over my face. "They're so perfect! She's gonna love them! I love them! And I love you so much!"

He accepted my embrace, caressing my back with his firm precise hands before his mouth found mine. Full of aching and longing, his kiss was deep and brisk, nibbling on my bottom lip. Happy to follow his lead, I backed up toward the bed. Every muscle in my body constricted as the weight of his pinned me to the bed. The volume of the television rose a few decibels with the commercial break. His hands lifted my nightgown, invigorated to find I'd already removed my underwear. Twenty-five minutes of brisk lovemaking later, I exhaled and snuggled next to my husband, studying his face as he drifted off to sleep. It seemed a shame to wake him but I couldn't help myself.

"When are you going to give Mia the toys?"

"What toys?" was his groggy reply.

"The toys in the basement. The stuffed animals in the bag near your tools. I was going to bring them up, but—"

His eyelids flew open. "You did not—"

"No. I thought you probably wanted to do it yourself."

He relaxed onto his side, muttering that we would discuss it in the morning.

Staring at his back I wondered what I'd said wrong. Did he misunderstand? I was happy. I wasn't trying to take over. He bought the gifts, of course, I'd let him do the gift-giving. I just wanted to know when it would happen.

"Is it for Christmas?"

"Go to sleep, Nicole."

"I just wanna know, so I know how much stuff to buy them. I was thinking about getting a new tree, a bigger one. I don't think Mia's ever had a Christmas tree. I know she doesn't have any toys. I don't want to overwhelm her."

But the conversation was over. His breathing slowed and the slight whistle I'd become familiar with breezed from his nostrils. With the aid of the remote control the late-late-night television show disappeared into blackness. I tossed and turned trying to find my own sleep.

When did he have time to go shopping? And why would he hide the toys from me? Keep it secret from me? I could've easily found a space for them in our closet, and Mya and the kids would've been no wiser. A pain seared into my gut and rose to my chest. The stuffed animals weren't for Mia at all.

"I want them to stay here. Permanently." I swallowed hard, staring up at the ceiling, as he stirred next to me. "Jean-Louis?"

"Not this again."

"Yes, this again. She's my sister."

A second later we were face to face. No visages of sleep visible in his features. "You will stop this." His jawline firmed, and my fortunate husband declared the option impossible.

"Who are they for?"

"The toys are for our children. Maybe you've given up but I haven't. I won't."

"I... I never said–

"You don't have to say it. It is obvious." He shot up, his voice following in the same manner. "You'll have to forgive me if I don't accept your sister's bastards as replacements!" He jumped out of bed, fumbling around for his slippers, and said, "This is why I do not want her here! She is a bad influence on you! They all are. Do you think I do not see these things? Do you think I am blind?"

"Please, keep your voice down." I pushed myself up to a sitting position, letting my eyes drift to the closed door leading into the hallway.

"You think I do not see the way she looks at me?"

"She looks at everybody that way."

"YOU ARE A FOOL! SHE HATES ME! HATES YOUR HUSBAND, AND STILL YOU BRING HER INTO OUR HOME!"

"Stop saying that!" Before I knew it, I'd flung off the covers, and I was rounding the bedpost, closing the distance between us. Didn't have an agenda other than to make him be decent, to make him understand how hurtful he was being, but he didn't know that. He'd misunderstood my action. I understood that the split second before his hand made contact across my face.

I gasped, pressing my hand to my cheek. The wetness seemed to spring up out of nowhere, my tears. "YOU HIT ME!"

"I..."

His apology barely got off the ground before the bedroom door was thrown open, and in its place stood a very pissed Morrow girl.

"MYA, DON'T! IT'S OKAY!"

I don't think my sister heard me because she charged at him, both hands jutted out in front of her until she had the collar of his sleepshirt in her grasp. She stood three inches or so higher than him anyway and watching as he struggled to free himself, I immediately understood the shame he must've felt. She released him, and he hit the wall with a thud.

"Don't you ever–"

"Mya, I'm okay," I pleaded with her.

"–put your hands on her again. Ever!" My sister's voice trembled, on the verge of losing control.

Did he know that? Did he know what awaited him on the other side of Mya's self-control? I couldn't see past her to him, but the answer came to me anyway. He couldn't have known. I'd been careful to leave that part out. He wouldn't have believed me anyway. No man would ever take a woman seriously as a physical threat.

"GET OUT! GET OUT MY HOUSE Y-YOU JUNKIE WHORE!"

"Fine by me." Mya threw a glance over her shoulder at me, but I was speechless. Tried to muster up an apology, but the words just piled up in my throat, a sluggish muddy clog in my airway.

"Get out or I call the police!"

She nodded. "You do that. I'll tell them what you did to my sister."

My heart skipped a beat. What he'd done to me? How did she know? When did she...what had he done to me? The carpet fibers rose before me like a wild field, growing until each was as tall as me. He'd struck me. That's what she meant. She would tell the police that he'd struck me. But what would they do? Didn't they have better things to pursue—murderers, rapists, burglars? Couldn't go after every man that struck his wife in a fit of anger.

"Nicole. Tell her to go. Tell her."

Oh, God, no! This isn't the way it's supposed to go! They were my blessing!

Mya's sigh thundered in my ear, and I realized she'd wrapped me in her arms, pressed her warm chest to mine. My sister loved me even though I was failing her.

"M-Mya?"

"It's okay," she whispered in my ear. "I'll call and check on you tomorrow." She turned, glared at my husband, and escaped to the guest room to pack.

72
MYA

"DID HE PUT HIS HANDS ON YOU?"

Mia was snuggled up between the two of us as the bus screeched to a stop. She let loose a yawn, then relaxed into his armpit.

"Mya, tell me if he did, and I'll—"

"You'll what?" I snapped at him. I'd reached a new level of pissed off. First him and his bad habits, then Nikki's little troll, and now he was insinuating I couldn't take care of myself. Didn't he know me at all? Well, Nikki's husband knew. If he ain't know before, he knew now. Nobody fucks with the Morrow girls. He oughta be grateful it was just me. If Jackie had been there, we'd have his ass buried in the backyard by now.

"I missed you, you know," Darien confessed to my reflection in the window. "You miss me?"

I didn't. Having him to come rescue us from Nikki's didn't mean I was ready to fall back into the normal rhythm of things. I just needed an extra set of hands to carry stuff.

"It'll be different this time. I promise. People at the school talking about giving me a promotion to head custodian. Means benefits and steady money. Okay? You can go get your GED like we always talked about. Go on to college even."

Nikki went to college. One full year. Jackie was in college now, didn't know how much time she actually spent at the place. One of us should actually do the thing right. Maybe it would be Natalie.

"Mya?"

"I heard you."

"You know you could do it. As smart as you are."

"College costs money."

"I'll pay for it." His eyes glistened proudly.

A good girlfriend would've accepted the offer without any hesitation. She'd smile and swoon and lace him with robust platitudes of gratitude, instead of recalling the broken promises that littered the past.

"Mya, let me make it up to you. Okay? I know you're pissed, but just give me a chance, and I'll make it better."

He wasn't a bad person. There were yards between Nikki's little demon and Darien, but still a tiny voice in my head accused me of turning into my sister. After all, I could've left Darien years ago, but I'd stayed. I knew what was in his heart. Knew the man that he was fighting so hard to become. And he deserved it. After everything he deserved to have folks look upon him with respect instead of shooing him away or looking right through him as if he didn't exist. Mia, Alan, and I might've been the only proof that he'd returned from the war a full-fledged human being.

"What are you thinking?" he asked, just as the baby bristled a bit against my chest.

The bus rocked side to side, picking up speed as the early morning traffic parted. Probably should've lied. Told him I was thinking about getting back to Lakeview Terrace in time for him to make it to school. Told him I was thinking about checking on Mama. Or any number of plausible answers. But I stayed quiet.

THIS TIME WILL BE DIFFERENT, HE SAID again with unworthiness burned into his retinas. The blood-red circles and their miniscule spidery veins pulsated with each breath he took. Begging. On his knees, he pleaded with me to believe him. This time would be different. He loved me. He'd die for me. He would stay straight for me.

Never seen a man cry until the mysterious soldier boy. On the outside he was old and crusty and more than a little musty, but his insides were sweet as jam. The kind of sweetness that made me believe in everything that wasn't in me. Tears and hugs and coy kisses with come-hither-stares. They'd never been me, and he didn't mind. All he asked was that I loved him.

He'd dropped to the floor the second we entered the room. "Mya, I swear...," he was mumbling. His arms stretched out as if to offer himself to a spiteful god. "Never again. Never, never, ever again."

I nodded. "All right. Get up."

"I can't live without you and the kids."

I nodded again but turned to the starry sky outside our window before his hands touched me. It'd been broken since the day we moved into room 222 at Lakeview Terrace, a motel with neither a view nor a lake.

"I'm gonna get us outta here. I swear. A real nice place."

"Nice places require security deposits."

I heaved my duffel bag onto the bed that we were to share and set my mind to unpacking.

Nobody would understand why I went back to this man who only made my life infinitely more complicated, but he'd made significant progress. Holding down a full-time job was a major accomplishment. I think it helped that it was at a school. Being around kids helped him beat back his demons.

"Let me help you."

"Don't need any help." I laid the stack of clean clothes in the first drawer on top of a clean towel. He sank into the foot of the bed, watching as I carried stacks of sweaters, baby onesies, and underwear, then tucked rolls of socks in the spaces between them.

"How you get all that into one drawer is beyond me. Sure you wasn't in the service?"

"We go sleep now?" Mia sat up on the bed next to us rubbing her eyes. She yawned and reached blindly for whoever was closest. Wrapped her arms around his neck and rested her head on his shoulder as he whispered sweet nothings in her ear.

No one would understand why I did what I did unless they'd seen the two of them together. He loved her so intensely that DNA didn't matter. Protected her before she was even born. Fed her out of the goodness of his heart. I wasn't the sort to believe in fairy tales, but because of him, my daughter did.

She stretched out on the bed next to her brother, eyelids closed, breathing steady, dreaming of the day to come.

"She's down."

"I see that."

"Mya, please...look at me. At least look at me. You're here, but you're not here. I know you're mad, and I can take that. I deserve it. I just gotta know that you still love me."

I'd left my sister's house with less than I'd brought there. I spun the duffel bag around searching each compartment for a diaper or two that might've made the return trip.

"Mya."

"I love you."

"You're just saying that."

"No." I exhaled and paused long enough for him to feel my eyes on his. "I do. But I'm tired of this. You are better...than this..."

Seconds later his arms were around me, pulling me into his promises of a better life. He withdrew slowly before he was ready because he knew I wasn't ready for physical contact. Eased out of the dark green jacket he'd worn every day since his discharge, folded it neatly, and placed it on the dresser with the patch that read Lt. Allen facing up.

"We're outta diapers."

"I'll go get some." He reached for his jacket.

"No. I'll do it."

"Mya, I can get diapers. I'm not gonna fuck that up. You should lie down and get some sleep. He'll be up soon, you know."

I did know. Couldn't help but know. My milk was fighting for more room in my ever-expanding chest. But still..."I said I'll go."

Last time he went out for diapers, he didn't come back for three hours. And he'd forgotten all about the diapers.

"Mya—"

"I'll go and be right back. Ten minutes."

73
JACKIE

THE POLICE SAID I WAS FOUND IN the bushes, my upper body hidden by the many branches and leaves. When they pulled me out, it was clear my face had taken quite a beating although nothing was broken. Just bruised. A rib. My cheekbone. My pride. I stood at the spot, remembering all that I could about the moments leading up to it. Ten feet ahead and around the corner stood Kem's apartment building. Three blocks behind me, the bar. Across the street was a currency exchange. I'd never paid any attention to it before. I'd followed Kem down there once, keeping him company while he paid his electricity bill but didn't remember a thing about the place.

Hiding behind a pair of sunglasses, my hair pulled back into a bun, I barely looked like me. Didn't help any that under my leather coat I was wearing one of Heziah's favorite dress shirts, the one with a white-and-black pattern of suits—clubs, hearts, spades—hanging loose over a pair of blue jeans. I'd been an easy mark. Hard to admit, but it was the truth. It wouldn't happen again, that much I was sure of because I would find them. Whoever they were, wherever they lived, I'd search them out. I waited for a break in the traffic, then crossed the street.

At four o'clock in the afternoon, it was only servicing a handful of customers. The vending machines in the corner offered up blow-pops, stickers, and gumballs sprinkled with a sugary replica of confetti, all for a quarter. Something to keep the kiddies busy while their mothers took care of business probably. An older gentleman tucked his wallet into his back pocket and nodded in my direction as he slipped out the front door. The windows framing the door looked out onto the street but were covered in a thin bluish plastic that was hell to see through. I sighed. Possibility number one down the drain.

Kem's neighbor heard a scuffle, a woman's screams, and dialed 911. She hadn't seen a thing. Apparently, no one had since the cops had yet to arrest anyone.

I had only one idea left. A drunk girl gets robbed as she walks down the street, it wasn't a crime that screamed premeditation or conspiracy. I'd simply been an opportunity that presented itself. In the right place at the right time. Perhaps they had been walking down the opposite side of the street and caught sight of little old me. Maybe they'd been present in the blurry crowd from the bar, leering from some dark corner and following as I left. Or just maybe they'd been cashing a check or paying a bill...

"Next. Ma'am?" The clerk beckoned me forward. "Can I help you?" He asked, clearly bored out of his mind.

"Yes. I'd like to see your security footage from last Friday. Please." I tacked on a smile as if it were a perfectly legitimate request.

"Umm...I don't think..."

"Well, maybe you didn't hear. A very nice, very attractive young lady was attacked just across the street, and she comes from a very important family, if you catch my drift."

He did but didn't yet know what to make of the information.

"They've hired me to look into the matter. And I'm sure they'd be very grateful when I tell them how helpful you..." I stole a quick peek at his nametag. "Ben Milford...how helpful you've been. Could even be a reward in it for you."

"A reward?"

"Yup. And why not? Without good Samaritans such as yourself, justice would be deaf, dumb, and blind. Don't you think?"

MOST CUSTOMERS STOOD PATIENTLY IN LINE WAITING to do their business, only two stood out. Two men no older than twenty-five, one black the other white or Hispanic, the video wasn't of the best quality. They came in, engrossed in their own conversation, lingered in a corner observing the long line of customers. The time stamp in the bottom right corner read 5:36. After work must've been the busiest time of day.

I eased to the edge of Kem's futon, both arms wrapped around my waist, waiting for one or both of the men to turn and give me a good view of their faces. It never happened. Or if it did, I wasn't paying attention.

A key rattled, and the front door swung open. My lover's face flashed surprise and then affection at seeing me in his living room.

"Hi."

"I didn't know you were here. When did you get here?" He was sitting by my side in seconds, leaving the door wide open. "Oh, mami."

The collar of his jacket brushed against my cheek, damp and smelling of his crisp woodsy aftershave as he embraced me. It was all I could do not to succumb to the warmth of his touch. It was all I wanted, all I could think about, even if I had forbidden myself from acknowledging it. I had other, more pressing, matters to attend to, so I kept my breaths short and focused on the door as it moved ever so slightly with the breeze. Why'd he leave it open? What if someone had left the door to the building open? That would explain the wind. Anyone could walk up the steps and into the apartment. Anyone.

He gazed after me, not bothering to hide the rejection he felt as I turned the locks and set the chain in place.

Mya had come by to check on him for me. She said he hadn't been home. I didn't want to think about where he'd been but couldn't help it as he gazed up at my sunglasses.

"How are you, mami?"

"Fine. You?"

He didn't have an answer for me. Instead he tugged at the rubberband stretched across his wrist, snapping it against his skin. If I'd followed my first mind, I would've descended upon him and freed him from the rhythm of tension and pain, kissed him until he knew none of this was his fault. But I stood frozen like the video on the television screen, unsure of whether that instinct was something to trust or hold at bay.

"You look good," I said.

"I want you to tell me everything that happened."

"I went to the bar for drinks. Got robbed on the way back."

He glared at the floor then at me as if I were keeping a secret. "I do not—I can handle it. Tell me...the truth."

"That is the truth."

"Did they..."

"They took the few dollars I had. That's it."

He sprung up defiantly, closed the space between us with slow cautious steps, and removed my sunglasses. Once he'd satisfied himself that I was indeed telling the whole truth, Kem's mouth fed hungrily on mine. He'd missed me more than I expected or maybe he was just grateful that I wasn't dead. In either case, he left me breathless and aroused as he knelt before me and took my hand in his.

"I will never love another woman as I love you. You are my heart and soul. Marry me?"

Oh, no. No. No. No! Damn it!

"Mami? Say something."

Now everything was ruined. Those idiots ruined it. Had I dreamed of Kem proposing one day? Yeah, but not like this. Not because he felt guilty.

"I...I really am fine. You don't...you don't have to do this. I'm okay."

"I do have to do this."

"No, Kem—"

"I do it because it is true. It is what's in my heart. Loving you, taking care of you is all that I want for the rest of my life."

"What about—"

"I only want you. No one else. What do you say, mami? Will you let me love you?"

Nikki crossed my mind. Never thought I'd ever think she was right about something, but apparently I was the marrying kind.

MYA

THE DEAD OF NIGHT SURROUNDING LAKEVIEW TERRACE held just as many quirks as any other time of day. A woman whose clothes were more off than on cackled from the doorway of her room on the first floor, stopping suddenly as I walked past. A dog made his way across the concrete lot and plopped down before a door that I assumed led to his owner. But no one argued. No one screamed. No one stopped to gaze at the sky either. They lounged about, crowded in rooms with open doors or around trashcans with flaming centers.

The tension seizing my chest reminded me that I was on the clock, so I increased my pace.

At the fullest stage of pregnancy, I'd wrapped myself in a wool cape but was happy to shed it for the moment. Happy also to have my own feet not the monstrous things that had grown so large I had to wear the soldier boy's boots. Bit by bit, I was adjusting myself to life in my original body. Another month or two, and I'd be back to my normal size.

Mia said she liked the soft me, but she was just a child. Thoughts of her fawning over her baby brother brought a smile to my face, and I flipped the hood on my sweatshirt up, tightening the strings to block the cold from assaulting my ears. She'd begged me enough for a baby sister that I thought she'd start roaring when I told her he was a boy. Although in fairness I wasn't sure she understood that there was a difference.

Nikki had taken one look at my baby and bit back bitter tears. She meant well. She was the natural between us. She'd been practicing for the mothering role for some twenty-odd years, but her time hadn't come yet. And Jackie was disappointed. She had been positive I was having a girl. She called herself, ensuring that by performing some ritual she'd heard about involving a string and a piece of jewelry. Well, we had Mia. If Jackie wanted another girl, she could have one herself 'cause nothing else was coming out of me.

I hurried across the street to the convenience store. The lights were ablaze despite the late hour.

"Well, hello, my friend! Cold?" Arif Abu was a rotund man with a very detailed memory. He managed to remember all of his customers, their names, and most purchased items. He chuckled as I shivered and let the heat of his store penetrate my cold bones. "Let me guess. Milk and diapers."

I nodded.

"Where is Darien?" he asked, pointing to the middle aisle where he kept the diapers.

"With the kids."

"I would not let my wife go out at this time of night."

"Yeah, well, I'm not his wife," I replied, studying the various brands and sizes.

"I do not understand you women today. In my day, there was none of this having children before marriage, but you think you can do everything."

I decided on the cheapest brand in size one and headed to the back of the store for a quart of milk. He continued the conversation even though I was only half paying attention. He wondered if it was a cultural thing or an age thing.

"My sweet mother once said—" But he didn't finish that sentence. The bells over the door rang as it opened then closed with a swoosh.

Whole milk or reduced-fat? White or chocolate? Mia had been a good girl as of late. She deserved a treat.

"Move it, old man! Every fuckin' penny!"

"Why do you do this? I am not rich!"

Clutching the cold container in one hand and the package of diapers under my arm, I dropped to the floor in a squat. He hadn't seen me.

"Where are you going? You have what you want! Leave! Leave now!"

"Shut up! or I'll blow you back to Fuck-istan!"

"Nothing back there!"

But his footsteps continued down the right aisle toward the freezer section. Inch by inch, I moved into the far left aisle, praying he was too drunk or high to check the reflection of the mirror positioned in the corner of the ceiling.

The knock-knock rattling of a tiny piece inside an aluminum can filled the space between us. The diaper package began to squirm under my arm, and I held my breath, waiting to find out if he'd heard it.

Maybe he wasn't armed. But then why would Arif give him money? He had to be armed.

The sound of an aerosol spray interrupted my thoughts, and I finally understood what the thief was doing at the freezer section.

Arif had come out from behind the counter, enraged. Money was one thing, but he couldn't stand by and let this fool denigrate his store. It was foolish, his pride, but it was also my opening. A distraction. If I stayed low, I could slip past all three aisles and out the door. I took another breath to steady myself. I would do it. It was the smart move. I bounced on the balls of my feet, preparing mentally for my flight, took the first step, and then...

Bang. The gun exploded. Once. Twice more. An oomph hit the floor, sounding like a sack of flour. And then the spray can continued.

Move, Mya. Go. Get out.

But it was no use. My feet didn't work. My legs wouldn't respond. Was I even breathing? Yes. My chest rose and fell. Therefore, I was breathing. I was alive.

The bells over the door let out a delicate melody as the familiar swoosh cut off the wintery winds determined to enter the store. A dark red substance slowly trickled across the grout lines in the floor, searching out safety. Arif!

The diapers fell into the path of the blood, the milk quickly forgotten as I ran to the center aisle. His chest had exploded, but he was still alive, reaching for me and pointing at his wounds. I needed something to stop the blood.

"It's okay. He's gone. It's okay." I heard my own voice.

So much blood. Soaking into my jeans now, oozing through my fingers. I needed something!

"Don't go. Don't leave me." His fingers latched on to my wrist.

"It's okay. I'm gonna stop the bleeding. Then I've gotta call somebody."

Blood gurgled in his throat, distorting his words, but it didn't matter. It was clear. He didn't want to die alone.

I tried to envision where the telephone was. I couldn't afford to waste a minute looking for it. But then I heard the sirens. Eight, maybe six, blocks away. It was going to be okay. Someone heard the shots. Help was coming. I smiled at him. It was going to be okay. He'd have a scar or two. Darien and I would visit him in the hospital and joke about how tough the old man was. Everything was going to...

The gurgles came faster, louder, the flow of blood stopped. His head fell to one side.

Do something, Mya!

Left hand over right, I pressed down into his chest....Where did I learn that? Again. Again.

The sirens were getting closer. No free lunch, I heard my daddy say. Folks don't owe you a damn thing, he'd said.

They'd want to question me. The police. There would be forms to be filled out. Address? Telephone number? I was covered in blood with five bucks in my back pocket. They weren't gonna take my word for anything. They'd be at Lakeview Terrace, poking around and asking questions, before I could say Mya Ann Morrow. Wouldn't take them long to put it together. Hookers. Drugs. Felonies and misdemeanors. I was one of them—guilty by association.

The sirens were blaring on top of us now, but I knew the layout of the store. Trembling, I ducked under the counter, squeezed down the corridor and leaned full force on the back door. I broke into the night with only one thing on my mind. Soldier boy. The kids. Our family didn't work without me. I was the glue.

A blinding white light cut through the night and car doors slammed left and right.

"FREEZE! DON'T MOVE!"

"HANDS ON YOUR HEAD!"

75
NIKKI

"The trick is to even it out with a tad of concealer, not too much." Darlene tended to my cheek with expert strokes. Cosmetics were her only worldly sin although to look at her you wouldn't know it. "There. Good as new."

My complexion had improved so much no one would know. I looked younger, happier, nothing like myself. I wondered if Jean-Louis would find the new me attractive, then quickly banished the thought.

"What's wrong? You don't like it?"

"No, I do. Thank you."

Darlene returned her chosen tools to their rightful places in her kit and began tending to the unseen wounds. "Every marriage has its challenges."

"The reverend ever hit you?"

She paused briefly and zipped the small pink bag. "No. But that doesn't mean we haven't faced our own demons. You know what you need to do. Give it up to Jesus. Nothing is impossible for him. Ask him for the strength to forgive and to save your marriage." She shuffled around the bedroom tiding up as she went, leaving me to stare at my brand-new reflection.

Each of my sisters looked like Mama, but I never did, not to me at least. I was always rounder in all the wrong places. Flat, squarish even, in some places, but I had Mama's eyes. And I had her voice in my head. Mama ain't believe in forgiveness.

"You pray on it last night?"

"Yes, ma'am."

"Good. Now that you've had a chance to rest and think on it, everything gonna work out just fine."

It was her way of telling me I needed to go back to my husband. Couldn't be a married woman living under somebody else's roof, especially the reverend's. His congregation was always coming by for one reason or another. They would start asking questions.

"I'm not sure I can go back." I turned away from my reflection to face her. "I know I should, but..."

She nodded. "Being a good Christian ain't the easiest thing in the world. I know you know that. Lots of people have taken the easy way out. Foresaking their vows, the commitment they made before God to love, honor, and cherish through the good and the bad." She knelt at the foot of the bed, tucking in the sheets before draping the blanket on top. Now the bed looked good as new just like my face. "You talked to him?"

I hadn't. He'd sent flowers. Written a short plea on the card for my return, but I hadn't responded. Truth was I was so glad the flowers came to the right place. Last thing I wanted was Mama to find out. I guess he knew me well enough to know I wouldn't have gone there. Couldn't help wondering though...maybe she knew anyway. Didn't think Mya would tell her, but at times Mama didn't need to be told anything. It was that special power she had that came from having six of us. She always seemed to know when one of us was in trouble.

Darlene opened the drawer to the nightstand and moved the Bible from inside it to the center of the bed. Our eyes met, and she slipped out of the room, leaving me alone with my conscience.

76
PECAN

WELL, GOOD MORNING, MRS. JENKINS. MR. JENKINS." The man in the white coat breezed by us, settling into his desk and thumbing through a stack of files for the one with my name on it. "Test results are in." He scanned the first page, then the second.

Heziah squeezed my hand, nearly crushing my fingers.

"Looks good."

It was the same comment he made last month. Then in the very next breath said he wanted to test me again in thirty days to make sure the cancer was really gone.

"Yup. White blood cell count looks good. Lymph nodes look good." He smiled. "Mrs. Jenkins, I think we can say that you're in remission."

"The cancer? It's gone?" Heziah broke into a grin, clapped his hands, and nearly jumped across the desk to shake the man's hand. "Thank you! Thank you, Dr. Seers! Baby, you hear that? It's gone! Belinda?"

A gasp broke free from my chest, and I swear the air never tasted so sweet.

"Come on, sweetheart. Let's get out of here." Heziah was giddy as a chile. Pulling me into the elevator, ignoring everybody else while he doted on me with kisses. "I'm gonna take you away. A vacation. Just you and me."

"We can't afford a vacation."

But he'd already moved on to making a list of all the places we could go. I smiled, intertwined my fingers into his, and followed him through the crowded lobby. We'd have to tell the girls. Was nice to have some good news for once. My girls needed something concrete to point to as proof that the world wasn't such a bad place. Now they had it. We had it. I was still young, had plenty of years ahead of me. I'd get to see them graduate, get married to good men, and have families of their own. Be a grandma. A great-grandma! I laughed.

"You like that one, huh? Lake Geneva's nice. Been there once before. We can go fishing and horseback riding..."

"Whatever you want." I slipped on my mittens and fumbled with Heziah's coat's zipper. "I don't care."

"Belinda?"

"Yeah."

"I..." My Heziah was doing battle with his tears. He was a good man. Done everything right and was still faced with losing me. But now he was free of all that worry. His face tilted down toward mine, brushing his nose against mine.

"Let's go home."

Soon as I said it, I knew what I had to do. Wouldn't be no home if it wasn't for Clara. She'd saved me. Loved me. Brought out the mama in me. And now that I was going to be around for a while, I would do right by her.

WASN'T RIGHT KEEPING GOOD NEWS A SECRET, so Heziah and me told the very first folks we set eyes on. Nat and the twins. They couldn't contain their excitement and set about putting together a party. Leaving messages all over town for their sisters, popping popcorn, slicing up fruit. We managed to scrounge up a few chocolate bars and split them up between the five of us. For our part, Heziah and I figured they could have a nice supper with vegetables tomorrow. Today was for celebrating.

"Mama, it's Nikki! Can I tell her?"

I took the phone from Jenna just in time. She hadn't quite mastered the art of surprises. "Hi, baby."

Proved me right. Good news was badly needed. Nikki got a whiff of it and automatically assumed something bad was about to happen. So I told her flat out.

"Doctor say they got all the cancer. Yup. All gone. Your auntie Helen gonna be over in a little while. We celebrating. So, you bring yourself on home soon as you can, all right? Baby?"

She was so happy, she was crying.

I laughed for the second time that day. "And if you talk to your sisters–Mya? No, I ain't heard from her, but if you do go ahead and tell her the news. Tell her I wanna see her. Jackie too. Okay, baby. See you soon."

11 MYA

IT WAS A MISUNDERSTANDING—A DRAWN-OUT, ONE-FOR-THE-RECORD-BOOKS MISUNDERSTANDING, so I explained it all again. The metal cuffs had begun to weigh heavily on my wrists, but if I kept them at a 30-degree angle, they didn't bite at my skin.

"So, Jane Doe...you expect us to believe you were present at the scene of a robbery homicide, but you didn't see anything, didn't do anything, and you just had to run out the back door?"

They didn't like me. After six hours of interrogation, the tag team of detectives had made that abundantly clear. They didn't bother with the good cop/bad cop dichotomy. Their distaste for me was equal. At first I thought that was their act. That they expected me to try to win them over, expected me to be one of those girls that couldn't stand for someone to dislike them.

"Yes."

"Yes, what?"

"Yes, that's what happened."

"And where did the blood come from again?"

The blood. I closed my eyes but I could still see the dark red mass spreading from his body. Feel the warm stickiness seeping into my jeans and coursing through my fingers. His life was in my hands. Should I have done CPR sooner? Faster?

"Arif."

"So, you knew the victim?"

"I guess."

How much did anybody know anybody else? I knew him enough to speak to him. He knew me enough to ask about Darien and Mia. And if I was a few pennies or even a dollar short, I'd come to expect that he'd forgive it.

"The cash register was empty. Where did you hide the money?"

"I didn't. I told you. It wasn't me."

"That's right," his partner chimed in, chuckling. "She was only there to get diapers. She's innocent. You must think we're a couple of simpletons, huh?"

Was I supposed to deny that? Claim that they were some Rhodes scholars or something?

"Look at her. She thinks she's smarter than us."

"Hey, missy." The fat one waved his thumb back and forth, indicating himself and his partner. "We ain't the ones living on the street, begging for hard-working people's spare change."

"I don't beg."

"She doesn't beg," the funny one mocked me. "What you do then? Stand on a corner?" He knelt, so he could see me sweat. "What do you do for those crumbled up sticky dollar bills?"

The metal nipped at my wrists reminding me to keep the anger under wraps. They couldn't keep this up forever. I'd stick to my story and they'd have to let me go. Then they'd better hope we never ran into each other in a dark alley.

"If we run your description by vice, any chance something interesting might come up?"

"That's why she won't give us her name because she's gotta long list of priors. Ain't that right, sweetheart?"

They paced in opposite directions, a choreographed routine they knew well, and waited for me to give an inch.

"We have you sneaking out the back door soaked in his blood."

"Maybe she had a crisis of conscience. Her boyfriend or pimp or whoever did the shooting, left her there to take the rap. That what happened?"

"Did he take the money with him?"

"Yes." I exhaled hard, my skin tingling from the effort the word drew from my body.

"Now we're getting somewhere." The shorter detective pulled up a chair and sat down, looking at me anew. "Where can we find him? What's his name?"

"I told you. I don't know him."

"She ain't gonna give him up. Are you?"

"She'll give him up if she knows what's good for her."

"We're running your prints right now. We're gonna find out who you are, your last known address, any known acquaintances...you might as well give it up now."

They ain't know I'd spent my whole life practicing for this moment. I could hold my tongue. I could keep a secret. I could be quiet as a mouse. I'd never played poker a day in my life, but I had the face for it.

"See. Told you. She's not gonna give him up."

"Guess she's not as smart as she thinks she is. Let's throw her in lockup. Maybe that'll change her mind."

"I get a phone call."

"You not even here! I mean, not like we gotta name to process. So you, princess, ain't owed a damn thing."

"Besides, you just wanna warn your boyfriend anyway. He left you behind. Sure you wanna keep protecting him?"

The he they were talking about didn't exist, but try as I might, I couldn't think of one piece of evidence of that fact. Not one solid fact that proved my story. All of which was secondary to my real concern. Soldier boy. One look at him, and it wouldn't take much for these two geniuses to convince themselves that he was the real thief, the real murderer.

"Stand up. Down to the tombs you go."

"Wait. There's a security camera. In the store. Check the tape. You'll see for yourself."

The twosome glanced at each other. Then one opened the door while the other led me to it.

"No tape. Security system been down for a few months according to the victim's family. Contrary to what you might think, Miss Doe, this ain't our first rodeo."

78

JACKIE

THE FLIGHT ATTENDANT WAS ASKING EVERYONE TO return to their seats for the landing. Her comrades were patrolling the aisles collecting trash. So it was the perfect opportunity to relieve the unattended cart of a few bottles. I eased out of the cramped restroom and discretely palmed two of the pocket-sized glass bottles before returning to my seat in coach.

"Look what I found."

Kem shook his head in mock disapproval.

"What? Clearly I'm terrified of flying. I need this."

"And me? What is my excuse for drinking at ten o'clock in the morning?"

"You're celebrating your impending marriage to a remarkable woman." I grinned and handed him the wee bottle of Champagne.

We'd taken the first flight to Las Vegas without a second thought. Maxed out his credit card on the reservations and had only one bag between the two of us. Kem insisted that we only needed swimwear to begin with because we would spend the first hours as husband and wife as God had intended. Naked and sublimely happy.

"So? Elvis?" I covered my mouth to hide the belch I'd been fighting for the last hour.

"They have chapels. We will pick one of them. A man in a suit will marry us with elevator music in the background."

"I want Elvis!"

"No Elvis!"

"Why do you hate Elvis?" I collapsed into a fit of giggles. "Or Big Bird! I want Big Bird!"

"That's it. I cannot marry you."

"Okay, fine. Have it your way, Delgado. Boring man in a suit with watered-down jazz in the background. But just so we're clear, I'm telling my grandkids that I wanted Elvis, but you were a big old fuddy-duddy."

The landing was bumpy even by a veteran flier's standards, but I barely noticed. Couldn't get enough of the man who'd stolen my heart. His lips, supple one minute, passionate the next. His smoldering stare setting my body on fire. No girl had ever been luckier.

"Don't look," whispered the irate mom of two as she shepherded her little ones into the ladies' room. Shame on you! was truly what she was saying to us.

Kem's chuckles interrupted the rhythm of our kisses, and my fingers slowly began to withdraw from his back. Wasn't like we were naked, humping each other against the wall. It was just a little kiss.

"Okay, I really have to go now," I added, wiggling as I pulled out of the embrace.

"One more minute."

"No! Kem! I gotta go!"

Damn man. All he had to do was whip it out. I had to pray there wasn't a line. That the toilets were all functioning. That there was enough toilet paper. And then do the get out of my panties dance. Taking flight on my tippy-toes, I darted into the terminal's restroom and locked myself in the first available stall, grinning like a madwoman at the floor. Had I ever been this happy? Maybe once as a child. A warm spring day that held nothing but imaginative play with my sisters. One of those rare moments where the real world fell away, leaving only what we could dream up.

"How do you do?" Upon my exit I nodded to the middle-aged prude standing at the sinks with a boy and girl. Wasn't in me to hold anything against her. In fact, I pitied her. Poor woman didn't know what it was like to be on the verge of the happiest day of her life. Washed my hands, shook the water off, and went in search of paper towels. Was then that I caught a glimpse of myself in the mirror. How could I have forgotten? I hadn't even bothered to cover the bruise with makeup. And Kem wouldn't let me hide behind my sunglasses, kept insisting that he wanted to see my eyes.

He loved my eyes. Well, at least that explained the looks we kept getting. People thought I was fawning all over a man that had hit me.

"Ready, mami?"

I nodded, taking the sunglasses from the side pocket on our bag. We stepped out in perfect time to catch the desert's sunset. Ripe and brilliant, the hues of red and orange stretched across the horizon.

"Have you ever seen anything so beautiful?"

"Yes," he whispered, brushing his hand against my shoulder until the strap of my tank top fell exposing inches of skin.

"Let's get a cab." His bicep flexed against my chest as he shifted the bag from his left to right hand. His fingers settling underneath my bosom.

"Kem." I tried again, but he just moaned in reply, words were too much work.

Sounds were all he could manage.

"There's one." I waved it down, dragging him along. But once inside what little self-control we had evaporated. I'd never seen him so publicly affectionate and never been so grateful to be wearing jeans as I playfully fended off his advances.

"I want to touch you." He seized the bottom of my tank. "I want to touch...my wife."

"But I'm not—" My body shuddered as his attentions infiltrated my brassiere, and I gave up the pointless resistance, instead pulling his body on top of mine.

We arrived at the hotel fifteen minutes later, flushed and moist. My breasts, which had been exposed in the cab, were now covered, but when the air conditioning hit the recently suckled skin, I felt like sex walking. Didn't help that Kem was enjoying every step I took, staring at the puckered knots that stood out so proudly.

"Cold?"

"Shut up." I made a move to search the bag for a jacket but lying on top was the bra I'd happily discarded in favor of fifteen minutes of pleasure. I blushed instead.

"Here. Let me hold you."

We stepped into the check-in line with Kem facing the clerk and me pressed against him.

"Well, you're happy."

"Si, mami. Never been happier. Tonight will be the happiest night of my life."

"Tonight? You don't want to wait until tomorrow?"

"I cannot wait. The next time I make love to you, you have to be my wife. And for that I cannot wait much longer."

"Or what? You'll turn to dust?" I was clearly joking, but Kem didn't look amused. Must've been the altar boy in him. We'd hit our threshold of premarital sex, and there was no going back. The line moved along until we were next, and I realized what was coming. They would want to know whom they were renting a room to—mister and missus or a mister and a miss. Could it really be that big of a difference?

"Good evening, sir. Do you have a reservation?"

"Delgado."

"And how long will you two be staying with us, Mr. Delgado?"

"Just one night."

"I see." She smirked. "Will one key be sufficient?"

"Yes."

"Two," I corrected him. Wasn't that I planned on going anywhere without him, but the helpful little clerk with all her assumptions needed to be put in her place. I wasn't his one-night stand or worse. "And can you recommend a chapel nearby? Please. My fiancé and I would really appreciate it."

With room keys tucked in our pockets and a map of the strip unfolded before me, Kem and I made our way to the elevators. The doors closed quietly, and he pressed the button labeled 5.

"You did not like her."

"I didn't like what she was implying." I replied, scanning the map for the intersection nearest the hotel.

"What was she implying?" Kem frowned, watching the numbers flash over the doors.

"That I'm a slut."

"I don't think she was implying that. Why would she think that?"

"It's just how women are."

The elevator chimed, doors parted, and off we went in search of room 522.

79
NIKKI

"WHAT BRINGS YOU BOTH HERE TODAY?"

Despite the fact that Dr. Abbott came highly recommended and that she passed Jean-Louis's personal screening, he didn't appear at all relieved to be sitting across from her.

"Nikki? Why don't you start?"

"I-I've been staying with my foster parents the last two days. Because he and I had a fight. But we...umm...we want to work it out."

"Jean-Louis. Can you tell me what the fight was about?"

"I try to be a good husband to her, but nothing I do is good enough. Her family hates me, and they are trying to turn her against me."

"That's not true!"

"They do not hate me? Her sister attacked me! In my home, she attacked me!"

I don't know what bothered me more that he wanted to make it all about my family or that he was forcing me to fill in all the gory details.

"Is this true, Nikki?" Dr. Abbott studied me over the rim of her glasses.

"Technically. But..."

"Yes?" She prodded.

"Mya was only protecting me."

"She burst into our bedroom! Threw me against the wall! She's homeless, you know." He shook his head in disbelief. "It is a sad story, I admit. This is why I let her stay in our guest room, but—"

"She didn't do anything wrong. She was just protecting me. That's how my sister is." Couldn't help glaring at the man I'd married. If he said one more word that was more false than true, I was gonna scream. "He's the one that owes her an apology. And...and me too. He hit me. That's why Mya came bursting in..."

I watched as Dr. Abott's demeanor changed. The reservation melted, her features softened, she glanced from him to me and down at her notebook. "I see," she replied to buy herself some time to find the objectivity that her profession required. "Is this the first time that you've hit your wife?"

"It was a mistake. I do not hit my wife."

"Except for this one time? Correct?"

"She can tell you. I do not hit her. I have never hit her."

"Except for this time."

"Yes." He shifted against the love seat's cushions, uncrossing then recrossing his legs. "It was a difficult night."

"Well, it's good that you both have decided to engage in couple's therapy."

"Can you help us? Help us save our marriage? I don't believe in divorce. My parents got divorced, and I don't want that for us."

"What do you want, Nikki?"

"I just want him to love me, so we can be happy."

"And Jean-Louis?"

"All I want is for my wife to be happy."

She nodded, walked to her desk, and returned with a planner. "Then let's schedule your next appointment."

SILENCE FILLED THE CAR ON THE RIDE home. I had been right to tell Dr. Abbott the truth, but I couldn't deny the morsel of guilt that had wedged itself into my moment of common sense. Her job was to help us. She couldn't do her job if she didn't have all the facts. I gazed at my husband wondering if he was going to hold a grudge against me. I didn't wanna turn into Mama.

Everything I'd done had been in effort to not be Mama. I doubted Mama had ever really loved Daddy, and she wasn't the follow-my-heart type of woman. But I had. I'd followed my heart. Followed my faith. And they both led me to Jean-Louis.

"Honey?" My fingers softly caressed his hand as he changed gears. "What did you think of the doctor?"

"If you like her, then I am happy."

I nodded. He was happy that I was returning home. He'd missed me like I missed him.

80
JACKIE

"WELCOME HOME, MRS. DELGADO." KEM LIFTED ME by the waist and carried me over the threshold with my bosom nestled against his chin. And before my feet hit the floor, his lips met mine.

"Mmm, now wait a minute."

"No, I don't think so."

"Kem!" My cheeks had begun to hurt from smiling so hard. "I don't remember saying anything about changing my name."

"Oh?" He matched me step for step as I walked backward into the apartment. "You must take me for some new-age hippie sort of husband."

"Call it what you like. But I'm a Morrow girl. Always have been, always will be."

The sweetness of his moist lips returned, and the flutter in my heart was almost enough to make me forget what we were discussing.

"The bag."

"It's not going anywhere."

"You never know. It might just sprout legs and walk off."

He chuckled and returned to the doorway to collect our things. A few seconds was exactly what I needed to catch my breath. Maybe this was what people were talking about when they said honeymooners. Eventually, it would wear off and I'd be able to think clearly around him.

"You really do not want to take my name?" He locked the door and joined me on the futon. "I think I'm hurt."

"Don't be hurt, my love. I did just marry you."

He nodded. "I get it, intellectually. I mean why should you change your name? Maybe we should pick a new name. And we'll both change our names."

"God, I love you."

"I am wonderful."

"And thoughtful."

"Yes, that too."

"And very sexy."

"As are you, mami."

"Wait."

"Why?" He paused, his face inches from mine, our bodies already connected from the chest down. All we'd done in the last forty-eight hours was make love. Was that normal? What if that's all we had? What if all that lovemaking overwhelmed my birth control, and I got pregnant with triplets or something?

"Umm...I'm hungry."

His eyebrows arched high in disbelief, but then he smiled as if he'd just read my mind. "I will feed you then." He stood. "I will feed my wife." He smiled, checking the thermostat as he passed it and disappeared down the hallway.

Damn. How'd I get so lucky? Me? Jackie Morrow?

I absentmindedly reached for the remote and the television came back to life. A black-and-white scene took over the screen. Not a figure had moved. I hit play and watched the people resume their movements. Why had I been so sure I'd find the robbers on this videotape? Maybe the two men in the corner didn't even know each other. Maybe they really just wanted a few gumballs.

"Okay, mami. I have red and white." Kem returned holding two bottles of wine.

"I thought you were cooking."

"I will. Liquor first. Red or white. Red and I will make steak. White... fish."

"White."

"As you wish." But before he could hurry back to the kitchen, the static-filled videotape caught his attention. "What's this?"

"Security footage from the currency exchange around the corner. I was looking for the guys that attacked me."

"Why?"

"Why?"

"Yes, why? Why would you do that? That is the police's job."

"I know."

"Then why would you be looking for them?"

"I was just curious. Thought I could help. Make myself useful." Possibly redeem myself for being an easy mark.

Kem bent over, taking the remote from my fingers and suddenly the television screen faded to black. "Help me in the kitchen. I will show you how to make the best perch you've ever tasted."

WE HADN'T BEEN APART FOR MORE THAN a minute, an impossible standard to keep up for the entirety of our marriage, but we were going to try anyway. Kem took my hand as I stepped off the bus, and we made our way toward campus. The commute from the north side to Hyde Park was a long one. Parking on campus was insane, so Kem opted not to drive. The band had practice, but not for a few hours, so he was happy to follow me to my afternoon classes.

"What are you going to do for two hours?"

He shrugged and moved his guitar case from his right to left hand. "Bookstore."

"What?"

"You have a bookstore?"

"Yeah. Do you want me to show you where it is?"

Kem smiled. "I will find it if I get bored. Then we'll meet here after your last class."

"Promise?"

"I promise."

I sighed as the prestigious New England-style building began to peek through the trees. Five of my six classes were overcrowded lectures, including this one.

"I bet if you come in, they won't even notice. Don't laugh at me."

"You are not tired of me yet?"

"Never."

"No. I think I will wait for you out here. Chemistry 101 doesn't sound like my cup of tea." Kem pointed to an oak tree in the quad and gently tapped his guitar case. "I have a song I want to work on first anyway. You go. Study. Learn. Get As."

I sat in the back row, twirling a black pen I'd found on the floor. Getting to class on time was going to be a headache from here on out. I began writing out a list of things to do. I wondered if I could get a credit to my account if I gave up my dorm room.

"Hey, Jackie. Finally decided to come to class, huh?" Lisa shuffled into the aisle and claimed the seat next to me.

"Only missed one class."

"One class and two labs. Remember? You asked me for the notes. Speaking of..." She unzipped her bag and lifted out photocopied pages from her notebook. "Here you go."

"Thanks."

"So, what'd you do this weekend?"

"Got married."

"Seriously?" My friend laughed so loud the last few students trickling in stopped and turned to look at us.

"I did."

"Where's the ring?"

"Don't have one yet. He's a starving artist. I'm a starving student."

"And you got married? What did your family say?"

"Shh." I pointed in the direction of the stage as the professor began the day's lecture.

Chemistry wasn't exactly my cup of tea either, but it was mandatory for all freshmen. Had to get at least a B to maintain my financial aid. So, I scribbled the date and time across the top of a fresh page in my notebook. I would take notes. I would not miss any more classes.

"You tell them?" she whispered.

"Not yet."

Just because most college students weren't married didn't mean I couldn't make it work.

"THEY WILL BE THRILLED TO SEE YOU again." Kem was more than ready to welcome me back into the band. "You will like the new sound we're working on. It is a little funk and a lot of blues."

We hurried down the street, turned the corner, and continued down the alley. I wasn't planning on singing, but I got the sense Kem hadn't picked up on that. I was following him to practice like he'd followed me to class. I was going to sit in the corner of the garage, going over my class notes and possibly reread a few chapters from the textbook.

"Did you hear me, mami?"

"Yeah."

"And Clark is working on a cover of a song I think you will like." He smiled knowingly and pushed open the gate then the door to the garage.

Nothing had changed other than the music. Clark and his drums. Jess and the keyboard. They were both surprised to set eyes on me. Funny how it took me leaving the band for them to give my suggestions any weight.

"So that's why we couldn't get this guy the last few days. You had him!"

"Ha-ha. Funny."

Kem pulled me close, bursting to share the news. My head dropped against his shoulder, and I nuzzled my nose against his neck, taking another hit of his scent.

"No!" Jesse was in shock. I didn't blame him. "When? How?"

"We flew to Vegas. It was lovely. Right, mami?"

I nodded.

"Next chance we get, I'm taking her home with me."

"Kem." I blushed even harder at such a blatant mention of his desire.

"No, I mean home. Columbia. For you to meet my family."

"Oh."

"You young'uns..." Clark wrestled both of us into a hug. "Well, congratulations. Hope you don't mind we're gonna have to steal your husband away for a few months. Did you tell her?"

"Tell me what?"

"Oh. We are going on tour." Kem smiled, and it all fell into place.

This was why he wanted me back in the band. He couldn't bear to be apart from me. I began stroking his hair, doting on my altogether perfect man.

"I think we should hear the set with some vocals, and since Jackie is here...wouldn't it be perfect to debut our new sound with her voice?"

"I'm sold," was Clark's immediate reply, and Jess's consent wasn't far behind.

"So, mami? What do you say? Ready to hit the stage again?"

I had been smiling throughout their conversation, but it had more to do with how Kem's cheeks perked up every time he said my name than the actual content. I wasn't there to sing. I had a corner and a textbook with my name on it.

"Mami?"

"Umm..."

"Jackie, if it's about before..."

"It's not."

"Mami, what's wrong?"

This time Kem followed my lead. Stepping over dismantled boxes and packing paper, we found a private corner.

"I don't think I should go. I've got school."

"You have Christmas break coming up. Come out with us for a few weeks." His hands worked their magic up and down my arms before settling on my hips. "I can't be apart from you that long."

"I know. Me either."

"So, then you will come?"

I nodded. It would only be for a few weeks.

HAPPY BRIDES—HAPPY WIVES WEREN'T DISAPPOINTED, AND I was happy, ipso facto, I couldn't be disappointed. I had the most perfect man, and he couldn't get enough of me. I might even realize my dream of becoming a superstar. Everything was perfect. Still, I sat up in bed, slipped on one of Kem's tee shirts, and tried to wish away the melancholy that had infiltrated my sleep.

Maybe it was Mama. I glanced at the cordless sitting on top of the tray beside the bed but couldn't bring myself to call her. She'd been doing well. I'd drive myself crazy thinking the worst every other minute.

Maybe it was school. I hadn't been a very good student and finals were around the corner.

Hugged my knees to my chest and considered the obvious. Vegas. It was sudden. I didn't do well with change. But then nothing had changed.

Kem's side of the bed lay empty and cold. That was different. That must've been what woke me up. He'd been gone from the bed for a while.

I peeked out into the hall and saw no sign of him in the kitchen. The floor boards squeaked subtly as I headed toward the front of the apartment. Hushed voices grew louder with each step, and then there he was, sitting on the coffee table. The light from the television broke through the night, creating a silhouette of his body.

"Kem?"

"Jackie." His face fell, pain replacing his usual optimism. "I was going to come get you..."

I didn't hear another word although I could see his lips were moving. The blonde sitting behind the desk was telling the good folks of Chicago about the latest in a string of convenience store attacks. A murder on the north side. My sister's face flashed on the screen, and the word suspect thundered in my ears.

"If anyone has any information about this woman or her known associates, please contact your local police precinct."

81
PECAN

NOTHING IN THE WORLD COULD PREPARE A Mama for the pain of her daughters following in her footsteps. They sat with me, Jackie on my right, Nikki on my left, both letting me clutch their hands—Nikki praying in hushed tones, and Jackie stewing in negativity. The three of us waited from sunup to sundown.

Chicago police had set their minds to not doing us any favors. Said they ain't have nobody by the name of Mya Morrow. Took one of the detectives, a fat one sucking on a cigar, to figure it all out. She'd come in as a Jane Doe. Nearly killed me because only one reason my child would be a Jane Doe, if she was dead. But she was alive and kicking it seemed. Cops didn't wanna let us see her. Said we ain't have the right. None of us was lawyers. But then the fat little dick beckoned me to his desk with a glint in his eye.

"Mrs. Morrow, I just have a few questions about your daughter if you don't mind." That made two of us.

"Her birthdate for one. Marital status and a list of her friends, if you please." He pushed a pad of paper and an ink pen in my direction.

Already felt like we'd made a mistake coming down here to claim her. Every corner of the room held cops whispering and shooting looks at us, like we held the key to some big mystery.

"Why you don't ask her?"

He took the unlit cigar out of his mouth and laid it across the rim of his coffee cup, pushing his tongue against the inside of his cheek. "She hasn't been the most cooperative."

"I want to see her."

"In due time. First, I need a few answers."

"No offense, but what you need ain't so high on my list of priorities. You have my daughter locked up, and I wanna know why."

"She's a person of interest in a string of robberies."

"Television said something about murder."

"That too."

"Mya ain't kill or rob nobody. It ain't in her."

He nodded, figuring I was like all mamas, blind to the truth about our children. Wish I could've been, but that wasn't in me, not where Mya was concerned. If he'd said she'd gotten into a fight, I'd have believed that. Just like I'd have believed she had a good reason for it. But stealing, my girl wouldn't do. Ain't one day passed that she'd taken more than she was due. And she wouldn't kill nobody for anything. In her mind, wasn't no-good reason for that.

"She can be a little hard-headed." I stared at the blank piece of paper, resisting the pull to pick up the pen. "She's smart. If she's not answering your questions, then she got a reason. Let me talk to her. Make her understand."

He made a big show of considering my request. Leaning back in his chair until its front legs were up in the air, then they came down hard.

"All right, Mrs. Morrow. I'm not such a hard-ass I'd deny a mother from seeing her child. But the minute it's over, I expect some answers. And I'll need to see some identification." He beckoned over one of the uniformed officers. "Something with your full name and address on it."

The officer whistled as he led me down a dark corridor. Had to have been colder inside than it was outside. Was probably all the concrete. Concrete and bars, folks with sad eyes and big mouths shouting to be heard over the din. Couldn't imagine my baby being among them. Even when the police took me into custody, they ain't put me in a place like this.

"Here we go."

We stopped outside a dark cell. The metal frame bed held a thin mattress without a sheet in sight. The last bit of light fell on a toilet nailed into the wall, and in the darkness, something moved.

"Mama?"

"Open this up."

His keys rattled as he did as I asked, and then the bars slid shut as soon as I was inside. He stood guard anyway, but I barely noticed.

"Baby? Come on in the light, so I can see you."

She stood, arms folded under her chest, her hair in one long braid over her shoulder. Wasn't until I went in to hug her, and she stepped back, that I realized she was covered in blood.

"It ain't mine. I'm okay."

"No, you not!"

The dark red smudges along the curve of her jaw had turned a flaky rust color, and my child, who couldn't care less how she looked, receded into the darkness of her cell.

"What happened? Why these people think you..."

She didn't answer me right away. Didn't move or sigh or anything.

"Mya?"

"I was there to get diapers. A guy came in, robbed the owner, shot him, and left."

"So you're a witness."

She shook her head. "I didn't see anything. And I sort of ran away after..."

"You were scared. You were afraid. That don't make you guilty!"

"The cops were coming."

"They should understand! Folks go through traumatic experiences, and they wanna run away. That's how it is."

"I was running from the cops."

I looked her in the eye, grabbed hold of her arms and said, "You ain't do nothing wrong. You hear me?"

She finally relaxed enough to let me put my arms around her.

"Your sisters are here. Jackie and Nikki. They wanted to come see you, but they would only let me in. That detective gotta lot of questions."

"Mama?"

"Yes, baby."

"I'm sorry."

"It's all right. Okay? You gonna be okay. We'll get you outta here."

"No, I'm sorry about...how I was...back when..."

I didn't need to hear anymore. Just held her tighter.

82 MYA

WHATEVER MAMA SAID TO THE BOYS IN blue put a fire under their behinds, but it didn't move them one bit closer to my truth. They let me clean up and handed me an orange jumpsuit with B66739 in faded black stencils over my heart. After they properly outfitted my cell, I actually got a few hours' sleep before they came back.

"Let's go, Morrow. Lawyer's here."

Ross Brooks was a veteran in the public defender's office. An unassuming little white man with wisps of gray hair above his ears, a hard nose, and spectacles that just wouldn't stay put.

"I'm Ross Brooks. Sit down, Miss Morrow."

I sat.

"You are being charged with robbery homicide. Guilty or not guilty?"

"Not guilty."

He nodded and pushed one of two stacks of paper in my direction and handed me a pen. "Sign here and every other place you see is marked. Police are still building their case unofficially, so that should work in your favor. Any witnesses?"

"No."

"Anybody hear you talking about the store before or after?"

"Why would I be talking about–"

"Just answer my questions, miss."

"No. Except Dee. He knew I was going."

"Own any weapons?"

"A few knives."

"Got permits for those?" He asked not looking up from the file with my name on it.

"Didn't know you needed permits for knives."

"Anybody know you have them? Ever used them on anyone or displayed them in a public fashion?"

"Yeah."

He passed me one clean sheet of paper and said, "Write down the dates, names, and locations."

He didn't ask me about the robbery or Arif. He wanted Darien's full name and contact information, but I feigned ignorance. Wasn't about to give up my family to this man I'd only just met.

"Miss Morrow, why haven't you cooperated with the police?"

"Don't trust 'em."

"Well, you're going to have to trust me."

It was the first time he'd actually looked at me.

I pointed at the legal pad on his side of the table and tore off another sheet. Trust was a bit of a stretch, but I had no problem testing him.

"Give this to my sister Jackie." I folded the page into perfect thirds then in half and wrote Kem's address on the center line. "Don't read it."

"Fine." He accepted it without a second thought and moved on with his agenda. "Arraignment is set for Monday. This is where you'll enter a plea of not guilty, and the judge will decide bail. Any questions?"

"What's the likelihood he'll dismiss this thing?"

Ross Brooks stood and slipped the pages I'd signed into his briefcase. "Judge Pearson? Not likely."

83

NIKKI

"I JUST CAN'T BELIEVE THIS IS HAPPENING."

It was all I could think to say to break the silence. Jackie just stared out the window. The brake lights of the car in front of us flashed, and I pushed the pedal to the floor. I much preferred highway driving to the streets, but neither the Stevenson nor the Dan Ryan would bring us any closer to our destination.

"It's like we're cursed or something."

As soon as the words were out of my mouth, I regretted them, but at least that got my sister's attention. Mama was careful to put a positive spin on it, smiling and declaring the whole thing a misunderstanding, but nobody who knew her believed it. Mya had been out of our reach for so long, we all secretly feared something like this might happen.

"There it is." Jackie pointed to the neon sign, and I turned into the parking lot. "Doesn't look that bad."

It looked horrible. Made my skin crawl as the tires rolled over the loose gravel.

Jackie unfolded the piece of paper with the address and room number and replied, "Two twenty-two. You wanna wait here?"

"No."

Jackie thought she was doing me a favor, but I wasn't gonna relax until we were all out of there.

We climbed the rickety metal staircase to the second floor and went left until we noticed the numbers on the doors were only getting bigger. Then turned and headed to the right. It was a horrid shame. My sister could've had a good life. She didn't deserve this.

Jackie paused outside the door and stared at me. "Fix your face."

How exactly was I supposed to look? Wasn't like I was calling on a neighbor for a cup of sugar. I doubted anybody there even had sugar. They probably ate crap and slept half their lives away. But I smiled and Jackie knocked, tucking the paper into the back pocket of her jeans. At least my sister had the fortitude to dress appropriately. It was the only time I'd seen her wear a turtleneck. Meant I didn't have to worry about her getting raped on the way back to the car.

The curtains swayed softly, but the movement didn't give us any clue to what waited inside the dark room. Jackie knocked again, and the door opened a crack. One droopy eye and then another appeared, blinking erratically at the early morning light. I nodded, confirming for Jackie that he was in fact the notorious Dee.

"Hi, I'm Jackie Morrow. I think you know my sister Nikki. Mya sent us."

"One second."

The door slammed shut, leaving us standing on the outside. Was a good thing Mama didn't come. She didn't need to see this. The door opened after some shuffling noises, and we stepped inside.

"She okay?"

"She's in jail," I snapped.

He stared at the floor. I wasn't telling him anything he didn't already know. It had been on the news the last two nights. It was in the papers. He knew and he hadn't done a thing about it.

"Hi, auntie." Mia waved from the foot of the bed. She was eating cereal off a Styrofoam plate.

"How are you, sweetheart?" I smiled, running my fingers through her hair. Her face was clean, her breath smelled of toothpaste, and she appeared to be in good spirits.

"You bring my mommy from work?"

"No...no, honey, but she asked me to come see you."

"How long she gonna be at work? Dee says she'll be home soon. Why she not take me with her?" Mia hopped down from the bed, spilling

Cheerios across the floor. "Take me to her."

I wasn't prepared for this. Mya told us to bring baby formula, but that was all. I tried to think of what my sister would say if she were there, but nothing came to mind other than, "Your mom wants you to eat your breakfast."

She walked to the dresser and tilted the half-empty box until her plate was once again full. Then returned the box to its place, next to a row of baby bottles, each one filled with water. Jackie had been conversing with Dee, neither of them paying any attention to the two of us.

"Excuse me. You haven't been feeding the baby tap water have you? Newborns can't drink water."

Jackie's eyes darted between us, and she sighed. "Can't hurt, right? Not like it's poison or something."

"He's on the breast." The man whose parenting skills were in question explained. "Soon as Mya gets back he'll be okay." He went quiet as I unwrapped the container of baby formula and set a gallon of nursery water on the dresser. "He's on the breast," he repeated.

"Mya sent this." I'd already read the instructions, so I began mixing bottles.

"She's just covering all the bases," I heard Jackie say. "It might take another day or two before we get this whole thing straightened out.

"So, you've seen her?"

"No, but Mama says she's okay. Stubborn. But you know how she is."

"Yeah..."

Even I heard the smile in his voice. Maybe I'd been too hard on this man. If Mya loved him, then there had to be something good about him.

"She just wanted us to come by and check on you all."

"You mean make sure I'm not fucking up."

"Make sure you have everything you need," Jackie corrected him with a smile. "Is there anything else you guys need? We can run to the store for you."

I added three fresh bottles to the mini-fridge and went about mixing up one more which I intended to feed to my nephew before we left.

"I...I been thinking about moving on...from here. Folks been talking about what happened. And about us. Eventually one of 'em is gonna go to the cops."

I turned around in time to see Jackie nod and hand him the piece of paper. He read it silently and sank into the bed closest to the window. "They really think she did this..."

"They think she was partners with somebody who did it. A man."

"Auntie, I can't see."

"Sorry." I hurried away from the television and joined the conversation. I hadn't read Mya's note, but seeing his reaction, I realized most of it was meant for him.

"Okay." His voice turned brittle with conviction, and he returned to his full height. "Okay, then we'll go to umm...Good Shepherd. Tell her she can find us there. Okay?"

"What exactly is Good Shepherd?"

"Church shelter."

"Well, don't you think the kids really need some stability right now—"

"Nikki," Jackie whispered urgently, but I ignored her.

"Why don't you let me take them for a while. Just until Mya gets out. She said something about you having to go to work anyway."

He double-checked the note, then asked Jackie if that was what Mya really wanted, and I held my breath. Jackie and I were never of the same mind. I couldn't remember the last time she'd backed me up on anything.

"I think she wanted us to help you. So, whatever you think is best."

He nodded and wandered over to the window, turning the note over and over in his hands. Then finally said, "What about you?"

"Me?" Jackie shifted her weight and squeezed her hands into her back pockets.

"Yeah. You live nearby, right?"

"I could take them. Sure."

"No, she can't. She's in school. She doesn't have one clue what to do with kids."

"I'm not a freaking idiot. I've babysat Mia more times than I can count."

"But you live in a dorm."

"I live with Kem."

"In a one-bedroom apartment."

"They're family. We can make it work."

"Don't you wanna run that by your boyfriend first?"

"Don't listen to Nikki. Kem will be fine with it. And if I have to, I'll take a semester off. That way I can have them during the day, and you can visit anytime you want or even take them at night if you want. It'll be fine."

"I can ask the school to put me on the night shift. If you can watch them for a few hours in the day, so I can sleep..."

They had both lost their minds. It was like I wasn't even in the room. Jackie spoke and he nodded. He spoke and she nodded. But then I remembered. They were both drug addicts, so of course, they thought each other made sense.

I made one last appeal for sanity. "I've got plenty of room, and Mia's already familiar with my house." It should've cinched it. I was clearly the logical choice.

But he still wasn't convinced and said, "What about your husband?"

"Oh, he won't mind."

"Liar." Jackie shifted her weight again, folding her arms under her chest. "Last thing that man wants is more Morrows under his roof."

I would've killed her, but he spoke first. "Well, I want them close by so..."

"Good. Then it's settled." Jackie hugged her new friend, and the two of them darted around the room packing things.

It wasn't just for my benefit, I argued with myself. The little ones would obviously be better off with me than with Jackie. She couldn't even take care of herself, much less another human being. Not that I was wishing my sister would fail. That wouldn't be Christian-like. I sighed and tapped the garage opener, pulling into the dimly lit space next to my husband's car. One night. I was giving myself one night to mourn my bad luck, then tomorrow, I'd call Jackie and work out a babysitting schedule. If it meant I had to go into the city, then I would. We were family after all.

"Where were you?" He sat at the counter, an open bottle of mineral water and glass of water at his elbow.

"I had to help Jackie do something."

"Ah, yes. Jackie."

He'd only set eyes on her a handful of times, but whenever the conversation turned to her, his lips puckered and his voice dropped an octave. It only made sense. I was the plain, responsible sister and she...she was not.

"Hungry?"

I'd found a recipe for a French casserole, prepared it, and stuck it in the fridge. The glass dish couldn't go straight into the oven, so I set it on the counter to warm to room temperature. It was enough to feed four. Maybe I'd bring the leftovers to Jackie. Poor Kem probably hadn't had a home-cooked meal the entire span of their relationship.

"Darlene called."

"I'll call her tomorrow."

"Fine." He stood, walked slowly toward me. "How is your sister?"

"Jackie? She's fine. The same as far as I can tell."

"Good. She is the only one of you who doesn't hate me."

I didn't have the heart to correct him.

"Dinner won't take long. Twenty-thirty minutes at the most. Can I ask you something?"

My sister was in jail. For all her flaws and mistakes, I couldn't imagine anyone thinking she deserved that. So, I did the unthinkable. I asked my husband to help.

"Think of it as smoothing things over with my family."

He returned to his station and gulped down what was left of his water. Then returned the glass to the counter with a clang.

"Please. Mama's doing everything she can to scrape up some money for bail, but that might not even happen if we don't get her a halfway decent lawyer...Jean-Louis? Say something. I know you two have had your differences—"

"You mean when she attacked me?"

"Please. For me."

84
PECAN

ONCE SHE WAS DONE SWEARING UP A storm, Clara reminded me that everything happens for a reason. Me and Ricky happened, so I could have my girls. And because of the divorce, I had this house. Soon as they came of age, the girls got to split Ricky's life insurance. Nikki paid for a year at that snooty Christian college with hers and should've had some left, but there was a rumor that she'd ended up paying for her wedding ring and possibly a good portion of her wedding with what she had left. How that man talked my child into that I'll never know.

Now Jackie, I had to talk fast just to get her to put it toward her schooling, and Mya, she wouldn't even discuss it with me. Wouldn't sign the papers to have the money transferred into her name. Wouldn't admit that the money even existed. So, I sat at the kitchen table, searching through the most recent statements to find the latest one. Dragged my finger across the bottom of the page to the balance, was more money than I'd ever see. At least he managed to do one good thing for my girls.

"Belinda?"

"I'm okay."

Heziah had taken to checking on me every hour or so. First thing out his mouth when he walked into a room was to ask me if I was okay.

"You need to get some sleep."

I nodded. Couldn't sleep and worry at the same time, so it sounded like a good idea. "You think they'll let me put Mya's money up for bail?"

"I think it won't come to that. The judge is gonna set this thing straight, and there's gonna be some apologies. That's what I think. Now come to bed."

"Guess we'll see, huh? Tomorrow?"

"Tomorrow." Heziah took my hand and I followed his lead.

85
JACKIE

COULDN'T SHAKE IT LOOSE. THE ALARM CLOCK announced a new day, and it started all over again. Thoughts that had finally receded into the back of my mind returned again, picking up exactly where they left off. Mya. I stumbled into the bathroom and pointed the tube of toothpaste at my toothbrush. Mya. My sister was a morning person. Was she awake? Had she slept at all? Was she even alive? How many people get killed waiting for trial? Cold water flowed at a steady stream, slowly filling the basin, lifting the frothy blue remnants of saliva and toothpaste from the walls of the sink. I smiled in the mirror. We had the same smile, but most folks didn't know that because my sister hardly ever showed her teeth. I'd given up trying to keep my unruly mane straight, instead pulling it back into a somewhat tidy ponytail, the tail end of which reminded me of a scarecrow. Mya's hair was always well-behaved. My sister and her hair never got into any trouble that I didn't pull her into, and yet, here I was secretly, happily married while she was locked behind bars.

"Morning, mami." Kem traipsed past me with a long vibrating yawn and lifted the toilet seat.

"You're seriously gonna do that in front of me?"

He yawned again, bouncing slightly on the balls of his feet as the last ounces of urine left his body.

"So this is marriage, huh? Pissing in front of each other?"

"What time do we have to be at the courthouse?"

"Oh, about that...you don't have to—"

"Of course, I will." His voice rose to be heard over the flush.

We traded places, so he could wash his hands. I lowered the seat, the cover, and sat down. Kem shook the last drops of water from his hands and began running them through his hair until he was satisfied that there were no more tangles.

"I can be ready in ten minutes." He leaned toward the mirror, digging the sleep out of the corners of his eyes.

We weren't morning people. We were breakfast at noon, up until dawn sort of people, and yet there he was promising to change for little old me.

"Kids'll be here soon," I didn't think I'd have to remind him, but apparently I did.

"I'm gonna stay until the kids get here. Make sure you guys are okay, then run like hell to the courthouse. Mama said for us to be there at eight, but hopefully I won't miss anything."

"I thought that was tonight."

"What?"

"The kids."

That had been the plan—school during the day, my niece and nephew at night—but the more time that passed, the more convinced Dee became that they should be with me not just at night but all day. It honestly wasn't my doing although I could imagine Nikki's expression when she found out. She'd probably think I'd manipulated him into handing over his kids just to piss her off. Like it was my life's ambition to steal everything she wanted.

"Mami?"

"Darien couldn't switch shifts. We'll have them days and nights. If that's okay."

"Of course, it's fine. Whatever they need." He gave a sad nod. "I just thought he'd want to be there. In court. Today."

"You don't know my sister. If she saw him, she'd wanna know why he wasn't with the kids or at work. Mya's all about the bottom line. That's her idea of romance."

"So, I'll stay here with the kids. But you're still going?"

"Yeah."

Kem's chest rose and fell just as he attempted a smile. "You're a good sister."

"I just couldn't say no. Something about him...the way he asked me... it was like..."

Kem sat before me on the edge of the tub, hands perched on his knees, bracing himself for what he was about to hear.

"I don't know. There's something off with him—"

"What do you mean?"

"No, not like that. It's just..." I wasn't an expert on the man, but I didn't need to be to understand that he was desperate. So desperate for something good that he'd convinced himself he was unworthy of having it. So, he was pushing everything away. Pushing it away before he lost it.

"Mami?"

"He's a good guy, I think. Just needs some help. It won't be forever. I just think he needs a break from the kids. You don't mind, do you?"

"I just said of course not. I am here for whatever you need. That's why I wanted to be there for you. At the courthouse. For you to lean on."

"I spent all night leaning on you."

"That's not what I mean." But his eyes sparkled at the memory. "I told my family. About you. About us."

I nodded, pointing at the tin box sitting against the base of the tub. "I need a little pick me up."

He passed me the stash and continued with his story while I searched under the bags of pot and piles of cigarette papers.

Old school Catholics generally weren't the run off to Vegas and elope type of folks. Kem took his time finding words that took some of the sting out of their reaction. It wasn't me they rejected, it was how everything happened so quickly and so far away from them.

"They want to meet you."

"So, they can have me killed?"

"That's not funny," he snapped.

"Want some?" I offered after a hearty snort of angel dust. After all, he was as much a morning person as I.

"Maybe we should take a break. For now...from the blow and reefer."

"Because I made a bad joke?"

"Because like you said, your family needs you right now. Mya...the kids...your mom..."

"Yeah, Kem. I get it."

"It's a tough time—"

"I got it. I'll stop. Okay? Now, if you don't mind, I'd like to get in the shower."

86
PECAN

SWARMS OF FOLKS FLOWED DOWN THE CORRIDOR, some of them angrily buzzing about parking tickets, others more somber, but most didn't carry the weight of anything at all, wearing faces that said it was like any other day. A work day. They'd clock in and clock out and get paid at the end of the week. Showing up here didn't mean their lives were taking an unexpected turn, about to be ruined beyond all belief, nope it was just Monday to them.

"There's Nikki." Heziah nodded in the direction of the last door on our left. She was standing side by side with a petite woman in a pants suit. Her hard face was fixed to do business.

"We late?"

"No, I just got here early. This is Mrs. Krakowski. She's Mya's new attorney. Jean-Louis hired her. This is my mother and stepfather."

"How do you do?"

"Nice to meet you." Heziah shook her hand briefly.

Even with all that was going on, Nikki couldn't resist celebrating. That toad of a man finally did something decent. She stared at me as if she expected to see a visual change in my opinion of him.

"They bring Mya out yet?"

"Not yet, Mrs. Jenkins. See most times they wait until thirty minutes before the case is called to bring the accused out, but I'll get five minutes with her beforehand to introduce myself and let the court services officer know that I'll be taking over the defense."

"She comes highly recommended."

The woman nodded appreciatively then shifted her attention to the man dressed up like a security guard and followed him into a door marked Court Personnel Only.

"Where's Jackie?"

"She'll be here." I answered, but my mind had begun to wander. Somewhere behind that door, my baby was waiting for this nightmare to be over. Made me think of that night she ran away from home. Worst night of my life. Imagining where she was, if she was cold or hungry or what she was thinking.

"I'm sure she's just running late," Heziah was saying as he studied the faces in the crowd. "She'll be here."

"Mama, you wanna sit down? We can wait for her inside."

87

JACKIE

I WAS WELL ACQUAINTED WITH THE TASTE, AND no longer needed the fruity sweetness. That left only one reason to submerge the liquor in fruit punch. Mama. She was upset enough as it was, she didn't need to worry about me on top of it. Besides, I was fine. I was good.

"Excuse me."

"No, my fault." I smiled at the woman with wide shoulders and reoriented myself to the layout of the courthouse.

I'd ignored the signs forbidding food and beverages at the entrance, but the reminder posted outside the courtroom prompted a quick swig. From here on out, there would be no more drinking, I promised myself and slipped inside.

The mood was dull, the walls covered in cheap beige paint, and the security guard shushed me as I entered. Why? I don't know. I hadn't said anything. Maybe it was my feet. Sometimes they got loud when I least expected them to.

The judge was a tidy Asian woman whose head barely made an appearance over the bench. She looked fair enough, so I smiled and imagined myself as an emissary on my sister's behalf, conveying the message that we were reasonable people, not killers.

"Jackie." Nikki reached into the aisle and pulled me into the pew beside her. "You're late!" she whispered. "But you haven't missed anything. They haven't gotten to Mya yet." She nodded to the wall on our left where a row of convicts sat.

Mya's direct stare zeroed in on me, and I waved sheepishly. She looked all right, but that didn't surprise me. If anybody could handle this horrible misunderstanding, it was Mya. She'd always been the most composed of us.

"You all right?" Mama leaned around Nikki to touch my hand.

"Fine. I missed the bus."

She understood, completely unaware that I missed the bus, so I could stop at the neighborhood liquor store. But then why would she suspect that? I'd been sober for years as far as Mama was concerned. It honestly said more about them, than it did about me that they expected me to give up all substances, especially at a time like this. But even though they didn't understand me, I couldn't have loved my family any more. Even Nikki, who sat rigidly, clinging to my hand. I'd had nineteen years as the middle child of Ricky and Pecan Morrow. Wasn't a thing my mama or sisters could do that would surprise me. Twenty-four hours ago, I would've said the same about Kem, but I'd have been wrong. Clearly I didn't know him as well as I thought. I'd thought we were the same, him and me, but no.

Nikki's elbow plummeted against my side just as I heard, "State versus Mya Morrow. Charge of robbery homicide."

An old man rose from his seat and met my sister at the defense table as he introduced himself to the court.

"But that's not..." Nikki swallowed hard, and her head began bobbing, trying to get a look at every face in the courtroom. Damn booze. I'd missed something.

"Miss Morrow. How do you plead?"

"Not guilty."

"The state requests remand your honor. Miss Morrow has no ties to the community and has impeded the police at every turn. We believe that if set free, she will continue to prey on the community."

"Your honor, my client has never had so much as a parking ticket—"

"She has no address. No job. No phone number. Not even a driver's license, so of course, she's never had a parking ticket!

"She is very close to her family who is here in the courtroom, your honor."

"Bail is set at five hundred thousand dollars. Next case."

"Half a million dollars! Are they serious?"

A glance from Mya was all it took for me to hold my tongue. She was the queen of quiet strength, and the least I could do was keep mum. Nikki took my hand and led the four of us out into the hall, and the sensation hit me again. Proof that I really had missed something. My sister was never getting out! Why hadn't I seen it before? Didn't they see it? My heart hiccupped in my chest, and tears threatened to spring from my eyes. But I was the only one. Heziah, Nikki, Mama they all shared the same expression.

"I can't believe she did that."

"Nikki, it's her choice." Heziah sighed.

"I hand-wrapped her a competent and very free attorney, and she practically spits in my face!"

"Who? Mya? Who spit in your face?"

All conversation came to an end as the door to the courtroom opened, and the man who introduced himself as my sister's representative stepped into the hall.

"Mrs. Jenkins. Mr. Jenkins. Good to see you both again. I'm going to move for a speedy trial, and hopefully, she won't spend too long in custody unless you have fifty thousand? For bail?"

"I'll put up the house."

"Belinda, wait a minute—"

But Mama had made up her mind. It was her one and only asset. The only good thing Ricky Morrow had left her. The one thing Mya ran from with consistency. Seemed poetic that it would be the key to Mya's freedom.

"That's our home," Heziah was saying. "Where would we live?"

"It will only be a problem if your daughter violates the conditions."

"Mya wouldn't do that," Nikki insisted, but it didn't put Heziah's mind at ease.

"Take the insurance money. My cut." I didn't want it anyway, and what better cause than my sister?

"Jackie, baby, are you sure? What about school?"

"Can't just leave her in there."

"No. We can't," Heziah stated simply. "But your mother and I won't stand for you sacrificing your education. We'll work it out. It's not for you girls to worry about. Okay?"

MYA

IF SOMEBODY HAD ASKED ME A WEEK ago if I had a good imagination, I'd have said yeah, but I would've been wrong. Never in a million years would I have imagined I'd be walking down the steps of the Cook County Correctional Facility on a temporary release. And folks was serious about the temporary part.

Had a long list of things I was forbidden from doing or else I'd end up right back there.

A car horn broke into the starry December night, and I spared a moment to thank my creator. Wasn't positive how much he had to do with me ending up in jail, but my exodus had his fingerprints all over it.

"Miss Morrow."

As far as public defenders went, Brooks had a good handle on things. He reached over and unlocked the car door. Waited patiently for me to buckle up, then asked where I wanted to be dropped off.

"My mama's house."

"All right."

I'd gone back and forth on it for the last hour. My kids were with Jackie supposedly, but my sister was a night owl. When normal folks were turning in and winding down, Jackie was fired up and ready to go. And I'd heard she'd gone back to singing at that club, which meant my kids ended up in one of two places. If I had a good grip on the conditions of my bail, and I liked to think I did, then it wasn't in my best interest to stop by Nikki's this time of night. Or on any day going forward, if I was completely honest. Scared me, but the truth was I didn't trust myself around her husband. Didn't know what I was liable to do. Worst case scenario, I'd end up serving life instead of ten to twenty.

"Your folks expecting you?"

"I didn't call them if that's what you mean."

Traffic was almost nil, but the stoplights had it out for us. Wouldn't have bothered me a week ago, but every minute I wasted standing still was another minute my kids were left wondering if I'd abandoned them.

"There is something I want to discuss with you, if you're not too tired."

"Go ahead." I stared at the gas station on the corner, wondering what brought the drivers out of their warm homes, surely it had to be more than gas.

"I'd like to try to get you a plea deal on the table. Robbery homicide carries with it a sentence of ten-to-twenty years, and if they try to tie the other cases to yours, it could be as much as forty-five years." He paused for effect. "So, the way this works is we have to have something to barter. So, if you know anything about–"

"I don't."

"If you know anything about the other robberies, then you tell me, and I'll float it along to try to get you a reduced sentence."

I nodded. Wasn't until I heard him exhale that I understood he took the gesture as a confession. "I get it. But I don't know anything. It wasn't me."

"I understand, but maybe you heard something about it from–"

"I don't know anything."

"Well, just think it over."

The car veered to the left, merging onto the Dan Ryan Expressway. He turned the dial on the radio, oblivious to the fact that he'd drawn my undivided attention. Couldn't blame him for being jaded, but I expected him to be able to see the truth when it was sitting right next to him. Maybe not the judge, and definitely not the prosecutor, but the man representing me...he should see it.

"HI, MAMA."

"Oh, baby...come here. You okay?" She held me for a second then ushered me inside and locked the door. "You're so cold. Where's your coat?"

"I'm fine."

Didn't have the heart to tell her I was wearing it. Two sweatshirts, a turtleneck, and a tank top.

The first floor was dark with the exception of the golden glow illuminating the first ten stairs. Mama moved toward them, and it was the first time in months I'd gotten a good look at her without her wig on. Nikki was right. Looking at her straight on, she didn't look quite like herself, but she wasn't the frail cancer patient anymore either. She must've felt my thoughts because she raised her hand to tug at the strands of hair that had grown back, wishing them longer.

"You look good, Mama."

"Some girls can carry short hair. I just ain't one of them."

"Sure you are. Looks good on you." I felt my gaze drifting up the stairs but forced it to stay focused. "Can I stay here?"

Her response was a cross between a sob and a whimper. And if I had any doubt, she pulled me into a longer hug. It was my house she said. Always would be.

I followed a few steps behind her, expecting to find an empty bedroom in need of fresh linen, but we stopped outside her bedroom, and she waited for my eyes to adjust to the darkness. Two lumps lay sound asleep beneath Mama's heavy quilt. One surrounded by pillows, the other arms and legs stretched out, resembling an X with hair.

"Go on, baby. They been waiting on you."

NIKKI

I was happy to do it. Jean-Louis too." I smiled and rearranged the presents under the Christmas tree to accommodate my contributions.

"Somebody's gonna be one happy little girl." I'd written "from Aunt Nikki and Uncle J-L" on each card even though Mia was too young to read it.

"Pretty wrapping paper. Mama, you see Nikki's presents?" Nat pointed at the slowly expanding pile. "Where's mine?"

"What do you mean?" Heziah looked up from the newspaper that had captured his attention. "You're a teenager now. Too old for Christmas."

"I never said that!"

"Sure you did." The pages rustled as he went from the business section to travel.

"He just playing with you, baby. You all got presents under the tree." Mama returned with a pitcher of eggnog then joined me and Mia on the sofa.

Mia couldn't take her eyes away from the stairs. Glancing over at the slightest sound, looking for Mya to come down and join us. Mama tried to reassure her, saying Mya would be down soon as she finished feeding the baby, but Mia was about two seconds from running upstairs anyway.

"Did everyone get something for Mya?"

"I did. I got her a set of watercolors," Nat admitted. "I hope she likes it."

Mya was gonna hate it, but I smiled anyway. Most Sunday dinners we never knew if she'd show up, and it didn't get any better around the holidays. On top of that, she was impossible to shop for, nothing at all like me. I was easy to please.

"Somebody call Jackie." Mama sighed, tired after cooking all morning. "Folks can't be waiting forever. Got everybody in here starving," she said and pushed the plate of chips and dip closer to the twins.

Nat was happy to volunteer, but before she could get out of the living room, the doorbell rang. "That's probably her now." My sister hurried into the hall.

The front door protested loudly as the cold air rushed into the house. The bottom half of Heziah's newspaper fluttered in the breeze, and I reached for the blanket tossed over the back of the sofa.

I'd prepared for questions about my husband's absence, but so far everybody was distracted with other things. That would change once Jackie showed up no doubt. She couldn't resist an opportunity like this. Here we were—the whole family, even Mya. Everyone except him. Wasn't like they ever made an effort to make him feel welcomed. From the very beginning, they'd made it clear what they thought of him.

"Jackie, baby, that you?" Mama called out. "Get on in here and stop letting all the heat out."

But the only response was from Nat. Her voice was muffled by the heavy winds. Wasn't until Mama joined her that we got an inkling that something was wrong.

Heziah was up first, then me. Trembling, Nat met us in the hallway with wide eyes. "I... I didn't know what to say. Sh-She just kept saying these things."

"Who?"

"Get off my property!"

Nat froze in my arms. The two of us, wrapped up in a blanket, watched as Heziah tried to pull Mama away from the woman with the microphone.

"She ain't do nothing wrong! You oughta be ashamed—"

"Just like you, Mrs. Jenkins? Where do you think your daughter got her violent streak from? You? Or her father? Do you regret killing him now that you see what it's done to your daughter?"

"There's no story here. Move on." The wind suddenly reversed course, aiding in Heziah's effort to close the door on the determined reporter and her cadre. But it wasn't enough to bring Mama any kind of peace. "Belinda, calm down."

"What's wrong with these fools? They think they can just knock on my damn door!"

"Mama!" Nat gasped. Wasn't everyday that Mama swore.

"Sorry, baby," she muttered.

"Upstairs," I whispered into her ear, leading her toward the stairs. "Come on."

Once we reached the second floor, that was where my plan ended. The drama downstairs was barely audible, not to mention upstairs was where all the heat was. Nat knocked on the door to Jackie's bedroom and pushed it in enough to stick her head inside. Mya sat in the center of the bed with Alan tucked in the nook of her arm. The tension melted from my baby sister's body as soon as she stepped in the room. She oooed and ahhed over the new baby, kissing his toes. Wasn't Christian-like to believe in magical powers, but if we had superpowers, that would've been Natalie's. She forgot so easily, the pain never got to leave its mark.

"What's wrong?" Mya asked, looking at me.

"Nothing. You almost done?"

"Yeah. Why?"

"Everybody's waiting for Jackie to show up so we can eat."

One thing had nothing to do with the other, but it was the first thing that came to mind. The only thing I could think to say that would keep my real thoughts hidden. We couldn't just have a normal family dinner without feelings of resentment and ghosts taking up space at the table.

"Nikki?"

Mya had given Nat the baby to burb and was focused on me. Even before I worked up the smile I wore on a daily basis, she was ready to call me on it. Must've been her time in jail. Normally she wouldn't have spent more than a second pondering what was going on with me.

"What's wrong?"

"You mad at me?" I hadn't planned to say it, but there it was, laid out on the bed between us. "I shouldn't have—I mean I should've stopped..."

Mya blinked slow and deliberate, her features returning to their covert positions. Nobody wanted to be on her bad side, least of all me, but I couldn't rightly say that I was. When she finally sighed, I realized she wasn't mad, she wasn't even disappointed. It was what she expected from me. She expected I'd submit to Jean-Louis's will.

"It's just when you dismissed the lawyer… I thought it was because of me. You don't know this, but I had to work really hard to get Jean-Louis to pay for it. To convince him, I mean…"

She nodded. Still not surprised.

"It was an olive branch," I explained.

"I ain't mad at you, Nikki."

"Are you sure because—"

"You want me to be?"

"No."

"Then let it be. I ain't mad at you. Not mad at anybody really. Just don't wanna owe anybody anything."

"Mommy! You take too long!" Mia's tiny body burst into the room and scaled the bed to declare, "I been waiting."

90
JACKIE

I WAS ALMOST TWO HOURS BEHIND SCHEDULE. MAMA had called first thing in the morning to say Mya was home, so she wanted to have a family supper. I'd promised to be there at five even though I had midterms to study for and band practice at three.

Mama had stopped asking about school, and I was afraid to bring it up. Afraid she'd see through my lies and start worrying or worse yet, she'd be disappointed in me. So, I'd promised with a smile on my face and hoped she could feel my happiness over the phone.

"Mami? Where are you?" Kem stole a glance at me.

"Think it's gonna be a blizzard?" I'd been staring out the passenger window since he started the car.

"I hope not. I need new tires."

She'd been thrilled when I dropped off the kids. Didn't question why I needed to study when I should've been sleeping. Just took them in and put them to bed. Was a good thing I guess since Mya ended up there.

"Mami?"

Maybe the nightmare was finally over and we could relax. It'd done what it was supposed to do– brought us closer. Now we'd have that happily ever after folks was always talking about.

"We should tell them. Tonight." Kem removed one hand from the steering wheel to intertwine it with mine. "It is good news. Now is the time to share it."

"I wonder if Mya's talked to Dee."

His hands returned to ten and two. Gripping the steering wheel with intense concentration. His long fingers flexing against the leather. He would stop talking now. It was a side of Kem I didn't know existed. He hated to argue, didn't like to push, so he chose to be silent instead.

"Probably not," I answered my own question. "Not like he has a phone. When I see her tonight I'll tell her to look for him at Good Samaritan. Or was it Good Shepherd?"

Kem's car skidded to a stop, and he turned in his seat to study the parking space behind us. We were three houses down. The city had yet to send the snow plow down Mama's street, so the car rolled over the snow packed in uneven layers over the road. There were inconvenient piles where there should've been cars, a sign of the residents trying to pitch in. And not to mention a gutter full of sludge.

"Damn." I sighed. "I love these boots."

"I know. Too bad they are not made for snow."

"But they're pretty." I pouted, waiting for at least a grin, but Kem only grimaced as he wrestled the car into the space. I gazed over my shoulder at the house. "I hope they haven't started without me."

"Without us, you mean."

"Right. Without us. You know my family's crazy about you."

"Are they?"

"Of course. Not as much as I am, but still it's something."

Finally! The beginnings of a smile. He slid the key out of the ignition and leaned over for a kiss, a flash of the happiness that lingered before us. We had the rest of our lives to beat folks over the head with it. What was the rush? We braved the cold winds and hurried up the icy walk hand in hand.

"Jackie's here!" Jenna took off down the hall while Kem and I looked for space on the coatrack.

Heziah had opened the door with clear reservation as if he'd been expecting Jehovah's Witnesses instead of family. "How's the roads?"

"All right," Kem replied.

"Good. Everyone's in the dining room."

A PRIVATE MOMENT WITH MY FAVORITE SISTER was all I wanted, but my niece wasn't about to abandon her throne. She sat a top Mya's lap, dominating the conversation with news of her imaginary friends, cartoon characters, and the tangential question or two.

"When we go back to Dee?"

"Later." Mya's gaze locked on mine. I'd finally met the famous Dee, and the pieces were falling into place. Mia wouldn't even let go of the man until she was certain he'd be back for her at a specified time.

"I gotta potty," she announced and hopped down. "Stay here."

We nodded our agreement and watched as she left the door to my bedroom open. "She's a bossy little thing."

"I know." Mya smiled after her firstborn, then pulled the covers up to her waist. "I must be coming down with something. Can't stay warm to save my life."

Four days in jail left its mark on her. Even a blind man could see that my sister looked upon the world anew. She marveled at the snow, savored each bite of food, and shed the solemn exterior that had been hers for quite some time. I had my sister back.

"What?"

"Just missed you is all."

She smiled. "How's your case coming? They find the guys yet?"

A vision of a bunch of jolly white guys with badges pinned to their massive chests, sitting around eating doughnuts and talking with their mouths' full, burrowed its way into my mind. I hadn't heard from the police since they questioned me and didn't expect I would. Maybe there was a possibility before the name Morrow meant anything to them, but no way they were gonna put themselves out on account of me, not now.

"You remember anything new?" Mya wanted to know. Leaning forward like it was her job to piece together what happened to me. "Even something small might help."

"Don't matter." I shrugged. "Wasn't like the twenty bucks they stole was gonna change my life."

My sister didn't like that. She fixed her stare on me, refusing to let my words carry any weight.

"I'm not holding my breath. Look what they did to you. Either the cops are a bunch of fools or they so corrupt they don't give a damn about justice."

"Don't say that," Mya snapped then scooted around until she found a more comfortable position.

I wondered if she was gonna pick up the line Mama had been using. It was all a mistake, and the good folks would figure that out sooner or later. She didn't. She reminded me that the thieves sent me to the hospital. That I had stitches and bruised ribs. The money wasn't what mattered, but somebody had to pay for the violence. I turned onto my back, starring up at the ceiling. Of all the people in the world to have an opinion about the dedicated officers in law enforcement, I never expected my sister to be so blind. Even now, she had faith in them. Maybe it was a residual effect of her childhood. All those mystery novels had warped Mya's brain. She was determined to believe the good guys always won in the end. Didn't she know that nobody was who they said they were? The good guys or the bad.

"How's school? Jackie?"

"Fine."

"Fine?"

"Mostly fine." I replied emphatically but couldn't keep a straight face. "Not like they're gonna kick me out or anything, but I'm definitely not getting any awards this semester. But then I ain't the one with brains in this family, am I?"

"Guess not."

"Ugh!" I whipped the pillow that had been kind enough to cushion my head toward her face. "What about you and Darien, huh? You gonna keep hiding him from us? I see what you see in him by the way. He's got that rustic Rastafarian thing going on."

Mya's laugh nearly knocked me off the bed, and before long, we were giggling like two school girls, that is until we had an unexpected visitor.

"Nice that you two are up here having a ball while the rest of us are scrubbing pots and pans." Nikki held a tray wedged between her waist and wrist and made a straight line for my bedside table to add the water glass and empty baby bottles to the pile of dishes she'd already collected. "Don't worry about us mere mortals."

"Aww, Nikki, come on, take a break."

"I wouldn't want to interrupt."

"You're not," Mya replied, nudging me slightly. "Right? Sit. Join us."

"Maybe for a minute." She sank into the foot of the bed, balancing the tray on her lap. And she waited, glancing from me to Mya, waiting for either of us to say something.

Didn't feel like fighting, so for once, I didn't know what to say. My efforts at small talk were never taken well. Couldn't ask her about her day because she took it as me poking fun at how much she didn't do in a day. Couldn't ask about her husband for the same reason. Mya's eyes shifted left to right as she studied the blanket across her legs, probably thinking the same thing.

"I was just asking Mya about Dee."

"Oh? What about him?"

"About sex. About his sex."

Mya's eyes opened wide, boring holes into the side of my head.

"She was gonna tell me—"

"Okay." A second later Nikki was on her feet. "I don't need to know any of that."

"Jackie's just teasing you."

"No, it's fine. Somebody's gotta help Mama with the dishes."

"I'm back, Mommy." Mia slipped past Nikki and reclaimed her position on Mya's lap.

It wasn't my fault Nikki was wrapped so tight, I wanted to say. She could've just rolled her eyes at me and changed the subject. Wasn't like I made her get up and leave.

91
PECAN

CAN'T SAY I'D EVER BEEN MORE PROUD of my girls—of what they'd done or who they were. I couldn't control the world, couldn't make it into a nice cushy place, but maybe I didn't have to because my girls could handle it. They were strong and smart and good. I sighed, cradling my grandson against my chest. I was a long way from Hattiesburg, Mississippi—the only child of a heartbroken man. Had me a family. Folks to ask after me even though I wasn't complaining none.

"Mama, can I hold the baby?"

"Okay, but he's not like one of your dolls. You gotta support his head."

Jenna followed my directions to the tee, glancing up at me to make sure she was doing it correctly.

"Callie, baby, you wanna hold him too?" But my youngest looked petrified at the notion. "Maybe when he gets bigger, huh? Newborn babies used to scare me too. Never even changed a diaper until I had Nikki."

A nerve-racking sound vibrated off the windows of my house. Wasn't quite the sound of danger just intense frustration. Leaning over the back of the sofa, I parted the curtains to take a peek. Heziah and Kem had been at it for a while. Both wrapped up in scarves and gloves, trying to make the winter safe and accommodating. Kem held the shovel, plunging it against the freezing pavement and packing pounds of snow against the fence. Heziah followed in the wake of Kem's work, sprinkling salt down the steps and over the sidewalk. They hadn't said more than a few words to each other, but they worked well together. Maybe by next Christmas, they'd be the best of friends.

"Mama, can I talk to you about something?" Nikki appeared at my side, drying her hands on the apron tied around her waist. She focused on the twins and said, "In private."

"Y'all take the baby in the kitchen."

Of all my girls, I worried about Nikki the most. Worried she'd end up like me or worse. Worried she'd blame herself for it. And the more I tried to guide her, the harder she resisted. So, when the sofa cushions bent to accommodate her, I tried to find the same softness in me. Wasn't every day she trusted me enough to ask for anything.

"I been thinking about something," she started. "About Mya. About her situation...and heaven-forbid, if she does end up going back to jail..." Nikki's lips formed a tight line as she reconsidered the right words to use. "I'm worried about the kids."

"That's not gonna happen. Okay? These folks just made a mistake is all. Everything's gonna be just fine."

"But, Mama, what if it isn't? What's gonna happen to Mia and Alan? He can't take care of them! You should've seen the way they were living—"

"Nikki—"

"I'm just saying one of us should be their guardian. Just in case."

Then it hit me. What worried me most about Nikki was her lack of protective instincts, at least when it came to herself. She'd wanted love, wanted a family more than anything. Nobody should want others more than they want themselves.

"Mama, I think it should be me. Jackie can't take care of them, and you shouldn't have to..."

"You mean you think I might get sick again."

She gasped, staring at me like a deer caught in the middle of the road.

"It's okay, baby. I think it's good that you thinking ahead. It ain't an easy conversation to have with a mama though, least of all one that might lose her kids."

Nikki nodded, staring at her hands. "I know Jackie's her favorite."

"You girls...ain't no favorites. You all sisters. Same blood run through your veins."

"If you back me up, I think Mya might agree. Will you? Please."

Of all the things she could've asked for, of course, my child went and picked the one thing I couldn't give her. But the lie had already taken up residence on my tongue, just waiting for permission to taste the free air. Wasn't like Mya needed my thoughts on the subject no way. What I said wouldn't make one bit of difference to anyone except Nikki.

"Mama? I...I know you think I should just wait until I'm older, but—"

"It ain't your age that I gotta problem with. It's your husband. Now, I'm gonna tell you this because I love you. You my blood. Just like Mia and the baby. And I wouldn't trust that man of yours to look after a dog let alone my blood." Tingles ran across my body while I watched her soak it all in. Mothering ways always came to me with a smidgen of doubt. Never was 100 percent sure I was doing it right. "I don't think your sister's gonna ask my opinion, but if she does that's what I'm gonna tell her. I know it hurts you to hear it, and that don't bring me any happiness."

"Right." She finally managed a reply. The quietness had receded into the blind spot of her anger. "I just thought maybe now...maybe...but you're gonna always hate him."

Nikki's eyes grew hard with the knowledge that her husband wasn't about to buy his way into my family. Not with fancy lawyers or expensive toys. She'd made herself into an extension of him. My beautiful girl with her chubby cheeks and heart of gold. My firstborn. Only got one firstborn. Remembering her first steps brought a weary smile to my lips. The mama I was back then wouldn't have seen this coming, maybe she'd even have given her son-in-law a second chance. Too bad for him that he got me instead.

"You hate him don't you?"

"Don't hate nobody. What I said was I don't trust him."

"Because of that joke he told? Mama you know how crazy that sounds?"

I did. I also knew he'd done a helluva lot more than joke about putting my black behind on the curb. The joke was just all he'd done that I could prove. "Fine, Nikki. Then I guess I'm crazy."

"You are! You're just—you won't even give him a chance! Not even for me! Don't matter at all that he loves me does it? He'd do anything for me. He would."

He ain't need to do anything other than let her go. Then maybe I could see my way to feeling different about the man. If he moved on before he caused any more damage to my girl. But n'all. Had his hooks in her real good. So good, I ain't even blink when she laid it out like I knew she would. The ultimatum. If I loved her, then I had to respect their marriage. She was a good wife. Sticking up for her husband. Taking his side over her crazy-ass mama.

"Otherwise I c-can't be in your life." She stood, arms folded tightly, only seconds from the door. "Mama?"

I nodded. "I hear you, baby. But I ain't gonna say anything new. You just go on and do what you gotta do."

92
MYA

FELONY ROBERRY. TEN YEARS."

"You have no evidence linking my client to this crime or any other crime."

"Other than the blood?"

"What?"

"The blood. The victim's blood was on her clothes, her shoes, her hands. Her DNA found on the body. Her fingerprints in the store. And six cops saw her fleeing the scene."

It was all circumstantial. He'd explained to me earlier. None of it spelled out murder, but that didn't mean they couldn't spin a story that sounded like murder.

"You agreed to consider a deal."

The prosecutor shrugged, leaning backward in his chair. "Ten years is what I'm authorized to offer, but she's gotta cop to the other two robberies and give us the shooter."

"Seven years. She gives you the shooter and you drop the other two holdups since you can't even place her there."

I had a natural poker face, but now that I really needed it, it was nowhere to be found. Couldn't stop glaring at the men discussing my future like I wasn't even in the room. If it wasn't the asshole who would've sooner sent me up river than look into my eyes, then it was the man who was supposed to defend me, basically confessing he didn't believe any parts of my story.

"Eight years. I might be able to swing eight years."

"I need to talk it over with my client."

"No need."

"Actually, Mya—"

"No. I'm not doing eight years."

"Five with good behavior."

"I don't care. Not doing it."

The prosecutor chuckled, gathered his things, and walked out the door. Didn't matter to me how much of a fool he thought I was because I wasn't a big enough fool to do time for something I ain't do.

Brooks closed the door behind his buddy, then faced me like he was my daddy about to punish me for insubordination. "That was a good deal."

"Funny. Seemed like a waste of time to me."

"Trust me. I'm the professional here."

"Yeah? Then get me off, professional. That sounds like a good deal to me. So, the next time you pull me away from my family to discuss a deal... it better come with an apology for putting me outta the Christmas spirit."

"Miss Morrow, I'm doing my very best for you here. I am. They may not have much of a case, but you don't have a defense! And their nothing is gonna look a lot heavier than your nothing when we put it in front of the court." Brooks dove into his briefcase and came out with a current copy of the Sun-Times. "Have you seen this?"

I'd barely glanced at it. Preferred my fiction to have a plot instead of bogus headlines. "Says you were in foster care. That true?"

"What's that got to do with anything?"

"Also says your mother killed your father. Bashed his head in right in front of you."

I winced. "Well, if it's in the paper it must be true."

"Miss Morrow, please stay with me here. I'm trying to keep you out of prison."

"Not sure how chasing old ghosts keeps me outta prison."

"Juries don't convict people that look like them. You, my dear...look like a criminal. If we go to trial, you'll have to answer for all of this."

"No."

"Yes." He nodded as if I were merely ill-informed. "I believe you will. Now, I can pull out the violins, but you'll need to get on the stand and denounce or explain your colorful background."

"Move on."

The folds of skin between his eyes popped out like wrinkles in the bed sheet. His eyebrows became slanted and short, just like his words. I wasn't even on the stand, but there I was getting the hostile-witness treatment.

"Miss Morrow—"

"Not trying to be difficult here. Really, I'm not. But I ain't talking about any of that. You put me on the stand, and I'll say just that. Nothing else."

Didn't know what to say anyway. My mama killed my daddy. I hadn't seen it but I couldn't say it didn't affect me. Couldn't say it was right or wrong either.

"Miss Morrow, I'm on your side."

"Yeah? I'm still not talking about any of that."

He could try me if he wanted to. Folks that knew me would advise against it, and I got the feeling that he knew that. I'd given him the truth, and if he couldn't work with that...well, I guess I was screwed.

93 PECAN

NATASHA STRAYHEN WAS HER NAME. SHE'D PUT together enough of the truth that it looked like she knew what she was talking about. This woman that never met me and didn't know my girls had convinced all of Chicago that she was the authority on us.

"Belinda, come on. Put that away."

No chance in that. Hadn't put it down since I got a minute to myself. Had six other ones stacked up next to the door. I'd liberated them from my neighbors' yards before they got home from work.

Heziah sat across the kitchen table from me, sipping his third cup of coffee. Needed that many cups to keep up with me. I was bouncing off the walls.

"Who the hell does she think she is?"

"She's just doing her job."

"Stop saying that."

"Nobody is gonna read it anyway. Tomorrow it's gonna be lining the trash bin."

"But it ain't tomorrow. It's today. And today's paper got Mya's face splashed across page nine, calling her a...a..." I glanced down searching again for the exact phrase. "A by-product of the cycle of violence. I'm gonna show her some violence. She wanna see violence? Let her bring her flat behind up on my stoop again!"

"Belinda."

"Quit calling my name."

His hand shot across the table to cover mine. I'd given up smoking, but the impulse was alive and well in my joints. My fingers jumped about restlessly tapping the table.

"I need a cigarette."

"No, you don't. You need to let go of the paper and go upstairs to put the girls to bed."

I shook my head, feeling every bit of my age plus a few more to grow on. This woman and her words had taken apart my life. She wasn't the first, truth be told, but she was the most recent to say it was me and my choices that had ruined my girls. And she had the ear of the whole city.

"Morrow was as brutal a specimen as Chicago had seen in decades. The power in his reach was only rivaled by his prowess against the ropes. It's possible there hasn't been a boxer like Ricky Morrow since."

"Stop reading that."

"He killed a man once. You know that? She missed that part." I tossed the pages on the table. "The man's widow wrote Ricky a letter. 'Course he ain't read it. I told him about it, and he sent the woman fifty dollars and went about his business."

"Let's go to bed."

Wasn't it enough I'd made supper, cleaned up, even made small talk with the girls? Spent the whole day thinking about things I couldn't say and now he couldn't wait to shut me up.

"She don't deserve this. Mya. I did what I did true enough, but—"

"You protected yourself. No shame in that." Heziah shook his head defiantly, warding off the past that had crept into my kitchen. "Nobody in their right mind would hold that against you."

Nobody except Ricky's favorite child. Maybe she ain't hate me anymore. Maybe she was even close to forgiveness but I wasn't about to fool myself into thinking that was the same as the love every girl supposed to have for her mama. Might never be, and I'd have to make my peace with that. Someday when all of this was done, I'd sit down with her. I'd tell her everything. Tell her how the twins really came to be and about my nervous breakdown. It would ruin any love she still had for her daddy but at least she'd know the truth. Know where I went and why. Then maybe she'd understand that when her daddy showed up again...showed up and beat

Louis half to death, meaning to do the same to me. She'd better understand where I was coming from. I'd wished Ricky dead a long time before then, that's true. But I had my reasons. Reasons no woman should have to bear. All this Strayhen woman had done with her damn interpretation was mix things up. Who did she think she was saving with that article? She could crucify me all she wanted, and it wouldn't bring Ricky back from the dead. Woman acted like it was her personal duty to let the world know Mya was my child. Make sure she ain't get away like I did. The woman clearly wasn't in her right mind.

"Belinda? Come on, honey. I see how tired you are."

"This just one more thing for her to blame me for."

"Who? Mya? Did she say something?"

"No."

"Of course not. Because you don't have any say over what this Strayhen woman writes in the paper. Mya's a smart girl. She knows that."

"Maybe she ain't seen it yet."

Heziah took me by the hand and led the way to the stairs. He meant well, always thinking things out so they made sense, but some things ain't work like that. Folks could hide 'em even try to talk themselves out of 'em but they couldn't help their feelings.

94
JACKIE

"DO ANY OF THEM LOOK FAMILIAR, MISS Morrow?"

I'd told the detectives that I didn't get a good look but they insisted I come down to the station anyway. "Look carefully now."

Each face in the row wore the same disinterested expression. All of them within a few inches in height and the same dark complexion. Maybe this was a test. They were trying to prove that the attack never happened. That I was a liar. Or maybe they were all innocent, and the cops were using me to railroad a good and decent person.

"Miss Morrow?"

Well, fuck if I was going to help them do that! These weren't the same assholes who had picked Mya up, but all cops tended to look alike. Lord knows they all marched to the same beat. The chatty one gave a nod, and his partner pressed a button then instructed the line of men to turn to their right.

"I never saw them. I told you that."

"Take a look."

"I am looking!"

"Look again. And concentrate. Is he there?"

We'd gone through the same process with a row of fair-complexioned men as well. None of them looked familiar either.

"Can I go now?"

"Don't you want us to catch them?"

"I want to go home."

"Let her go, Otis."

So go, I did. Down the bright hall, past the suspects chained to the bench waiting for questioning, and to the clerk who had stuttered at my last name. Never heard anybody struggle with Morrow, not until this week. Classmates whispering behind my back, cops studying me up and down like I might be carrying a bomb to blow them all to kingdom come. The scrawny gatekeeper pushed the clipboard in my direction. I signed my name in the sign out column and kept moving toward the sunshine.

"WHERE WERE YOU?" SAID THE BLINDING VOICE in the sky.

Wasn't it enough that mere mortals thought I was up to no-good, now God was persecuting me too.

"You—look at me. Look at me!" He said.

I wondered if other folks knew how demanding the Lord was. I mean after all he did come up with Ten Commandment's like five wouldn't do.

There was a commotion nearby, the screech of tin against porcelain. Cold porcelain, so hard it pushed my neck into an awkward position as I relaxed against it. Darkness fell in a gentle wave then repealed itself only to fall again.

"What did you take?"

Who? Me? I wasn't a thief!

"Mami, look at me. What did you take?"

There was a rush of water and even though my senses were limited, I could tell he'd plugged the tub. A light mist sprinkled my face.

"Come on, mami. Come on. Help me. Get up."

My bare feet slipped against the tile floor, and I clutched to his shirt, while fighting off the darkness. It was useless to fight. I knew that now. Good guys never won. Good guys weren't even good.

"Hey! Mami! Hey! Open your eyes!"

My body slumped into the tub, still and numb, as the water weighed us down. Kem leaned over me, a wet washcloth in his hand. Kem was my angel. The dry tickle in my throat turned into a coughing fit, and I realized I'd been drooling. Drooling in front of my angel.

"No, it's okay. You're gonna be okay." He stroked my face calmly with the towel.

The darkness was gone, but she left behind a gray field of guilt. What a terrible wife I was, making him worry. I smiled and tried to lift my hand to shoo away the towel but only managed to tread water. "I'm okay. Just sleepy." If only I could get a few hours of sleep...

"No, mami. Wake up. Eyes open. There you go. Good. Look at me. Stay with me."

The tub was full now. My blouse floated away from my body with each slit still buttoned. I remembered. The lineup. One by one they'd come in, and I looked for any sign of guilt, but there was none. Nothing in their eyes but boredom. They were there, I could feel it. They were right there. If only I could remember what they looked like.

My hand finally broke free of the water and connected with his. "I'm awake now. I'm okay."

He nodded, stood, and helped me out of the tub. Quickly peeled the wet layers of clothing from my body until I was standing there naked. I smiled, but he didn't notice. Covered me in towels instead, like he was drying off a child. A naughty child.

"What were you thinking? Where did you get that?" His head jerked to the bathroom floor. The lighter, spoon, and needle lay discarded and partially hidden by the toilet.

"I tried something new."

He glared at the floor, seething with rage. Then turned on his heels.

"Kem?" I shivered and stumbled a few feet behind him down the hall. "Kem, I'm sorry. I won't do it again. I promise. I didn't even like it—"

He whipped around so fast I almost ran into him.

"It was just a one-time thing."

"You swear to me?"

I nodded, my high souring as I waited for him to wrap me in his arms. "Tell me you love me, okay?" Silence filled the emptiness between us. Drops of water slid down my legs to the floor, and I gripped tighter to the towels. "Kem?"

It was painfully obvious he wasn't going to swoop in with a heartfelt hug. Wasn't going to whisper sweet nothings in my ear.

"I love you....You're my husband."

"Am I?"

"Of course."

A second passed. His penetrating stare interrupted by the flicker of his long lashes. "When are you going to tell your family?"

"Soon."

"When? Do you think it was easy for me? To tell mine? But I did."

"I know–"

"I am trying to be here for you, but you won't let me!"

"I–"

"Where were you? Today. This morning. You went to the police station didn't you?"

I nodded, realizing I'd forgotten to erase the detective's message from the answering machine.

"Why didn't you tell me?"

"You like to sleep in so–"

"You can't stop lying can you?" He grabbed handfuls of air, pitching them over my head with enough force to stun a seasoned batter. "Who am I to you? Am I anything at all? Or just someone to fuck you?"

"Okay, overreacting much? I was doing you a favor. Kem! Don't walk away from– Hey! I'm still talking!"

I dropped one towel on the floor of the bedroom, so I could stop picking up dust and dirt with my wet feet. Wiped my feet across it and wrapped the remaining towel lengthwise around my body, tucking it into my cleavage.

"Kem."

An armful of clothes fell in a heap across the bed. He began packing. "You're leaving me?"

"I'm going on tour. Alone, but I am going. I have to make some money."

"Bullshit! You're just pissed I got high without you! Well, I'm sorry my whole fucking world doesn't revolve around you. If that's what you want, then you got the wrong girl."

"I see that."

"Oh, yeah? WELL, GOOD! GO! RUN AWAY! SOON AS I NEED YOU! MY SISTER'S GOING TO JAIL, AND ALL YOU CAN THINK ABOUT IS YOURSELF!"

95 PECAN

I'D BEEN SEARCHING THE WANT ADS WHEN the phone rang. Sitting in the kitchen trying to convince myself that the time was right for me to go back to work. Bills were piling up, and a second mortgage was hanging over our heads, not to mention more mouths to feed. Even with work wasn't much I could do about it, given the pitiful wage I was worth.

The newspaper rustled as I turned the page and an ad for Chicago City Colleges popped out at me. For all the hell I rose about my girls taking their schooling seriously, I hadn't finished high school. Could have. I'd been a smart girl, but sometime between now and then, I'd forgotten what that felt like—to be thought of as smart.

Then the phone rang.

Maybe I wasn't perfect as a mama, but I never been confused about who my girls were. Nikki and her wide-eyed sweetness or Mya's quiet spirit bursting to be set free, and the fight in Jackie that put her at odds with folks whether she meant it or not. With all the drama of the older three's teenage years, I was in danger of losing sight of the younger ones. I could feel my attention wavering. Could be looking right at Jenna, and my mind would wander after Mya. Had to make it stay put. Focus. So, when the school called to tell me there was a problem with Nat, I hurried down there. Sat outside the principal's office wringing my hands.

"Mrs. Jenkins?"

"Yes."

"The principal will see you now."

I nodded, rose, and walked through the oper doorway.

Principal Burgess was a dark-skinned man with a sprinkling of gray hair across his lip and head. Looked like a man who was tough but fair. He was new to the school, but he'd seen his fair share of trouble.

"Mrs. Jenkins, please. Have a seat."

So I did. Perfect posture and all. Waiting for him to tell me Nat had been hurt or something like that.

"We've never had any trouble with Natalie before. Her teachers say she's a wonderful addition. Kind. Respectful."

I nodded, breathing slowly as the idea took hold that Nat wasn't hurt. "Where is she?"

"She's in the library finishing her test. There was an incident," he said, then pressed both lips firmly together. "She had an outburst during the test. As you can imagine, quiet is necessary during tests. Her teacher sent her down here, and I sent her to the library."

"What kind of outburst?"

"She screamed at another student."

"What he do?"

"She."

"What did she do?"

"Mrs. Jenkins—"

I shook my head. "Don't need it spoon-fed to me. Just tell me what happened."

"It seems some of the students were making comments. Inappropriate and rightly insensitive, but we cannot tolerate disruptive behavior regardless of the circumstances."

"This girl, she get sent to the library too?"

"She'll have detention."

I nodded, thanked the man, and stood up to leave. All my girls had come through the neighborhood school. I'd been called in to the principal's office more times than I'd like to remember. Mostly for fighting. Mostly for Jackie. I knew the layout and found the library without any trouble. It was empty except for the librarian and my girl. Saw only the top of her head. She'd fallen asleep on her arm.

"Nat, baby?" I took the seat next to her, rubbing her back.

She looked up, blinking the sleep from her mind. Sat back in her chair and waited for her punishment.

"You okay?"

"Yes, Mama. I'm fine. I'm sorry."

"You wanna tell me what happened?"

She shrugged. The simple gesture barely noticeable inside her sweater.

"They teasing you about your sister? About Mya?" She stared at the edge of the table. "About me?"

"Not really. Xavier said he saw a picture of Mya. Said she was...umm..."

I held my breath, my mind spinning with the worst insult a stranger could utter about my family. Took me a minute to realize things had gone in a different direction.

"He brought it in, the clipping from the paper, and they was passing it around—all the boys saying how they would...how they liked her...and... and Dominique started this list of all the girls in the class." Nat's eyes began to water. "With her at the top and me at the bottom."

I wasn't getting it. It was about Mya, but it wasn't. What kinda list had the power to make my girl yell and cry?

"They said I got the ugly and Mya got all the pretty..."

A part of me relaxed, even wanted to smile. Wasn't some big conspiracy. Wasn't even life or death. Was just some stupid kids making their stupid-ness known. But I wiped all that from my face and pretended like it was worst thing I'd ever heard.

"Assholes!"

"Mama!" Nat gasped, then smiled sheepishly.

"Fools don't know what to do with themselves. You just ignore them. You just as pretty as anybody. And unlike them, you pretty on the inside too."

THE WINTERY WINDS HAD BEGUN TO FIX their sights on snow. Buttoned my coat from knee to neck and wrapped my scarf tight before pushing the double doors open. It was a dry sort of cold, but it would change in a day or two, and then the first flakes would begin to fall. I took the steps from the high school in quick succession, braving the unforgiving burst of cold that nearly drove me back inside. I knew exactly what I needed to do. I'd go back to retail. See Mya through this little issue she was having and put her back on the right track. She was too smart to have her life destroyed by this nonsense. And Nikki? Well, my first born would just have to learn her lesson on her own. Hopefully, sooner rather than later.

MYA

IS THAT HIM?" JACKIE STOOD ON HER tippy-toes, leaning side to side, peering through the crowd. "That's him, right?"

The little man my sister had picked out walked past us and hurried into the courtroom two doors down. My lawyer was late.

The prosecutor convinced the judge that we should wrap the trial up in time for Christmas. He said the victim's family deserved not to have this hanging over their heads.

"You don't have to stand out here with me. Go back inside," she said, eyeballing me but refusing to say what was on her mind.

I was painfully aware that I'd been fidgeting with my clothes off and on since we arrived. I'd gone through three separate outfits before settling on this one. It was one of Mama's skirt suits. Couldn't fit any of her shoes though, so I grabbed a pair from the first secondhand shop I saw. I'd worn hand-me-downs before, practically lived in them, but this was different. None of it was me.

"Mya?"

"I'm gonna stay out here with you. They'll call me when it's time."

She nodded and resumed her dutiful search of all the faces that stepped off the escalator. I should've been excited to get this over with. Clear my name. Get back to my life. I sighed and forced my hands into a static position. I'd woken up at the crack of dawn in a panic. Slipped out before everybody woke and went searching for soldier boy. The school said he didn't work there anymore, and the folks at Good Shepherd didn't take messages. He was in the wind, and Mia wouldn't stop pestering me about finding him. Wasn't her fault. Was a good thing really. She had no clue what all was going on.

"Don't worry. Okay?"

I nodded.

Arif's family was sitting in the first row. His mother, wife, and two sons. The women and the little boy looked at me with billowing sorrow in their eyes. The older son, his dark stare burned like the fires of hell. He hated me. I didn't blame him.

"Your hair looks pretty." Jackie smiled. "I don't know why you never wear it down."

"Gets in the way."

"In the way of what, Mya? Ain't like you're a brain surgeon or something." She abandoned her search to face me, chewing on her lip as she considered whether to continue sharing her thoughts.

"What?"

"You know folks might be a little more accommodating to you if you didn't try so hard to look..." Jackie's lips parted as she took a breath. "Not nice."

"I look not nice?"

"If you let yourself look nice I mean, then maybe—"

"I'll try to remember that the next time I get arrested."

"I didn't mean it like that."

"Mya Morrow?" The young man appeared suddenly before us, juggling several file folders and a cup of coffee. The strong roast nearly sent me gagging into the nearest restroom. "Miss Morrow?" he asked again and took a deep breath to steady himself. "I'm James Booker, I'll be representing you from now on."

"How old are you?" Jackie demanded to know.

He smiled uncomfortably and admitted he was new. "But I've been following your case."

"Where's Brooks?"

"Who? Oh, he retired. But I read your statement." He shoved the files back into his briefcase and gestured toward the courtroom doors. "And apart from a few questions I have, which I think we can handle later, I think you've got a good case." He smiled. "Shall we?"

"MAMA, IT WAS HORRIBLE! THE MEDICAL EXAMINER got up there talking all this science mumbo jumbo, and the man didn't have one thing to say! Just sat there, tapping his pen on the table. I don't think he's even a real lawyer."

Jackie dialed the dramatics way up for this performance. She hadn't stopped talking since we walked through the door. Plopped down on the sofa next to Mama and let loose. Mama had Mia asleep across her lap. She didn't move an inch except to stroke Mia's back. Every now and then her face contracted as she tried to absorb but not get weighed down by what my sister was saying. Jackie had her thinking they were ready to lock me up and throw away the key.

"It's a fucking conspiracy, I'm telling you!"

"Watch your language." Mama nodded in the direction of the twins.

"Her lawyer just suddenly up and retires out of the fucking blue?"

"Jackie," Mama warned her again on reflex.

"They're trying to screw us over!"

After changing into more comfortable clothes, I found myself leaning against the wall, eavesdropping. Folks were walking on eggshells around me. Nobody said what they really thought. Nobody but Jackie.

Booker was green, but at least he wasn't jaded. And he believed me. That had to be worth something.

"Pssst." Nat beckoned me into the kitchen then handed me the phone.

"Hello?"

"How you doing, baby girl?" said a weathered voice that made my heart skip a beat. It was Aunt Clara. Nobody called me baby girl except for her and my daddy.

"Fine. You?"

"As good as can be expected for an old broad. I want you to know I been praying for you."

I nodded.

"I'm coming up there to see y'all after the new year. You take care now."

"I will."

"Put your mama on the phone."

JACKIE STAYED FOR SUPPER, AND AFTER, WE locked ourselves in her room. We sat on the floor with my kids asleep on the bed above us. The closet light was on to break up the darkness as we whispered back and forth. She and Kem were having problems. Even though she smiled when she said he was giving her some space, I knew she was heartbroken.

"You moving back home?"

She took a moment to think it over, then nodded. It was probably for the best. When it came to guys, Jackie went from zero to sixty in no time at all. She got serious about Kem way too fast. I was searching for the words to say as much when she interrupted my thoughts.

"I think I broke it." Jackie stifled a yawn and blinked the tears from her eyes. "Kem and me. It was perfect and...I ruined it." She paused, waiting for me to add something comforting.

"There's more fish in the sea, right?"

"Not like Kem."

Right. Well, technically we're all different, so nobody is like anybody. Don't say that, Mya. I cleared my throat to buy myself some time. Was about to confess the truth, that sometimes love just sucks. No ifs, ands, or buts about it. Just flat out sucks.

Then she said, "We got married."

"What?"

"In Vegas. A few weeks ago," she whispered with big eyes on the verge of losing hope. "Don't say anything okay?"

"Why?"

"Because I don't know how to tell Mama. You know how she is..."

"No, why—" I stopped. I didn't want to be insensitive. Most folks knew off the bat what not to say, but I wasn't one of them. "I mean, I know y'all care about each other, and all, but..."

"I love him. Seemed like a good idea at the time. You never thought about marrying Darien? Y'all got two kids together." She pointed out as if I needed a reminder.

"Maybe someday." I shrugged.

Jackie stretched out on her back, folded her hands over her stomach and seamlessly changed the subject. She would rededicate herself to her studies, foresaking all men, even if she happened to be married to them. Said the new year was going to be different. By some stroke of destiny, she'd gotten into the most elusive college in the state. Only made sense that she took advantage of that. Besides, she'd decided what she wanted to do with her degree.

"I'm gonna be a lawyer," she announced with a twinge of pride. "Gonna right wrongs and stand up for the little people."

I nodded and lay down beside her. "Mama's gonna love that."

"You could go to school too, and then we could both be lawyers. We'd start our own firm and be like...Morrow and Morrow...kicking ass and taking names."

I tried to see the world she painted. Smiled when she did and kept quiet while she talked. It made sense for her, not me. Last thing I wanted was to spend my days knee-deep in other folks' problems. Not to mention I'd lose seven years of my life while fancy educators told me what to think and what to do. Seven years not making a dime. No. I had two kids to take care of...

"Mya, you listening?"

"Yeah."

She went on to describe the office we would have. With its sophisticated decor and handsome male receptionist. We'd make tons of money and have very important friends. And she'd get one of those closets that operated on remote to house her very fashionable wardrobe.

"And you can wear pants suits," she added to reassure me.

I sat up to open the drawer on the bedside table and remove the towel I'd folded and hid there. Jackie kept talking as I unwrapped the contents. Then she sat back on her elbows and her eyes rested on the ornamental handles. I'd traded the pistol Ramon had given me years ago for weapons I was more comfortable with. The larger blade wore a leather sheath, the smaller one was a switchblade.

"Pick one."

"Damn, Mya." She reached for the full-size weapon, gently withdrawing it from its protective covering until the metal gleamed in the dim light of the bedroom.

"Careful. It's sharp."

Before its full length was exposed, Jackie returned it to its sheath and reached for the switchblade instead.

I nodded. "Easier to control. Last thing you want is somebody taking it from you and using it on you." I leaned over to show her how to open it. "It's a just-in-case kinda weapon. Just in case somebody gets up on you. That's when you pull this. When they're too close to see it coming."

"Damn, Mya. Where you learn this?"

I shrugged. "Life."

97
MYA

ALL THE LEGAL THRILLERS I READ DIDN'T prepare me for the real thing. First of all, there was no jury. And the trial wasn't drawn out like I expected. It started on December 17 and lasted five days. The prosecution took up most of that time putting on their case. The coroner's report, the arresting officers, two witnesses that said I was capable with a knife, which didn't seem related at all considering Arif was killed by a gun. Then his family took the stand. Prosecutor said it was to explain why the security cameras were down, but it became clear that it wasn't about that when the man asked what Arif meant to the family.

Booker shot up, "Objection, your honor!"

"Overruled."

I sat back, watching the spectacle, overcome with indifference one minute and fiery frustration the next. Nikki took the stand on my behalf, but she was a terrible liar and couldn't convince somebody of the truth if she was under pressure. Heziah did better. I'd forgotten how much of my life he'd been around for—my childhood, my adolescence. Forgotten how much he'd cared about me and how well he knew me.

"Mr. Jenkins, you'd say just about anything to save Miss Morrow from prison, wouldn't you?"

Nikki had been hoping the good reverend would show up, but I knew better. He may have been the silver bullet we needed, but what could he say? He hadn't seen me since I was thirteen. And I hadn't left the best impression on God's servant. We'd run out of witnesses.

The four of us ate a quick lunch, chewing in silence. Booker sat a few tables over writing furiously in his notebook. Occasionally, he flipped through the thin file folder that must've been left for him by Brooks.

We returned to the courtroom with five minutes to spare and settled into our seats. "Booker?"

"Yeah," he replied without looking up from his notes.

"Put me on the stand."

Our eyes met.

He stuttered, "I...I...I don't know if that's the best idea."

He had wide round eyes, a squarish head, and copper skin. His physical build said he wasn't a stranger to sports, but he wasn't a maniac either. I'd only known him a few days but I trusted him.

"You get on the stand, and the prosecution's gonna ask a whole lotta questions you don't wanna answer."

Didn't matter anymore. Who knew what happened better than me? Who was gonna stand up for me better than I could?

"Put me on the stand."

THE JUDGE FIXED ME WITH AN AUTHORITATIVE stare. "Miss Morrow, you must answer the question. Do you need it repeated for you?"

I didn't.

"Harry—Harold I mean. Harold Perkins." Sounded like a real enough person to me.

"How long have you lived with Mr. Perkins?" Booker rose from his chair. "An estimate is fine."

"Off and on for three or four years."

"And on the night of December 17, he sent you to the store to get diapers?"

"I sent myself."

"Please tell us what you found when you arrived at the store."

"It was empty. Except for Arif and me."

"But it didn't stay that way for long, did it? Tell us what happened next."

"I got the diapers. Went back to the freezer section to get some milk. Heard somebody come in, but I didn't think much of it until the guy demanded money. Then I hit the floor and tried to stay low so he wouldn't see me. He must've gotten the money because Arif kept trying to get him to leave, but he was spray painting the freezer section. Arif got mad, came from behind the counter...I heard a gunshot."

"Thank you, Miss Morrow."

Booker reclaimed his chair, and my gaze wandered first to Arif's family then to mine. I was thankful to have Mama looking after my kids, but all I wanted was to see her face looking back at me.

"Miss Morrow." The prosecutor was a polished man. He leaned back in his chair, a snarky grin on his face, and prepared to run me down. "You're a rather tall woman. What? Five ten?"

"Five eight."

"All right, five eight. Think back to the night. Standing up, could you see over the shelves?"

"It wasn't a big store if that's what you're getting at."

"You were standing up when the assailant walked in. At your height, was it possible to see him?"

"Yeah, I guess."

"But you didn't turn around. Is that correct?"

"Yeah."

"So, if we follow your version of the crime. You didn't see him, but could he have seen you? Don't you think a man who enters an establishment intent on robbing it, vandalizing it, and beating–possibly killing–the owner would look around before he did anything?"

"I don't know. Maybe."

"I think he would. I think he'd probably scope the place out first. He'd notice there was a third person there. And I don't think he'd leave her alive to tell the tale."

"Counselor." The judge cleared his throat. "Get to a question."

He nodded, catapulted himself out of his chair, and buttoned his jacket as he made his next point. "Harold Perkins. Is he in the courtroom today?"

"No."

"Has he ever been in the courtroom? To show his support? According to you, the two of you have been an item for sometime, so he's here, right?" He pivoted slightly to feign studying the crowd. "Hmm. Interesting. He's not here, is he? This Harold Perkins?"

"No."

"And you never saw the man you say actually killed Mr. Hassan? Never met him before in your life, so you say. But what if you had?"

"I didn't."

"Let's say hypothetically that you did. Let's say you knew him. The two of you were...involved. In love even. That would explain why you would want to protect him, right? Hide his identity from the police? And one way to do that would be to say...that you didn't see a thing."

"I'm not lying. I don't lie."

"Oh, really!" His face broke into a grin as wide as all outside. "You've never lied before? Never? You receive benefits from the state do you not? For five years now, correct?"

"Yeah."

"Any idea what your address of record is? It's your mother's house, isn't it?"

"Yes."

"Even though you moved out when you were...sixteen, is that correct?"

"Yeah but–"

"Did you ever report that Mr. Perkins was living with you?"

"No."

"So, you do lie. Seems like you've been getting away with it until now."

"Objection!"

"Sustained."

"Miss Morrow, I have one more question for you. The blood. Tell us how you got the victim's blood all over you."

"I tried to help him. To stop the bleeding."

"You tried to help..." He pretended to ponder. "I suppose that's a possibility. Is it also possible that you bent over the body to rifle through his pockets?"

The room began spinning. Blood rushed to my face. My ears picked up every possible sound until it all blended together. I'd made a mistake. This was a horrible mistake.

"Okay, let's say you didn't rifle through his pockets. Is it possible that when Mr. Hassan was shot, his body spun in such a way that he collided with you, maybe even falling on top of you?"

"Objection, Your Honor, my client isn't an expert in...in..."

"It's fine. I have no more questions."

98
PECAN

MIA MADE A MAD DASH FOR THE front door at the first click of the keys. My grandbaby loved her mama something fierce. Acted like they hadn't spent no time away from each other her whole life. Scared me. Somebody so little and innocent...if things took a turn...

"Mommy! Where you go?"

The three of them hurried in from the cold. Heziah closed the door behind them, and Jackie was the first to come on in the living room. Could tell just from the look on her face that I'd missed something important.

"What happened?"

Her face did a sad twitch that was supposed to be an attempt at a smile. And she reached for the baby, cuddling her face in his belly, getting lost in the scent of his sweetness.

"It's over, for now." Heziah sighed, standing back, so Mya could enter first, her feet clobbering across the floor in secondhand pumps.

Mia was wrapped around her mama with unflinching devotion. Legs cinched around Mya's waist, arms clutching her neck. Hadn't seen my girl cry in...I don't know when, but she was damn close.

"Jackie, take the kids on upstairs. Get them ready for their nap."

"I don't want no nap. Mommy, when we go get Dee?"

Mya's eyes slid shut, and a whimper parted her lips as she sank into the sofa.

"Jackie—"

"No, it's okay." Mya said.

My girl was back.

"I wanna do it." Mya stood. Taking the stairs at a slow pace with Jackie following a safe distance behind them.

"What happened?"

Heziah crossed the room and pulled me into a hug. Wasn't for me though. He was the one needed it. "I tried," he mumbled into my shoulder.

"That good, huh? Nikki show up?"

He nodded. Leaned back enough to study my face, then kissed me like it might be the last time. "Took the judge ten minutes to decide. Guilty."

99 MYA

AFTER THE INITIAL BURST OF ENERGY, MIA went down easy. She was tired. Mama had been right about that. I sat on the edge of the bed, looking over them, wondering how any parent could walk away without so much as a word. Was there even such a thing as the right words? How does a mother say goodbye to her child?

Maybe I'd start with something like "Mommy has to go away for a while."

"Take me with you," she'd say.

"I can't. Kids can't come."

I touched her hairline with just a faint brush of my fingertips, careful not to disturb her sleep. I wanted to scoop her up in my arms and get lost in her warmth. Instead, I concentrated. Allowed only the slightest touch, matching my breathing to the slow pace of hers. She needed the sleep. The sleep would help prepare her for what was coming next. I'd tell her the truth. The judge—no, the police—she understood what the police were. I'd tell her they thought I did something bad, and they wanted to punish me for it.

"What'd you do?"

"Nothing. I'm innocent. It's all a mistake."

"Did you tell 'em it was a mistake? You should tell 'em, Mommy."

"I did tell them."

"Then why you have to go?"

I was so involved in the scene playing out in my head that I didn't even notice the flurry of noises going on behind me. Not until Jackie heaved a suitcase on the foot of the bed.

"What are you doing?"

"Can't take that much. Just the essentials." She yanked out the top drawer on her bureau and tossed in some of my underwear. "We'll go when it gets dark. After everybody's asleep."

"Jackie?"

She'd been quiet the whole ride home. Now I knew why. She'd been plotting. Defiant to the end. Even when we were little, she was the one always resisting the rules, fighting the inevitability of the world we lived in, fighting Daddy every chance she got. I took a deep breath in through my nostrils, closed my eyes, and let the oxygen disseminate throughout my body. I would have to make a choice. Maybe Darien saw it coming, and that's why he disappeared. To make it easier on me, he took himself out of the equation. That just left Nikki, Jackie, and Mama.

"Don't worry about money. I got you. Once we get to the border, we'll find one of those people that sneak folks into the country and get them to sneak you out. That simple."

Jackie had lost her mind, and chaos was sure to follow. I wasn't surprised. If anybody knew my sister, I did. It made the choice easier.

"You're smart. You'll learn the language. We'll go down and visit you. It'll be fine. Mama's gonna worry, but no way around that."

"Stop."

"No," she replied without a moment's pause. "I got it worked out. See Kem left his car here and what he doesn't know won't hurt him. I can drive y'all down to the border—"

"You can't drive."

"It's a technicality! I can drive! I just don't have a license yet."

The suitcase was nearly full, and Jackie had only packed my things. She seemed to come to the realization as soon as I did and tossed the first layer onto the floor, replacing it with Mia's clothes, clean bottles, and diapers.

"Mama would lose the house."

"Fuck the house. It's Daddy's house."

"Jackie."

"You can't just sit around waiting for the other shoe to drop! Who are you? 'Cause the sister I know wouldn't just roll over." She glared at me. "Well?" she demanded, one hand on her hip, the other clenched into a fist. "We can't just do nothing!"

"Shh!"

The carpet barely moved under our feet as I dragged her into the hallway and closed the bedroom door behind us.

"Prison! Mya!" she shouted as if I were fuzzy about the concept of criminal punishment. "We gotta right to—"

"Not we. Me. It's my business, not yours."

The twins emerged from their bedroom. Nat from hers. Mama and Heziah were on the stairs. All of us watching as Jackie cut loose.

"Don't you do that! You are my sister! My blood! What happens to you happens to me! Even if you do run away. Even if I don't see you for months or years or..." Tears welled up in her eyes, and I looked away.

"All right, now." It was Mama. As stern as she'd ever been. Joined us on the second floor and slowly walked over to put her arms around Jackie. "You done said enough. Time for quiet."

Mama's chest muffled the sound of my sister's cries. The snotty blubbery kinda cries. The ones that broke your heart if you heard 'em. Her sobs washed over us all, drowning our family in the unfairness of it all. Nobody moved. Nobody fought it. Jackie sobbed some more, her knees wavering under the weight of it all. Her legs couldn't have been stronger than a pair of limp noodles, but Mama held her up. Struck me how much strength it took to keep my sister upright when she was falling to pieces. I'd always known I was strong. I'd just assumed I got it from my daddy. Was a lot of things I thought I knew, but I didn't.

"You pull yourself together, you hear?" Mama whispered. "You do it right now."

Thirty seconds later, Mama withdrew her support and turned to face the rest of us. "Ain't gonna be no pity in this house tonight. We gonna have a nice supper—whatever Mya wants. Potato salad, meatloaf, whatever. And we gonna spend the night enjoying each other's company."

All was quiet.

"Mama?"

"Yes, baby?" She turned to me.

"Fried chicken? Greens. And potato salad."

"You want anything sweet?"

My sister wiped the tears from her eyes and reclaimed her natural posture. Our eyes met.

"German chocolate cake."

100 MYA

WITH THE SUNRISE, CAME THE BEGINNINGS OF a new life. A life without cool breezes on summer days, and the warmth of sunshine on my face. A life that held few surprises, good ones anyway. Where family only existed on weekends and in letters. Where the best of me became a nugget of weakness to be hidden and suppressed. The start of a life that settled for good enough. A life with concrete floors, a maze of locked doors, and only the dream of a window. Life at Beaumont Correctional Facility for Women.

"Count your blessings," Darlene Pratt used to say. I'd roll my eyes and sulk instead. But that was then. Now, sitting on the steel-frame bed, hands clasped between my knees, I counted the seconds until the cockroach would cross the threshold of my cell on its way to visit another prisoner. One Mississippi.

Never felt one way or the other about bugs. Guess that was a blessing. Mama couldn't stand the sight of anything with more than three legs. She'd run screaming through the house, pointing in the general direction of the perpetrator until me or Aunt Clara killed it and cleaned up all the evidence.

Two Mississippi.

Prisoners like me were sequestered into a tightly controlled population. Seventy-five cages, all in need of some repair, with only a view of the bars to feed our imaginations. Forced into faded blue jumpsuits. Scratchy but comfortable. Allowed one hour of daily exercise. I wondered if the outdoor space would be big enough for me to run. I nodded to myself.

It probably was. Wouldn't be much of a point otherwise.

Three Mississippi.

Hadn't met my cellmate yet. I was alone. I could do alone. Four Mississippi.

Or was it the quiet that I relished? Hard to have quiet in a house full of people. My people...my kids...I closed my eyes, breathing slowly in through my nose and out a few seconds later. Then once more until I no longer saw their faces looking back at me.

Five, six, seven Mississippi.

Nikki promised to bring Mia and Alan every weekend. Probably wasn't realistic, but she insisted. She promised to give them a good life. The best of everything. I nodded and tuned her out as she explained all she had planned. My kids would have it easy. A nice comfortable life. That's all I needed to know.

Booker was already working on my appeal. He was smart and losing didn't fit with his perception of himself. After the sentencing, he laid out his plan. Not that I knew the possible from the impossible. Not yet anyway.

I'd heard there was a library on the grounds somewhere. I would do what I should've done from the beginning. I'd study up. Between Booker and me, we'd find a flaw in the prosecution's case—some matter of legal fact they'd ignored—and all this would be like a bad dream. Nine months was all I needed, maybe a year tops.

Dear reader,

Thank you for taking this journey with me! I hope you are enjoying it as much as I enjoyed writing it. It is my mission to develop stories that reflect what women are going through. If you saw yourself or were touched by something in this book, please share that with someone. We are our sister's keeper and together we can empower one another.

Although this was the second novel in the series, the Morrow family saga is just beginning. If you came to *Blue Sky* without reading *How to Knock a Bravebird from Her Perch*, I apologize for the spoilers, because as a huge fan of series fiction I despise spoilers! But, if you want to know more about the girls's childhood, life with Ricky Morrow, and his death *How to Knock a Bravebird from Her Perch* is the novel for that.

As always, please take some time to leave a review either on Amazon, Goodreads, or whatever outlet you purchased this book from. Other readers are counting on you! And I always quote the first 10 reviews on my website!

Until we meet again...

Enjoy the journey,

D. Bryant Simmons

D. Bryant Simmons is an award-winning author who pens realistic fiction that straddles the line between art and social commentary.

She is currently hard at work on *The Morrow Girls Series*, a family saga that spans three generations of women.

Simmons incorporates meaty topics, such as domestic violence, addiction, and mental illness into her fiction. She believes novels can act as agents of change and hopes that her writing will inspire and empower women.

D. Bryant Simmons resides in Chicago, Illinois.

www.themorrowgirls.com
dbs@themorrowgirls.com

@DBryantSimmons
facebook.com/morrowgirls
pinterest.com/dbryantsimmons
plus.google.com/+dbryantsimmons